THE VOYAGE
OF THE
DAWN TREADER

S

The first part of the
VOYAGE

About here they
joined the ship

FELIMATH   THE LONE ISLANDS
DOORN   AVRA

THE GREAT EASTERN OCEAN

The CHRONICLES *of* NARNIA

The CHRONICLES of NARNIA

C. S. LEWIS

BOOK 5

THE VOYAGE
OF THE
DAWN TREADER

Illustrated by Pauline Baynes

HarperTrophy
A Division of HarperCollins*Publishers*

The Voyage of the *Dawn Treader*
Copyright © 1952 by C. S. Lewis (Pte) Limited
Copyright renewed 1980 by C. S. Lewis (Pte) Limited

Library of Congress Cataloging-in-Publication Data
Lewis, C. S. (Clive Staples), 1898–1963.
    The voyage of the Dawn Treader / C. S. Lewis ; illustrated by Pauline Baynes.
        p.   cm. — (The Chronicles of Narnia ; bk. 5)
    Summary: Lucy and Edmund, accompanied by their peevish cousin Eustace, sail to
the land of Narnia where Eustace is temporarily transformed into a green dragon be-
cause of his selfish behavior and skepticism.
    ISBN 0-06-023486-5. — ISBN 0-06-023487-3 (lib. bdg.)
    ISBN 0-06-447107-1 (pbk.)
    [1. Fantasy.]   I. Baynes, Pauline, ill.   II. Title.   III. Series: Lewis, C. S. (Clive
Staples), 1898–1963.   Chronicles of Narnia   (HarperCollins (Firm)) ; bk. 5.
PZ7.L58474Vo   1994   93-11515
[Fic]—dc20   CIP
                                                                                      AC

Typography by Nicholas Krenitsky
◆
First Harper Trophy Edition, 1994

To Geoffrey Barfield

CAST OF CHARACTERS

ASLAN. The King, Lord of the whole wood, and son of the Emperor across the Sea. Aslan is the Lion, the Great Lion. He comes and goes as and when he pleases; he comes to overthrow the witch and save Narnia. Aslan appears in all seven books.

DIGORY KIRKE. Digory was there at the very beginning in *The Magician's Nephew*, and he is also in *The Lion, the Witch and the Wardrobe*. If it were not for Digory's courage, we might never have heard of Narnia. Find out why in *The Magician's Nephew*.

POLLY PLUMMER. Polly is the first person to leave our world. She and Digory take part in the very beginning of everything in *The Magician's Nephew*.

JADIS. The last Queen of Charn, which she herself destroyed. Jadis arrives in Narnia with Digory and Polly in *The Magician's Nephew* and has taken over the land as the White Witch in *The Lion, the Witch and the Wardrobe*. Completely evil, she is also very dangerous, even in *The Silver Chair*.

UNCLE ANDREW. Mr. Andrew Ketterley thinks he is a magician, but like all who meddle with magic, he doesn't really know what he is doing. The results are dire in *The Magician's Nephew*.

THE PEVENSIES.

Peter Pevensie, King Peter the Magnificent, the High King

Susan Pevensie, Queen Susan the Gentle

Edmund Pevensie, King Edmund the Just

Lucy Pevensie, Queen Lucy the Valiant

The four Pevensies, brothers and sisters, visited Narnia at the time of the winter rule of the White Witch. They remained there for many Narnian years and established the Golden Age of Narnia. Peter is the oldest, followed by Susan, then Edmund and Lucy. They are all in *The Lion, the Witch and the Wardrobe* and *Prince Caspian*. Edmund and Lucy are also in *The Voyage of the* Dawn Treader; Edmund, Lucy, and Susan appear in *The Horse and His Boy*; and Peter, Edmund, and Lucy appear in *The Last Battle*.

SHASTA. There is a mystery about this adopted son of a Calormene fisherman. He is not what he seems, as he himself discovers in *The Horse and His Boy*.

BREE. This great war horse is also unusual. He was kidnapped as a foal from the forests of Narnia and sold as a slave-horse in Calormen, a country across Archenland and far to the south of Narnia. His real adventures begin when he tries to escape in *The Horse and His Boy*.

ARAVIS. Aravis is a Tarkheena, a Calormene

noblewoman, but even so she has many good points, and they come to light in *The Horse and His Boy*.

HWIN. Hwin is a good-natured, sensible horse. Another slave taken from Narnia, she and Aravis become friends in *The Horse and His Boy*.

PRINCE CASPIAN. He is the nephew of King Miraz and is known as Caspian the Tenth, Son of Caspian, and the True King of Narnia (King of Old Narnians). He is also called a Telmarine of Narnia, Lord of Cair Paravel, and Emperor of the Lone Islands. He appears in *Prince Caspian*, *The Voyage of the* Dawn Treader, *The Silver Chair*, and *The Last Battle*.

MIRAZ. Miraz is a Telmarine from the land of Telmar, far beyond the Western Mountains (originally the ancestors of the Telmarines came from our world), and the usurper of the throne of Narnia in *Prince Caspian*.

REEPICHEEP. Reepicheep is the Chief Mouse. He is the self-appointed humble servant to Prince Caspian, and perhaps the most valiant knight in all of Narnia. His chivalry is unsurpassed, as also are his courage and skill with the sword. Reepicheep appears in *Prince Caspian*, *Th: Voyage of the* Dawn Treader, and *The Last Eattle*.

EUSTACE CLARENCE SCRUBB. Eustace is a cousin of the Pevensie family whom Edmund and Lucy must go and visit. He finds Narnia something of a shock. He appears in *The Voyage of the Dawn Treader*, *The Silver Chair*, and *The Last Battle*.

JILL POLE. Jill is the heroine of *The Silver Chair*; she goes to Narnia with Eustace on his second Narnian adventure. She also comes to aid Narnia in *The Last Battle*.

PRINCE RILIAN. The son of King Caspian the Tenth, Rilian is the lost Prince of Narnia; find him in *The Silver Chair*.

PUDDLEGLUM. Puddleglum is a Marsh-wiggle from the Eastern Marshes of Narnia. He is tall, and his very serious demeanor masks a true heart of great courage. He appears in *The Silver Chair* and *The Last Battle*.

KING TIRIAN. Noble and brave, Tirian is the last King of Narnia. He and his friend Jewel, a Unicorn, fight *The Last Battle*.

SHIFT. An old and ugly Ape, Shift decides that he should be in charge of Narnia and starts things that he can't stop in *The Last Battle*.

PUZZLE. Puzzle, a donkey, never meant any harm—you see, he's not really very clever. And Shift deceives him in *The Last Battle*.

CONTENTS

1

THE PICTURE
IN THE BEDROOM

There was a boy called Eustace Clarence
Scrubb, and he almost deserved it. His parents
called him Eustace Clarence and masters called
him Scrubb. I can't tell you how his friends
spoke to him, for he had none. He didn't call his
Father and Mother "Father" and "Mother," but
Harold and Alberta. They were very up-to-date
and advanced people. They were vegetarians,
non-smokers and teetotalers and wore a special
kind of underclothes. In their house there was
very little furniture and very few clothes on beds
and the windows were always open.

Eustace Clarence liked animals, especially beetles, if they were dead and pinned on a card. He liked books if they were books of information and had pictures of grain elevators or of fat foreign children doing exercises in model schools.

Eustace Clarence disliked his cousins the four Pevensies, Peter, Susan, Edmund and Lucy. But he was quite glad when he heard that Edmund and Lucy were coming to stay. For deep down inside him he liked bossing and bullying; and, though he was a puny little person who couldn't have stood up even to Lucy, let alone Edmund, in a fight, he knew that there are dozens of ways to give people a bad time if you are in your own home and they are only visitors.

Edmund and Lucy did not at all want to

come and stay with Uncle Harold and Aunt Alberta. But it really couldn't be helped. Father had got a job lecturing in America for sixteen weeks that summer, and Mother was to go with him because she hadn't had a real holiday for ten years. Peter was working very hard for an exam and he was to spend the holidays being coached by old Professor Kirke in whose house these four children had had wonderful adventures long ago in the war years. If he had still been in that house he would have had them all to stay. But he had somehow become poor since the old days and was living in a small cottage with only one bedroom to spare. It would have cost too much money to take the other three all to America, and Susan had gone.

Grown-ups thought her the pretty one of the family and she was no good at school work (though otherwise very old for her age) and Mother said she "would get far more out of a trip to America than the youngsters." Edmund and Lucy tried not to grudge Susan her luck, but it was dreadful having to spend the summer holidays at their Aunt's. "But it's far worse for me," said Edmund, "because you'll at least have a room of your own and I shall have to share a bedroom with that record stinker, Eustace."

The story begins on an afternoon when Edmund and Lucy were stealing a few precious minutes alone together. And of course they were talking about Narnia, which was the name of their own private and secret country. Most of us, I suppose, have a secret country but for most of us it is only an imaginary country. Edmund and Lucy were luckier than other people in that respect. Their secret country was real. They had already visited it twice; not in a game or a dream but in reality. They had got there of course by Magic, which is the only way of getting to Narnia. And a promise, or very nearly a promise, had been made them in Narnia itself that they would some day get back. You may imagine that they talked about it a good deal, when they got the chance.

They were in Lucy's room, sitting on the edge of her bed and looking at a picture on the opposite wall. It was the only picture in the house that they liked. Aunt Alberta didn't like it at all (that was why it was put away in a little back room upstairs), but she couldn't get rid of it because it had been a wedding present from someone she did not want to offend.

It was a picture of a ship—a ship sailing straight toward you. Her prow was gilded and shaped like the head of a dragon with wide-open mouth. She had only one mast and one large, square sail which was a rich purple. The sides of the ship—what you could see of them where the gilded wings of the dragon ended—were green. She had just run up to the top of one glorious blue wave, and the nearer slope of that wave came down toward you, with streaks and bubbles on it. She was obviously running fast before a gay wind, listing over a little on her port side. (By the way, if you are going to read this story at all, and if you don't know already, you had better get it into your head that the left of a ship when you are looking ahead, is *port*, and the right is *starboard*.) All the sunlight fell on her from that side, and the water on that side was full of greens and purples. On the other, it was darker blue from the shadow of the ship.

"The question is," said Edmund, "whether it doesn't make things worse, *looking* at a Narnian ship when you can't get there."

"Even looking is better than nothing," said Lucy. "And she is such a very Narnian ship."

"Still playing your old game?" said Eustace Clarence, who had been listening outside the door and now came grinning into the room. Last year, when he had been staying with the Pevensies, he had managed to hear them all talking of Narnia and he loved teasing them about it. He thought of course that they were making it all up; and as he was far too stupid to make anything up himself, he did not approve of that.

"You're not wanted here," said Edmund curtly.

"I'm trying to think of a limerick," said Eustace. "Something like this:

"Some kids who played games about Narnia
Got gradually balmier and balmier—"

"Well *Narnia* and *balmier* don't rhyme, to begin with," said Lucy.

"It's an assonance," said Eustace.

"Don't ask him what an assy-thingummy is," said Edmund. "He's only longing to be asked. Say nothing and perhaps he'll go away."

Most boys, on meeting a reception like this, would either have cleared out or flared up. Eustace did neither. He just hung about grinning, and presently began talking again.

"Do you like that picture?" he asked.

"For heaven's sake don't let him get started about Art and all that," said Edmund hurriedly, but Lucy, who was very truthful, had already said, "Yes, I do. I like it very much."

"It's a rotten picture," said Eustace.

"You won't see it if you step outside," said Edmund.

"Why do you like it?" said Eustace to Lucy.

"Well, for one thing," said Lucy, "I like it because the ship looks as if it was really moving.

And the water looks as if it was really wet. And the waves look as if they were really going up and down."

Of course Eustace knew lots of answers to this, but he didn't say anything. The reason was that at that very moment he looked at the waves and saw that they did look very much indeed as if they were going up and down. He had only once been in a ship (and then only as far as the Isle of Wight) and had been horribly seasick. The look of the waves in the picture made him feel sick again. He turned rather green and tried another look. And then all three children were staring with open mouths.

What they were seeing may be hard to believe when you read it in print, but it was almost as hard to believe when you saw it happening. The things in the picture were moving. It didn't look at all like a cinema either; the colors were too real and clean and out-of-doors for that. Down went the prow of the ship into the wave and up went a great shock of spray. And then up went the wave behind her, and her stern and her deck became visible for the first time, and then disappeared as the next wave came to meet her and her bows went up again. At the same moment an exercise book which had been lying beside Edmund on the bed flapped, rose and sailed through the air to the wall behind him, and Lucy felt all her hair whipping round her face as it does on a windy day. And this was a windy day; but the wind was blowing out of the picture toward them. And suddenly with the wind came the noises—the swishing of waves and the slap of water against the ship's sides and the creaking and the over-all high steady roar of air and water. But it was the smell, the wild, briny smell, which really convinced Lucy that she was not dreaming.

"Stop it," came Eustace's voice, squeaky with fright and bad temper. "It's some silly trick you two are playing. Stop it. I'll tell Alberta—Ow!"

The other two were much more accustomed to adventures, but, just exactly as Eustace Clarence said "Ow," they both said "Ow" too. The reason was that a great cold, salt splash had broken right out of the frame and they were breathless from the smack of it, besides being wet through.

"I'll smash the rotten thing," cried Eustace; and then several things happened at the same time. Eustace rushed toward the picture. Edmund, who knew something about magic, sprang after him, warning him to look out and not to be a fool. Lucy grabbed at him from the other side and was dragged forward. And by this time either they had grown much smaller or the

picture had grown bigger. Eustace jumped to try to pull it off the wall and found himself standing on the frame; in front of him was not glass but real sea, and wind and waves rushing up to the frame as they might to a rock. He lost his head and clutched at the other two who had jumped up beside him. There was a second of struggling and shouting, and just as they thought they had got their balance a great blue roller surged up round them, swept them off their feet, and drew them down into the sea. Eustace's despairing cry suddenly ended as the water got into his mouth.

Lucy thanked her stars that she had worked hard at her swimming last summer term. It is true that she would have got on much better if she had used a slower stroke, and also that the water felt a great deal colder than it had looked while it was only a picture. Still, she kept her head and kicked her shoes off, as everyone ought to do who falls into deep water in their clothes. She even kept her mouth shut and her eyes open. They were still quite near the ship; she saw its green side towering high above them, and people looking at her from the deck. Then, as one might have expected, Eustace clutched at her in a panic and down they both went.

When they came up again she saw a white figure diving off the ship's side. Edmund was close beside her now, treading water, and had caught the arms of the howling Eustace. Then someone else, whose face was vaguely familiar, slipped an arm under her from the other side. There was a lot of shouting going on from the ship, heads crowding together above the bulwarks, ropes being thrown. Edmund and the stranger were fastening ropes round her. After that followed what seemed a very long delay during which her face got blue and her teeth began chattering. In reality the delay was not very long; they were waiting till the moment when she could be got on board the ship without being dashed against its side. Even with all their best endeavors she had a bruised knee when she finally stood, dripping and shivering, on the deck. After her Edmund was heaved up, and then the miserable Eustace. Last of all came the stranger—a golden-headed boy some years older than herself.

"Ca—Ca—Caspian!" gasped Lucy as soon

as she had breath enough. For Caspian it was; Caspian, the boy king of Narnia whom they had helped to set on the throne during their last visit. Immediately Edmund recognized him too. All three shook hands and clapped one another on the back with great delight.

"But who is your friend?" said Caspian almost at once, turning to Eustace with his cheerful smile. But Eustace was crying much harder than any boy of his age has a right to cry when nothing worse than a wetting has happened to him, and would only yell out, "Let me go. Let me go back. I don't *like* it."

"Let you go?" said Caspian. "But where?"

Eustace rushed to the ship's side, as if he expected to see the picture frame hanging above the sea, and perhaps a glimpse of Lucy's bedroom. What he saw was blue waves flecked with foam, and paler blue sky, both spreading without a break to the horizon. Perhaps we can hardly blame him if his heart sank. He was promptly sick.

"Hey! Rynelf," said Caspian to one of the sailors. "Bring spiced wine for their Majesties. You'll need something to warm you after that dip." He called Edmund and Lucy their Majesties because they and Peter and Susan had all been Kings and Queens of Narnia long before his time. Narnian time flows differently from ours. If you spent a hundred years in Narnia, you would still come back to our world at the very same hour of the very same day on which you left. And then, if you went back to Narnia after spending a week here, you might find that a thousand Narnian years had passed, or only a day, or no time at all. You never know till you get there. Consequently, when the Pevensie children had returned to Narnia last time for their second visit, it was (for the Narnians) as if King Arthur came back to Britain, as some people say he will. And I say the sooner the better.

Rynelf returned with the spiced wine steaming in a flagon and four silver cups. It was just what one wanted, and as Lucy and Edmund sipped it they could feel the warmth going right down to their toes. But Eustace made faces and spluttered and spat it out and was sick again and began to cry again and asked if they hadn't any Plumptree's Vitaminized Nerve Food and could it be made with distilled water and anyway he insisted on being put ashore at the next station.

"This is a merry shipmate you've brought us, Brother," whispered Caspian to Edmund with a chuckle; but before he could say anything more Eustace burst out again.

"Oh! Ugh! What on earth's *that*! Take it away, the horrid thing."

He really had some excuse this time for feeling a little surprised. Something very curious indeed had come out of the cabin in the poop and was slowly approaching them. You might call it—and indeed it was—a Mouse. But then it was a Mouse on its hind legs and stood about two feet high. A thin band of gold passed round its head under one ear and over the other and in this was stuck a long crimson feather. (As the Mouse's fur was very dark, almost black, the effect was bold and striking.) Its left paw rested on the hilt of a sword very nearly as long as its tail. Its balance, as it paced gravely along the swaying deck, was perfect, and its manners courtly. Lucy and Edmund recognized it at once—

Reepicheep, the most valiant of all the Talking Beasts of Narnia, and the Chief Mouse. It had won undying glory in the second Battle of Beruna. Lucy longed, as she had always done, to take Reepicheep up in her arms and cuddle him. But this, as she well knew, was a pleasure she could never have: it would have offended him deeply. Instead, she went down on one knee to talk to him.

Reepicheep put forward his left leg, drew back his right, bowed, kissed her hand, straightened himself, twirled his whiskers, and said in his shrill, piping voice:

"My humble duty to your Majesty. And to King Edmund, too." (Here he bowed again.) "Nothing except your Majesties' presence was lacking to this glorious venture."

"Ugh, take it away," wailed Eustace. "I hate mice. And I never could bear performing animals. They're silly and vulgar and—and sentimental."

"Am I to understand," said Reepicheep to Lucy after a long stare at Eustace, "that this singularly discourteous person is under your Majesty's protection? Because, if not—"

At this moment Lucy and Edmund both sneezed.

"What a fool I am to keep you all standing here in your wet things," said Caspian. "Come on below and get changed. I'll give you my cabin of course, Lucy, but I'm afraid we have no women's clothes on board. You'll have to make do with some of mine. Lead the way, Reepicheep, like a good fellow."

"To the convenience of a lady," said Reepicheep, "even a question of honor must give way—at least for the moment—" and here he looked very hard at Eustace. But Caspian hustled them on and in a few minutes Lucy found herself passing through the door into the stern cabin. She fell in love with it at once—the three square windows that looked out on the blue, swirling water astern, the low cushioned benches round three sides of the table, the swinging silver lamp overhead (Dwarfs' work, she knew at once by its exquisite delicacy) and the flat gold image of Aslan the Lion on the forward wall above the door. All this she took in in a flash, for Caspian immediately opened a door on the starboard side, and said, "This'll be your room, Lucy. I'll just get some dry things for myself"—he was rummaging in one of the lockers while he spoke—"and then leave you to change. If you'll fling your wet things outside the door I'll get them taken to the galley to be dried."

Lucy found herself as much at home as if she had been in Caspian's cabin for weeks, and the motion of the ship did not worry her, for in the old days when she had been a queen in Narnia she had done a good deal of voyaging. The cabin was very tiny but bright with painted panels (all birds and beasts and crimson dragons and vines) and spotlessly clean. Caspian's clothes were too big for her, but she could manage. His shoes, sandals and sea-boots were hopelessly big but she did not mind going barefoot on board ship. When she had finished dressing she looked out of her window at the water rushing past and took a long deep breath. She felt quite sure they were in for a lovely time.

ON BOARD
THE *DAWN TREADER*

"Ah, there you are, Lucy," said Caspian. "We were just waiting for you. This is my captain, the Lord Drinian."

A dark-haired man went down on one knee and kissed her hand. The only others present were Reepicheep and Edmund.

"Where is Eustace?" asked Lucy.

"In bed," said Edmund, "and I don't think we can do anything for him. It only makes him worse if you try to be nice to him."

"Meanwhile," said Caspian, "we want to talk."

"By Jove, we do," said Edmund. "And first, about time. It's a year ago by our time since we left you just before your coronation. How long has it been in Narnia?"

"Exactly three years," said Caspian.

"All going well?" asked Edmund.

"You don't suppose I'd have left my kingdom and put to sea unless all was well," answered the King. "It couldn't be better. There's no trouble at all now between Telmarines, Dwarfs, Talking Beasts, Fauns and the rest. And we gave those troublesome giants on the frontier such a good beating last summer that they pay us tribute now. And I had an excellent person to leave as Regent while I'm away—Trumpkin, the Dwarf. You remember him?"

"Dear Trumpkin," said Lucy, "of course I do. You couldn't have made a better choice."

"Loyal as a badger, Ma'am, and valiant as— as a Mouse," said Drinian. He had been going to say "as a lion" but had noticed Reepicheep's eyes fixed on him.

"And where are we heading for?" asked Edmund.

"Well," said Caspian, "that's rather a long story. Perhaps you remember that when I was a child my usurping uncle Miraz got rid of seven friends of my father's (who might have taken my part) by sending them off to explore the unknown Eastern Seas beyond the Lone Islands."

"Yes," said Lucy, "and none of them ever came back."

"Right. Well, on my coronation day, with Aslan's approval, I swore an oath that, if once I established peace in Narnia, I would sail east myself for a year and a day to find my father's friends or to learn of their deaths and avenge them if I could. These were their names: the Lord Revilian, the Lord Bern, the Lord Argoz, the Lord Mavramorn, the Lord Octesian, the Lord Restimar, and—oh, that other one who's so hard to remember."

"The Lord Rhoop, Sire," said Drinian.

"Rhoop, Rhoop, of course," said Caspian. "That is my main intention. But Reepicheep here has an even higher hope." Everyone's eyes turned to the Mouse.

"As high as my spirit," it said. "Though perhaps as small as my stature. Why should we not come to the very eastern end of the world? And what might we find there? I expect to find Aslan's own country. It is always from the east, across the sea, that the great Lion comes to us."

"I say, that *is* an idea," said Edmund in an awed voice.

"But do you think," said Lucy, "Aslan's country would be that sort of country—I mean, the sort you could ever *sail* to?"

"I do not know, Madam," said Reepicheep. "But there is this. When I was in my cradle a wood woman, a Dryad, spoke this verse over me:

> *Where sky and water meet,*
> *Where the waves grow sweet,*
> *Doubt not, Reepicheep,*
> *To find all you seek,*
> *There is the utter East.*

"I do not know what it means. But the spell of it has been on me all my life."

After a short silence Lucy asked, "And where are we now, Caspian?"

"The Captain can tell you better than I," said Caspian, so Drinian got out his chart and spread it on the table.

"That's our position," he said, laying his finger on it. "Or was at noon today. We had a fair wind from Cair Paravel and stood a little north for Galma, which we made on the next day. We were in port for a week, for the Duke of Galma made a great tournament for His Majesty and there he unhorsed many knights—"

"And got a few nasty falls myself, Drinian. Some of the bruises are there still," put in Caspian.

"—And unhorsed many knights," repeated Drinian with a grin. "We thought the Duke would have been pleased if the King's Majesty would have married his daughter, but nothing came of that—"

"Squints, and has freckles," said Caspian.

"Oh, poor girl," said Lucy.

"And we sailed from Galma," continued Drinian, "and ran into a calm for the best part of two days and had to row, and then had wind again and did not make Terebinthia till the fourth day from Galma. And there their King sent out a warning not to land for there was sickness in Terebinthia, but we doubled the cape and put in at a little creek far from the city and watered. Then we had to lie off for three days before we got a southeast wind and stood out for Seven Isles. The third day out a pirate (Terebinthian by her rig) overhauled us, but when she saw us well armed she stood off after some shooting of arrows on either part—"

"And we ought to have given her chase and boarded her and hanged every mother's son of them," said Reepicheep.

"—And in five days more we were in sight of Muil, which, as you know, is the westernmost of the Seven Isles. Then we rowed through the straits and came about sundown into Redhaven on the isle of Brenn, where we were very lovingly feasted and had victuals and water at will. We left Redhaven six days ago and have made marvelously good speed, so that I hope to see the Lone Islands the day after tomorrow. The sum is, we are now nearly thirty days at sea and have sailed more than four hundred leagues from Narnia."

"And after the Lone Islands?" said Lucy.

"No one knows, your Majesty," answered Drinian. "Unless the Lone Islanders themselves can tell us."

"They couldn't in our days," said Edmund.

"Then," said Reepicheep, "it is after the Lone Islands that the adventure really begins."

Caspian now suggested that they might like to be shown over the ship before supper, but Lucy's conscience smote her and she said, "I think I really must go and see Eustace. Seasickness is horrid, you know. If I had my old cordial with me I could cure him."

"But you have," said Caspian. "I'd quite forgotten about it. As you left it behind I thought it might be regarded as one of the royal treasures and so I brought it—if you think it ought to be wasted on a thing like seasickness."

"It'll only take a drop," said Lucy.

Caspian opened one of the lockers beneath the bench and brought out the beautiful little diamond flask which Lucy remembered so well. "Take back your own, Queen," he said. They then left the cabin and went out into the sunshine.

In the deck there were two large, long hatches, fore and aft of the mast, and both open, as they always were in fair weather, to let light and air into the belly of the ship. Caspian led them down a ladder into the after hatch. Here they found themselves in a place where benches for rowing ran from side to side and the light came in through the oarholes and danced on the roof. Of course Caspian's ship was not that horrible thing, a galley rowed by slaves. Oars were used only when wind failed or for getting in and out of harbor and everyone (except Reepicheep whose legs were too short) had often taken a turn. At each side of the ship the space under the benches was left clear for the rowers' feet, but all down the center there was a kind of pit which went down to the very keel and this was filled with all kinds of things— sacks of flour, casks of water and beer, barrels of pork, jars of honey, skin bottles of wine, apples, nuts, cheeses, biscuits, turnips, sides of bacon. From the roof—that is, from the under side of the deck—hung hams and strings of onions, and also the men of the watch off-duty in their hammocks. Caspian led them aft, stepping from bench to bench; at least, it was stepping for him, and something between a step and a jump for Lucy, and a real long jump for Reepicheep. In this way they came to a partition with a door in it. Caspian opened the door and led them into a cabin which filled the stern underneath the deck cabins in the poop. It was of course not so nice. It was very low and the sides sloped together as they went down so that there was hardly any floor; and though it had windows of thick glass, they were not made to open because they were under water. In fact at this very moment, as the ship pitched they were alternately golden with sunlight and dim green with the sea.

"You and I must lodge here, Edmund," said Caspian. "We'll leave your kinsman the bunk and sling hammocks for ourselves."

"I beseech your Majesty—" said Drinian.

"No, no shipmate," said Caspian, "we have argued all that out already. You and Rhince" (Rhince was the mate) "are sailing the ship and will have cares and labors many a night when we are singing catches or telling stories, so you and he must have the port cabin above. King Edmund and I can lie very snug here below. But how is the stranger?"

Eustace, very green in the face, scowled and asked whether there was any sign of the storm getting less. But Caspian said, "What storm?"

and Drinian burst out laughing.

"Storm, young master!" he roared. "This is as fair weather as a man could ask for."

"Who's that?" said Eustace irritably. "Send him away. His voice goes through my head."

"I've brought you something that will make you feel better, Eustace," said Lucy.

"Oh, go away and leave me alone," growled Eustace. But he took a drop from her flask, and though he said it was beastly stuff (the smell in the cabin when she opened it was delicious) it is certain that his face came the right color a few moments after he had swallowed it, and he must have felt better because, instead of wailing about the storm and his head, he began demanding to be put ashore and said that at the first port he would "lodge a disposition" against them all with the British Consul. But when Reepicheep asked what a disposition was and how you lodged it (Reepicheep thought it was some new way of arranging a single combat) Eustace could only reply, "Fancy not knowing that." In the end they succeeded in convincing Eustace that they were already sailing as fast as they could toward the nearest land they knew, and that they had no more power of sending him back to Cambridge—which was where Uncle Harold lived—than of sending him to the moon. After that he sulkily agreed to put on the fresh clothes which had been put out for him and come on deck.

Caspian now showed them over the ship, though indeed they had seen most of it already. They went up on the forecastle and saw the look-out man standing on a little shelf inside the gilded dragon's neck and peering through its open mouth. Inside the forecastle was the galley (or ship's kitchen) and quarters for such people as the boatswain, the carpenter, the cook and the master-archer. If you think it odd to have the galley in the bows and imagine the smoke from its chimney streaming back over the ship, that is because you are thinking of steamships where there is always a headwind. On a sailing

ship the wind is coming from behind, and anything smelly is put as far forward as possible.
They were taken up to the fighting-top, and at
first it was rather alarming to rock to and fro
there and see the deck looking small and far
away beneath. You realized that if you fell there
was no particular reason why you should fall on
board rather than in the sea. Then they were
taken to the poop, where Rhince was on duty
with another man at the great tiller, and behind
that the dragon's tail rose up, covered with gild-
ing, and round inside it ran a little bench. The
name of the ship was *Dawn Treader*. She was
only a little bit of a thing compared with one of
our ships, or even with the cogs, dromonds, car-
racks and galleons which Narnia had owned
when Lucy and Edmund had reigned there under Peter as the High King, for nearly all naviga-
tion had died out in the reigns of Caspian's
ancestors. When his uncle, Miraz the usurper,
had sent the seven lords to sea, they had had to
buy a Galmian ship and man it with hired
Galmian sailors. But now Caspian had begun to

teach the Narnians to be sea-faring folk once more, and the *Dawn Treader* was the finest ship he had built yet. She was so small that, forward of the mast, there was hardly any deck room between the central hatch and the ship's boat on one side and the hen-coop (Lucy fed the hens) on the other. But she was a beauty of her kind, a "lady" as sailors say, her lines perfect, her colors pure, and every spar and rope and pin lovingly made. Eustace of course would be pleased with nothing, and kept on boasting about liners and motorboats and aeroplanes and submarines ("As if *he* knew anything about them," muttered Edmund), but the other two were delighted with the *Dawn Treader*, and when they returned aft to the cabin and supper, and saw the whole western sky lit up with an immense crimson sunset, and felt the quiver of the ship, and tasted the salt on their lips, and thought of unknown lands on the Eastern rim of the world, Lucy felt that she was almost too happy to speak.

What Eustace thought had best be told in his own words, for when they all got their clothes back, dried, next morning, he at once got out a little black notebook and a pencil and started to keep a diary. He always had this notebook with him and kept a record of his marks in it, for though he didn't care much about any subject for its own sake, he cared a great deal about marks and would even go to people and say, "I got so much. What did you get?" But as he didn't seem likely to get many marks on the *Dawn Treader* he now started a diary. This was the first entry.

"*August 7th*. Have now been twenty-four hours on this ghastly boat if it isn't a dream. All the time a frightful storm has been raging (it's a good thing I'm not seasick). Huge waves keep coming in over the front and I have seen the boat nearly go under any number of times. All the others pretend to take no notice of this, either from swank or because Harold says one of the most cowardly things ordinary people do is to shut their eyes to Facts. It's madness to come out into the sea in a rotten little thing like this. Not much bigger than a lifeboat. And, of course, absolutely primitive indoors. No proper saloon, no radio, no bathrooms, no deck-chairs. I was dragged all over it yesterday evening and it would make anyone sick to hear Caspian showing off his funny little toy boat as if it was the *Queen Mary*. I tried to tell him what real ships are like, but he's too dense. E. and L., *of course*, didn't back me up. I suppose a kid like L. doesn't realize the danger and E. is buttering up C. as everyone does here. They call him a King. I said I was a Republican but he had to ask me what that meant! He doesn't seem to know anything at all. *Needless to say* I've been put in the worst cabin of the boat, a perfect dungeon, and Lucy has been given a whole room on deck to herself, almost a nice room compared with the rest of this place. C. says that's because she's a girl. I tried to make him see what Alberta says, that all that sort of thing is really lowering girls but he was too dense. Still, he might see that I shall be ill if I'm kept in that *hole* any longer. E. says we mustn't grumble because C. is sharing it with us himself to make room for L. As if that didn't make it more crowded and far worse. Nearly forgot to say that there is also a kind of Mouse thing that gives everyone the most frightful cheek. The others can put up with it if they like but I shall twist his tail pretty soon if he tries it on me. The food is frightful too."

The trouble between Eustace and Reepicheep arrived even sooner than might have been expected. Before dinner next day, when the others were sitting round the table waiting (being at sea gives one a magnificent appetite), Eustace came rushing in, wringing his hand and shouting out:

"That little brute has half killed me. I insist on it being kept under control. I could bring an action against you, Caspian. I could order you to have it destroyed."

At the same moment Reepicheep appeared. His sword was drawn and his whiskers looked very fierce but he was as polite as ever.

"I ask your pardons all," he said, "and especially her Majesty's. If I had known that he would take refuge here I would have awaited a more reasonable time for his correction."

"What on earth's up?" asked Edmund.

What had really happened was this. Reepicheep, who never felt that the ship was getting on fast enough, loved to sit on the bulwarks far forward just beside the dragon's head, gazing out at the eastern horizon and singing softly in his little chirruping voice the song the Dryad had made for him. He never held on to anything, however the ship pitched, and kept his balance with perfect ease; perhaps his long

tail, hanging down to the deck inside the bulwarks, made this easier. Everyone on board was familiar with this habit, and the sailors liked it because when one was on look-out duty it gave one somebody to talk to. Why exactly Eustace had slipped and reeled and stumbled all the way forward to the forecastle (he had not yet got his sea-legs) I never heard. Perhaps he hoped he would see land, or perhaps he wanted to hang about the galley and scrounge something. Anyway, as soon as he saw that long tail hanging down—and perhaps it was rather tempting—he thought it would be delightful to catch hold of it, swing Reepicheep round by it once or twice upside-down, then run away and laugh. At first the plan seemed to work beautifully. The Mouse was not much heavier than a very large cat. Eustace had him off the rail in a trice and very silly he looked (thought Eustace) with his little limbs all splayed out and his mouth

open. But unfortunately Reepicheep, who had fought for his life many a time, never lost his head even for a moment. Nor his skill. It is not very easy to draw one's sword when one is swinging round in the air by one's tail, but he did. And the next thing Eustace knew was two agonizing jabs in his hand which made him let go of the tail; and the next thing after that was that the Mouse had picked itself up again as if it were a ball bouncing off the deck, and there it was facing him, and a horrid long, bright, sharp thing like a skewer was waving to and fro within an inch of his stomach. (This doesn't count as below the belt for mice in Narnia because they can hardly be expected to reach higher.)

"Stop it," spluttered Eustace, "go away. Put that thing away. It's not safe. Stop it, I say. I'll tell Caspian. I'll have you muzzled and tied up."

"Why do you not draw your own sword, poltroon!" cheeped the Mouse. "Draw and fight or I'll beat you black and blue with the flat."

"I haven't got one," said Eustace. "I'm a pacifist. I don't believe in fighting."

"Do I understand," said Reepicheep, withdrawing his sword for a moment and speaking very sternly, "that you do not intend to give me satisfaction?"

"I don't know what you mean," said Eustace, nursing his hand. "If you don't know how to take a joke I shan't bother my head about you."

"Then take that," said Reepicheep, "and that—to teach you manners—and the respect due to a knight—and a Mouse—and a Mouse's tail—" and at each word he gave Eustace a blow with the side of his rapier, which was thin, fine, dwarf-tempered steel and as supple and effective as a birch rod. Eustace (of course) was at a school where they didn't have corporal punishment, so the sensation was quite new to him. That was why, in spite of having no sea-legs, it took him less than a minute to get off that forecastle and cover the whole length of the deck and burst in at the cabin door—still hotly pursued by Reepicheep. Indeed it seemed to Eustace that the rapier as well as the pursuit was hot. It might have been red-hot by the feel.

There was not much difficulty in settling the matter once Eustace realized that everyone took the idea of a duel seriously and heard Caspian offering to lend him a sword, and Drinian and Edmund discussing whether he ought to be handicapped in some way to make up for his being so much bigger than Reepicheep. He apologized sulkily and went off with Lucy to have his hand bathed and bandaged and then went to his bunk. He was careful to lie on his side.

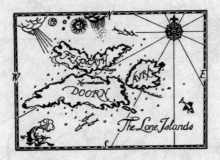

THE LONE ISLANDS

"Land in sight," shouted the man in the bows.

Lucy, who had been talking to Rhince on the poop, came pattering down the ladder and raced forward. As she went she was joined by Edmund, and they found Caspian, Drinian and Reepicheep already on the forecastle. It was a coldish morning, the sky very pale and the sea very dark blue with little white caps of foam, and there, a little way off on the starboard bow, was the nearest of the Lone Islands, Felimath, like a low green hill in the sea, and behind it, further off, the gray slopes of its sister Doorn.

"Same old Felimath! Same old Doorn," said

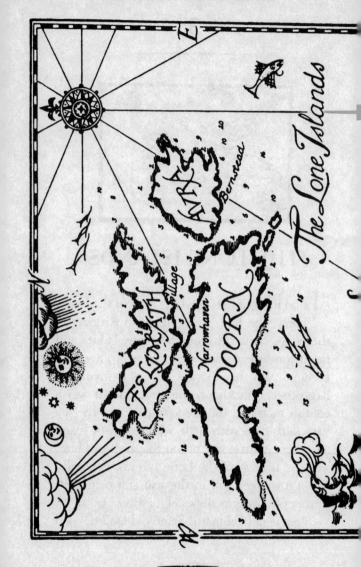

Lucy, clapping her hands. "Oh—Edmund, how long it is since you and I saw them last!"

"I've never understood why they belong to Narnia," said Caspian. "Did Peter the High King conquer them?"

"Oh no," said Edmund. "They were Narnian before our time—in the days of the White Witch."

(By the way, I have never yet heard how these remote islands became attached to the crown of Narnia; if I ever do, and if the story is at all interesting, I may put it in some other book.)

"Are we to put in here, Sire?" asked Drinian.

"I shouldn't think it would be much good landing on Felimath," said Edmund. "It was almost uninhabited in our days and it looks as if it was the same still. The people lived mostly on Doorn and a little on Avra—that's the third one; you can't see it yet. They only kept sheep on Felimath."

"Then we'll have to double that cape, I suppose," said Drinian, "and land on Doorn. That'll mean rowing."

"I'm sorry we're not landing on Felimath," said Lucy. "I'd like to walk there again. It was so lonely—a nice kind of loneliness, and all grass and clover and soft sea air."

"I'd love to stretch my legs too," said Caspian. "I tell you what. Why shouldn't we go ashore in the boat and send it back, and then we could walk across Felimath and let the *Dawn Treader* pick us up on the other side?"

If Caspian had been as experienced then as he became later on in this voyage he would not have made this suggestion; but at the moment it seemed an excellent one. "Oh do let's," said Lucy.

"You'll come, will you?" said Caspian to Eustace, who had come on deck with his hand bandaged.

"Anything to get off this blasted boat," said Eustace.

"Blasted?" said Drinian. "How do you mean?"

"In a civilized country like where I come from," said Eustace, "the ships are so big that when you're inside you wouldn't know you were at sea at all."

"In that case you might just as well stay ashore," said Caspian. "Will you tell them to lower the boat, Drinian?"

The King, the Mouse, the two Pevensies, and Eustace all got into the boat and were pulled to the beach of Felimath. When the boat had left them and was being rowed back they all turned and looked round. They were surprised at how small the *Dawn Treader* looked.

Lucy was of course barefoot, having kicked off her shoes while swimming, but that is no hardship if one is going to walk on downy turf. It was delightful to be ashore again and to smell the earth and grass, even if at first the ground seemed to be pitching up and down like a ship, as it usually does for a while if one has been at sea. It was much warmer here than it had been on board and Lucy found the sand pleasant to her feet as they crossed it. There was a lark singing.

They struck inland and up a fairly steep, though low, hill. At the top of course they looked back, and there was the *Dawn Treader* shining like a great bright insect and crawling slowly northwestward with her oars. Then they went over the ridge and could see her no longer.

Doorn now lay before them, divided from Felimath by a channel about a mile wide; behind it and to the left lay Avra. The little white town of Narrowhaven on Doorn was easily seen.

"Hullo! What's this?" said Edmund suddenly.

In the green valley to which they were descending six or seven rough-looking men, all armed, were sitting by a tree.

"Don't tell them who we are," said Caspian.

"And pray, your Majesty, why not?" said

Reepicheep who had consented to ride on Lucy's shoulder.

"It just occurred to me," replied Caspian, "that no one here can have heard from Narnia for a long time. It's just possible they may not still acknowledge our over-lordship. In which case it might not be quite safe to be known as the King."

"We have our swords, Sire," said Reepicheep.

"Yes, Reep, I know we have," said Caspian. "But if it is a question of re-conquering the three islands, I'd prefer to come back with a rather larger army."

By this time they were quite close to the strangers, one of whom—a big black-haired fellow—shouted out, "A good morning to you."

"And a good morning to you," said Caspian.

"Is there still a Governor of the Lone Islands?"

"To be sure there is," said the man, "Governor Gumpas. His Sufficiency is at Narrowhaven. But you'll stay and drink with us."

Caspian thanked him, though neither he nor the others much liked the look of their new acquaintance, and all of them sat down. But hardly had they raised their cups to their lips when the black-haired man nodded to his companions and, as quick as lightning, all the five visitors found themselves wrapped in strong arms. There was a moment's struggle but all the advantages were on one side, and soon everyone was disarmed and had their hands tied behind their backs—except Reepicheep, writhing in his captor's grip and biting furiously.

"Careful with that beast, Tacks," said the Leader. "Don't damage him. He'll fetch the best price of the lot, I shouldn't wonder."

"Coward! Poltroon!" squeaked Reepicheep. "Give me my sword and free my paws if you dare."

"Whew!" whistled the slave merchant (for that is what he was). "It can talk! Well I never did. Blowed if I take less than two hundred crescents for him." The Calormen crescent, which is the chief coin in those parts, is worth about a third of a pound.

"So that's what you are," said Caspian. "A kidnapper and slaver. I hope you're proud of it."

"Now, now, now, now," said the slaver. "Don't you start any jaw. The easier you take it, the pleasanter all round, see? I don't do this for fun. I've got my living to make same as anyone else."

"Where will you take us?" asked Lucy, getting the words out with some difficulty.

"Over to Narrowhaven," said the slaver. "For market day tomorrow."

"Is there a British Consul there?" asked Eustace.

"Is there a which?" said the man.

But long before Eustace was tired of trying to explain, the slaver simply said, "Well, I've had enough of this jabber. The Mouse is a fair treat but this one would talk the hind leg off a donkey. Off we go, mates."

Then the four human prisoners were roped together, not cruelly but securely, and made to march down to the shore. Reepicheep was carried. He had stopped biting on a threat of having his mouth tied up, but he had a great deal to say, and Lucy really wondered how any man could bear to have the things said to him which were said to the slave dealer by the Mouse. But the slave dealer, far from objecting, only said "Go on" whenever Reepicheep paused for

breath, occasionally adding, "It's as good as a play," or, "Blimey, you can't help almost thinking it knows what it's saying!" or "Was it one of you what trained it?" This so infuriated Reepicheep that in the end the number of things he thought of saying all at once nearly suffocated him and he became silent.

When they got down to the shore that looked toward Doorn they found a little village and a long-boat on the beach and, lying a little further out, a dirty bedraggled looking ship.

"Now, youngsters," said the slave dealer, "let's have no fuss and then you'll have nothing to cry about. All aboard."

At that moment a fine-looking bearded man came out of one of the houses (an inn, I think) and said:

"Well, Pug. More of your usual wares?"

The slaver, whose name seemed to be Pug, bowed very low, and said in a wheedling kind of voice, "Yes, please your Lordship."

"How much do you want for that boy?" asked the other, pointing to Caspian.

"Ah," said Pug, "I knew your Lordship would pick on the best. No deceiving your Lordship with anything second rate. That boy, now, I've taken a fancy to him myself. Got kind of fond of him, I have. I'm that tender-hearted I didn't ever ought to have taken up this job. Still, to a customer like your Lordship—"

"Tell me your price, carrion," said the Lord sternly. "Do you think I want to listen to the rigmarole of your filthy trade?"

"Three hundred crescents, my Lord, to your honorable Lordship, but to anyone else—"

"I'll give you a hundred and fifty."

"Oh please, please," broke in Lucy. "Don't separate us, whatever you do. You don't know—" But then she stopped for she saw that Caspian didn't even now want to be known.

"A hundred and fifty, then," said the Lord. "As for you, little maiden, I am sorry I cannot buy you all. Unrope my boy, Pug. And look—treat these others well while they are in your hands or it'll be the worse for you."

"Well!" said Pug. "Now who ever heard of a

gentleman in my way of business who treated his stock better than what I do? Well? Why, I treat 'em like my own children."

"That's likely enough to be true," said the other grimly.

The dreadful moment had now come. Caspian was untied and his new master said, "This way, lad," and Lucy burst into tears and Edmund looked very blank. But Caspian looked over his shoulder and said, "Cheer up. I'm sure it will come all right in the end. So long."

"Now, missie," said Pug. "Don't you start taking on and spoiling your looks for the market tomorrow. You be a good girl and then you won't have nothing to cry *about*, see?"

Then they were rowed out to the slave-ship and taken below into a long, rather dark place, none too clean, where they found many other unfortunate prisoners; for Pug was of course a pirate and had just returned from cruising among the islands and capturing what he could. The children didn't meet anyone whom they knew; the prisoners were mostly Galmians and Terebinthians. And there they sat in the straw and wondered what was happening to Caspian and tried to stop Eustace talking as if everyone except himself was to blame.

Meanwhile Caspian was having a much more interesting time. The man who had bought him led him down a little lane between two of the village houses and so out into an open place behind the village. Then he turned and faced him.

"You needn't be afraid of me, boy," he said. "I'll treat you well. I bought you for your face. You reminded me of someone."

"May I ask of whom, my Lord?" said Caspian.

"You remind me of my master, King Caspian of Narnia."

Then Caspian decided to risk everything on one stroke.

"My Lord," he said, "I *am* your master. I am Caspian, King of Narnia."

"You make very free," said the other. "How shall I know this is true?"

"Firstly by my face," said Caspian. "Secondly because I know within six guesses who you are. You are one of those seven lords of Narnia whom my Uncle Miraz sent to sea and whom I have come out to look for—Argoz, Bern, Octesian, Restimar, Mavramorn, or—or—I have forgotten the others. And finally, if your Lordship will give me a sword I will prove on any man's body in clean battle that I am Caspian the son of Caspian, lawful King of Narnia, Lord of Cair Paravel, and Emperor of the Lone Islands."

"By heaven," exclaimed the man, "it is his father's very voice and trick of speech. My liege—your Majesty—" And there in the field he knelt and kissed the King's hand.

"The moneys your Lordship disbursed for our person will be made good from our own treasury," said Caspian.

"They're not in Pug's purse yet, Sire," said the Lord Bern, for he it was. "And never will be, I trust. I have moved His Sufficiency the Governor a hundred times to crush this vile traffic in man's flesh."

"My Lord Bern," said Caspian, "we must talk of the state of these Islands. But first what is your Lordship's own story?"

"Short enough, Sire," said Bern. "I came thus far with my six fellows, loved a girl of the islands, and felt I had had enough of the sea. And there was no purpose in returning to Narnia while your Majesty's uncle held the reins. So I married and have lived here ever since."

"And what is this governor, this Gumpas, like? Does he still acknowledge the King of Narnia for his lord?"

"In words, yes. All is done in the King's name. But he would not be best pleased to find a real, live King of Narnia coming in upon him. And if your Majesty came before him alone and unarmed—well he would not deny his allegiance, but he would pretend to disbelieve you. Your Grace's life would be in danger. What following has your Majesty in these waters?"

"There is my ship just rounding the point," said Caspian. "We are about thirty swords if it came to fighting. Shall we not have my ship in and fall upon Pug and free my friends whom he holds captive?"

"Not by my counsel," said Bern. "As soon as there was a fight two or three ships would put out from Narrowhaven to rescue Pug. Your Majesty must work by a show of more power than you really have, and by the terror of the King's name. It must not come to plain battle. Gumpas is a chicken-hearted man and can be over-awed."

After a little more conversation Caspian and Bern walked down to the coast a little west of the village and there Caspian winded his horn. (This was not the great magic horn of Narnia, Queen Susan's Horn: he had left that at home for his regent Trumpkin to use if any great need fell upon the land in the King's absence.) Drinian, who was on the lookout for a signal, recognized the royal horn at once and the *Dawn Treader* began standing in to shore. Then the boat put off again and in a few moments Caspian and the Lord Bern were on deck explaining the situation to Drinian. He, just like Caspian, wanted to lay the *Dawn Treader* alongside the slave-ship at once and board her, but Bern made the same objection.

"Steer straight down this channel, captain," said Bern, "and then round to Avra where my own estates are. But first run up the King's banner, hang out all the shields, and send as many men to the fighting-top as you can. And about five bowshots hence, when you get open sea on your port bow, run up a few signals."

"Signals? To whom?" said Drinian.

"Why, to all the other ships we haven't got but which it might be well that Gumpas thinks we have."

"Oh, I see," said Drinian, rubbing his hands. "And they'll read our signals. What shall I say? *Whole fleet round the South of Avra and assemble at—?*"

"Bernstead," said the Lord Bern. "That'll do excellently. Their whole journey—if there *were* any ships—would be out of sight from Narrowhaven."

Caspian was sorry for the others languishing in the hold of Pug's slave-ship, but he could not help finding the rest of that day enjoyable. Late in the afternoon (for they had to do all by oar), having turned to starboard round the northeast end of Doorn and port again round the point of

Avra, they entered into a good harbor on Avra's southern shore where Bern's pleasant lands sloped down to the water's edge. Bern's people, many of whom they saw working in the fields, were all freemen and it was a happy and prosperous fief. Here they all went ashore and were royally feasted in a low, pillared house overlooking the bay. Bern and his gracious wife and merry daughters made them good cheer. But after dark Bern sent a messenger over by boat to Doorn to order some preparations (he did not say exactly what) for the following day.

4

WHAT CASPIAN
DID THERE

Next morning the Lord Bern called his guests early, and after breakfast he asked Caspian to order every man he had into full armor. "And above all," he added, "let everything be as trim and scoured as if it were the morning of the first battle in a great war between noble kings with all the world looking on." This was done; and then in three boatloads Caspian and his people, and Bern with a few of his, put out for Narrowhaven. The King's flag flew in the stern of his boat and his trumpeter was with him.

When they reached the jetty at Narrowhaven, Caspian found a considerable crowd assembled to meet them. "This is what I sent word about last night," said Bern. "They are all friends of mine and honest people." And as soon as Caspian stepped ashore the crowd broke out into hurrahs and shouts of, "Narnia! Narnia! Long live the King." At the same moment—and this was also due to Bern's messengers—bells began ringing from many parts of the town. Then Caspian caused his banner to be advanced and his trumpet to be blown and every man drew his sword and set his face into a joyful sternness, and they marched up the street so that the street shook, and their armor shone (for it was a sunny morning) so that one could hardly look at it steadily.

At first the only people who cheered were those who had been warned by Bern's messenger and knew what was happening and wanted it to happen. But then all the children joined in because they liked a procession and had seen very few. And then all the schoolboys joined in because they also liked processions and felt that the more noise and disturbance there was the less likely they would be to have any school that morning. And then all the old women put their heads out of doors and windows and began chattering and cheering because it was a king, and what is a governor compared with that? And all

the young women joined in for the same reason and also because Caspian and Drinian and the rest were so handsome. And then all the young men came to see what the young women were looking at, so that by the time Caspian reached the castle gates, nearly the whole town was shouting; and where Gumpas sat in the castle, muddling and messing about with accounts and forms and rules and regulations, he heard the noise.

At the castle gate Caspian's trumpeter blew a blast and cried, "Open for the King of Narnia, come to visit his trusty and well-beloved servant the governor of the Lone Islands." In those days everything in the islands was done in a slovenly, slouching manner. Only the little postern opened, and out came a tousled fellow with a dirty old hat on his head instead of a helmet, and a rusty old pike in his hand. He blinked at the flashing figures before him. "Carn—seez—fishansy," he mumbled (which was his way of saying, "You can't see His Sufficiency"). "No interviews without 'pointments 'cept 'tween nine 'n' ten p.m. second Saturday every month."

"Uncover before Narnia, you dog," thundered the Lord Bern, and dealt him a rap with his gauntleted hand which sent his hat flying from his head.

"'Ere? Wot's it all about?" began the doorkeeper, but no one took any notice of him. Two of Caspian's men stepped through the postern and after some struggling with bars and bolts (for everything was rusty) flung both wings of the gate wide open. Then the King and his followers strode into the courtyard. Here a number of the governor's guards were lounging about and several more (they were mostly wiping their mouths) came tumbling out of various doorways. Though their armor was in a disgraceful condition, these were fellows who might have fought if they had been led or had known what was happening; so this was the dangerous moment. Caspian gave them no time to think.

"Where is the captain?" he asked.

"I am, more or less, if you know what I mean," said a languid and rather dandified young person without any armor at all.

"It is our wish," said Caspian, "that our royal visitation to our realm of the Lone Islands should, if possible, be an occasion of joy and not of terror to our loyal subjects. If it were not for that, I should have something to say about the state of your men's armor and weapons. As it is, you are pardoned. Command a cask of wine to be opened that your men may drink our health. But at noon tomorrow I wish to see them here in this courtyard looking like men-at-arms and not like vagabonds. See to it on pain of our extreme displeasure."

The captain gaped but Bern immediately cried, "Three cheers for the King," and the soldiers, who had understood about the cask of wine even if they understood nothing else, joined in. Caspian then ordered most of his own men to remain in the courtyard. He, with Bern and Drinian and four others, went into the hall.

Behind a table at the far end with various secretaries about him sat his Sufficiency, the Governor of the Lone Islands. Gumpas was a bilious-looking man with hair that had once been red and was now mostly gray. He glanced up as the strangers entered and then looked down at his papers saying automatically, "No interviews without appointments except between nine and ten p.m. on second Saturdays."

Caspian nodded to Bern and then stood aside. Bern and Drinian took a step forward and each seized one end of the table. They lifted it,

and flung it on one side of the hall where it rolled over, scattering a cascade of letters, dossiers, ink-pots, pens, sealing-wax and documents. Then, not roughly but as firmly as if their hands were pincers of steel, they plucked Gumpas out of his chair and deposited him, facing it, about four feet away. Caspian at once sat down in the chair and laid his naked sword across his knees.

"My Lord," said he, fixing his eyes on Gumpas, "you have not given us quite the welcome we expected. We are the King of Narnia."

"Nothing about it in the correspondence," said the governor. "Nothing in the minutes. We have not been notified of any such thing. All irregular. Happy to consider any applications—"

"And we are come to inquire into your Sufficiency's conduct of your office," continued Caspian. "There are two points especially on which I require an explanation. Firstly I find no record that the tribute due from these Islands to the crown of Narnia has been received for about a hundred and fifty years."

"That would be a question to raise at the Council next month," said Gumpas. "If anyone moves that a commission of inquiry be set up to report on the financial history of the islands at the first meeting next year, why then . . ."

"I also find it very clearly written in our

laws," Caspian went on, "that if the tribute is not delivered the whole debt has to be paid by the Governor of the Lone Islands out of his private purse."

At this Gumpas began to pay real attention. "Oh, that's quite out of the question," he said. "It is an economic impossibility—er—your Majesty must be joking."

Inside, he was wondering if there were any way of getting rid of these unwelcome visitors. Had he known that Caspian had only one ship and one ship's company with him, he would have spoken soft words for the moment, and hoped to have them all surrounded and killed during the night. But he had seen a ship of war sail down the straits yesterday and seen it signaling, as he supposed, to its consorts. He had not then known it was the King's ship for there was not wind enough to spread the flag out and make the golden lion visible, so he had waited further developments. Now he imagined that Caspian had a whole fleet at Bernstead. It would never have occurred to Gumpas that anyone would walk into Narrowhaven to take the islands with less than fifty men; it was certainly not at all the kind of thing he could imagine doing himself.

"Secondly," said Caspian, "I want to know why you have permitted this abominable and unnatural traffic in slaves to grow up here, contrary to the ancient custom and usage of our dominions."

"Necessary, unavoidable," said his Sufficiency. "An essential part of the economic development of the islands, I assure you. Our present burst of prosperity depends on it."

"What need have you of slaves?"

"For export, your Majesty. Sell 'em to Calormen mostly; and we have other markets. We are a great center of the trade."

"In other words," said Caspian, "you don't need them. Tell me what purpose they serve except to put money into the pockets of such as Pug?"

"Your Majesty's tender years," said Gumpas, with what was meant to be a fatherly smile, "hardly make it possible that you should understand the economic problem involved. I have statistics, I have graphs, I have—"

"Tender as my years may be," said Caspian, "I believe I understand the slave trade from within quite as well as your Sufficiency. And I do not see that it brings into the islands meat or bread or beer or wine or timber or cabbages or books or instruments of music or horses or armor or anything else worth having. But whether it does or not, it must be stopped."

"But that would be putting the clock back," gasped the governor. "Have you no idea of progress, of development?"

"I have seen them both in an egg," said Caspian. "We call it 'Going Bad' in Narnia. This trade must stop."

"I can take no responsibility for any such measure," said Gumpas.

"Very well, then," answered Caspian, "we relieve you of your office. My Lord Bern, come here." And before Gumpas quite realized what was happening, Bern was kneeling with his hands between the King's hands and taking the oath to govern the Lone Islands in accordance with the old customs, rights, usages and laws of Narnia. And Caspian said, "I think we have had enough of governors," and made Bern a Duke, the Duke of the Lone Islands.

"As for you, my Lord," he said to Gumpas, "I forgive you your debt for the tribute. But before noon tomorrow you and yours must be out of the castle, which is now the Duke's residence."

"Look here, this is all very well," said one of Gumpas's secretaries, "but suppose all you gentlemen stop play-acting and we do a little business. The question before us really is—"

"The question is," said the Duke, "whether you and the rest of the rabble will leave without a flogging or with one. You may choose which you prefer."

When all this had been pleasantly settled,

Caspian ordered horses, of which there were a few in the castle, though very ill-groomed, and he, with Bern and Drinian and a few others, rode out into the town and made for the slave market. It was a long low building near the harbor and the scene which they found going on inside was very much like any other auction; that is to say, there was a great crowd and Pug, on a platform, was roaring out in a raucous voice:

"Now, gentlemen, lot twenty-three. Fine Terebinthian agricultural laborer, suitable for the mines or the galleys. Under twenty-five years of age. Not a bad tooth in his head. Good, brawny fellow. Take off his shirt, Tacks, and let the gentlemen see. There's muscle for you! Look at the chest on him. Ten crescents from the gentleman in the corner. You must be joking, sir. Fifteen! Eighteen! Eighteen is bidden for lot twenty-three. Any advance on eighteen? Twenty-one. Thank you, sir. Twenty-one is bidden—"

But Pug stopped and gaped when he saw the mail-clad figures who had clanked up to the platform.

"On your knees, every man of you, to the King of Narnia," said the Duke. Everyone heard the horses jingling and stamping outside and many had heard some rumor of the landing and the events at the castle. Most obeyed. Those who did not were pulled down by their neighbors. Some cheered.

"Your life is forfeit, Pug, for laying hands on our royal person yesterday," said Caspian. "But your ignorance is pardoned. The slave trade was forbidden in all our dominions quarter of an hour ago. I declare every slave in this market free."

He held up his hand to check the cheering of the slaves and went on, "Where are my friends?"

"That dear little gel and the nice young gentleman?" said Pug with an ingratiating smile. "Why, they were snapped up at once—"

"We're here, we're here, Caspian," cried Lucy and Edmund together and, "At your service, Sire," piped Reepicheep from another corner. They had all been sold but the men who had bought them were staying to bid for other slaves and so they had not yet been taken away. The crowd parted to let the three of them out and there was great hand-clasping and greeting between them and Caspian. Two merchants of Calormen at once approached. The Calormen have dark faces and long beards. They wear flowing robes and orange-colored turbans, and they are a wise, wealthy, courteous, cruel and ancient people. They bowed most politely to

Caspian and paid him long compliments, all about the fountains of prosperity irrigating the gardens of prudence and virtue—and things like that—but of course what they wanted was the money they had paid.

"That is only fair, sirs," said Caspian. "Every man who has bought a slave today must have his money back. Pug, bring out your takings to the last minim." (A minim is the fortieth part of a crescent.)

"Does your good Majesty mean to beggar me?" whined Pug.

"You have lived on broken hearts all your life," said Caspian, "and if you *are* beggared, it is better to be a beggar than a slave. But where is my other friend?"

"Oh *him*?" said Pug. "Oh take *him* and welcome. Glad to have him off my hands. I've never seen such a drug in the market in all my born days. Priced him at five crescents in the end and even so nobody'd have him. Threw him in free with other lots and still no one would have him. Wouldn't touch him. Wouldn't look at him. Tacks, bring out Sulky."

Thus Eustace was produced, and sulky he certainly looked; for though no one would want to be sold as a slave, it is perhaps even more galling to be a sort of utility slave whom no one will buy. He walked up to Caspian and said, "I see. As usual. Been enjoying yourself somewhere while the rest of us were prisoners. I suppose you haven't even found out about the British Consul. Of course not."

That night they had a great feast in the castle of Narrowhaven and then, "Tomorrow for the beginning of our real adventures!" said Reepicheep when he had made his bows to everyone and went to bed. But it could not really be tomorrow or anything like it. For now they were preparing to leave all known lands and seas behind them and the fullest preparations had to be made. The *Dawn Treader* was emptied and drawn on land by eight horses over rollers and every bit of her was gone over by the most skilled shipwrights. Then she was launched again and victualed and watered as full as she could hold—that is to say for twenty-eight days. Even this, as Edmund noticed with disappointment, only gave them a fortnight's eastward sailing before they had to abandon their quest.

While all this was being done Caspian missed no chance of questioning all the oldest sea captains whom he could find in Narrowhaven to learn if they had any knowledge or even any rumors of land further to the east. He poured out many a flagon of the castle ale to weather-beaten men with short gray beards and clear blue eyes, and many a tall yarn he heard in

return. But those who seemed the most truthful could tell of no lands beyond the Lone Islands, and many thought that if you sailed too far east you would come into the surges of a sea without lands that swirled perpetually round the rim of the world—"And that, I reckon, is where your Majesty's friends went to the bottom." The rest had only wild stories of islands inhabited by headless men, floating islands, waterspouts, and a fire that burned along the water. Only one, to Reepicheep's delight, said, "And beyond that, Aslan's country. But that's beyond the end of the world and you can't get there." But when they questioned him he could only say that he'd heard it from his father.

Bern could only tell them that he had seen his six companions sail away eastward and that nothing had ever been heard of them again. He said this when he and Caspian were standing on the highest point of Avra looking down on the eastern ocean. "I've often been up here of a morning," said the Duke, "and seen the sun come up out of the sea, and sometimes it looked as if it were only a couple of miles away. And I've wondered about my friends and wondered what there really is behind that horizon. Nothing, most likely, yet I am always half ashamed that I stayed behind. But I wish your Majesty wouldn't go. We may need your help here. This closing the slave market might make a new world; war with Calormen is what I foresee. My liege, think again."

"I have an oath, my lord Duke," said Caspian. "And anyway, what *could* I say to Reepicheep?"

5

THE STORM
AND WHAT CAME OF IT

It was nearly three weeks after their landing
that the *Dawn Treader* was towed out of Narrowhaven harbor. Very solemn farewells had been
spoken and a great crowd had assembled to see
her departure. There had been cheers, and tears
too, when Caspian made his last speech to the
Lone Islanders and parted from the Duke and
his family, but as the ship, her purple sail still
flapping idly, drew further from the shore, and
the sound of Caspian's trumpet from the poop
came fainter across the water, everyone became
silent. Then she came into the wind. The sail

swelled out, the tug cast off and began rowing back, the first real wave ran up under the *Dawn Treader*'s prow, and she was a live ship again. The men off duty went below, Drinian took the first watch on the poop, and she turned her head eastward round the south of Avra.

The next few days were delightful. Lucy thought she was the most fortunate girl in the world, as she woke each morning to see the reflections of the sunlit water dancing on the ceiling of her cabin and looked round on all the nice new things she had got in the Lone Islands—seaboots and buskins and cloaks and jerkins and scarves. And then she would go on deck and take a look from the forecastle at a sea which was a brighter blue each morning and drink in an air that was a little warmer day by day. After that came breakfast and such an appetite as one only has at sea.

She spent a good deal of time sitting on the little bench in the stern playing chess with Reepicheep. It was amusing to see him lifting the pieces, which were far too big for him, with both paws and standing on tiptoes if he made a move near the center of the board. He was a good player and when he remembered what he was doing he usually won. But every now and then Lucy won because the Mouse did something quite ridiculous like sending a knight into the danger of a queen and castle combined. This happened because he had momentarily forgotten it was a game of chess and was thinking of a real battle and making the knight do what he would certainly have done in its place. For his mind was full of forlorn hopes, death-or-glory charges, and last stands.

But this pleasant time did not last. There came an evening when Lucy, gazing idly astern at the long furrow or wake they were leaving behind them, saw a great rack of clouds building itself up in the west with amazing speed. Then a gap was torn in it and a yellow sunset poured through the gap. All the waves behind them seemed to take on unusual shapes and the sea was a drab or yellowish color like dirty canvas. The air grew cold. The ship seemed to move uneasily as if she felt danger behind her. The sail would be flat and limp one minute and wildly full the next. While she was noting these things and wondering at a sinister change which had come over the very noise of the wind, Drinian cried, "All hands on deck." In a moment everyone became frantically busy. The hatches were battened down, the galley fire was put out, men went aloft to reef the sail. Before they had finished the storm struck them. It seemed to Lucy that a great valley in the sea opened just before their bows, and they rushed down into it, deeper down than she would have believed possible. A great gray hill of water, far higher than the mast, rushed to meet them; it looked certain death but they were tossed to the top of it. Then the ship seemed to spin round. A cataract of water poured over the deck; the poop and forecastle were like two islands with a fierce sea between them. Up aloft the sailors were lying out along the yard desperately trying to get control of the sail. A broken rope stood out sideways in the wind as straight and stiff as if it was a poker.

"Get below, Ma'am," bawled Drinian. And Lucy, knowing that landsmen—and landswomen—are a nuisance to the crew, began to obey. It was not easy. The *Dawn Treader* was listing terribly to starboard and the deck sloped like the roof of a house. She had to clamber round to the top of the ladder, holding on to the rail, and then stand by while two men climbed up it, and then get down it as best she could. It was well she was already holding on tight for at the foot of the ladder another wave roared across the deck, up to her shoulders. She was already almost wet through with spray and rain but this was colder. Then she made a dash for the cabin door and got in and shut out for a moment the appalling sight of the speed with which they were rushing into the dark, but not of course the horrible confusion of creakings, groanings, snap-

pings, clatterings, roarings and boomings which only sounded more alarming below than they had done on the poop.

And all next day and all the next it went on. It went on till one could hardly even remember a time before it had begun. And there always had to be three men at the tiller and it was as much as three could do to keep any kind of a course. And there always had to be men at the pump. And there was hardly any rest for anyone, and nothing could be cooked and nothing could be dried, and one man was lost overboard, and they never saw the sun.

When it was over Eustace made the following entry in his diary:

"*September 3.* The first day for ages when I have been able to write. We had been driven before a hurricane for thirteen days and nights. I know that because I kept a careful count, though the others all say it was only twelve. *Pleasant* to be embarked on a dangerous voyage with people who can't even count right! I have had a ghastly time, up and down enormous waves hour after hour, usually wet to the skin, and not even an *attempt* at giving us proper meals. Needless to say there's no wireless or even a rocket, so no chance of signaling anyone for help. It all proves what I keep on telling them, the madness of setting out in a rotten little tub like this. It would be bad enough even if one was with decent people instead of fiends in human form. Caspian and Edmund are simply brutal to me. The night we lost our mast (there's only a stump left now), though I was *not at all* well, they forced me to come on deck and work like a slave. Lucy shoved her oar in by saying that Reepicheep was longing to go only he was too small. I wonder she doesn't see that everything that little beast does is all for the sake of *showing off.* Even at her age she ought to have that amount of sense. Today the beastly boat is level at last and the sun's out and we have all been jawing about what to do. We have food enough, pretty beastly stuff most of it, to last for sixteen days. (The poultry were all washed over-board. Even if they hadn't been, the storm would have stopped them laying.) The real trouble is water. Two casks seem to have got a leak knocked in them and are empty. (Narnian efficiency again.) On short rations, half a pint a day each, we've got enough for twelve days. (There's still lots of rum and wine but even *they* realize that would only make them thirstier.)

"If we could, of course, the sensible thing would be to turn west at once and make for the Lone Islands. But it took us eighteen days to get where we are, running like mad with a gale be-hind us. Even if we got an east wind it might take us far longer to get back. And at present there's no sign of an east wind—in fact there's no wind at all. As for rowing back, it would take far too long and Caspian says the men couldn't row on half a pint of water a day. I'm pretty sure this is wrong. I tried to explain that perspiration really cools people down, so the men would need less water if they were working. He didn't take any notice of this, which is always his way when he can't think of an answer. The others all voted for going *on* in the hope of finding land. I felt it my duty to point out that we didn't know there *was* any land ahead and tried to get them to see the dangers of *wishful thinking*. Instead of producing a better plan they had the cheek to ask me what I proposed. So I just explained coolly and quietly that I had been kidnapped and brought away on this *idiotic* voyage without my consent, and it was hardly *my* business to get *them* out of their scrape.

"*September 4*. Still becalmed. Very short rations for dinner and I got less than anyone. Caspian is very clever at helping and thinks I don't see! Lucy for some reason tried to make up to me by offering me some of hers but that *interfering prig* Edmund wouldn't let her. Pretty hot sun. Terribly thirsty all evening.

"*September 5*. Still becalmed and very hot. Feeling rotten all day and am sure I've got a temperature. Of course they haven't the sense to keep a thermometer on board.

"*September 6*. A horrible day. Woke up in the night *knowing* I was feverish and *must* have a drink of water. Any doctor would have said so. Heaven knows I'm the last person to try to get any unfair advantage but I never *dreamed* that this water-rationing would be meant to apply to a sick man. In fact I would have woken the others up and asked for some only I thought it would be selfish to wake them. So I just got up and took my cup and tiptoed out of the Black Hole we slept in, taking great care not to disturb Caspian and Edmund, for they've been sleeping badly since the heat and the short water began. I always try to consider others whether they are nice to me or not. I got out all right into the big room, if you can call it a room, where the rowing benches and the luggage are. The thing of water is at this end. All was going beautifully, but before I'd drawn a cupful who should catch me but that *little spy* Reep. I tried to explain that I was going on deck for a breath of air (the business about the water had nothing to do with him) and he asked me why I had a cup. He made such a noise that the whole ship was roused. They treated me scandalously. I asked, as I think anyone would have, why Reepicheep was sneaking about the water cask in the middle of the night. He said that as he was too small to be any use on deck, he did sentry over the water every night so that one more man could go to sleep. Now comes their rotten unfairness: they all believed *him*. Can you beat it?

"I had to apologize or the dangerous little brute would have been at me with his sword. And then Caspian showed up in his true colors as a brutal tyrant and said out loud for everyone to hear that anyone found 'stealing' water in future would 'get two dozen.' I didn't know what this meant till Edmund explained to me. It comes in the sort of books those Pevensie kids read.

"After this cowardly threat Caspian changed

his tune and started being *patronizing*. Said he was sorry for me and that everyone felt just as feverish as I did and we must all make the best of it, etc., etc. Odious stuck-up prig. Stayed in bed all day today.

"*September* 7. A little wind today but still from the west. Made a few miles eastward with part of the sail, set on what Drinian calls the jury-mast—that means the bowsprit set upright and tied (they call it 'lashed') to the stump of the real mast. Still terribly thirsty.

"*September* 8. Still sailing east. I stay in my bunk all day now and see no one except Lucy till the two *fiends* come to bed. Lucy gives me a little of her water ration. She says girls don't get as thirsty as boys. I had often thought this but it ought to be more generally known at sea.

"*September* 9. Land in sight; a very high mountain a long way off to the southeast.

"*September* 10. The mountain is bigger and clearer but still a long way off. Gulls again today for the first time since I don't know how long.

"*September* 11. Caught some fish and had them for dinner. Dropped anchor at about 7 P.M. in three fathoms of water in a bay of this mountainous island. That idiot Caspian wouldn't let us go ashore because it was getting dark and he was afraid of savages and wild beasts. Extra water ration tonight."

❖　　❖　　❖

What awaited them on this island was going to concern Eustace more than anyone else, but it cannot be told in his words because after September 11 he forgot about keeping his diary for a long time.

When morning came, with a low, gray sky but very hot, the adventurers found they were in a bay encircled by such cliffs and crags that it was like a Norwegian fjord. In front of them, at the head of the bay, there was some level land heavily overgrown with trees that appeared to be cedars, through which a rapid stream came out. Beyond that was a steep ascent ending in a jagged ridge and behind that a vague darkness of mountains which ran into dull-colored clouds so that you could not see their tops. The nearer cliffs, at each side of the bay, were streaked here and there with lines of white which everyone knew to be waterfalls, though at that distance they did not show any movement or make any noise. Indeed the whole place was very silent and the water of the bay as smooth as glass. It reflected every detail of the cliffs. The scene would have been pretty in a picture but was rather oppressive in real life. It was not a country that welcomed visitors.

The whole ship's company went ashore in two boatloads and everyone drank and washed

deliciously in the river and had a meal and a rest
before Caspian sent four men back to keep the
ship, and the day's work began. There was
everything to be done. The casks must be
brought ashore and the faulty ones mended if

possible and all refilled; a tree—a pine if they could get it—must be felled and made into a new mast; sails must be repaired; a hunting party organized to shoot any game the land might yield; clothes to be washed and mended; and countless small breakages on board to be set right. For the *Dawn Treader* herself—and this was more obvious now that they saw her at a distance—could hardly be recognized as the same gallant ship which had left Narrowhaven. She looked a crippled, discolored hulk which anyone might have taken for a wreck. And her officers and crew were no better—lean, pale, red-eyed from lack of sleep, and dressed in rags.

As Eustace lay under a tree and heard all these plans being discussed his heart sank. Was there going to be no rest? It looked as if their first day on the longed-for land was going to be quite as hard work as a day at sea. Then a delightful idea occurred to him. Nobody was looking—they were all chattering about their ship as if they actually liked the beastly thing. Why shouldn't he simply slip away? He would take a stroll inland, find a cool, airy place up in the mountains, have a good long sleep, and not rejoin the others till the day's work was over. He felt it would do him good. But he would take great care to keep the bay and the ship in sight so as to be sure of his way back. He wouldn't like to be left behind in this country.

He at once put his plan into action. He rose quietly from his place and walked away among the trees, taking care to go slowly and in an aimless manner so that anyone who saw him would think he was merely stretching his legs. He was surprised to find how quickly the noise of conversation died away behind him and how very silent and warm and dark green the wood became. Soon he felt he could venture on a quicker and more determined stride.

This soon brought him out of the wood. The ground began sloping steeply up in front of him. The grass was dry and slippery but manageable if he used his hands as well as his feet, and though he panted and mopped his forehead a good deal, he plugged away steadily. This showed, by the way, that his new life, little as he suspected it, had already done him some good; the old Eustace, Harold and Alberta's Eustace, would have given up the climb after about ten minutes.

Slowly, and with several rests, he reached the ridge. Here he had expected to have a view into the heart of the island, but the clouds had now come lower and nearer and a sea of fog was rolling to meet him. He sat down and looked back. He was now so high that the bay looked small beneath him and miles of sea were visible.

Then the fog from the mountains closed in all round him, thick but not cold, and he lay down and turned this way and that to find the most comfortable position to enjoy himself.

But he didn't enjoy himself, or not for very long. He began, almost for the first time in his life, to feel lonely. At first this feeling grew very gradually. And then he began to worry about the time. There was not the slightest sound. Suddenly it occurred to him that he might have

been lying there for hours. Perhaps the others had gone! Perhaps they had let him wander away on purpose simply in order to leave him behind! He leaped up in a panic and began the descent.

At first he tried to do it too quickly, slipped on the steep grass, and slid for several feet. Then he thought this had carried him too far to the left—and as he came up he had seen precipices on that side. So he clambered up again, as near as he could guess to the place he had started from, and began the descent afresh, bearing to his right. After that things seemed to be going better. He went very cautiously, for he could not see more than a yard ahead, and there was still perfect silence all around him. It is very unpleasant to have to go cautiously when there is a voice inside you saying all the time, "Hurry, hurry, hurry." For every moment the terrible idea of being left behind grew stronger. If he had understood Caspian and the Pevensies at all he would have known, of course, that there was not the least chance of their doing any such thing. But he had persuaded himself that they were all fiends in human form.

"At last!" said Eustace, as he came slithering down a slide of loose stones (*scree*, they call it) and found himself on the level. "And now, where are those trees? There *is* something dark ahead. Why, I do believe the fog is clearing."

It was. The light increased every moment and made him blink. The fog lifted. He was in an utterly unknown valley and the sea was nowhere in sight.

6

THE ADVENTURES OF
EUSTACE

At that very moment the others were washing
hands and faces in the river and generally
getting ready for dinner and a rest. The three
best archers had gone up into the hills north of
the bay and returned laden with a pair of wild
goats which were now roasting over a fire.
Caspian had ordered a cask of wine ashore,
strong wine of Archenland which had to be
mixed with water before you drank it, so there
would be plenty for all. The work had gone well
so far and it was a merry meal. Only after
the second helping of goat did Edmund say,

"Where's that blighter Eustace?"

Meanwhile Eustace stared round the unknown valley. It was so narrow and deep, and the precipices which surrounded it so sheer, that it was like a huge pit or trench. The floor was grassy though strewn with rocks, and here and there Eustace saw black burnt patches like those you see on the sides of a railway embankment in a dry summer. About fifteen yards away from him was a pool of clear, smooth water. There was, at first, nothing else at all in the valley; not an animal, not a bird, not an insect. The sun beat down and grim peaks and horns of mountains peered over the valley's edge.

Eustace realized of course that in the fog he had come down the wrong side of the ridge, so he turned at once to see about getting back. But as soon as he had looked he shuddered. Apparently he had by amazing luck found the only possible way down—a long green spit of land, horribly steep and narrow, with precipices on either side. There was no other possible way of getting back. But could he do it, now that he saw what it was really like? His head swam at the very thought of it.

He turned round again, thinking that at any rate he'd better have a good drink from the pool first. But as soon as he had turned and before he had taken a step forward into the valley he

heard a noise behind him. It was only a small noise but it sounded loud in that immense silence. It froze him dead-still where he stood for a second. Then he slewed round his neck and looked.

At the bottom of the cliff a little on his left hand was a low, dark hole—the entrance to a cave perhaps. And out of this two thin wisps of smoke were coming. And the loose stones just beneath the dark hollow were moving (that was the noise he had heard) just as if something were crawling in the dark behind them.

Something *was* crawling. Worse still, something was coming out. Edmund or Lucy or you would have recognized it at once, but Eustace had read none of the right books. The thing that came out of the cave was something he had never even imagined—a long lead-colored snout, dull red eyes, no feathers or fur, a long lithe body that trailed on the ground, legs whose elbows went up higher than its back like a spider's, cruel claws, bat's wings that made a rasping noise on the stones, yards of tail. And the lines of smoke were coming from its two nostrils. He never said the word *Dragon* to himself. Nor would it have made things any better if he had.

But perhaps if he had known something about dragons he would have been a little surprised at this dragon's behavior. It did not sit up and clap its wings, nor did it shoot out a stream of flame from its mouth. The smoke from its nostrils was like the smoke of a fire that will not last much longer. Nor did it seem to have noticed Eustace. It moved very slowly toward the pool—slowly and with many pauses. Even in his fear Eustace felt that it was an old, sad creature. He wondered if he dared make a dash for the ascent. But it might look round if he made any noise. It might come more to life. Perhaps it was only shamming. Anyway, what was the use of trying to escape by climbing from a creature that could fly?

It reached the pool and slid its horrible scaly chin down over the gravel to drink: but before it had drunk there came from it a great croaking or clanging cry and after a few twitches and convulsions it rolled round on its side and lay perfectly still with one claw in the air. A little dark blood gushed from its wide-opened mouth. The smoke from its nostrils turned black for a moment and then floated away. No more came.

For a long time Eustace did not dare to move. Perhaps this was the brute's trick, the way it lured travelers to their doom. But one couldn't wait forever. He took a step nearer, then two steps, and halted again. The dragon remained motionless; he noticed too that the red fire had gone out of its eyes. At last he came up to it. He was quite sure now that it was

dead. With a shudder he touched it; nothing happened.

The relief was so great that Eustace almost laughed out loud. He began to feel as if he had fought and killed the dragon instead of merely seeing it die. He stepped over it and went to the pool for his drink, for the heat was getting unbearable. He was not surprised when he heard a peal of thunder. Almost immediately afterward the sun disappeared and before he had finished his drink big drops of rain were falling.

The climate of this island was a very unpleasant one. In less than a minute Eustace was wet to the skin and half blinded with such rain as one never sees in Europe. There was no use trying to climb out of the valley as long as this lasted. He bolted for the only shelter in sight—the dragon's cave. There he lay down and tried to get his breath.

Most of us know what we should expect to find in a dragon's lair, but, as I said before, Eustace had read only the wrong books. They had a lot to say about exports and imports and governments and drains, but they were weak on dragons. That is why he was so puzzled at the surface on which he was lying. Parts of it were too prickly to be stones and too hard to be thorns, and there seemed to be a great many round, flat things, and it all clinked when he moved. There was light enough at the cave's mouth to examine it by. And of course Eustace found it to be what any of us could have told him in advance—treasure. There were crowns (those were the prickly things), coins, rings, bracelets, ingots, cups, plates and gems.

Eustace (unlike most boys) had never thought much of treasure but he saw at once the use it would be in this new world which he had so foolishly stumbled into through the picture in Lucy's bedroom at home. "They don't have any tax here," he said, "and you don't have to give treasure to the government. With some of this stuff I could have quite a decent time here— perhaps in Calormen. It sounds the least phony of these countries. I wonder how much I can carry? That bracelet now—those things in it are probably diamonds—I'll slip that on my own wrist. Too big, but not if I push it right up here above my elbow. Then fill my pockets with diamonds—that's easier than gold. I wonder when this infernal rain's going to let up?" He got into a less uncomfortable part of the pile, where it was mostly coins, and settled down to wait. But a bad fright, when once it is over, and especially a bad fright following a mountain walk, leaves you very tired. Eustace fell asleep.

By the time he was sound asleep and snoring the others had finished dinner and become seriously alarmed about him. They shouted, "Eustace! Eustace! Coo-ee!" till they were hoarse and Caspian blew his horn.

"He's nowhere near or he'd have heard that," said Lucy with a white face.

"Confound the fellow," said Edmund. "What on earth did he want to slink away like this for?"

"But we must do something," said Lucy. "He may have got lost, or fallen into a hole, or been captured by savages."

"Or killed by wild beasts," said Drinian.

"And a good riddance if he has, *I* say," muttered Rhince.

"Master Rhince," said Reepicheep, "you never spoke a word that became you less. The creature is no friend of mine but he is of the Queen's blood, and while he is one of our fellowship it concerns our honor to find him and to avenge him if he is dead."

"Of course we've got to find him (if we *can*)," said Caspian wearily. "That's the nuisance of it. It means a search party and endless trouble. Bother Eustace."

Meanwhile Eustace slept and slept—and slept. What woke him was a pain in his arm. The moon was shining in at the mouth of the cave, and the bed of treasures seemed to have grown much more comfortable: in fact he could hardly feel it at all. He was puzzled by the pain in his arm at first, but presently it occurred to him that the bracelet which he had shoved up above his elbow had become strangely tight. His arm must have swollen while he was asleep (it was his left arm).

He moved his right arm in order to feel his left, but stopped before he had moved it an inch and bit his lip in terror. For just in front of him, and a little on his right, where the moonlight fell clear on the floor of the cave, he saw a hideous shape moving. He knew that shape: it was a dragon's claw. It had moved as he moved his hand and became still when he stopped moving his hand.

"Oh, what a fool I've been," thought Eustace. "Of course, the brute had a mate and it's lying beside me."

For several minutes he did not dare to move a muscle. He saw two thin columns of smoke going up before his eyes, black against the moonlight; just as there had been smoke coming from the other dragon's nose before it died. This was so alarming that he held his breath. The two columns of smoke vanished. When he could hold his breath no longer he let it out stealthily; instantly two jets of smoke appeared again. But even yet he had no idea of the truth.

Presently he decided that he would edge

very cautiously to his left and try to creep out of the cave. Perhaps the creature was asleep—and anyway it was his only chance. But of course before he edged to the left he looked to the left. Oh horror! There was a dragon's claw on that side too.

No one will blame Eustace if at this moment he shed tears. He was surprised at the size of his own tears as he saw them splashing on to the treasure in front of him. They also seemed strangely hot; steam went up from them.

But there was no good crying. He must try to crawl out from between the two dragons. He began extending his right arm. The dragon's fore-leg and claw on his right went through exactly the same motion. Then he thought he would try his left. The dragon limb on that side moved too.

Two dragons, one on each side, mimicking whatever he did! His nerve broke and he simply made a bolt for it.

There was such a clatter and rasping, and clinking of gold, and grinding of stones, as he rushed out of the cave that he thought they were both following him. He daren't look back. He rushed to the pool. The twisted shape of the dead dragon lying in the moonlight would have been enough to frighten anyone but now he hardly noticed it. His idea was to get into the water.

But just as he reached the edge of the pool two things happened. First of all, it came over him like a thunder-clap that he had been running on all fours—and why on earth had he been doing that? And secondly, as he bent toward the water, he thought for a second that yet another dragon was staring up at him out of the pool. But in an instant he realized the truth. The dragon face in the pool was his own reflection. There was no doubt of it. It moved as he moved: it opened and shut its mouth as he opened and shut his.

He had turned into a dragon while he was asleep. Sleeping on a dragon's hoard with greedy, dragonish thoughts in his heart, he had become a dragon himself.

That explained everything. There had been no two dragons beside him in the cave. The claws to right and left had been his own right and left claws. The two columns of smoke had been coming from his own nostrils. As for the pain in his left arm (or what had been his left arm) he could now see what had happened by squinting with his left eye. The bracelet which had fitted very nicely on the upper arm of a boy was far too small for the thick, stumpy foreleg of a dragon. It had sunk deeply into his scaly flesh and there was a throbbing bulge on each side of it. He tore at the place with his dragon's teeth but could not get it off.

In spite of the pain, his first feeling was one of relief. There was nothing to be afraid of any more. He was a terror himself now and nothing in the world but a knight (and not all of those) would dare to attack him. He could get even with Caspian and Edmund now—

But the moment he thought this he realized that he didn't want to. He wanted to be friends. He wanted to get back among humans and talk and laugh and share things. He realized that he was a monster cut off from the whole human race. An appalling loneliness came over him. He began to see that the others had not really been fiends at all. He began to wonder if he himself had been such a nice person as he had always supposed. He longed for their voices. He would have been grateful for a kind word even from Reepicheep.

When he thought of this the poor dragon that had been Eustace lifted up its voice and wept. A powerful dragon crying its eyes out under the moon in a deserted valley is a sight and a sound hardly to be imagined.

At last he decided he would try to find his way back to the shore. He realized now that

Caspian would never have sailed away and left him. And he felt sure that somehow or other he would be able to make people understand who he was.

He took a long drink and then (I know this sounds shocking, but it isn't if you think it over) he ate nearly all the dead dragon. He was half-way through it before he realized what he was doing; for, you see, though his mind was the mind of Eustace, his tastes and his digestion

were dragonish. And there is nothing a dragon likes so well as fresh dragon. That is why you so seldom find more than one dragon in the same country.

Then he turned to climb out of the valley. He began the climb with a jump and as soon as he jumped he found that he was flying. He had quite forgotten about his wings and it was a great surprise to him—the first pleasant surprise he had had for a long time. He rose high into the air and saw innumerable mountain-tops spread out beneath him in the moonlight. He could see the bay like a silver slab and the *Dawn Treader* lying at anchor and camp fires twinkling in the woods beside the beach. From a great height he launched himself down toward them in a single glide.

Lucy was sleeping very soundly for she had sat up till the return of the search party in hope of good news about Eustace. It had been led by Caspian and had come back late and weary. Their news was disquieting. They had found no trace of Eustace but had seen a dead dragon in a valley. They tried to make the best of it and everyone assured everyone else that there were not likely to be more dragons about, and that one which was dead at about three o'clock that afternoon (which was when they had seen it) would hardly have been killing people a very few hours before.

"Unless it ate the little brat and died of him: he'd poison anything," said Rhince. But he said this under his breath and no one heard it.

But later in the night Lucy was wakened, very softly, and found the whole company gathered close together and talking in whispers.

"What is it?" said Lucy.

"We must all show great constancy," Caspian was saying. "A dragon has just flown over the tree-tops and lighted on the beach. Yes, I am afraid it is between us and the ship. And arrows are no use against dragons. And they're not at all afraid of fire."

"With your Majesty's leave—" began Reepicheep.

"No, Reepicheep," said the King very firmly, "you are *not* to attempt a single combat with it. And unless you promise to obey me in this matter I'll have you tied up. We must just keep close watch and, as soon as it is light, go down to the beach and give it battle. I will lead. King Edmund will be on my right and the Lord Drinian on my left. There are no other arrangements to be made. It will be light in a couple of hours. In an hour's time let a meal be served out and what is left of the wine. And let everything be done silently."

"Perhaps it will go away," said Lucy.

"It'll be worse if it does," said Edmund, "because then we shan't know where it is. If there's a wasp in the room I like to be able to see it."

The rest of the night was dreadful, and when the meal came, though they knew they ought to eat, many found that they had very poor appetites. And endless hours seemed to pass before the darkness thinned and birds began chirping here and there and the world got colder and wetter than it had been all night and Caspian said, "Now for it, friends."

They got up, all with swords drawn, and formed themselves into a solid mass with Lucy in the middle and Reepicheep on her shoulder. It was nicer than the waiting about and everyone felt fonder of everyone else than at ordinary times. A moment later they were marching. It grew lighter as they came to the edge of the wood. And there on the sand, like a giant lizard, or a flexible crocodile, or a serpent with legs, huge and horrible and humpy, lay the dragon.

But when it saw them, instead of rising up and blowing fire and smoke, the dragon retreated—you could almost say it waddled—back into the shallows of the bay.

"What's it wagging its head like that for?" said Edmund.

"And now it's nodding," said Caspian.

"And there's something coming from its eyes," said Drinian.

"Oh, can't you see," said Lucy. "It's crying. Those are tears."

"I shouldn't trust to that, Ma'am," said Drinian. "That's what crocodiles do, to put you off your guard."

"It wagged its head when you said that," remarked Edmund. "Just as if it meant No. Look, there it goes again."

"Do you think it understands what we're saying?" asked Lucy.

The dragon nodded its head violently.

Reepicheep slipped off Lucy's shoulder and stepped to the front.

"Dragon," came his shrill voice, "can you understand speech?"

The dragon nodded.

"Can you speak?"

It shook its head.

"Then," said Reepicheep, "it is idle to ask you your business. But if you will swear friendship with us raise your left foreleg above your head."

It did so, but clumsily because that leg was sore and swollen with the golden bracelet.

"Oh look," said Lucy, "there's something wrong with its leg. The poor thing—that's probably what it was crying about. Perhaps it came to us to be cured like in Androcles and the lion."

"Be careful, Lucy," said Caspian. "It's a very clever dragon but it may be a liar."

Lucy had, however, already run forward, followed by Reepicheep, as fast as his short legs could carry him, and then of course the boys and Drinian came too.

"Show me your poor paw," said Lucy. "I might be able to cure it."

The dragon-that-had-been-Eustace held out its sore leg gladly enough, remembering how Lucy's cordial had cured him of seasickness before he became a dragon. But he was disappointed. The magic fluid reduced the swelling and eased the pain a little but it could not dissolve the gold.

Everyone had now crowded round to watch the treatment, and Caspian suddenly exclaimed, "Look!" He was staring at the bracelet.

HOW THE
ADVENTURE ENDED

"Look at what?" said Edmund.

"Look at the device on the gold," said Caspian.

"A little hammer with a diamond above it like a star," said Drinian. "Why, I've seen that before."

"Seen it!" said Caspian. "Why, of course you have. It is the sign of a great Narnian house. This is the Lord Octesian's arm-ring."

"Villain," said Reepicheep to the dragon, "have you devoured a Narnian lord?" But the dragon shook his head violently.

"Or perhaps," said Lucy, "this *is* the Lord Octesian, turned into a dragon—under an enchantment, you know."

"It needn't be either," said Edmund. "All dragons collect gold. But I think it's a safe guess that Octesian got no further than this island."

"Are you the Lord Octesian?" said Lucy to the dragon, and then, when it sadly shook its head, "Are you someone enchanted—someone human, I mean?"

It nodded violently.

And then someone said—people disputed afterward whether Lucy or Edmund said it first—"You're not—not Eustace by any chance?"

And Eustace nodded his terrible dragon head and thumped his tail in the sea and everyone skipped back (some of the sailors with ejaculations I will not put down in writing) to avoid the enormous and boiling tears which flowed from his eyes.

Lucy tried hard to console him and even screwed up her courage to kiss the scaly face, and nearly everyone said "Hard luck" and several assured Eustace that they would all stand by him and many said there was sure to be some way of disenchanting him and they'd have him as right as rain in a day or two. And of course they were all very anxious to hear his story, but he couldn't speak. More than once in the days that followed he attempted to write it for them on the sand. But this never succeeded. In the first place Eustace (never having read the right books) had no idea how to tell a story straight. And for another thing, the muscles and nerves of the dragon-claws that he had to use had never learned to write and were not built for writing anyway. As a result he never got nearly to the end before the tide came in and washed away all the writing except the bits he had already trodden on or accidentally swished out with his tail. And all that anyone had seen would be something like this—the dots are for the bits he had smudged out—

I WNET TO SLEE . . . RGOS AGRONS I MEAN DRANGONS CAVE CAUSE ITWAS DEAD AND AINING SO HAR . . . WOKE UP AND COU . . . GET OFFF MI ARM OH BOTHER . . .

It was, however, clear to everyone that Eustace's character had been rather improved by becoming a dragon. He was anxious to help. He flew over the whole island and found that it was all mountainous and inhabited only by wild goats and droves of wild swine. Of these he brought back many carcasses as provisions for the ship. He was a very humane killer too, for he could dispatch a beast with one blow of his tail so that it didn't know (and presumably still doesn't know) it had been killed. He ate a few himself, of course, but always alone, for now that he was a dragon he liked his food raw but he could never bear to let others see him at his messy meals. And one day, flying slowly and wearily but in great triumph, he bore back to camp a great tall pine tree which he had torn up by the roots in a distant valley and which could be made into a capital mast. And in the evening if it turned chilly, as it sometimes did after the heavy rains, he was a comfort to everyone, for the whole party would come and sit with their backs against his hot sides and get well warmed and dried; and one puff of his fiery breath would light the most obstinate fire. Sometimes he would take a select party for a fly on his back, so that they could see wheeling below them the green slopes, the rocky heights, the narrow pit-like valleys and far out over the sea to the eastward a spot of darker blue on the blue horizon which might be land.

The pleasure (quite new to him) of being liked and, still more, of liking other people, was what kept Eustace from despair. For it was very dreary being a dragon. He shuddered whenever he caught sight of his own reflection as he flew

over a mountain lake. He hated the huge bat-like wings, the saw-edged ridge on his back, and the cruel, curved claws. He was almost afraid to be alone with himself and yet he was ashamed to be with the others. On the evenings when he was not being used as a hot-water bottle he would slink away from the camp and lie curled up like a snake between the wood and the water. On such occasions, greatly to his surprise, Reepicheep was his most constant comforter. The noble Mouse would creep away from the merry circle at the camp fire and sit down by the dragon's head, well to the windward to be out of the way of his smoky breath. There he would explain that what had happened to Eustace was a striking illustration of the turn of Fortune's wheel, and that if he had Eustace at his own house in Narnia (it was really a hole not a house and the dragon's head, let alone his body, would not have fitted in) he could show him more than a hundred examples of emperors, kings, dukes, knights, poets, lovers, astronomers, philosophers, and magicians, who had fallen from prosperity into the most distressing circumstances, and of whom many had recovered and lived happily ever afterward. It did not, perhaps, seem so very comforting at the time, but it was kindly meant and Eustace never forgot it.

But of course what hung over everyone like a cloud was the problem of what to do with their dragon when they were ready to sail. They tried not to talk of it when he was there, but he couldn't help overhearing things like, "Would he fit all along one side of the deck? And we'd have to shift all the stores to the other side down below so as to balance," or, "Would towing him be any good?" or "Would he be able to keep up by flying?" and (most often of all), "But how are we to feed him?" And poor Eustace realized more and more that since the first day he came on board he had been an unmitigated nuisance and that he was now a greater nuisance still. And this ate into his mind, just as that bracelet ate into his foreleg. He knew that it only made it worse to tear at it with his great teeth, but he couldn't help tearing now and then, especially on hot nights.

✣ ✣ ✣

About six days after they had landed on Dragon Island, Edmund happened to wake up very early one morning. It was just getting gray so that you could see the tree-trunks if they were between you and the bay but not in the other direction. As he woke he thought he heard something moving, so he raised himself on one elbow and looked about him: and presently he thought he saw a dark figure moving on the seaward side of the wood. The idea that at once occurred to his mind was, "Are we so sure there are no natives on this island after all?" Then he thought it was Caspian—it was about the right size—but he knew that Caspian had been sleeping next to him and could see that he hadn't moved. Edmund made sure that his sword was in its place and then rose to investigate.

He came down softly to the edge of the wood and the dark figure was still there. He saw now that it was too small for Caspian and too big for Lucy. It did not run away. Edmund drew his sword and was about to challenge the stranger when the stranger said in a low voice, "Is that you, Edmund?"

"Yes. Who are you?" said he.

"Don't you know me?" said the other. "It's me—Eustace."

"By jove," said Edmund, "so it is. My dear chap—"

"Hush," said Eustace and lurched as if he were going to fall.

"Hello!" said Edmund, steadying him. "What's up? Are you ill?"

Eustace was silent for so long that Edmund thought he was fainting; but at last he said, "It's been ghastly. You don't know . . . but it's all right now. Could we go and talk somewhere? I don't want to meet the others just yet."

"Yes, rather, anywhere you like," said Edmund. "We can go and sit on the rocks over there. I say, I *am* glad to see you—er—looking yourself again. You must have had a pretty beastly time."

They went to the rocks and sat down looking out across the bay while the sky got paler and paler and the stars disappeared except for one very bright one low down and near the horizon.

"I won't tell you how I became a—a dragon till I can tell the others and get it all over," said Eustace. "By the way, I didn't even know it *was* a dragon till I heard you all using the word when I turned up here the other morning. I want to tell you how I stopped being one."

"Fire ahead," said Edmund.

"Well, last night I was more miserable than ever. And that beastly arm-ring was hurting like anything—"

"Is that all right now?"

Eustace laughed—a different laugh from any Edmund had heard him give before—and slipped the bracelet easily off his arm. "There it is," he said, "and anyone who likes can have it as far as I'm concerned. Well, as I say, I was lying awake and wondering what on earth would become of me. And then—but, mind you, it may have been all a dream. I don't know."

"Go on," said Edmund, with considerable patience.

"Well, anyway, I looked up and saw the very last thing I expected: a huge lion coming slowly toward me. And one queer thing was that there was no moon last night, but there was moonlight where the lion was. So it came nearer and nearer. I was terribly afraid of it. You may think that, being a dragon, I could have knocked any lion out easily enough. But it wasn't that kind of fear. I wasn't afraid of it eating me, I was just afraid of *it*—if you can understand. Well, it came close up to me and looked straight into my eyes. And I shut my eyes tight. But that wasn't any good because it told me to follow it."

"You mean it spoke?"

"I don't know. Now that you mention it, I don't think it did. But it told me all the same. And I knew I'd have to do what it told me, so I got up and followed it. And it led me a long way into the mountains. And there was always this moonlight over and round the lion wherever we went. So at last we came to the top of a mountain I'd never seen before and on the top of this mountain there was a garden—trees and fruit and everything. In the middle of it there was a well.

"I knew it was a well because you could see the water bubbling up from the bottom of it: but it was a lot bigger than most wells—like a very big, round bath with marble steps going down into it. The water was as clear as anything and I thought if I could get in there and bathe it would ease the pain in my leg. But the lion told me I must undress first. Mind you, I don't know if he said any words out loud or not.

"I was just going to say that I couldn't undress because I hadn't any clothes on when I suddenly thought that dragons are snaky sort of things and snakes can cast their skins. Oh, of course, thought I, that's what the lion means. So I started scratching myself and my scales began coming off all over the place. And then I scratched a little deeper and, instead of just scales coming off here and there, my whole skin started peeling off beautifully, like it does after an illness, or as if I was a banana. In a minute or two I just stepped out of it. I could see it lying there beside me, looking rather nasty. It was a most lovely feeling. So I started to go down into the well for my bathe.

"But just as I was going to put my feet into the water I looked down and saw that they were all hard and rough and wrinkled and scaly just as they had been before. Oh, that's all right, said I, it only means I had another smaller suit on underneath the first one, and I'll have to get out of it too. So I scratched and tore again and this underskin peeled off beautifully and out I stepped and left it lying beside the other one and went down to the well for my bathe.

"Well, exactly the same thing happened again. And I thought to myself, oh dear, how ever many skins have I got to take off? For I was longing to bathe my leg. So I scratched away for the third time and got off a third skin, just like the two others, and stepped out of it. But as soon as I looked at myself in the water I knew it had been no good.

"Then the lion said—but I don't know if it spoke—'You will have to let me undress you.' I was afraid of his claws, I can tell you, but I was pretty nearly desperate now. So I just lay flat down on my back to let him do it.

"The very first tear he made was so deep that I thought it had gone right into my heart. And when he began pulling the skin off, it hurt worse than anything I've ever felt. The only thing that made me able to bear it was just the pleasure of feeling the stuff peel off. You know— if you've ever picked the scab of a sore place. It hurts like billy-oh but it *is* such fun to see it coming away."

"I know exactly what you mean," said Edmund.

"Well, he peeled the beastly stuff right off— just as I thought I'd done it myself the other three times, only they hadn't hurt—and there it was lying on the grass: only ever so much thicker, and darker, and more knobbly-looking than the others had been. And there was I as smooth and soft as a peeled switch and smaller than I had been. Then he caught hold of me—I didn't like that much for I was very tender underneath now that I'd no skin on—and threw me into the water. It smarted like anything but only for a moment. After that it became perfectly delicious and as soon as I started swimming and splashing I found that all the pain had gone from my arm. And then I saw why. I'd turned into a boy again. You'd think me simply phony if I told you how I felt about my own arms. I know they've no muscle and are pretty mouldy compared with Caspian's, but I was so glad to see them.

"After a bit the lion took me out and dressed me—"

"Dressed you. With his paws?"

"Well, I don't exactly remember that bit. But he did somehow or other: in new clothes—the same I've got on now, as a matter of fact. And then suddenly I was back here. Which is what makes me think it must have been a dream."

"No. It wasn't a dream," said Edmund.

"Why not?"

"Well, there are the clothes, for one thing. And you have been—well, un-dragoned, for another."

"What do you think it was, then?" asked Eustace.

"I think you've seen Aslan," said Edmund.

"Aslan!" said Eustace. "I've heard that name mentioned several times since we joined the *Dawn Treader*. And I felt—I don't know what—I hated it. But I was hating everything then. And by the way, I'd like to apologize. I'm afraid I've been pretty beastly."

"That's all right," said Edmund. "Between ourselves, you haven't been as bad as I was on my first trip to Narnia. You were only an ass, but I was a traitor."

"Well, don't tell me about it, then," said Eustace. "But who is Aslan? Do you know him?"

"Well—he knows me," said Edmund. "He is the great Lion, the son of the Emperor-beyond-the-Sea, who saved me and saved Narnia. We've all seen him. Lucy sees him most often. And it may be Aslan's country we are sailing to."

Neither said anything for a while. The last bright star had vanished and though they could not see the sunrise because of the mountains on their right, they knew it was going on because the sky above them and the bay before them turned the color of roses. Then some bird of the parrot kind screamed in the wood behind them, they heard movements among the trees, and finally a blast on Caspian's horn. The camp was astir.

Great was the rejoicing when Edmund and the restored Eustace walked into the breakfast circle round the camp fire. And now of course everyone heard the earlier part of his story. People wondered whether the other dragon had killed the Lord Octesian several years ago or whether Octesian himself had been the old dragon. The jewels with which Eustace had crammed his pockets in the cave had disappeared along with the clothes he had then been wearing: but no one, least of all Eustace himself, felt any desire to go back to that valley for more treasure.

In a few days now the *Dawn Treader*, re-masted, repainted, and well stored, was ready to sail. Before they embarked Caspian caused to be cut on a smooth cliff facing the bay the words:

DRAGON ISLAND
discovered by
CASPIAN X, KING OF NARNIA, *etc.*
in the fourth year
of his reign.
Here, as we suppose,
THE LORD OCTESIAN
had his death

It would be nice, and fairly nearly true, to say that "from that time forth Eustace was a different boy." To be strictly accurate, he began to be a different boy. He had relapses. There were

still many days when he could be very tiresome. But most of those I shall not notice. The cure had begun.

The Lord Octesian's arm ring had a curious fate. Eustace did not want it and offered it to Caspian and Caspian offered it to Lucy. She did not care about having it. "Very well, then, catch as catch can," said Caspian and flung it up in the air. This was when they were all standing looking at the inscription. Up went the ring, flashing in the sunlight, and caught, and hung, as neatly as a well-thrown quoit, on a little projection on the rock. No one could climb up to get it from below and no one could climb down to get it from above. And there, for all I know, it is hanging still and may hang till that world ends.

TWO NARROW ESCAPES

Everyone was cheerful as the *Dawn Treader* sailed from Dragon Island. They had fair winds as soon as they were out of the bay and came early next morning to the unknown land which some of them had seen when flying over the mountains while Eustace was still a dragon. It was a low green island inhabited by nothing but rabbits and a few goats, but from the ruins of stone huts, and from blackened places where fires had been, they judged that it had been peopled not long before. There were also some bones and broken weapons.

"Pirates' work," said Caspian.

"Or the dragon's," said Edmund.

The only other thing they found here was a little skin boat, or coracle, on the sands. It was made of hide stretched over a wicker framework. It was a tiny boat, barely four feet long, and the paddle which still lay in it was in proportion. They thought that either it had been made for a child or else that the people of that country had been Dwarfs. Reepicheep decided to keep it, as it was just the right size for him; so it was taken on board. They called that land Burnt Island, and sailed away before noon.

For some five days they ran before a south-southeast wind, out of sight of all lands and seeing neither fish nor gull. Then they had a day that rained hard till the afternoon. Eustace lost two games of chess to Reepicheep and began to get like his old and disagreeable self again, and Edmund said he wished they could have gone to America with Susan. Then Lucy looked out of the stern windows and said:

"Hello! I do believe it's stopping. And what's *that?*"

They all tumbled up to the poop at this and found that the rain had stopped and that Drinian, who was on watch, was also staring hard at something astern. Or rather, at several things. They looked a little like smooth rounded rocks, a whole line of them with intervals of about forty feet in between.

"But they can't be rocks," Drinian was saying, "because they weren't there five minutes ago."

"And one's just disappeared," said Lucy.

"Yes, and there's another one coming up," said Edmund.

"And nearer," said Eustace.

"Hang it!" said Caspian. "The whole thing is moving this way."

"And moving a great deal quicker than we can sail, Sire," said Drinian. "It'll be up with us in a minute."

They all held their breath, for it is not at all nice to be pursued by an unknown something either on land or sea. But what it turned out to be was far worse than anyone had suspected. Suddenly, only about the length of a cricket pitch from their port side, an appalling head reared itself out of the sea. It was all greens and vermilions with purple blotches—except where shellfish clung to it—and shaped rather like a horse's, though without ears. It had enormous eyes, eyes made for staring through the dark depths of the ocean, and a gaping mouth filled with double rows of sharp fish-like teeth. It came up on what they first took to be a huge neck, but as more and more of it emerged everyone knew that this was not its neck but its body and that at last they were seeing what so many people have foolishly wanted to see—the great Sea Serpent. The folds of its gigantic tail could be seen far away, rising at intervals from the surface. And now its head was towering up higher than the mast.

Every man rushed to his weapon, but there was nothing to be done, the monster was out of reach. "Shoot! Shoot!" cried the Master Bowman, and several obeyed, but the arrows glanced off the Sea Serpent's hide as if it was iron-plated. Then, for a dreadful minute, everyone was still, staring up at its eyes and mouth and wondering where it would pounce.

But it didn't pounce. It shot its head forward across the ship on a level with the yard of the mast. Now its head was just beside the fighting-top. Still it stretched and stretched till its head was over the starboard bulwark. Then down it began to come—not onto the crowded deck but into the water, so that the whole ship was under an arch of serpent. And almost at once that arch began to get smaller: indeed on the starboard the Sea Serpent was now almost touching the *Dawn Treader*'s side.

Eustace (who had really been trying very hard to behave well, till the rain and the chess put him back) now did the first brave thing he had ever done. He was wearing a sword that

Caspian had lent him. As soon as the serpent's body was near enough on the starboard side he jumped on to the bulwark and began hacking at it with all his might. It is true that he accomplished nothing beyond breaking Caspian's second-best sword into bits, but it was a fine thing for a beginner to have done.

Others would have joined him if at that moment Reepicheep had not called out, "Don't fight! Push!" It was so unusual for the Mouse to advise anyone not to fight that, even in that terrible moment, every eye turned to him. And when he jumped up on to the bulwark, forward of the snake, and set his little furry back against its huge scaly, slimy back, and began pushing as hard as he could, quite a number of people saw what he meant and rushed to both sides of the ship to do the same. And when, a moment later, the Sea Serpent's head appeared again, this time on the port side, and this time with its back to them, then everyone understood.

The brute had made a loop of itself round the *Dawn Treader* and was beginning to draw the loop tight. When it got quite tight—snap!—there would be floating matchwood where the ship had been and it could pick them out of the water one by one. Their only chance was to push the loop backward till it slid over the stern; or else (to put the same thing another way) to push the ship forward out of the loop.

Reepicheep alone had, of course, no more chance of doing this than of lifting up a cathedral, but he had nearly killed himself with trying before others shoved him aside. Very soon the whole ship's company except Lucy and the Mouse (which was fainting) was in two long lines along the two bulwarks, each man's chest to the back of the man in front, so that the weight of the whole line was in the last man, pushing for their lives. For a few sickening seconds (which seemed like hours) nothing appeared to happen. Joints cracked, sweat dropped, breath came in grunts and gasps. Then they felt that the ship was moving. They saw that the snake-loop was further from the mast than it had been. But they also saw that it was smaller. And now the real danger was at hand. Could they get it over the poop, or was it already too tight? Yes. It would just fit. It was resting on the poop rails. A dozen or more sprang up on the poop. This was far better. The Sea Serpent's body was so low now that they could make a line across the poop and push side by side. Hope rose high till everyone remembered the high carved stern, the dragon tail, of the *Dawn Treader*. It would be quite impossible to get the brute over that.

"An axe," cried Caspian hoarsely, "and still

shove." Lucy, who knew where everything was, heard him where she was standing on the main deck staring up at the poop. In a few seconds she had been below, got the axe, and was rushing up the ladder to the poop. But just as she reached the top there came a great crashing noise like a tree coming down and the ship rocked and darted forward. For at that very moment, whether because the Sea Serpent was being pushed so hard, or because it foolishly decided to draw the noose tight, the whole of the carved stern broke off and the ship was free.

The others were too exhausted to see what Lucy saw. There, a few yards behind them, the loop of Sea Serpent's body got rapidly smaller and disappeared into a splash. Lucy always said (but of course she was very excited at the moment, and it may have been only imagination) that she saw a look of idiotic satisfaction on the creature's face. What is certain is that it was a very stupid animal, for instead of pursuing the ship it turned its head round and began nosing all along its own body as if it expected to find the wreckage of the *Dawn Treader* there. But the *Dawn Treader* was already well away, running before a fresh breeze, and the men lay and sat panting and groaning all about the deck, till presently they were able to talk about it, and then to laugh about it. And when some rum had been served out they even raised a cheer; and everyone praised the valor of Eustace (though it hadn't done any good) and of Reepicheep.

After this they sailed for three days more and saw nothing but sea and sky. On the fourth day the wind changed to the north and the seas began to rise; by the afternoon it had nearly become a gale. But at the same time they sighted land on their port bow.

"By your leave, Sire," said Drinian, "we will try to get under the lee of that country by rowing and lie in harbor, maybe till this is over." Caspian agreed, but a long row against the gale did not bring them to the land before evening. By the last light of that day they steered into a natural harbor and anchored, but no one went ashore that night. In the morning they found themselves in the green bay of a rugged, lonely-looking country which sloped up to a rocky summit. From the windy north beyond that summit clouds came streaming rapidly. They lowered the boat and loaded her with any of the water casks which were now empty.

"Which stream shall we water at, Drinian?" said Caspian as he took his seat in the stern-sheets of the boat. "There seem to be two coming down into the bay."

"It makes little odds, Sire," said Drinian. "But I think it's a shorter pull to that on the starboard—the eastern one."

"Here comes the rain," said Lucy.

"I should think it does!" said Edmund, for it was already pelting hard. "I say, let's go to the other stream. There are trees there and we'll have some shelter."

"Yes, let's," said Eustace. "No point in getting wetter than we need."

But all the time Drinian was steadily steering to the starboard, like tiresome people in cars who continue at forty miles an hour while you are explaining to them that they are on the wrong road.

"They're right, Drinian," said Caspian. "Why don't you bring her head round and make for the western stream?"

"As your Majesty pleases," said Drinian a little shortly. He had had an anxious day with the weather yesterday, and he didn't like advice from landsmen. But he altered course; and it turned out afterward that it was a good thing he did.

By the time they had finished watering, the rain was over and Caspian, with Eustace, the Pevensies, and Reepicheep, decided to walk up to the top of the hill and see what could be seen. It was a stiffish climb through coarse grass and heather and they saw neither man nor beast, except seagulls. When they reached the top they saw that it was a very small island, not more than twenty acres; and from this height the sea looked larger and more desolate than it did from the deck, or even the fighting-top, of the *Dawn Treader*.

"Crazy, you know," said Eustace to Lucy in a low voice, looking at the eastern horizon. "Sailing on and on into *that* with no idea what we may get to." But he only said it out of habit, not really nastily as he would have done at one time.

It was too cold to stay long on the ridge for the wind still blew freshly from the north.

"Don't let's go back the same way," said Lucy as they turned; "let's go along a bit and come down by the other stream, the one Drinian wanted to go to."

Everyone agreed to this and after about fifteen minutes they were at the source of the second river. It was a more interesting place than they had expected; a deep little mountain lake, surrounded by cliffs except for a narrow channel on the seaward side out of which the water flowed. Here at last they were out of the wind, and all sat down in the heather above the cliff for a rest.

All sat down, but one (it was Edmund) jumped up again very quickly.

"They go in for sharp stones on this island," he said, groping about in the heather. "Where is the wretched thing? . . . Ah, now I've got it . . . Hullo! It wasn't a stone at all, it's a sword-hilt. No, by jove, it's a whole sword; what the rust has left of it. It must have lain here for ages."

"Narnian, too, by the look of it," said Caspian, as they all crowded round.

"I'm sitting on something too," said Lucy. "Something hard." It turned out to be the remains of a mail shirt. By this time everyone was on hands and knees, feeling in the thick heather in every direction. Their search revealed, one by one, a helmet, a dagger, and a few coins; not Calormen crescents but genuine Narnian "Lions" and "Trees" such as you might see any day in the market-place of Beaversdam or Beruna.

"Looks as if this might be all that's left of one of our seven lords," said Edmund.

"Just what I was thinking," said Caspian. "I wonder which it was. There's nothing on the dagger to show. And I wonder how he died."

"And how we are to avenge him," added Reepicheep.

Edmund, the only one of the party who had read several detective stories, had meanwhile been thinking.

"Look here," he said, "there's something very fishy about this. He can't have been killed in a fight."

"Why not?" asked Caspian.

"No bones," said Edmund. "An enemy might take the armor and leave the body. But who ever heard of a chap who'd won a fight carrying away the body and leaving the armor?"

"Perhaps he was killed by a wild animal," Lucy suggested.

"It'd be a clever animal," said Edmund, "that would take a man's mail shirt off."

"Perhaps a dragon?" said Caspian.

"Nothing doing," said Eustace. "A dragon couldn't do it. I ought to know."

"Well, let's get away from the place, anyway," said Lucy. She had not felt like sitting down again since Edmund had raised the question of bones.

"If you like," said Caspian, getting up. "I don't think any of this stuff is worth taking away."

They came down and round to the little opening where the stream came out of the lake, and stood looking at the deep water within the circle of cliffs. If it had been a hot day, no doubt some would have been tempted to bathe and everyone would have had a drink. Indeed, even as it was, Eustace was on the very point of stooping down and scooping up some water in his hands when Reepicheep and Lucy both at the same moment cried, "Look," so he forgot about his drink and looked into the water.

The bottom of the pool was made of large grayish-blue stones and the water was perfectly clear, and on the bottom lay a life-size figure of a man, made apparently of gold. It lay face downward with its arms stretched out above its head. And it so happened that as they looked at it, the clouds parted and the sun shone out. The golden shape was lit up from end to end. Lucy thought it was the most beautiful statue she had ever seen.

"Well!" whistled Caspian. "That was worth coming to see! I wonder, can we get it out?"

"We can dive for it, Sire," said Reepicheep.

"No good at all," said Edmund. "At least, if it's really gold—solid gold—it'll be far too heavy

to bring up. And that pool's twelve or fifteen feet deep if it's an inch. Half a moment, though. It's a good thing I've brought a hunting spear with me. Let's see what the depth *is* like. Hold on to my hand, Caspian, while I lean out over the water a bit." Caspian took his hand and Edmund, leaning forward, began to lower his spear into the water.

Before it was half-way in Lucy said, "I don't believe the statue is gold at all. It's only the light. Your spear looks just the same color."

"What's wrong?" asked several voices at once; for Edmund had suddenly let go of the spear.

"I couldn't hold it," gasped Edmund. "It seemed so *heavy*."

"And there it is on the bottom now," said Caspian, "and Lucy is right. It looks just the same color as the statue."

But Edmund, who appeared to be having some trouble with his boots—at least he was bending down and looking at them—straightened himself all at once and shouted out in the sharp voice which people hardly ever disobey:

"Get back! Back from the water. All of you. At once!!"

They all did and stared at him.

"Look," said Edmund, "look at the toes of my boots."

"They look a bit yellow," began Eustace.

"They're gold, solid gold," interrupted Edmund. "Look at them. Feel them. The leather's pulled away from it already. And they're as heavy as lead."

"By Aslan!" said Caspian. "You don't mean to say—?"

"Yes, I do," said Edmund. "That water turns things into gold. It turned the spear into gold, that's why it got so heavy. And it was just lapping against my feet (it's a good thing I wasn't barefoot) and it turned the toe-caps into gold. And that poor fellow on the bottom—well, you see."

"So it isn't a statue at all," said Lucy in a low voice.

"No. The whole thing is plain now. He was here on a hot day. He undressed on top of the cliff—where we were sitting. The clothes have rotted away or been taken by birds to line nests with; the armor's still there. Then he dived and—"

"Don't," said Lucy. "What a horrible thing."

"And what a narrow shave *we've* had," said Edmund.

"Narrow indeed," said Reepicheep. "Anyone's finger, anyone's foot, anyone's whisker, or anyone's tail, might have slipped into the water at any moment."

"All the same," said Caspian, "we may as well test it." He stooped down and wrenched up a spray of heather. Then, very cautiously, he knelt beside the pool and dipped it in. It was heather that he dipped; what he drew out was a perfect model of heather made of the purest gold, heavy and soft as lead.

"The King who owned this island," said Caspian slowly, and his face flushed as he spoke, "would soon be the richest of all Kings of the world. I claim this land forever as a Narnian possession. It shall be called Goldwater Island. And I bind all of you to secrecy. No one must know of this. Not even Drinian—on pain of death, do you hear?"

"Who are you talking to?" said Edmund. "I'm no subject of yours. If anything it's the other way round. I am one of the four ancient sovereigns of Narnia and you are under allegiance to the High King my brother."

"So it has come to that, King Edmund, has it?" said Caspian, laying his hand on his sword-hilt.

"Oh, stop it, both of you," said Lucy. "That's the worst of doing anything with boys. You're all such swaggering, bullying idiots—oooh!—" Her voice died away into a gasp. And everyone else saw what she had seen.

Across the gray hillside above them—gray,

for the heather was not yet in bloom—without noise, and without looking at them, and shining as if he were in bright sunlight though the sun had in fact gone in, passed with slow pace the hugest lion that human eyes have ever seen. In describing the scene Lucy said afterward, "He was the size of an elephant," though at another time she only said, "The size of a cart-horse." But it was not the size that mattered. Nobody dared to ask what it was. They knew it was Aslan.

And nobody ever saw how or where he went. They looked at one another like people waking from sleep.

"What were we talking about?" said Caspian. "Have I been making rather an ass of myself?"

"Sire," said Reepicheep, "this is a place with a curse on it. Let us get back on board at once. And if I might have the honor of naming this island, I should call it Deathwater."

"That strikes me as a very good name, Reep," said Caspian, "though now that I come to think of it, I don't know why. But the weather seems to be settling and I dare say Drinian would like to be off. What a lot we shall have to tell him."

But in fact they had not much to tell for the memory of the last hour had all become confused.

"Their Majesties all seemed a bit bewitched when they came aboard," said Drinian to Rhince some hours later when the *Dawn Treader* was once more under sail and Deathwater Island already below the horizon. "Something happened to them in that place. The only thing I could get clear was that they think they've found the body of one of these lords we're looking for."

"You don't say so, Captain," answered Rhince. "Well, that's three. Only four more. At this rate we might be home soon after the New Year. And a good thing too. My baccy's running a bit low. Good night, Sir."

9

THE ISLAND
OF THE VOICES

And now the winds which had so long been
from the northwest began to blow from the west
itself and every morning when the sun rose out
of the sea the curved prow of the *Dawn Treader*
stood up right across the middle of the sun.
Some thought that the sun looked larger than it
looked from Narnia, but others disagreed. And
they sailed and sailed before a gentle yet steady
breeze and saw neither fish nor gull nor ship nor
shore. And stores began to get low again, and it
crept into their hearts that perhaps they might
have come to a sea which went on forever. But

when the very last day on which they thought they could risk continuing their eastward voyage dawned, it revealed, right ahead between them and the sunrise, a low land lying like a cloud.

They made harbor in a wide bay about the middle of the afternoon and landed. It was a very different country from any they had yet seen. For when they had crossed the sandy beach they found all silent and empty as if it were an uninhabited land, but before them there were level lawns in which the grass was as smooth and short as it used to be in the grounds of a great English house where ten gardeners were kept. The trees, of which there were many, all stood well apart from one another, and there were no broken branches and no leaves lying on the ground. Pigeons sometimes cooed but there was no other noise.

Presently they came to a long, straight, sanded path with not a weed growing on it and trees on either hand. Far off at the other end of this avenue they now caught sight of a house— very long and gray and quiet-looking in the afternoon sun.

Almost as soon as they entered this path Lucy noticed that she had a little stone in her shoe. In that unknown place it might have been wiser for her to ask the others to wait while she

took it out. But she didn't; she just dropped quietly behind and sat down to take off her shoe. Her lace had got into a knot.

Before she had undone the knot the others were a fair distance ahead. By the time she had got the stone out and was putting the shoe on again she could no longer hear them. But almost at once she heard something else. It was not coming from the direction of the house.

What she heard was a thumping. It sounded as if dozens of strong workmen were hitting the ground as hard as they could with great wooden mallets. And it was very quickly coming nearer. She was already sitting with her back to a tree, and as the tree was not one she could climb, there was really nothing to do but to sit dead still and press herself against the tree and hope she wouldn't be seen.

Thump, thump, thump . . . and whatever it was must be very close now for she could feel the ground shaking. But she could see nothing. She thought the thing—or things—must be just behind her. But then there came a thump on the path right in front of her. She knew it was on the path not only by the sound but because she saw the sand scatter as if it had been struck a heavy blow. But she could see nothing that had struck it. Then all the thumping noises drew together about twenty feet away from her and suddenly ceased. Then came the Voice.

It was really very dreadful because she could still see nobody at all. The whole of that parklike country still looked as quiet and empty as it had looked when they first landed. Nevertheless, only a few feet away from her, a voice spoke. And what it said was:

"Mates, now's our chance."

Instantly a whole chorus of other voices replied, "Hear him. Hear him. 'Now's our chance,' he said. Well done, Chief. You never said a truer word."

"What I say," continued the first voice, "is, get down to the shore between them and their boat, and let every mother's son look to his weapons. Catch 'em when they try to put to sea."

"Eh, that's the way," shouted all the other voices. "You never made a better plan, Chief. Keep it up, Chief. You couldn't have a better plan than that."

"Lively, then, mates, lively," said the first voice. "Off we go."

"Right again, Chief," said the others. "Couldn't have a better order. Just what we were going to say ourselves. Off we go."

Immediately the thumping began again—very loud at first but soon fainter and fainter, till it died out in the direction of the sea.

Lucy knew there was no time to sit puzzling as to what these invisible creatures might be. As soon as the thumping noise had died away she got up and ran along the path after the others as quickly as her legs would carry her. They must at all costs be warned.

While this had been happening the others had reached the house. It was a low building—only two stories high—made of a beautiful mellow stone, many-windowed, and partially covered with ivy. Everything was so still that Eustace said, "I think it's empty," but Caspian silently pointed to the column of smoke which rose from one chimney.

They found a wide gateway open and passed

through it into a paved courtyard. And it was here that they had their first indication that there was something odd about this island. In the middle of the courtyard stood a pump, and beneath the pump a bucket. There was nothing odd about that. But the pump handle was moving up and down, though there seemed to be no one moving it.

"There's some magic at work here," said Caspian.

"Machinery!" said Eustace. "I do believe we've come to a civilized country at last."

At that moment Lucy, hot and breathless, rushed into the courtyard behind them. In a low

voice she tried to make them understand what she had overheard. And when they had partly understood it even the bravest of them did not look very happy.

"Invisible enemies," muttered Caspian. "And cutting us off from the boat. This is an ugly furrow to plow."

"You've no idea what *sort* of creatures they are, Lu?" asked Edmund.

"How can I, Ed, when I couldn't see them?"

"Did they sound like humans from their footsteps?"

"I didn't hear any noise of feet—only voices and this frightful thudding and thumping—like a mallet."

"I wonder," said Reepicheep, "do they become visible when you drive a sword into them?"

"It looks as if we shall find out," said Caspian. "But let's get out of this gateway. There's one of these gentry at that pump listening to all we say."

They came out and went back on to the path where the trees might possibly make them less conspicuous. "Not that it's any good *really*," said Eustace, "trying to hide from people you can't see. They may be all round us."

"Now, Drinian," said Caspian. "How would it be if we gave up the boat for lost, went down to another part of the bay, and signaled to the *Dawn Treader* to stand in and take us aboard?"

"Not depth for her, Sire," said Drinian.

"We could swim," said Lucy.

"Your Majesties all," said Reepicheep, "hear me. It is folly to think of avoiding an invisible enemy by any amount of creeping and skulking. If these creatures mean to bring us to battle, be sure they will succeed. And whatever comes of it I'd sooner meet them face to face than be caught by the tail."

"I really think Reep is in the right this time," said Edmund.

"Surely," said Lucy, "if Rhince and the others on the *Dawn Treader* see us fighting on the shore they'll be able to do *something*."

"But they won't see us fighting if they can't see any enemy," said Eustace miserably. "They'll think we're just swinging our swords in the air for fun."

There was an uncomfortable pause.

"Well," said Caspian at last, "let's get on with it. We must go and face them. Shake hands all round—arrow on the string, Lucy—swords out, everyone else—and now for it. Perhaps they'll parley."

It was strange to see the lawns and the great trees looking so peaceful as they marched back to the beach. And when they arrived there, and saw the boat lying where they had left her, and the smooth sand with no one to be seen on it, more than one doubted whether Lucy had not merely imagined all she had told them. But before they reached the sand, a voice spoke out of the air.

"No further, masters, no further now," it said. "We've got to talk with you first. There's fifty of us and more here with weapons in our fists."

"Hear him, hear him," came the chorus. "That's our Chief. You can depend on what he says. He's telling you the truth, he is."

"I do not see these fifty warriors," observed Reepicheep.

"That's right, that's right," said the Chief Voice. "You don't see us. And why not? Because we're invisible."

"Keep it up, Chief, keep it up," said the Other Voices. "You're talking like a book. They couldn't ask for a better answer than that."

"Be quiet, Reep," said Caspian, and then added in a louder voice, "You invisible people, what do you want with us? And what have we done to earn your enmity?"

"We want something that little girl can do for us," said the Chief Voice. (The others explained that this was just what they would have said themselves.)

"Little girl!" said Reepicheep. "The lady is a queen."

"We don't know about queens," said the Chief Voice. ("No more we do, no more we do," chimed in the others.) "But we want something she can do."

"What is it?" said Lucy.

"And if it is anything against her Majesty's honor or safety," added Reepicheep, "you will wonder to see how many we can kill before we die."

"Well," said the Chief Voice. "It's a long story. Suppose we all sit down?"

The proposal was warmly approved by the other voices but the Narnians remained standing.

"Well," said the Chief Voice. "It's like this. This island has been the property of a great magician time out of mind. And we all are—or perhaps in a manner of speaking, I might say, we were—his servants. Well, to cut a long story short, this magician that I was speaking about, he told us to do something we didn't like. And why not? Because we didn't want to. Well, then, this same magician he fell into a great rage; for I ought to tell you he owned the island and he wasn't used to being crossed. He was terribly downright, you know. But let me see, where am I? Oh yes, this magician then, he goes upstairs (for you must know he kept all his magic things up there and we all lived down below), I say he goes upstairs and puts a spell on us. An uglifying spell. If you saw us now, which in my opinion you may thank your stars you can't, you wouldn't believe what we looked like before we were uglified. You wouldn't really. So there we all were so ugly we couldn't bear to look at one another. So then what did we do? Well, I'll tell you what we did. We waited till we thought this same magician would be asleep in the afternoon and we creep upstairs and go to his magic book, as bold as brass, to see if we can do anything about this uglification. But we were all of a sweat and a tremble, so I won't deceive you. But, believe me or believe me not, I do assure you that we couldn't find anything in the way of a spell for taking off the ugliness. And what with time getting on and being afraid that the old gentleman might wake up any minute—I was all of a muck sweat, so I won't deceive you—well, to cut a long story short, whether we did right or whether we did wrong, in the end we see a spell for making people invisible. And we thought we'd rather be invisible than go on being as ugly as all that. And why? Because we'd like it better. So my little girl, who's just about your little girl's age, and a sweet child she was before she was uglified, though now—but least said soonest mended—I say, my little girl she says the spell, for it's got to be a little girl or else the magician himself, if you see my meaning, for otherwise it won't work. And why not? Because nothing happens. So my Clipsie says the spell, for I ought to have told you she reads beautifully, and there we all were as invisible as you could wish to see. And I do assure you it was a relief not to see one another's faces. At first, anyway. But the long and the short of it is we're mortal tired of being invisible. And there's another thing. We never reckoned on this magician (the one I was telling you about before) going invisible too. But we haven't ever seen him since. So we don't know if he's dead, or gone away, or whether he's just sitting upstairs being invisible, and perhaps coming down and being invisible there. And, believe me, it's no manner of use listening because he always did go about with his bare feet on, making no more noise than a great big cat. And I'll tell all you gentlemen straight, it's getting more than what our nerves can stand."

Such was the Chief Voice's story, but very much shortened, because I have left out what the Other Voices said. Actually he never got out more than six or seven words without being interrupted by their agreements and encouragements, which drove the Narnians nearly out of their minds with impatience. When it was over there was a very long silence.

"But," said Lucy at last, "what's all this got to do with us? I don't understand."

"Why, bless me, if I haven't gone and left out the whole point," said the Chief Voice.

"That you have, that you have," roared the Other Voices with great enthusiasm. "No one couldn't have left it out cleaner and better. Keep it up, Chief, keep it up."

"Well, I needn't go over the whole story again," began the Chief Voice.

"No. Certainly not," said Caspian and Edmund.

"Well, then, to put it in a nutshell," said the Chief Voice, "we've been waiting for ever so long for a nice little girl from foreign parts, like it might be you, Missie—that would go upstairs and go to the magic book and find the spell that takes off the invisibleness, and say it. And we all swore that the first strangers as landed on this island (having a nice little girl with them, I mean, for if they hadn't it'd be another matter) we wouldn't let them go away alive unless they'd done the needful for us. And that's why, gentlemen, if your little girl doesn't come up to scratch, it will be our painful duty to cut all your throats. Merely in the way of business, as you might say, and no offense, I hope."

"I don't see all your weapons," said

Reepicheep. "Are they invisible too?" The words were scarcely out of his mouth before they heard a whizzing sound and next moment a spear had stuck, quivering, in one of the trees behind them.

"That's a spear, that is," said the Chief Voice.

"That it is, Chief, that it is," said the others. "You couldn't have put it better."

"And it came from my hand," the Chief Voice continued. "They get visible when they leave us."

"But why do you want *me* to do this?" asked Lucy. "Why can't one of your own people? Haven't you got any girls?"

"We dursen't, we dursen't," said all the Voices. "We're not going upstairs again."

"In other words," said Caspian, "you are asking this lady to face some danger which you daren't ask your own sisters and daughters to face!"

"That's right, that's right," said all the Voices cheerfully. "You couldn't have said it better. Eh, you've had some education, you have. Anyone can see that."

"Well, of all the outrageous—" began Edmund, but Lucy interrupted.

"Would I have to go upstairs at night, or would it do in daylight?"

"Oh, daylight, daylight, to be sure," said the Chief Voice. "Not at night. No one's asking you to do that. Go upstairs in the dark? Ugh."

"All right, then, I'll do it," said Lucy. "No," she said, turning to the others, "don't try to stop me. Can't you see it's no use? There are dozens of them there. We can't fight them. And the other way there *is* a chance."

"But a magician!" said Caspian.

"I know," said Lucy. "But he mayn't be as bad as they make out. Don't you get the idea that these people are not very brave?"

"They're certainly not very clever," said Eustace.

"Look here, Lu," said Edmund. "We really can't let you do a thing like this. Ask Reep, I'm sure he'll say just the same."

"But it's to save my own life as well as yours," said Lucy. "I don't want to be cut to bits with invisible swords any more than anyone else."

"Her Majesty is in the right," said Reepicheep. "If we had any assurance of saving *her* by battle, our duty would be very plain. It appears to me that we have none. And the service they ask of her is in no way contrary to her Majesty's honor, but a noble and heroical act. If the Queen's heart moves her to risk the magician, I will not speak against it."

As no one had ever known Reepicheep to be afraid of anything, he could say this without feeling at all awkward. But the boys, who had all been afraid quite often, grew very red. None the less, it was such obvious sense that they had to give in. Loud cheers broke from the invisible people when their decision was announced, and the Chief Voice (warmly supported by all the others) invited the Narnians to come to supper and spend the night. Eustace didn't want to accept, but Lucy said, "I'm sure they're not treacherous. They're not like that at all," and the others agreed. And so, accompanied by an enormous noise of thumpings (which became louder when they reached the flagged and echoing courtyard) they all went back to the house.

THE MAGICIAN'S BOOK

The invisible people feasted their guests royally. It was very funny to see the plates and dishes coming to the table and not to see anyone carrying them. It would have been funny even if they had moved along level with the floor, as you would expect things to do in invisible hands. But they didn't. They progressed up the long dining-hall in a series of bounds or jumps. At the highest point of each jump a dish would be about fifteen feet up in the air; then it would come down and stop quite suddenly about three feet from the floor. When the dish contained anything like soup or stew the result was rather disastrous.

"I'm beginning to feel very inquisitive about these people," whispered Eustace to Edmund. "Do you think they're human at all? More like huge grasshoppers or giant frogs, I should say."

"It does look like it," said Edmund. "But don't put the idea of the grasshoppers into Lucy's head. She's not too keen on insects; especially big ones."

The meal would have been pleasanter if it had not been so exceedingly messy, and also if the conversation had not consisted entirely of agreements. The invisible people agreed about everything. Indeed most of their remarks were the sort it would not be easy to disagree with: "What I always say is, when a chap's hungry, he likes some victuals," or "Getting dark now; always does at night," or even "Ah, you've come over the water. Powerful wet stuff, ain't it?" And Lucy could not help looking at the dark yawning entrance to the foot of the staircase—she could see it from where she sat—and wondering what she would find when she went up those stairs next morning. But it was a good meal otherwise, with mushroom soup and boiled chickens and hot boiled ham and gooseberries, redcurrants, curds, cream, milk, and mead. The others liked the mead but Eustace was sorry afterward that he had drunk any.

When Lucy woke up next morning it was like waking up on the day of an examination or a day when you are going to the dentist. It was a lovely morning with bees buzzing in and out of her open window and the lawn outside looking very like somewhere in England. She got up and dressed and tried to talk and eat ordinarily at breakfast. Then, after being instructed by the Chief Voice about what she was to do upstairs, she bid good-bye to the others, said nothing, walked to the bottom of the stairs, and began going up them without once looking back.

It was quite light, that was one good thing. There was, indeed, a window straight ahead of her at the top of the first flight. As long as she was on that flight she could hear the *tick-tock-tick-tock* of a grandfather clock in the hall below. Then she came to the landing and had to turn to her left up the next flight; after that she couldn't hear the clock any more.

Now she had come to the top of the stairs. Lucy looked and saw a long, wide passage with a large window at the far end. Apparently the passage ran the whole length of the house. It was carved and paneled and carpeted and very many doors opened off it on each side. She stood still and couldn't hear the squeak of a mouse, or the buzzing of a fly, or the swaying of a curtain, or anything—except the beating of her own heart.

"The last doorway on the left," she said to herself. It did seem a bit hard that it should be the last. To reach it she would have to walk past room after room. And in any room there might be the magician—asleep, or awake, or invisible, or even dead. But it wouldn't do to think about that. She set out on her journey. The carpet was so thick that her feet made no noise.

"There's nothing whatever to be afraid of yet," Lucy told herself. And certainly it was a quiet, sunlit passage; perhaps a bit too quiet. It would have been nicer if there had not been strange signs painted in scarlet on the doors— twisty, complicated things which obviously had a meaning and it mightn't be a very nice meaning either. It would have been nicer still if there weren't those masks hanging on the wall. Not that they were exactly ugly—or not so very ugly—but the empty eye-holes did look queer, and if you let yourself you would soon start imagining that the masks were doing things as soon as your back was turned to them.

After about the sixth door she got her first real fright. For one second she felt almost certain that a wicked little bearded face had popped out of the wall and made a grimace at her. She forced herself to stop and look at it. And it was not a face at all. It was a little mirror just the size and shape of her own face, with hair

on the top of it and a beard hanging down from it, so that when you looked in the mirror your own face fitted into the hair and beard and it looked as if they belonged to you. "I just caught my own reflection with the tail of my eye as I went past," said Lucy to herself. "That was all it was. It's quite harmless." But she didn't like the look of her own face with that hair and beard, and went on. (I don't know what the Bearded Glass was for because I am not a magician.)

Before she reached the last door on the left, Lucy was beginning to wonder whether the corridor had grown longer since she began her journey and whether this was part of the magic of the house. But she got to it at last. And the door was open.

It was a large room with three big windows and it was lined from floor to ceiling with books; more books than Lucy had ever seen before, tiny little books, fat and dumpy books, and books bigger than any church Bible you have ever seen, all bound in leather and smelling old and learned and magical. But she knew from her instructions that she need not bother about any of these. For *the* Book, the Magic Book, was lying on a reading-desk in the very middle of the room. She saw she would have to read it standing (and anyway there were no chairs) and also that she would have to stand with her back to the door while she read it. So at once she turned to shut the door.

It wouldn't shut.

Some people may disagree with Lucy about this, but I think she was quite right. She said she wouldn't have minded if she could have shut the door, but that it was unpleasant to have to stand in a place like that with an open doorway right behind your back. I should have felt just the same. But there was nothing else to be done.

One thing that worried her a good deal was the size of the Book. The Chief Voice had not been able to give her any idea whereabouts in the Book the spell for making things visible came. He even seemed rather surprised at her asking. He expected her to begin at the beginning and go on till she came to it; obviously he had never thought that there was any other way of finding a place in a book. "But it might take me days and weeks!" said Lucy, looking at the huge volume, "and I feel already as if I'd been in this place for hours."

She went up to the desk and laid her hand on the book; her fingers tingled when she touched it as if it were full of electricity. She tried to open it but couldn't at first; this, however, was only because it was fastened by two leaden clasps, and when she had undone these it opened easily enough. And what a book it was!

It was written, not printed; written in a clear, even hand, with thick downstrokes and thin upstrokes, very large, easier than print, and so beautiful that Lucy stared at it for a whole minute and forgot about reading it. The paper was crisp and smooth and a nice smell came from it; and in the margins, and round the big colored capital letters at the beginning of each spell, there were pictures.

There was no title page or title; the spells began straight away, and at first there was nothing very important in them. They were cures for warts (by washing your hands in moonlight in a silver basin) and toothache and cramp, and a spell for taking a swarm of bees. The picture of the man with toothache was so lifelike that it would have set your own teeth aching if you looked at it too long, and the golden bees which were dotted all round the fourth spell looked for a moment as if they were really flying.

Lucy could hardly tear herself away from that first page, but when she turned over, the next was just as interesting. "But I must get on," she told herself. And on she went for about thirty pages which, if she could have remembered them, would have taught her how to find buried treasure, how to remember things forgotten, how to forget things you wanted to forget, how to tell whether anyone was speaking the

Cure for warts: wash in a silver basin by moonlight.

truth, how to call up (or prevent) wind, fog, snow, sleet or rain, how to produce enchanted sleeps and how to give a man an ass's head (as they did to poor Bottom). And the longer she read the more wonderful and more real the pictures became.

Then she came to a page which was such a blaze of pictures that one hardly noticed the writing. Hardly—but she *did* notice the first words. They were, *An infallible spell to make beautiful her that uttereth it beyond the lot of mortals.* Lucy peered at the pictures with her face close to the page, and though they had seemed crowded and muddlesome before, she found she could now see them quite clearly. The first was a picture of a girl standing at a reading-desk reading in a huge book. And the girl was dressed exactly like Lucy. In the next picture Lucy (for the girl in the picture was Lucy herself) was standing up with her mouth open and a rather terrible expression on her face, chanting or reciting something. In the third picture the beauty beyond the lot of mortals had come to her. It was strange, considering how small the pictures had looked at first, that the Lucy in the picture now seemed quite as big as the real Lucy; and they looked into each other's eyes and the real Lucy looked away after a few minutes because she was dazzled by the beauty of the other Lucy; though she could still see a sort of likeness to herself in that beautiful face. And now the pictures came crowding on her thick and fast. She saw herself throned on high at a great tournament in Calormen and all the Kings of the world fought because of her beauty. After that it turned from tournaments to real wars, and all Narnia and Archenland, Telmar and Calormen, Galma and Terebinthia, were laid waste with the fury of the kings and dukes and great lords who fought for her favor. Then it changed and Lucy, still beautiful beyond the lot of mortals, was back in England. And Susan (who had always been the beauty of the family) came home from America. The Susan in the picture looked exactly like the real Susan only plainer and with a nasty expression. And Susan was jealous of the dazzling beauty of Lucy, but that didn't matter a bit because no one cared anything about Susan now.

"I *will* say the spell," said Lucy. "I don't care. I will." She said *I don't care* because she had a strong feeling that she mustn't.

But when she looked back at the opening words of the spell, there in the middle of the writing, where she felt quite sure there had been no picture before, she found the great face of a lion, of The Lion, Aslan himself, staring into hers. It was painted such a bright gold that it seemed to be coming toward her out of the page; and indeed she never was quite sure afterward that it hadn't really moved a little. At any rate she knew the expression on his face quite well. He was growling and you could see most of his teeth. She became horribly afraid and turned over the page at once.

A little later she came to a spell which would let you know what your friends thought about you. Now Lucy had wanted very badly to try the other spell, the one that made you beautiful beyond the lot of mortals. So she felt that to make up for not having said it, she really would say this one. And all in a hurry, for fear her mind would change, she said the words (nothing will induce me to tell you what they were). Then she waited for something to happen.

As nothing happened she began looking at the pictures. And all at once she saw the very last thing she expected—a picture of a third-class carriage in a train, with two schoolgirls sitting in it. She knew them at once. They were Marjorie Preston and Anne Featherstone. Only now it was much more than a picture. It was alive. She could see the telegraph posts flicking past outside the window. Then gradually (like when the radio is "coming on") she could hear what they were saying.

"Shall I see anything of you this term?" said Anne, "or are you still going to be all taken up with Lucy Pevensie."

"Don't know what you mean by *taken up*," said Marjorie.

"Oh yes, you do," said Anne. "You were crazy about her last term."

"No, I wasn't," said Marjorie. "I've got more sense than that. Not a bad little kid in her way. But I was getting pretty tired of her before the end of term."

"Well, you jolly well won't have the chance any other term!" shouted Lucy. "Two-faced little beast." But the sound of her own voice at once reminded her that she was talking to a picture and that the real Marjorie was far away in another world.

"Well," said Lucy to herself, "I did think better of her than that. And I did all sorts of things for her last term, and I stuck to her when not many other girls would. And she knows it too. And to Anne Featherstone, of all people! I wonder are all my friends the same? There are lots of other pictures. No. I won't look at any more. I won't, I won't"—and with a great effort she turned over the page, but not before a large, angry tear had splashed on it.

On the next page she came to a spell "for the refreshment of the spirit." The pictures were fewer here but very beautiful. And what Lucy found herself reading was more like a story than a spell. It went on for three pages and before she had read to the bottom of the page she had forgotten that she was reading at all. She was living in the story as if it were real, and all the pictures were real too. When she had got to the third page and come to the end, she said, "That is the loveliest story I've ever read or ever shall read in my whole life. Oh, I wish I could have gone on reading it for ten years. At least I'll read it over again."

But here part of the magic of the Book came into play. You couldn't turn back. The right-hand pages, the ones ahead, could be turned;

the left-hand pages could not.

"Oh, what a shame!" said Lucy. "I did so want to read it again. Well, at least I must remember it. Let's see . . . it was about . . . about . . . oh dear, it's all fading away again. And even this last page is going blank. This is a very queer book. How can I have forgotten? It was about a cup and a sword and a tree and a green hill, I know that much. But I can't remember and what *shall* I do?"

And she never could remember; and ever since that day what Lucy means by a good story is a story which reminds her of the forgotten story in the Magician's Book.

She turned on and found to her surprise a page with no pictures at all; but the first words were *A Spell to make hidden things visible*. She read it through to make sure of all the hard words and then said it out loud. And she knew at once that it was working because as she spoke the colors came into the capital letters at the top of the page and the pictures began appearing in the margins. It was like when you hold to the fire something written in Invisible Ink and the writing gradually shows up; only instead of the dingy color of lemon juice (which is the easiest Invisible Ink) this was all gold and blue and scarlet. They were odd pictures and contained many figures that Lucy did not much like the look of. And then she thought, "I suppose I've made everything visible, and not only the Thumpers. There might be lots of other invisible things hanging about a place like this. I'm not sure that I want to see them all."

At that moment she heard soft, heavy footfalls coming along the corridor behind her; and of course she remembered what she had been told about the Magician walking in his bare feet and making no more noise than a cat. It is always better to turn round than to have anything creeping up behind your back. Lucy did so.

Then her face lit up till, for a moment (but of course she didn't know it), she looked almost as beautiful as that other Lucy in the picture, and she ran forward with a little cry of delight and with her arms stretched out. For what stood in the doorway was Aslan himself, The Lion, the highest of all High Kings. And he was solid and real and warm and he let her kiss him and bury herself in his shining mane. And from the low, earthquake-like sound that came from inside him, Lucy even dared to think that he was purring.

"Oh, Aslan," said she, "it was kind of you to come."

"I have been here all the time," said he, "but

you have just made me visible."

"Aslan!" said Lucy almost a little reproachfully. "Don't make fun of me. As if anything *I* could do would make *you* visible!"

"It did," said Aslan. "Do you think I wouldn't obey my own rules?"

After a little pause he spoke again.

"Child," he said, "I think you have been eavesdropping."

"Eavesdropping?"

"You listened to what your two schoolfellows were saying about you."

"Oh that? I never thought that was eavesdropping, Aslan. Wasn't it magic?"

"Spying on people by magic is the same as spying on them in any other way. And you have misjudged your friend. She is weak, but she loves you. She was afraid of the older girl and said what she does not mean."

"I don't think I'd ever be able to forget what I heard her say."

"No, you won't."

"Oh dear," said Lucy. "Have I spoiled everything? Do you mean we would have gone on being friends if it hadn't been for this—and been really great friends—all our lives perhaps—and now we never shall."

"Child," said Aslan, "did I not explain to

you once before that no one is ever told *what would have happened?*"

"Yes, Aslan, you did," said Lucy. "I'm sorry. But please—"

"Speak on, dear heart."

"Shall I ever be able to read that story again; the one I couldn't remember? Will you tell it to me, Aslan? Oh do, do, do."

"Indeed, yes, I will tell it to you for years and years. But now, come. We must meet the master of this house."

THE DUFFLEPUDS
MADE HAPPY

Lucy followed the great Lion out into the passage and at once she saw coming toward them an old man, barefoot, dressed in a red robe. His white hair was crowned with a chaplet of oak leaves, his beard fell to his girdle, and he supported himself with a curiously carved staff. When he saw Aslan he bowed low and said,

"Welcome, Sir, to the least of your houses."

"Do you grow weary, Coriakin, of ruling such foolish subjects as I have given you here?"

"No," said the Magician, "they are very stupid but there is no real harm in them. I begin to grow rather fond of the creatures. Sometimes, perhaps, I am a little impatient, waiting for the day when they can be governed by wisdom instead of this rough magic."

"All in good time, Coriakin," said Aslan.

"Yes, all in very good time, Sir," was the answer. "Do you intend to show yourself to them?"

"Nay," said the Lion, with a little half-growl that meant (Lucy thought) the same as a laugh. "I should frighten them out of their senses. Many stars will grow old and come to take their rest in islands before your people are ripe for that. And today before sunset I must visit Trumpkin the Dwarf where he sits in the castle of Cair Paravel counting the days till his master Caspian comes home. I will tell him all your story, Lucy. Do not look so sad. We shall meet soon again."

"Please, Aslan," said Lucy, "what do you call *soon?*"

"I call all times soon," said Aslan; and instantly he was vanished away and Lucy was alone with the Magician.

"Gone!" said he, "and you and I quite crestfallen. It's always like that, you can't keep him; it's not as if he were a *tame* lion. And how did you enjoy my book?"

"Parts of it very much indeed," said Lucy. "Did you know I was there all the time?"

"Well, of course I knew when I let the Duffers make themselves invisible that you would be coming along presently to take the spell off. I wasn't quite sure of the exact day. And I wasn't especially on the watch this morning. You see they had made me invisible too and being invisible always makes me so sleepy. Heigh-ho—there I'm yawning again. Are you hungry?"

"Well, perhaps I am a little," said Lucy. "I've no idea what the time is."

"Come," said the Magician. "All times may be soon to Aslan; but in my home all hungry times are one o'clock."

He led her a little way down the passage and opened a door. Passing in, Lucy found herself in a pleasant room full of sunlight and flowers. The table was bare when they entered, but it was of course a magic table, and at a word from the old man the tablecloth, silver, plates, glasses and food appeared.

"I hope that is what you would like," said he. "I have tried to give you food more like the food of your own land than perhaps you have had lately."

"It's lovely," said Lucy, and so it was; an omelette, piping hot, cold lamb and green peas, a strawberry ice, lemon-squash to drink with the meal and a cup of chocolate to follow. But the magician himself drank only wine and ate only bread. There was nothing alarming about him, and Lucy and he were soon chatting away like old friends.

"When will the spell work?" asked Lucy. "Will the Duffers be visible again at once?"

"Oh yes, they're visible now. But they're probably all asleep still; they always take a rest in the middle of the day."

"And now that they're visible, are you going to let them off being ugly? Will you make them as they were before?"

"Well, that's rather a delicate question," said the Magician. "You see, it's only *they* who think they were so nice to look at before. They say they've been uglified, but that isn't what I called it. Many people might say the change was for the better."

"Are they awfully conceited?"

"They are. Or at least the Chief Duffer is, and he's taught all the rest to be. They always believe every word he says."

"We'd noticed that," said Lucy.

"Yes—we'd get on better without him, in a way. Of course I could turn him into something else, or even put a spell on him which would make them not believe a word he said. But I don't like to do that. It's better for them to admire him than to admire nobody."

"Don't they admire *you?*" asked Lucy.

"Oh, not *me*," said the Magician. "They wouldn't admire *me*."

"What was it you uglified them for—I mean, what they call *uglified?*"

"Well, they wouldn't do what they were told. Their work is to mind the garden and raise food—not for me, as they imagine, but for themselves. They wouldn't do it at all if I didn't make them. And of course for a garden you want water. There is a beautiful spring about half a mile away up the hill. And from that spring there flows a stream which comes right past the garden. All I asked them to do was to take their water from the stream instead of trudging up to the spring with their buckets two or three times a day and tiring themselves out besides spilling half of it on the way back. But they wouldn't see it. In the end they refused point blank."

"Are they as stupid as all that?" asked Lucy.

The Magician sighed. "You wouldn't believe the troubles I've had with them. A few months ago they were all for washing up the plates and knives before dinner: they said it saved time afterward. I've caught them planting boiled potatoes to save cooking them when they were dug up. One day the cat got into the dairy and twenty of them were at work moving all the milk out; no one thought of moving the cat. But I see you've finished. Let's go and look at the Duffers now they can be looked at."

They went into another room which was full of polished instruments hard to understand—such as Astrolabes, Orreries, Chronoscopes, Poesimeters, Choriambuses and Theodolinds—and here, when they had come to the window, the Magician said, "There. There are your Duffers."

"I don't see anybody," said Lucy. "And what are those mushroom things?"

The things she pointed at were dotted all over the level grass. They were certainly very like mushrooms, but far too big—the stalks about three feet high and the umbrellas about the same length from edge to edge. When she looked carefully she noticed too that the stalks joined the umbrellas not in the middle but at one side which gave an unbalanced look to them. And there was something—a sort of little bundle—lying on the grass at the foot of each stalk. In fact the longer she gazed at them the less like mushrooms they appeared. The umbrella part was not really round as she had thought at first. It was longer than it was broad, and it widened at one end. There were a great many of them, fifty or more.

The clock struck three.

Instantly a most extraordinary thing happened. Each of the "mushrooms" suddenly turned upside-down. The little bundles which had lain at the bottom of the stalks were heads and bodies. The stalks themselves were legs. But not two legs to each body. Each body had a single thick leg right under it (not to one side like the leg of a one-legged man) and at the end of it, a single enormous foot—a broad-toed foot with the toes curling up a little so that it looked rather like a small canoe. She saw in a moment why they had looked like mushrooms. They had been lying flat on their backs each with its single leg straight up in the air and its enormous foot spread out above it. She learned afterward that this was their ordinary way of resting; for

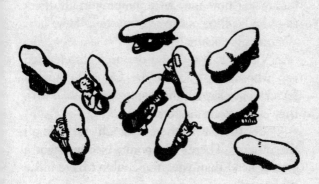

the foot kept off both rain and sun and for a Monopod to lie under its own foot is almost as good as being in a tent.

"Oh, the funnies, the funnies," cried Lucy, bursting into laughter. "Did *you* make them like that?"

"Yes, yes. I made the Duffers into Monopods," said the Magician. He too was laughing till the tears ran down his cheeks. "But watch," he added.

It was worth watching. Of course these little one-footed men couldn't walk or run as we do. They got about by jumping, like fleas or frogs. And what jumps they made!—as if each big foot were a mass of springs. And with what a bounce they came down; that was what made the thumping noise which had so puzzled Lucy yesterday. For now they were jumping in all directions and calling out to one another, "Hey, lads! We're visible again."

"Visible we are," said one in a tasseled red cap who was obviously the Chief Monopod. "And what I say is, when chaps are visible, why, they can see one another."

"Ah, there it is, there it is, Chief," cried all the others. "There's the point. No one's got a clearer head than you. You couldn't have made it plainer."

"She caught the old man napping, that little

girl did," said the Chief Monopod. "We've beaten him this time."

"Just what we were going to say ourselves," chimed the chorus. "You're going stronger than ever today, Chief. Keep it up, keep it up."

"But do they dare to talk about you like that?" said Lucy. "They seemed to be so afraid of you yesterday. Don't they know you might be listening?"

"That's one of the funny things about the Duffers," said the Magician. "One minute they talk as if I ran everything and overheard everything and was extremely dangerous. The next moment they think they can take me in by tricks that a baby would see through—bless them!"

"Will they have to be turned back into their proper shapes?" asked Lucy. "Oh, I do hope it wouldn't be unkind to leave them as they are. Do they really mind very much? They seem pretty happy. I say—look at that jump. What were they like before?"

"Common little dwarfs," said he. "Nothing like so nice as the sort you have in Narnia."

"It *would* be a pity to change them back," said Lucy. "They're so funny: and they're rather nice. Do you think it would make any difference if I told them that?"

"I'm sure it would—if you could get it into their heads."

"Will you come with me and try?"

"No, no. You'll get on far better without me."

"Thanks awfully for the lunch," said Lucy and turned quickly away. She ran down the stairs which she had come up so nervously that morning and cannoned into Edmund at the bottom. All the others were there with him waiting, and Lucy's conscience smote her when she saw their anxious faces and realized how long she had forgotten them.

"It's all right," she shouted. "Everything's all right. The Magician's a brick—and I've seen *Him*—Aslan."

After that she went from them like the wind and out into the garden. Here the earth was shaking with the jumps and the air ringing with the shouts of the Monopods. Both were redoubled when they caught sight of her.

"Here she comes, here she comes," they cried. "Three cheers for the little girl. Ah! She put it across the old gentleman properly, she did."

"And we're extremely regrettable," said the Chief Monopod, "that we can't give you the pleasure of seeing us as we were before we were uglified, for you wouldn't believe the difference, and that's the truth, for there's no denying we're mortal ugly now, so we won't deceive you."

"Eh, that we are, Chief, that we are," echoed the others, bouncing like so many toy balloons. "You've said it, you've said it."

"But I don't think you are at all," said Lucy, shouting to make herself heard. "I think you look very nice."

"Hear her, hear her," said the Monopods. "True for you, Missie. Very nice we look. You couldn't find a handsomer lot." They said this without any surprise and did not seem to notice that they had changed their minds.

"She's a-saying," remarked the Chief Monopod, "as how we looked very nice before we were uglified."

"True for you, Chief, true for you," chanted the others. "That's what she says. We heard her ourselves."

"I did *not*," bawled Lucy. "I said you're very nice *now*."

"So she did, so she did," said the Chief Monopod, "said we were very nice then."

"Hear 'em both, hear 'em both," said the Monopods. "There's a pair for you. Always right. They couldn't have put it better."

"But we're saying just the opposite," said Lucy, stamping her foot with impatience.

"So you are, to be sure, so you are," said the Monopods. "Nothing like an opposite. Keep it up, both of you."

"You're enough to drive anyone mad," said Lucy, and gave it up. But the Monopods seemed perfectly contented, and she decided that on the whole the conversation had been a success.

And before everyone went to bed that evening something else happened which made them even more satisfied with their one-legged condition. Caspian and all the Narnians went back as soon as possible to the shore to give their news to Rhince and the others on board the *Dawn Treader*, who were by now very anxious.

And, of course, the Monopods went with them, bouncing like footballs and agreeing with one another in loud voices till Eustace said, "I wish the Magician would make them inaudible instead of invisible." (He was soon sorry he had spoken because then he had to explain that an inaudible thing is something you can't hear, and though he took a lot of trouble he never felt sure that the Monopods had really understood, and what especially annoyed him was that they said in the end, "Eh, he can't put things the way our Chief does. But you'll learn, young man. Hark to *him*. He'll show you how to say things. There's a speaker for you!") When they reached the bay, Reepicheep had a brilliant idea. He had his little coracle lowered and paddled himself about in it till the Monopods were thoroughly interested. He then stood up in it and said, "Worthy and intelligent Monopods, you do not need boats. Each of you has a foot that will do instead. Just jump as lightly as you can on the water and see what happens."

The Chief Monopod hung back and warned the others that they'd find the water powerful wet, but one or two of the younger ones tried it almost at once; and then a few others followed their example, and at last the whole lot did the same. It worked perfectly. The huge single foot of a Monopod acted as a natural raft or boat, and when Reepicheep had taught them how to cut rude paddles for themselves, they all paddled about the bay and round the *Dawn Treader*, looking for all the world like a fleet of little canoes with a fat dwarf standing up in the extreme stern of each. And they had races, and bottles of wine were lowered down to them from the ship as prizes, and the sailors stood leaning over the ship's sides and laughed till their own sides ached.

The Duffers were also very pleased with their new name of Monopods, which seemed to them a magnificent name though they never got it right. "That's what we are," they bellowed. "Moneypuds, Pomonods, Poddymons. Just what it was on the tips of our tongue to call ourselves." But they soon got it mixed up with their old name of Duffers and finally settled down to calling themselves the Dufflepuds; and that is what they will probably be called for centuries.

That evening all the Narnians dined upstairs with the Magician, and Lucy noticed how different the whole top floor looked now that she was no longer afraid of it. The mysterious signs on the doors were still mysterious but now looked as if they had kind and cheerful meanings, and even the bearded mirror now seemed funny rather than frightening. At dinner everyone had by magic what everyone liked best to eat and drink, and after dinner the Magician did a very useful and beautiful piece of magic. He laid two blank sheets of parchment on the table and asked Drinian to give him an exact account of their voyage up to date: and as Drinian spoke, everything he described came out on the parchment in fine clear lines till at last each sheet was a splendid map of the Eastern Ocean, showing Galma, Terebinthia, the Seven Isles, the Lone Islands, Dragon Island, Burnt Island, Deathwater, and the land of the Duffers itself, all exactly the right sizes and in the right positions. They were the first maps ever made of those seas and better than any that have been made since without magic. For on these, though the towns and mountains looked at first just as they would on an ordinary map, when the Magician lent them a magnifying glass you saw that they were perfect little pictures of the real things, so that you could see the very castle and slave market and streets in Narrowhaven, all very clear though very distant, like things seen through the wrong end of a telescope. The only drawback was that the coastline of most of the islands was incomplete, for the map showed only what Drinian had seen with his own eyes. When they were finished the Magician kept one himself and presented the other to Caspian: it still hangs in his Chamber of Instruments at Cair Paravel. But the Magician could tell them nothing about seas or lands further east. He did, however, tell them that about seven years before a Narnian ship had put in at his waters and that she had on board the Lords Revilian, Argoz, Mavramorn and Rhoop: so they judged that the golden man they had seen lying in Deathwater must be the Lord Restimar.

Next day, the Magician magically mended the stern of the *Dawn Treader* where it had been damaged by the Sea Serpent and loaded her with useful gifts. There was a most friendly parting, and when she sailed, two hours after noon, all the Dufflepuds paddled out with her to the harbor mouth, and cheered until she was out of sound of their cheering.

THE DARK ISLAND

After this adventure they sailed on south and a little east for twelve days with a gentle wind, the skies being mostly clear and the air warm, and saw no bird or fish, except that once there were whales spouting a long way to starboard. Lucy and Reepicheep played a good deal of chess at this time. Then on the thirteenth day, Edmund, from the fighting-top, sighted what looked like a great dark mountain rising out of the sea on their port bow.

They altered course and made for this land, mostly by oar, for the wind would not serve them to sail northeast. When evening fell they were still a long way from it and rowed all night. Next morning the weather was fair but a flat calm. The dark mass lay ahead, much nearer and larger, but still very dim, so that some thought it was still a long way off and others thought they were running into a mist.

About nine that morning, very suddenly, it was so close that they could see that it was not land at all, nor even, in an ordinary sense, a mist. It was a Darkness. It is rather hard to describe, but you will see what it was like if you imagine yourself looking into the mouth of a railway tunnel—a tunnel either so long or so twisty that you cannot see the light at the far end. And you know what it would be like. For a few feet you would see the rails and sleepers and gravel in broad daylight; then there would come a place where they were in twilight; and then, pretty suddenly, but of course without a sharp dividing line, they would vanish altogether into smooth, solid blackness. It was just so here. For a few feet in front of their bows they could see the swell of the bright greenish-blue water. Beyond that, they could see the water looking pale and gray as it would look late in the evening. But beyond that again, utter blackness as if they had come to the edge of moonless and starless night.

Caspian shouted to the boatswain to keep her back, and all except the rowers rushed

forward and gazed from the bows. But there was nothing to be seen by gazing. Behind them was the sea and the sun, before them the Darkness.

"Do we go into this?" asked Caspian at length.

"Not by my advice," said Drinian.

"The Captain's right," said several sailors.

"I almost think he is," said Edmund.

Lucy and Eustace didn't speak but they felt very glad inside at the turn things seemed to be taking. But all at once the clear voice of Reepicheep broke in upon the silence.

"And why not?" he said. "Will someone explain to me why not."

No one was anxious to explain, so Reepicheep continued:

"If I were addressing peasants or slaves," he said, "I might suppose that this suggestion proceeded from cowardice. But I hope it will never be told in Narnia that a company of noble and royal persons in the flower of their age turned tail because they were afraid of the dark."

"But what manner of use would it be plowing through that blackness?" asked Drinian.

"Use?" replied Reepicheep. "Use, Captain? If by use you mean filling our bellies or our purses, I confess it will be no use at all. So far as I know we did not set sail to look for things useful but to seek honor and adventure. And here is as great an adventure as ever I heard of, and here, if we turn back, no little impeachment of all our honors."

Several of the sailors said things under their breath that sounded like "Honor be blowed," but Caspian said:

"Oh, *bother* you, Reepicheep. I almost wish we'd left you at home. All right! If you put it that way, I suppose we shall have to go on. Unless Lucy would rather not?"

Lucy felt that she would very much rather not, but what she said out loud was, "I'm game."

"Your Majesty will at least order lights?" said Drinian.

"By all means," said Caspian. "See to it, Captain."

So the three lanterns, at the stern, and the prow and the masthead, were all lit, and Drinian ordered two torches amidships. Pale and feeble they looked in the sunshine. Then all the men except some who were left below at the oars were ordered on deck and fully armed and posted in their battle stations with swords drawn. Lucy and two archers were posted on the fighting-top with bows bent and arrows on the string. Rynelf was in the bows with his line ready to take soundings. Reepicheep, Edmund, Eustace and Caspian, glittering in mail, were with him. Drinian took the tiller.

"And now, in Aslan's name, forward!" cried Caspian. "A slow, steady stroke. And let every man be silent and keep his ears open for orders."

With a creak and a groan the *Dawn Treader* started to creep forward as the men began to row. Lucy, up in the fighting-top, had a wonderful view of the exact moment at which they entered the darkness. The bows had already disappeared before the sunlight had left the stern. She saw it go. At one minute the gilded stern, the blue sea, and the sky, were all in broad daylight: next minute the sea and sky had vanished, the stern lantern—which had been hardly noticeable before—was the only thing to show where the ship ended. In front of the lantern she could see the black shape of Drinian crouching at the tiller. Down below her the two torches made visible two small patches of deck and gleamed on swords and helmets, and forward there was another island of light on the forecastle. Apart from that, the fighting-top, lit by the masthead light which was only just above her, seemed to be a little lighted world of its own floating in lonely darkness. And the lights themselves, as always happens with lights when you have to have them at the wrong time of day, looked lurid and unnatural. She also noticed that she was very cold.

How long this voyage into the darkness

lasted, nobody knew. Except for the creak of the rowlocks and the splash of the oars there was nothing to show that they were moving at all. Edmund, peering from the bows, could see nothing except the reflection of the lantern in the water before him. It looked a greasy sort of reflection, and the ripple made by their advancing prow appeared to be heavy, small, and lifeless. As time went on everyone except the rowers began to shiver with cold.

Suddenly, from somewhere—no one's sense of direction was very clear by now—there came a cry, either of some inhuman voice or else a voice of one in such extremity of terror that he had almost lost his humanity.

Caspian was still trying to speak—his mouth was too dry—when the shrill voice of Reepicheep, which sounded louder than usual in that silence, was heard.

"Who calls?" it piped. "If you are a foe we do not fear you, and if you are a friend your enemies shall be taught the fear of us."

"Mercy!" cried the voice. "Mercy! Even if you are only one more dream, have mercy. Take me on board. Take me, even if you strike me dead. But in the name of all mercies do not fade away and leave me in this horrible land."

"Where are you?" shouted Caspian. "Come aboard and welcome."

There came another cry, whether of joy or terror, and then they knew that someone was swimming toward them.

"Stand by to heave him up, men," said Caspian.

"Aye, aye, your Majesty," said the sailors. Several crowded to the port bulwark with ropes and one, leaning far out over the side, held the torch. A wild, white face appeared in the blackness of the water, and then, after some scrambling and pulling, a dozen friendly hands had heaved the stranger on board.

Edmund thought he had never seen a wilder-looking man. Though he did not otherwise look very old, his hair was an untidy mop of white, his face was thin and drawn, and, for clothing, only a few wet rags hung about him. But what one mainly noticed were his eyes, which were so widely opened that he seemed to have no eyelids at all, and stared as if in an agony of pure fear. The moment his feet reached the deck he said:

"Fly! Fly! About with your ship and fly! Row, row, row for your lives away from this accursed shore."

"Compose yourself," said Reepicheep, "and tell us what the danger is. We are not used to flying."

The stranger started horribly at the voice of

the Mouse, which he had not noticed before.

"Nevertheless you will fly from here," he gasped. "This is the Island where Dreams come true."

"That's the island I've been looking for this long time," said one of the sailors. "I reckon I'd find I was married to Nancy if we landed here."

"And I'd find Tom alive again," said another.

"Fools!" said the man, stamping his foot with rage. "That is the sort of talk that brought me here, and I'd better have been drowned or never born. Do you hear what I say? This is where dreams—dreams, do you understand— come to life, come real. Not daydreams: dreams."

There was about half a minute's silence and then, with a great clatter of armor, the whole crew were tumbling down the main hatch as quick as they could and flinging themselves on the oars to row as they had never rowed before; and Drinian was swinging round the tiller, and the boatswain was giving out the quickest stroke that had ever been heard at sea. For it had taken everyone just that half-minute to remember certain dreams they had had—dreams that make you afraid of going to sleep again—and to realize what it would mean to land on a country where dreams come true.

Only Reepicheep remained unmoved.

"Your Majesty, your Majesty," he said, "are you going to tolerate this mutiny, this poltroonery? This is a panic, this is a rout."

"Row, row," bellowed Caspian. "Pull for all our lives. Is her head right, Drinian? You can say what you like, Reepicheep. There are some things no man can face."

"It is, then, my good fortune not to be a man," replied Reepicheep with a very stiff bow.

Lucy from up aloft had heard it all. In an instant that one of her own dreams which she had tried hardest to forget came back to her as vividly as if she had only just woken from it. So *that* was what was behind them, on the island, in the darkness! For a second she wanted to go down to the deck and be with Edmund and Caspian. But what was the use? If dreams began coming true, Edmund and Caspian themselves might turn into something horrible just as she reached them. She gripped the rail of the fighting-top and tried to steady herself. They were rowing back to the light as hard as they could: it would be all right in a few seconds. But oh, if only it could be all right now!

Though the rowing made a good deal of noise it did not quite conceal the total silence which surrounded the ship. Everyone knew it would be better not to listen, not to strain his ears for any sound from the darkness. But no one could help listening. And soon everyone was hearing things. Each one heard something different.

"Do you hear a noise like . . . like a huge pair of scissors opening and shutting . . . over there?" Eustace asked Rynelf.

"Hush!" said Rynelf. "I can hear *them* crawling up the sides of the ship."

"*It's* just going to settle on the mast," said Caspian.

"Ugh!" said a sailor. "There are the gongs beginning. I knew they would."

Caspian, trying not to look at anything (especially not to keep looking behind him), went aft to Drinian.

"Drinian," he said in a very low voice. "How long did we take rowing in?—I mean rowing to where we picked up the stranger."

"Five minutes, perhaps," whispered Drinian. "Why?"

"Because we've been more than that already trying to get out."

Drinian's hand shook on the tiller and a line of cold sweat ran down his face. The same idea was occurring to everyone on board. "We shall never get out, never get out," moaned the rowers. "He's steering us wrong. We're going round and round in circles. We shall never get out."

The stranger, who had been lying in a huddled heap on the deck, sat up and burst out into a horrible screaming laugh.

"Never get out!" he yelled. "That's it. Of course. We shall never get out. What a fool I was to have thought they would let me go as easily as that. No, no, we shall never get out."

Lucy leant her head on the edge of the fighting-top and whispered, "Aslan, Aslan, if ever you loved us at all, send us help now." The darkness did not grow any less, but she began to feel a little—a very, very little—better. "After all, nothing has really happened to us yet," she thought.

"Look!" cried Rynelf's voice hoarsely from the bows. There was a tiny speck of light ahead, and while they watched a broad beam of light fell from it upon the ship. It did not alter the surrounding darkness, but the whole ship was lit up as if by searchlight. Caspian blinked, stared round, saw the faces of his companions all with wild, fixed expressions. Everyone was staring in the same direction: behind everyone lay his black, sharply edged shadow.

Lucy looked along the beam and presently saw something in it. At first it looked like a cross, then it looked like an aeroplane, then it looked like a kite, and at last with a whirring of wings it was right overhead and was an alba-

tross. It circled three times round the mast and
then perched for an instant on the crest of the
gilded dragon at the prow. It called out in a
strong sweet voice what seemed to be words
though no one understood them. After that it
spread its wings, rose, and began to fly slowly
ahead, bearing a little to starboard. Drinian
steered after it not doubting that it offered good
guidance. But no one except Lucy knew that as
it circled the mast it had whispered to her,
"Courage, dear heart," and the voice, she felt
sure, was Aslan's, and with the voice a delicious
smell breathed in her face.

In a few moments the darkness turned into
a grayness ahead, and then, almost before they
dared to begin hoping, they had shot out into
the sunlight and were in the warm, blue world
again. And all at once everybody realized that
there was nothing to be afraid of and never had
been. They blinked their eyes and looked about
them. The brightness of the ship herself aston-
ished them: they had half expected to find that
the darkness would cling to the white and the
green and the gold in the form of some grime or
scum. And then first one, and then another, began laughing.

"I reckon we've made pretty good fools of
ourselves," said Rynelf.

Lucy lost no time in coming down to the

deck, where she found the others all gathered round the newcomer. For a long time he was too happy to speak, and could only gaze at the sea and the sun and feel the bulwarks and the ropes, as if to make sure he was really awake, while tears rolled down his cheeks.

"Thank you," he said at last. "You have saved me from . . . but I won't talk of that. And now let me know who you are. I am a Telmarine of Narnia, and when I was worth anything men called me the Lord Rhoop."

"And I," said Caspian, "am Caspian, King of Narnia, and I sail to find you and your companions who were my father's friends."

Lord Rhoop fell on his knees and kissed the King's hand. "Sire," he said, "you are the man in all the world I most wished to see. Grant me a boon."

"What is it?" asked Caspian.

"Never to bring me back there," he said. He pointed astern. They all looked. But they saw only bright blue sea and bright blue sky. The Dark Island and the darkness had vanished for ever.

"Why!" cried Lord Rhoop. "You have destroyed it!"

"I don't think it was us," said Lucy.

"Sire," said Drinian, "this wind is fair for the southeast. Shall I have our poor fellows up and set sail? And after that, every man who can be spared, to his hammock."

"Yes," said Caspian, "and let there be grog all round. Heigh-ho, I feel I could sleep the clock round myself."

So all afternoon with great joy they sailed southeast with a fair wind. But nobody noticed when the albatross had disappeared.

THE THREE SLEEPERS

The wind never failed but it grew gentler every day till at length the waves were little more than ripples, and the ship glided on hour after hour almost as if they were sailing on a lake. And every night they saw that there rose in the east new constellations which no one had ever seen in Narnia and perhaps, as Lucy thought with a mixture of joy and fear, no living eye had seen at all. Those new stars were big and bright and the nights were warm. Most of them slept on deck and talked far into the night or hung over the ship's side watching the luminous dance of the foam thrown up by their bows.

On an evening of startling beauty, when the sunset behind them was so crimson and purple and widely spread that the very sky itself seemed to have grown larger, they came in sight of land on their starboard bow. It came slowly nearer and the light behind them made it look as if the capes and headlands of this new country were all on fire. But presently they were sailing along its coast and its western cape now rose up astern of them, black against the red sky and sharp as if it was cut out of cardboard, and then they could see better what this country was like. It had no mountains but many gentle hills with slopes like pillows. An attractive smell came from it—what Lucy called "a dim, purple kind of smell," which Edmund said (and Rhince thought) was rot, but Caspian said, "I know what you mean."

They sailed on a good way, past point after point, hoping to find a nice deep harbor, but had to content themselves in the end with a wide and shallow bay. Though it had seemed calm out at sea there was of course surf breaking on the sand and they could not bring the *Dawn Treader* as far in as they would have liked. They dropped anchor a good way from the beach and had a wet and tumbling landing in the boat. The Lord Rhoop remained on board the *Dawn Treader*. He wished to see no more islands. All the time that they remained in this country the sound of the long breakers was in their ears.

Two men were left to guard the boat and Caspian led the others inland, but not far because it was too late for exploring and the light would soon go. But there was no need to go far to find an adventure. The level valley which lay at the head of the bay showed no road or track or other sign of habitation. Underfoot was fine springy turf dotted here and there with a low bushy growth which Edmund and Lucy took for heather. Eustace, who was really rather good at botany, said it wasn't, and he was probably right; but it was something of very much the same kind.

When they had gone less than a bowshot from the shore, Drinian said, "Look! What's that?" and everyone stopped.

"Are they great trees?" said Caspian.

"Towers, I think," said Eustace.

"It might be giants," said Edmund in a lower voice.

"The way to find out is to go right in among them," said Reepicheep, drawing his sword and pattering off ahead of everyone else.

"I think it's a ruin," said Lucy when they had got a good deal nearer, and her guess was the best so far. What they now saw was a wide oblong space flagged with smooth stones and surrounded by gray pillars but unroofed. And from end to end of it ran a long table laid with a rich crimson cloth that came down nearly to the pavement. At either side of it were many chairs of stone richly carved and with silken cushions upon the seats. But on the table itself there was set out such a banquet as had never been seen, not even when Peter the High King kept his court at Cair Paravel. There were turkeys and geese and peacocks, there were boars' heads and sides of venison, there were pies shaped like ships under full sail or like dragons and elephants, there were ice puddings and bright lobsters and gleaming salmon, there were nuts and grapes, pineapples and peaches, pomegranates and melons and tomatoes. There were flagons of gold and silver and curiously-wrought glass; and the smell of the fruit and the wine blew toward them like a promise of all happiness.

"I *say!*" said Lucy.

They came nearer and nearer, all very quietly.

"But where are the guests?" asked Eustace.

"We can provide that, Sir," said Rhince.

"Look!" said Edmund sharply. They were actually within the pillars now and standing on the pavement. Everyone looked where Edmund had pointed. The chairs were not all empty. At the head of the table and in the two places beside it there was something—or possibly three somethings.

"What are *those*?" asked Lucy in a whisper. "It looks like three beavers sitting on the table."

"Or a huge bird's nest," said Edmund.

"It looks more like a haystack to me," said Caspian.

Reepicheep ran forward, jumped on a chair and thence on to the table, and ran along it, threading his way as nimbly as a dancer between jeweled cups and pyramids of fruit and ivory salt-cellars. He ran right up to the mysterious gray mass at the end: peered, touched, and then called out:

"These will not fight, I think."

Everyone now came close and saw that what

sat in those three chairs was three men, though **hard to recognize as men till you looked closely.** Their hair, which was gray, had grown over their eyes till it almost concealed their faces, and their beards had grown over the table, climbing round and entwining plates and goblets as brambles entwine a fence, until, all mixed in one great mat of hair, they flowed over the edge and down to the floor. And from their heads the hair hung over the backs of their chairs so that they were wholly hidden. In fact the three men were nearly all hair.

"Dead?" said Caspian.

"I think not, Sire," said Reepicheep, lifting one of their hands out of its tangle of hair in his two paws. "This one is warm and his pulse beats."

"This one, too, and this," said Drinian.

"Why, they're only asleep," said Eustace.

"It's been a long sleep, though," said Edmund, "to let their hair grow like this."

"It must be an enchanted sleep," said Lucy. "I felt the moment we landed on this island that it was full of magic. Oh! do you think we have perhaps come here to break it?"

"We can try," said Caspian, and began shaking the nearest of the three sleepers. For a moment everyone thought he was going to be successful, for the man breathed hard and muttered, "I'll go eastward no more. Out oars for Narnia." But he sank back almost at once into a yet deeper sleep than before: that is, his heavy head sagged a few inches lower toward the table and all efforts to rouse him again were useless. With the second it was much the same. "Weren't born to live like animals. Get to the east while you've a chance—lands behind the sun," and sank down. And the third only said, "Mustard, please," and slept hard.

"*Out oars for Narnia*, eh?" said Drinian.

"Yes," said Caspian, "you are right, Drinian. I think our quest is at an end. Let's look at their rings. Yes, these are their devices. This is the Lord Revilian. This is the Lord Argoz: and this, the Lord Mavramorn."

"But we can't wake them," said Lucy. "What are we to do?"

"Begging your Majesties' pardons all," said Rhince, "but why not fall to while you're discussing it? We don't see a dinner like this every day."

"Not for your life!" said Caspian.

"That's right, that's right," said several of the sailors. "Too much magic about here. The sooner we're back on board the better."

"Depend upon it," said Reepicheep, "it was from eating this food that these three lords came by a seven years' sleep."

"I wouldn't touch it to save my life," said Drinian.

"The light's going uncommon quick," said Rynelf.

"Back to ship, back to ship," muttered the men.

"I really think," said Edmund, "they're right. We can decide what to do with the three sleepers tomorrow. We daren't eat the food and there's no point in staying here for the night. The whole place smells of magic—and danger."

"I am entirely of King Edmund's opinion," said Reepicheep, "as far as concerns the ship's company in general. But I myself will sit at this table till sunrise."

"Why on earth?" said Eustace.

"Because," said the Mouse, "this is a very great adventure, and no danger seems to me so great as that of knowing when I get back to Narnia that I left a mystery behind me through fear."

"I'll stay with you, Reep," said Edmund.

"And I too," said Caspian.

"And me," said Lucy. And then Eustace volunteered also. This was very brave of him because never having read of such things or even heard of them till he joined the *Dawn Treader* made it worse for him than for the others.

"I beseech your Majesty—" began Drinian.

"No, my Lord," said Caspian. "Your place is with the ship, and you have had a day's work while we five have idled." There was a lot of argument about this but in the end Caspian had his way. As the crew marched off to the shore in the gathering dusk none of the five watchers, except perhaps Reepicheep, could avoid a cold feeling in the stomach.

They took some time choosing their seats at the perilous table. Probably everyone had the same reason but no one said it out loud. For it was really a rather nasty choice. One could hardly bear to sit all night next to those three terrible hairy objects which, if not dead, were certainly not alive in the ordinary sense. On the other hand, to sit at the far end, so that you would see them less and less as the night grew darker, and wouldn't know if they were moving, and perhaps wouldn't see them at all by about two o'clock—no, it was not to be thought of. So they sauntered round and round the table saying, "What about here?" and "Or perhaps a bit further on," or, "Why not on this side?" till at last they settled down somewhere about the middle but nearer to the sleepers than to the other end. It was about ten by now and almost dark. Those strange new constellations burned in the east. Lucy would have liked it better if they had been the Leopard and the Ship and other old friends of the Narnian sky.

They wrapped themselves in their sea cloaks and sat still and waited. At first there was some attempt at talk but it didn't come to much. And they sat and sat. And all the time they heard the waves breaking on the beach.

After hours that seemed like ages there came a moment when they all knew they had been dozing a moment before but were all suddenly wide awake. The stars were all in quite different positions from those they had last noticed. The sky was very black except for the faintest possible grayness in the east. They were cold, though thirsty, and stiff. And none of them spoke because now at last something was happening.

Before them, beyond the pillars, there was the slope of a low hill. And now a door opened in the hillside, and light appeared in the doorway, and a figure came out, and the door shut behind it. The figure carried a light, and this light was really all that they could see distinctly. It came slowly nearer and nearer till at last it stood right at the table opposite to them. Now they could see that it was a tall girl, dressed in a single long garment of clear blue which left her arms bare. She was bareheaded and her yellow hair hung down her back. And when they looked at her they thought they had never before known what beauty meant.

The light which she had been carrying was a tall candle in a silver candlestick which she now set upon the table. If there had been any wind off the sea earlier in the night it must have died down by now, for the flame of the candle burned as straight and still as if it were in a room with the windows shut and the curtains drawn. Gold and silver on the table shone in its light.

Lucy now noticed something lying lengthwise on the table which had escaped her attention before. It was a knife of stone, sharp as steel, a cruel-looking, ancient-looking thing.

No one had yet spoken a word. Then—Reepicheep first, and Caspian next—they all rose to their feet, because they felt that she was a great lady.

"Travelers who have come from far to Aslan's table," said the girl. "Why do you not eat and drink?"

"Madam," said Caspian, "we feared the food because we thought it had cast our friends into an enchanted sleep."

"They have never tasted it," she said.

"Please," said Lucy, "what happened to them?"

"Seven years ago," said the girl, "they came here in a ship whose sails were rags and her timbers ready to fall apart. There were a few others with them, sailors, and when they came to this table one said, 'Here is the good place. Let us set sail and reef sail and row no longer but sit down and end our days in peace!' And the second said, 'No, let us re-embark and sail for Narnia and the west; it may be that Miraz is dead.' But the third, who was a very masterful man, leaped up and said, 'No, by heaven. We are men and Telmarines, not brutes. What should we do but seek adventure after adventure? We have not long to live in any event. Let us spend what is left in seeking the unpeopled world behind the sunrise.' And as they quarreled he caught up the Knife of Stone which lies there on the table and would have fought with his comrades. But it is a thing not right for him to touch. And as his fingers closed upon the hilt, deep sleep fell upon all the three. And till the enchantment is undone they will never wake."

"What is this Knife of Stone?" asked Eustace.

"Do none of you know it?" said the girl.

"I—I think," said Lucy, "I've seen something like it before. It was a knife like it that the White Witch used when she killed Aslan at the Stone Table long ago."

"It was the same," said the girl, "and it was brought here to be kept in honor while the world lasts."

Edmund, who had been looking more and more uncomfortable for the last few minutes, now spoke.

"Look here," he said, "I hope I'm not a coward—about eating this food, I mean—and I'm sure I don't mean to be rude. But we have had a lot of queer adventures on this voyage of ours and things aren't always what they seem. When I look in your face I can't help believing all you say: but then that's just what might happen with a witch too. How are we to know you're a friend?"

"You can't know," said the girl. "You can only believe—or not."

After a moment's pause Reepicheep's small voice was heard.

"Sire," he said to Caspian, "of your courtesy fill my cup with wine from that flagon: it is too big for me to lift. I will drink to the lady."

Caspian obeyed and the Mouse, standing on the table, held up a golden cup between its tiny paws and said, "Lady, I pledge you." Then it fell to on cold peacock, and in a short while everyone else followed his example. All were very hungry and the meal, if not quite what you wanted for a very early breakfast, was excellent as a very late supper.

"Why is it called Aslan's table?" asked Lucy presently.

"It is set here by his bidding," said the girl, "for those who come so far. Some call this island the World's End, for though you can sail further, this is the beginning of the end."

"But how does the food *keep?*" asked the practical Eustace.

"It is eaten, and renewed every day," said the girl. "This you will see."

"And what are we to do about the Sleepers?" asked Caspian. "In the world from which my friends come" (here he nodded at Eustace and the Pevensies) "they have a story of a prince or a king coming to a castle where all the people lay in an enchanted sleep. In that story he could not dissolve the enchantment until he had kissed the Princess."

"But here," said the girl, "it is different. Here he cannot kiss the Princess till he has dissolved the enchantment."

"Then," said Caspian, "in the name of Aslan, show me how to set about that work at once."

"My father will teach you that," said the girl.

"Your father!" said everyone. "Who is he? And where?"

"Look," said the girl, turning round and pointing at the door in the hillside. They could see it more easily now, for while they had been talking the stars had grown fainter and great gaps of white light were appearing in the grayness of the eastern sky.

14

THE BEGINNING OF THE END OF THE WORLD

Slowly the door opened again and out there came a figure as tall and straight as the girl's but not so slender. It carried no light but light seemed to come from it. As it came nearer, Lucy saw that it was like an old man. His silver beard came down to his bare feet in front and his silver hair hung down to his heels behind and his robe appeared to be made from the fleece of silver sheep. He looked so mild and grave that once more all the travelers rose to their feet and stood in silence.

But the old man came on without speaking to the travelers and stood on the other side of the table opposite to his daughter. Then both of them held up their arms before them and turned to face the east. In that position they began to sing. I wish I could write down the song, but no one who was present could remember it. Lucy said afterward that it was high, almost shrill, but very beautiful, "A cold kind of song, an early morning kind of song." And as they sang, the gray clouds lifted from the eastern sky and the white patches grew bigger and bigger till it was all white, and the sea began to shine like silver. And long afterward (but those two sang all the time) the east began to turn red and at last, unclouded, the sun came up out of the sea and its long level ray shot down the length of the table on the gold and silver and on the Stone Knife.

Once or twice before, the Narnians had wondered whether the sun at its rising did not look bigger in these seas than it had looked at home. This time they were certain. There was no mistaking it. And the brightness of its ray on the dew and on the table was far beyond any morning brightness they had ever seen. And as Edmund said afterward, "Though lots of things happened on that trip which *sound* more exciting, that moment was really the most exciting."

For now they knew that they had truly come to the beginning of the End of the World.

Then something seemed to be flying at them out of the very center of the rising sun: but of course one couldn't look steadily in that direction to make sure. But presently the air became full of voices—voices which took up the same song that the Lady and her Father were singing, but in far wilder tones and in a language which no one knew. And soon after that the owners of these voices could be seen. They were birds, large and white, and they came by hundreds and thousands and alighted on everything; on the grass, and the pavement, on the table, on your shoulders, your hands, and your head, till it looked as if heavy snow had fallen. For, like snow, they not only made everything white but blurred and blunted all shapes. But Lucy, looking out from between the wings of the birds that covered her, saw one bird fly to the Old Man with something in its beak that looked like a little fruit, unless it was a little live coal, which it might have been, for it was too bright to look at. And the bird laid it in the Old Man's mouth.

Then the birds stopped their singing and appeared to be very busy about the table. When they rose from it again everything on the table that could be eaten or drunk had disappeared. These birds rose from their meal in their thou-

sands and hundreds and carried away all the things that could not be eaten or drunk, such as bones, rinds, and shells, and took their flight back to the rising sun. But now, because they were not singing, the whir of their wings seemed to set the whole air a-tremble. And there was the table pecked clean and empty, and the three old Lords of Narnia still fast asleep.

Now at last the Old Man turned to the travelers and bade them welcome.

"Sir," said Caspian, "will you tell us how to undo the enchantment which holds these three Narnian Lords asleep."

"I will gladly tell you that, my son," said the Old Man. "To break this enchantment you must sail to the World's End, or as near as you can come to it, and you must come back having left at least one of your company behind."

"And what must happen to that one?" asked Reepicheep.

"He must go on into the utter east and never return into the world."

"That is my heart's desire," said Reepicheep.

"And are we near the World's End now, Sir?" asked Caspian. "Have you any knowledge of the seas and lands further east than this?"

"I saw them long ago," said the Old Man, "but it was from a great height. I cannot tell you such things as sailors need to know."

"Do you mean you were flying in the air?" Eustace blurted out.

"I was a long way above the air, my son," replied the Old Man. "I am Ramandu. But I see that you stare at one another and have not heard this name. And no wonder, for the days when I was a star had ceased long before any of you knew this world, and all the constellations have changed."

"Golly," said Edmund under his breath. "He's a *retired* star."

"Aren't you a star any longer?" asked Lucy.

"I am a star at rest, my daughter," answered Ramandu. "When I set for the last time, decrepit and old beyond all that you can reckon, I was carried to this island. I am not so old now as I was then. Every morning a bird brings me a fire-berry from the valleys in the Sun, and each fire-berry takes away a little of my age. And when I have become as young as the child that was born yesterday, then I shall take my rising again (for we are at earth's eastern rim) and once more tread the great dance."

"In our world," said Eustace, "a star is a huge ball of flaming gas."

"Even in your world, my son, that is not what a star is but only what it is made of. And in this world you have already met a star: for I think you have been with Coriakin."

"Is he a retired star, too?" said Lucy.

"Well, not quite the same," said Ramandu. "It was not quite as a rest that he was set to govern the Duffers. You might call it a punishment. He might have shone for thousands of years more in the southern winter sky if all had gone well."

"What did he do, Sir?" asked Caspian.

"My son," said Ramandu, "it is not for you, a son of Adam, to know what faults a star can commit. But come, we waste time in such talk. Are you yet resolved? Will you sail further east and come again, leaving one to return no more, and so break the enchantment? Or will you sail westward?"

"Surely, Sire," said Reepicheep, "there is no question about that? It is very plainly part of our quest to rescue these three lords from enchantment."

"I think the same, Reepicheep," replied Caspian. "And even if it were not so, it would break my heart not to go as near the World's End as the *Dawn Treader* will take us. But I am thinking of the crew. They signed on to seek the seven lords, not to reach the rim of the Earth. If we sail east from here we sail to find the edge, the utter east. And no one knows how far it is. They're brave fellows, but I see signs that some of them are weary of the voyage and long to have our prow pointing to Narnia again. I don't think I should take them further without their knowledge and consent. And then there's the poor Lord Rhoop. He's a broken man."

"My son," said the star, "it would be no use, even though you wished it, to sail for the World's End with men unwilling or men deceived. That is not how great unenchantments are achieved. They must know where they go and why. But who is this broken man you speak of?"

Caspian told Ramandu the story of Rhoop.

"I can give him what he needs most," said Ramandu. "In this island there is sleep without stint or measure, and sleep in which no faintest footfall of a dream was ever heard. Let him sit beside these other three and drink oblivion till your return."

"Oh, do let's do that, Caspian," said Lucy. "I'm sure it's just what he would love."

At that moment they were interrupted by the sound of many feet and voices: Drinian and the rest of the ship's company were approaching. They halted in surprise when they saw Ramandu and his daughter; and then, because these were obviously great people, every man uncovered his head. Some sailors eyed the empty dishes and flagons on the table with eyes filled with regret.

"My lord," said the King to Drinian, "pray send two men back to the *Dawn Treader* with a message to the Lord Rhoop. Tell him that the last of his old shipmates are here asleep—a sleep without dreams—and that he can share it."

When this had been done, Caspian told the rest to sit down and laid the whole situation before them. When he had finished there was a long silence and some whispering until presently the Master Bowman got to his feet, and said:

"What some of us have been wanting to ask for a long time, your Majesty, is how we're ever to get home when we do turn, whether we turn here or somewhere else. It's been west and northwest winds all the way, barring an occasional calm. And if that doesn't change, I'd like to know what hopes we have of seeing Narnia again. There's not much chance of supplies lasting while we *row* all that way."

"That's landsman's talk," said Drinian. "There's always a prevailing west wind in these seas all through the late summer, and it always changes after the New Year. We'll have plenty of wind for sailing westward; more than we shall like from all accounts."

"That's true, Master," said an old sailor who was a Galmian by birth. "You get some ugly weather rolling up from the east in January and February. And by your leave, Sire, if I was in command of this ship, I'd say to winter here and begin the voyage home in March."

"What'd you eat while you were wintering here?" asked Eustace.

"This table," said Ramandu, "will be filled with a king's feast every day at sunset."

"Now you're talking!" said several sailors.

"Your Majesties and gentlemen and ladies all," said Rynelf, "there's just one thing I want to say. There's not one of us chaps as was pressed on this journey. We're volunteers. And there's some here that are looking very hard at that table and thinking about king's feasts who were talking very loud about adventures on the day we sailed from Cair Paravel, and swearing they wouldn't come home till we'd found the end of the world. And there were some standing on the quay who would have given all they had to come with us. It was thought a finer thing then to have a cabin-boy's berth on the *Dawn Treader* than to wear a knight's belt. I don't know if you get the hang of what I'm saying. But what I mean is that I think chaps who set out like us will look as silly as—as those Dufflepuds—if we come home and say we got to the beginning of the world's end and hadn't the heart to go further."

Some of the sailors cheered at this but some said that that was all very well.

"This isn't going to be much fun," whispered Edmund to Caspian. "What are we to do if half those fellows hang back?"

"Wait," Caspian whispered back. "I've still a card to play."

"Aren't you going to say anything, Reep?" whispered Lucy.

"No. Why should your Majesty expect it?"

answered Reepicheep in a voice that most people heard. "My own plans are made. While I can, I sail east in the *Dawn Treader*. When she fails me, I paddle east in my coracle. When she sinks, I shall swim east with my four paws. And when I can swim no longer, if I have not reached Aslan's country, or shot over the edge of the world in some vast cataract, I shall sink with my nose to the sunrise and Peepiceek will be head of the talking mice in Narnia."

"Hear, hear," said a sailor. "I'll say the same, barring the bit about the coracle, which wouldn't bear me." He added in a lower voice, "I'm not going to be outdone by a mouse."

At this point Caspian jumped to his feet. "Friends," he said, "I think you have not quite understood our purpose. You talk as if we had come to you with our hat in our hand, begging for shipmates. It isn't like that at all. We and our royal brother and sister and their kinsman and Sir Reepicheep, the good knight, and the Lord Drinian have an errand to the world's edge. It is our pleasure to choose from among such of you as are willing those whom we deem worthy of so high an enterprise. We have not said that any can come for the asking. That is why we shall now command the Lord Drinian and Master Rhince to consider carefully what men among you are the hardest in battle, the most skilled seamen, the purest in blood, the most loyal to our person, and the cleanest of life and manners; and to give their names to us in a schedule." He paused and went on in a quicker voice, "Aslan's mane!" he exclaimed. "Do you think that the privilege of seeing the last things is to be bought for a song? Why, every man that comes with us shall bequeath the title of Dawn Treader to all his descendants, and when we land at Cair Paravel on the homeward voyage he shall have either gold or land enough to make him rich all his life. Now—scatter over the island, all of you. In half an hour's time I shall receive the names that Lord Drinian brings me."

There was rather a sheepish silence and then the crew made their bows and moved away, one in this direction and one in that, but mostly in little knots or bunches, talking.

"And now for the Lord Rhoop," said Caspian.

But turning to the head of the table he saw that Rhoop was already there. He had arrived, silent and unnoticed, while the discussion was going on, and was seated beside the Lord Argoz. The daughter of Ramandu stood beside him as if she had just helped him into his chair; Ramandu stood behind him and laid both his hands on Rhoop's gray head. Even in daylight a faint silver light came from the hands of the star. There was a smile on Rhoop's haggard face. He held out one of his hands to Lucy and the other to Caspian. For a moment it looked as if he were going to say something. Then his smile brightened as if he were feeling some delicious sensation, a long sigh of contentment came from his lips, his head fell forward, and he slept.

"Poor Rhoop," said Lucy. "I *am* glad. He must have had terrible times."

"Don't let's even think of it," said Eustace.

Meanwhile Caspian's speech, helped perhaps by some magic of the island, was having just the effect he intended. A good many who had been anxious enough to *get* out of the voyage felt quite differently about being *left* out of it. And of course whenever any one sailor announced that he had made up his mind to ask for permission to sail, the ones who hadn't said this felt that they were getting fewer and more uncomfortable. So that before the half-hour was nearly over several people were positively "sucking up" to Drinian and Rhince (at least that was what they called it at my school) to get a good report. And soon there were only three left who didn't want to go, and those three were trying very hard to persuade others to stay with them. And very shortly after that there was only one left. And in the end he began to be afraid of being left behind all on his own and changed his mind.

At the end of the half-hour they all came trooping back to Aslan's Table and stood at one end while Drinian and Rhince went and sat down with Caspian and made their report; and Caspian accepted all the men but that one who had changed his mind at the last moment. His name was Pittencream and he stayed on the Island of the Star all the time the others were away looking for the World's End, and he very much wished he had gone with them. He wasn't the sort of man who could enjoy talking to Ramandu and Ramandu's daughter (nor they to him), and it rained a good deal, and though there was a wonderful feast on the Table every night, he didn't very much enjoy it. He said it gave him the creeps sitting there alone (and in the rain as likely as not) with those four Lords asleep at the end of the Table. And when the others returned he felt so out of things that he deserted on the voyage home at the Lone Islands, and went and lived in Calormen, where he told wonderful stories about his adventures at the End of the World, until at last he came to believe them himself. So you may say, in a sense, that he lived happily ever after. But he could never bear mice.

That night they all ate and drank together at the great Table between the pillars where the feast was magically renewed: and next morning the *Dawn Treader* set sail once more just when the great birds had come and gone again.

"Lady," said Caspian, "I hope to speak with you again when I have broken the enchantments." And Ramandu's daughter looked at him and smiled.

THE WONDERS
OF THE LAST SEA

Very soon after they had left Ramandu's country they began to feel that they had already sailed beyond the world. All was different. For one thing they all found that they were needing less sleep. One did not want to go to bed nor to eat much, nor even to talk except in low voices. Another thing was the light. There was too much of it. The sun when it came up each morning looked twice, if not three times, its usual size. And every morning (which gave Lucy the strangest feeling of all) the huge white birds, singing their song with human voices in a language no one knew, streamed overhead and vanished astern on their way to their breakfast at Aslan's Table. A little later they came flying back and vanished into the east.

"How beautifully clear the water is!" said Lucy to herself, as she leaned over the port side early in the afternoon of the second day.

And it was. The first thing that she noticed was a little black object, about the size of a shoe, traveling along at the same speed as the ship. For a moment she thought it was something floating on the surface. But then there came floating past a bit of stale bread which the cook had just thrown out of the galley. And the bit of bread looked as if it were going to collide with the black thing, but it didn't. It passed above it, and Lucy now saw that the black thing could not be on the surface. Then the black thing suddenly got very much bigger and flicked back to normal size a moment later.

Now Lucy knew she had seen something just like that happen somewhere else—if only she could remember where. She held her hand to her head and screwed up her face and put out her tongue in the effort to remember. At last she did. Of course! It was like what you saw from a train on a bright sunny day. You saw the black shadow of your own coach running along the fields at the same pace as the train. Then you went into a cutting; and immediately the same shadow flicked close up to you and got big, racing along the grass of the cutting-bank. Then you came out of the cutting and—flick!—once more the black shadow had gone back to its normal size and was running along the fields.

"It's our shadow!—the shadow of the *Dawn Treader*," said Lucy. "Our shadow running along on the bottom of the sea. That time when it got bigger it went over a hill. But in that case the water must be clearer than I thought! Good gracious, I must be seeing the bottom of the sea; fathoms and fathoms down."

As soon as she had said this she realized that the great silvery expanse which she had been seeing (without noticing) for some time was really the sand on the sea-bed and that all sorts of darker or brighter patches were not lights and shadows on the surface but real things on the bottom. At present, for instance, they were passing over a mass of soft purply green with a broad, winding strip of pale gray in the middle of it. But now that she knew it was on the bottom she saw it much better. She could see that bits of the dark stuff were much higher than other bits and were waving gently. "Just like trees in a wind," said Lucy. "And I do believe that's what they are. It's a submarine forest."

They passed on above it and presently the

pale streak was joined by another pale streak. "If I was down there," thought Lucy, "that streak would be just like a road through the wood. And that place where it joins the other would be a crossroads. Oh, I do wish I was. Hallo! the forest is coming to an end. And I do believe the streak really was a road! I can still see it going on across the open sand. It's a different color. And it's marked out with something at the edges— dotted lines. Perhaps they are stones. And now it's getting wider."

But it was not really getting wider, it was getting nearer. She realized this because of the way in which the shadow of the ship came rushing up toward her. And the road—she felt sure it was a road now—began to go in zigzags. Obviously it was climbing up a steep hill. And when she held her head sideways and looked back, what she saw was very like what you see when you look down a winding road from the top of a hill. She could even see the shafts of sunlight falling through the deep water onto the wooded valley—and, in the extreme distance, everything melting away into a dim greenness. But some places—the sunny ones, she thought—were ultramarine blue.

She could not, however, spend much time looking back; what was coming into view in the forward direction was too exciting. The road had apparently now reached the top of the hill and ran straight forward. Little specks were moving to and fro on it. And now something most wonderful, fortunately in full sunlight—or as full as it can be when it falls through fathoms of water—flashed into sight. It was knobbly and jagged and of a pearly, or perhaps an ivory, color. She was so nearly straight above it that at first she could hardly make out what it was. But everything became plain when she noticed its shadow. The sunlight was falling across Lucy's shoulders, so the shadow of the thing lay stretched out on the sand behind it. And by its shape she saw clearly that it was a shadow of towers and pinnacles, minarets and domes.

"Why!—it's a city or a huge castle," said Lucy to herself. "But I wonder why they've built it on top of a high mountain?"

Long afterward when she was back in England and talked all these adventures over with Edmund, they thought of a reason and I am pretty sure it is the true one. In the sea, the deeper you go, the darker and colder it gets, and it is down there, in the dark and cold, that dangerous things live—the squid and the Sea Serpent and the Kraken. The valleys are the wild, unfriendly places. The sea-people feel about their valleys as we do about mountains, and feel about their mountains as we feel about valleys. It is on the heights (or, as we would say, "in the shallows") that there is warmth and peace. The reckless hunters and brave knights of the sea go down into the depths on quests and adventures, but return home to the heights for rest and peace, courtesy and council, the sports, the dances and the songs.

They had passed the city and the sea-bed was still rising. It was only a few hundred feet below the ship now. The road had disappeared. They were sailing above an open park-like country, dotted with little groves of brightly-colored vegetation. And then—Lucy nearly squealed aloud with excitement—she had seen People.

There were between fifteen and twenty of them, and all mounted on sea-horses—not the tiny little sea-horses which you may have seen in museums but horses rather bigger than themselves. They must be noble and lordly people, Lucy thought, for she could catch the gleam of gold on some of their foreheads and streamers of emerald- or orange-colored stuff fluttered from their shoulders in the current. Then:

"Oh, bother these fish!" said Lucy, for a whole shoal of small fat fish, swimming quite close to the surface, had come between her and the Sea People. But though this spoiled her view it led to the most interesting thing of all. Suddenly a fierce little fish of a kind she had

never seen before came darting up from below, snapped, grabbed, and sank rapidly with one of the fat fish in its mouth. And all the Sea People were sitting on their horses staring up at what had happened. They seemed to be talking and laughing. And before the hunting fish had got back to them with its prey, another of the same kind came up from the Sea People. And Lucy was almost certain that one big Sea Man who sat on his sea-horse in the middle of the party had sent it or released it; as if he had been holding it back till then in his hand or on his wrist.

"Why, I do declare," said Lucy, "it's a hunting party. Or more like a hawking party. Yes, that's it. They ride out with these little fierce fish on their wrists just as we used to ride out with falcons on our wrists when we were Kings and Queens at Cair Paravel long ago. And then they fly them—or I suppose I should say *swim* them—at the others. How—"

She stopped suddenly because the scene was changing. The Sea People had noticed the *Dawn Treader*. The shoal of fish had scattered in every direction: the People themselves were coming up to find out the meaning of this big, black thing which had come between them and the sun. And now they were so close to the surface that if they had been in air, instead of water, Lucy could have spoken to them. There were men and women both. All wore coronets of some kind and many had chains of pearls. They wore no other clothes. Their bodies were the color of old ivory, their hair dark purple. The King in the center (no one could mistake him for anything but the King) looked proudly and fiercely into Lucy's face and shook a spear in his hand. His knights did the same. The faces of the ladies were filled with astonishment. Lucy felt sure they had never seen a ship or a human before—and how should they, in seas beyond the world's end where no ship ever came?

"What are you staring at, Lu?" said a voice close beside her.

Lucy had been so absorbed in what she was seeing that she started at the sound, and when she turned she found that her arm had gone "dead" from leaning so long on the rail in one position. Drinian and Edmund were beside her.

"Look," she said.

They both looked, but almost at once Drinian said in a low voice:

"Turn round at once, your Majesties—that's right, with our backs to the sea. And don't look as if we were talking about anything important."

"Why, what's the matter?" said Lucy as she obeyed.

"It'll never do for the sailors to see *all that*," said Drinian. "We'll have men falling in love with a sea-woman, or falling in love with the under-sea country itself, and jumping overboard. I've heard of that kind of thing happening before in strange seas. It's always unlucky to see *these* people."

"But we used to know them," said Lucy. "In the old days at Cair Paravel when my brother Peter was High King. They came to the surface and sang at our coronation."

"I think that must have been a different kind, Lu," said Edmund. "They could live in the air as well as under water. I rather think these can't. By the look of them they'd have surfaced and started attacking us long ago if they could. They seem very fierce."

"At any rate," began Drinian, but at that

moment two sounds were heard. One was a plop. The other was a voice from the fighting-top shouting, "Man overboard!" Then everyone was busy. Some of the sailors hurried aloft to take in the sail; others hurried below to get to the oars; and Rhince, who was on duty on the poop, began to put the helm hard over so as to come round and back to the man who had gone overboard. But by now everyone knew that it wasn't strictly a man. It was Reepicheep.

"Drat that mouse!" said Drinian. "It's more trouble than all the rest of the ship's company put together. If there is any scrape to be got into, in it will get! It ought to be put in irons—keel-hauled—marooned—have its whiskers cut off. Can anyone see the little blighter?"

All this didn't mean that Drinian really disliked Reepicheep. On the contrary he liked him very much and was therefore frightened about him, and being frightened put him in a bad temper—just as your mother is much angrier with you for running out into the road in front of a car than a stranger would be. No one, of course, was afraid of Reepicheep's drowning, for he was an excellent swimmer; but the three who knew what was going on below the water were afraid of those long, cruel spears in the hands of the Sea People.

In a few minutes the *Dawn Treader* had come round and everyone could see the black blob in the water which was Reepicheep. He was chattering with the greatest excitement but as his mouth kept on getting filled with water nobody could understand what he was saying.

"He'll blurt the whole thing out if we don't shut him up," cried Drinian. To prevent this he rushed to the side and lowered a rope himself, shouting to the sailors, "All right, all right. Back to your places. I hope I can heave a *mouse* up without help." And as Reepicheep began climbing up the rope—not very nimbly because his wet fur made him heavy—Drinian leaned over and whispered to him,

"Don't tell. Not a word."

But when the dripping Mouse had reached the deck it turned out not to be at all interested in the Sea People.

"Sweet!" he cheeped. "Sweet, sweet!"

"What are you talking about?" asked Drinian crossly. "And you needn't shake yourself all over *me*, either."

"I tell you the water's sweet," said the Mouse. "Sweet, fresh. It isn't salt."

For a moment no one quite took in the importance of this. But then Reepicheep once more repeated the old prophecy:

> *"Where the waves grow sweet,*
> *Doubt not, Reepicheep,*
> *There is the utter East."*

Then at last everyone understood.

"Let me have a bucket, Rynelf," said Drinian.

It was handed him and he lowered it and up it came again. The water shone in it like glass.

"Perhaps your Majesty would like to taste it first," said Drinian to Caspian.

The King took the bucket in both hands, raised it to his lips, sipped, then drank deeply and raised his head. His face was changed. Not only his eyes but everything about him seemed to be brighter.

"Yes," he said, "it is sweet. That's real water, that. I'm not sure that it isn't going to kill me. But it is the death I would have chosen—if I'd known about it till now."

"What do you mean?" asked Edmund.

"It—it's like light more than anything else," said Caspian.

"That is what it is," said Reepicheep. "Drinkable light. We must be very near the end of the world now."

There was a moment's silence and then Lucy

knelt down on the deck and drank from the bucket.

"It's the loveliest thing I have ever tasted," she said with a kind of gasp. "But oh—it's strong. We shan't need to *eat* anything now."

And one by one everybody on board drank. And for a long time they were all silent. They felt almost too well and strong to bear it; and presently they began to notice another result. As I have said before, there had been too much light ever since they left the island of Ramandu—the sun too large (though not too hot), the sea too bright, the air too shining. Now, the light grew no less—if anything, it increased—but they could bear it. They could look straight up at the sun without blinking. They could see more light than they had ever seen

before. And the deck and the sail and their own faces and bodies became brighter and brighter and every rope shone. And next morning, when the sun rose, now five or six times its old size, they stared hard into it and could see the very feathers of the birds that came flying from it.

Hardly a word was spoken on board all that day, till about dinner-time (no one wanted any dinner, the water was enough for them) Drinian said:

"I can't understand this. There is not a breath of wind. The sail hangs dead. The sea is as flat as a pond. And yet we drive on as fast as if there were a gale behind us."

"I've been thinking that, too," said Caspian. "We must be caught in some strong current."

"H'm," said Edmund. "That's not so nice if the World really has an edge and we're getting near it."

"You mean," said Caspian, "that we might be just—well, poured over it?"

"Yes, yes," cried Reepicheep, clapping his paws together. "That's how I've always imagined it—the World like a great round table and the waters of all the oceans endlessly pouring over the edge. The ship will tip up—stand on her head—for one moment we shall see over the edge—and then, down, down, the rush, the speed—"

"And what do you think will be waiting for us at the bottom, eh?" said Drinian.

"Aslan's country, perhaps," said the Mouse, its eyes shining. "Or perhaps there isn't any bottom. Perhaps it goes down for ever and ever. But whatever it is, won't it be worth anything just to have looked for one moment beyond the edge of the world."

"But look here," said Eustace, "this is all rot. The world's round—I mean, round like a ball, not like a table."

"*Our* world is," said Edmund. "But is this?"

"Do you mean to say," asked Caspian, "that you three come from a round world (round like a ball) and you've never told me! It's really too bad of you. Because we have fairy-tales in which there are round worlds and I always loved them. I never believed there were any real ones. But I've always wished there were and I've always longed to live in one. Oh, I'd give anything—I wonder why you can get into our world and we never get into yours? If only I had the chance! It must be exciting to live on a thing like a ball. Have you ever been to the parts where people walk about upside-down?"

Edmund shook his head. "And it isn't like that," he added. "There's nothing particularly exciting about a round world when you're there."

16

THE VERY END
OF THE WORLD

Reepicheep was the only person on board besides Drinian and the two Pevensies who had noticed the Sea People. He had dived in at once when he saw the Sea King shaking his spear, for he regarded this as a sort of threat or challenge and wanted to have the matter out there and then. The excitement of discovering that the water was now fresh had distracted his attention, and before he remembered the Sea People again Lucy and Drinian had taken him aside and warned him not to mention what he had seen.

As things turned out they need hardly have bothered, for by this time the *Dawn Treader* was gliding over a part of the sea which seemed to be uninhabited. No one except Lucy saw anything more of the People, and even she had only one short glimpse. All morning on the following day they sailed in fairly shallow water and the bottom was weedy. Just before midday Lucy saw a large shoal of fishes grazing on the weed. They were all eating steadily and all moving in the same direction. "Just like a flock of sheep," thought Lucy. Suddenly she saw a little Sea Girl of about her own age in the middle of them—a quiet, lonely-looking girl with a sort of crook in her hand. Lucy felt sure that this girl must be a shepherdess—or perhaps a fish-herdess—and that the shoal was really a flock at pasture. Both the fishes and the girl were quite close to the surface. And just as the girl, gliding in the shallow water, and Lucy, leaning over the bulwark, came opposite to one another, the girl looked up and stared straight into Lucy's face. Neither could speak to the other and in a moment the Sea Girl dropped astern. But Lucy will never forget her face. It did not look frightened or angry like those of the other Sea People. Lucy had liked that girl and she felt certain the girl had liked her. In that one moment they had somehow become friends. There does not seem to be much chance of their meeting again in that world or any other. But if ever they do they will rush together with their hands held out.

After that for many days, without wind in her shrouds or foam at her bows, across a waveless sea, the *Dawn Treader* glided smoothly east. Every day and every hour the light became more brilliant and still they could bear it. No one ate or slept and no one wanted to, but they drew buckets of dazzling water from the sea, stronger than wine and somehow wetter, more liquid, than ordinary water, and pledged one another silently in deep drafts of it. And one or two of the sailors who had been oldish men when the voyage began now grew younger every day. Everyone on board was filled with joy and excitement, but not an excitement that made one talk. The further they sailed the less they spoke, and then almost in a whisper. The stillness of that last sea laid hold on them.

"My Lord," said Caspian to Drinian one day, "what do you see ahead?"

"Sire," said Drinian, "I see whiteness. All along the horizon from north to south, as far as my eyes can reach."

"That is what I see too," said Caspian, "and I cannot imagine what it is."

"If we were in higher latitudes, your Majesty," said Drinian, "I would say it was ice.

But it can't be that; not here. All the same, we'd better get men to the oars and hold the ship back against the current. Whatever the stuff is, we don't want to crash into it at this speed!"

They did as Drinian said, and so continued to go slower and slower. The whiteness did not get any less mysterious as they approached it. If it was land it must be a very strange land, for it seemed just as smooth as the water and on the same level with it. When they got very close to it Drinian put the helm hard over and turned the *Dawn Treader* south so that she was broadside on to the current and rowed a little way southward along the edge of the whiteness. In so doing they accidentally made the important discovery that the current was only about forty feet wide and the rest of the sea as still as a pond. This was good news for the crew, who had already begun to think that the return journey to Ramandu's land, rowing against stream all the way, would be pretty poor sport. (It also explained why the shepherd girl had dropped so quickly astern. She was not in the current. If she had been she would have been moving east at the same speed as the ship.)

And still no one could make out what the white stuff was. Then the boat was lowered and it put off to investigate. Those who remained on the *Dawn Treader* could see that the boat pushed right in amidst the whiteness. Then they could hear the voices of the party in the boat (clear across the still water) talking in a shrill and surprised way. Then there was a pause while Rynelf in the bows of the boat took a sounding; and when, after that, the boat came rowing back there seemed to be plenty of the white stuff inside her. Everyone crowded to the side to hear the news.

"Lilies, your Majesty!" shouted Rynelf, standing up in the bows.

"*What* did you say?" asked Caspian.

"Blooming lilies, your Majesty," said Rynelf. "Same as in a pool or in a garden at home."

"Look!" said Lucy, who was in the stern of the boat. She held up her wet arms full of white petals and broad flat leaves.

"What's the depth, Rynelf?" asked Drinian.

"That's the funny thing, Captain," said Rynelf. "It's still deep. Three and a half fathoms clear."

"They can't be real lilies—not what we call lilies," said Eustace.

Probably they were not, but they were very like them. And when, after some consultation, the *Dawn Treader* turned back into the current and began to glide eastward through the Lily Lake or the Silver Sea (they tried both these names but it was the Silver Sea that stuck and is now on Caspian's map) the strangest part of their travels began. Very soon the open sea which they were leaving was only a thin rim of blue on the western horizon. Whiteness, shot with faintest color of gold, spread round them on every side, except just astern where their passage had thrust the lilies apart and left an open lane of water that shone like dark green glass. To look at, this last sea was very like the Arctic; and if their eyes had not by now grown as strong as eagles' the sun on all that whiteness—especially at early morning when the sun was hugest—would have been unbearable. And every evening the same whiteness made the daylight last longer. There seemed no end to the lilies. Day after day from all those miles and leagues of flowers there rose a smell which Lucy found it very hard to describe; sweet—yes, but not at all sleepy or overpowering, a fresh, wild, lonely smell that seemed to get into your brain and make you feel that you could go up mountains at a run or wrestle with an elephant. She and Caspian said to one another, "I feel that I can't stand much more of this, yet I don't want it to stop."

They took soundings very often but it was only several days later that the water became shallower. After that it went on getting shallower. There came a day when they had to row

out of the current and feel their way forward at a
snail's pace, rowing. And soon it was clear that
the *Dawn Treader* could sail no further east.
Indeed it was only by very clever handling that
they saved her from grounding.

"Lower the boat," cried Caspian, "and then
call the men aft. I must speak to them."

"What's he going to do?" whispered Eustace
to Edmund. "There's a queer look in his eyes."

"I think we probably all look the same," said
Edmund.

They joined Caspian on the poop and soon
all the men were crowded together at the foot of
the ladder to hear the King's speech.

"Friends," said Caspian, "we have now ful-
filled the quest on which you embarked. The
seven lords are all accounted for and as Sir
Reepicheep has sworn never to return, when you
reach Ramandu's Land you will doubtless find the
Lords Revilian and Argoz and Mavramorn
awake. To you, my Lord Drinian, I entrust this
ship, bidding you sail to Narnia with all the speed
you may, and above all not to land on the Island
of Deathwater. And instruct my regent, the
Dwarf Trumpkin, to give to all these, my shipmates, the rewards I promised them. They have
been earned well. And if I come not again it is
my will that the Regent, and Master Cornelius,
and Trufflehunter the Badger, and the Lord

Drinian choose a King of Narnia with the consent—"

"But, Sire," interrupted Drinian, "are you abdicating?"

"I am going with Reepicheep to see the World's End," said Caspian.

A low murmur of dismay ran through the sailors.

"We will take the boat," said Caspian. "You will have no need of it in these gentle seas and you must build a new one on Ramandu's island. And now—"

"Caspian," said Edmund suddenly and sternly, "you can't do this."

"Most certainly," said Reepicheep, "his Majesty cannot."

"No indeed," said Drinian.

"Can't?" said Caspian sharply, looking for a moment not unlike his uncle Miraz.

"Begging your Majesty's pardon," said Rynelf from the deck below, "but if one of us did the same it would be called deserting."

"You presume too much on your long service, Rynelf," said Caspian.

"No, Sire! He's perfectly right," said Drinian.

"By the Mane of Aslan," said Caspian, "I had thought you were all my subjects here, not my schoolmasters."

"I'm not," said Edmund, "and I say you can *not* do this."

"Can't again," said Caspian. "What do you mean?"

"If it please your Majesty, we mean *shall not*," said Reepicheep with a very low bow. "You are the King of Narnia. You break faith with all your subjects, and especially with Trumpkin, if you do not return. You shall not please yourself with adventures as if you were a private person. And if your Majesty will not hear reason it will be the truest loyalty of every man on board to follow me in disarming and binding you till you come to your senses."

"Quite right," said Edmund. "Like they did with Ulysses when he wanted to go near the Sirens."

Caspian's hand had gone to his sword hilt, when Lucy said, "And you've almost promised Ramandu's daughter to go back."

Caspian paused. "Well, yes. There is that," he said. He stood irresolute for a moment and then shouted out to the ship in general.

"Well, have your way. The quest is ended. We all return. Get the boat up again."

"Sire," said Reepicheep, "we do not *all* return. I, as I explained before—"

"Silence!" thundered Caspian. "I've been lessoned but I'll not be baited. Will no one silence that Mouse?"

"Your Majesty promised," said Reepicheep, "to be good lord to the Talking Beasts of Narnia."

"Talking beasts, yes," said Caspian. "I said nothing about beasts that never stop talking." And he flung down the ladder in a temper and went into the cabin, slamming the door.

But when the others rejoined him a little later they found him changed; he was white and there were tears in his eyes.

"It's no good," he said. "I might as well have behaved decently for all the good I did with my temper and swagger. Aslan has spoken to me. No—I don't mean he was actually here. He wouldn't fit into the cabin, for one thing. But that gold lion's head on the wall came to life and spoke to me. It was terrible—his eyes. Not that he was at all rough with me—only a bit stern at first. But it was terrible all the same. And he said—he said—oh, I can't bear it. The worst thing he could have said. You're to go on—Reep and Edmund, and Lucy, and Eustace; and I'm to go back. Alone. And at once. And what *is* the good of anything?"

"Caspian, dear," said Lucy. "You knew we'd have to go back to our own world sooner or later."

"Yes," said Caspian with a sob, "but this is sooner."

"You'll feel better when you get back to Ramandu's Island," said Lucy.

He cheered up a little later on, but it was a grievous parting on both sides and I will not dwell on it. About two o'clock in the afternoon, well victualed and watered (though they thought they would need neither food nor drink) and with Reepicheep's coracle on board, the boat pulled away from the *Dawn Treader* to row through the endless carpet of lilies. The *Dawn Treader* flew all her flags and hung out her shields to honor their departure. Tall and big and homelike she looked from their low position with the lilies all round them. And even before she was out of sight they saw her turn and begin rowing slowly westward. Yet though Lucy shed a few tears, she could not feel it as much as you might have expected. The light, the silence, the tingling smell of the Silver Sea, even (in some odd way) the loneliness itself, were too exciting.

There was no need to row, for the current drifted them steadily to the east. None of them slept or ate. All that night and all next day they glided eastward, and when the third day dawned—with a brightness you or I could not bear even if we had dark glasses on—they saw a wonder ahead. It was as if a wall stood up between them and the sky, a greenish-gray, trembling, shimmering wall. Then up came the sun, and at its first rising they saw it through the wall and it turned into wonderful rainbow colors. Then they knew that the wall was really a long, tall wave—a wave endlessly fixed in one place as you may often see at the edge of a waterfall. It seemed to be about thirty feet high, and the current was gliding them swiftly toward it. You

might have supposed they would have thought of their danger. They didn't. I don't think anyone could have in their position. For now they saw something not only behind the wave but behind the sun. They could not have seen even the sun if their eyes had not been strengthened by the water of the Last Sea. But now they could look at the rising sun and see it clearly and see things beyond it. What they saw—eastward, beyond the sun—was a range of mountains. It was so high that either they never saw the top of it or they forgot it. None of them remembers seeing any sky in that direction. And the mountains must really have been outside the world. For any mountains even a quarter of a twentieth of that height ought to have had ice and snow on them. But these were warm and green and full of forests and waterfalls however high you looked. And suddenly there came a breeze from the east, tossing the top of the wave into foamy shapes and ruffling the smooth water all round them. It lasted only a second or so but what it brought them in that second none of those three children will ever forget. It brought both a smell and a sound, a musical sound. Edmund and Eustace would never talk about it afterward. Lucy could only say, "It would break your heart." "Why," said I, "was it so sad?" "Sad!! No," said Lucy.

No one in that boat doubted that they were

seeing beyond the End of the World into Aslan's country.

At that moment, with a crunch, the boat ran aground. The water was too shallow now for it. "This," said Reepicheep, "is where I go on alone."

They did not even try to stop him, for everything now felt as if it had been fated or had happened before. They helped him to lower his little coracle. Then he took off his sword ("I shall need it no more," he said) and flung it far away across the lilied sea. Where it fell it stood upright with the hilt above the surface. Then he bade them good-bye, trying to be sad for their sakes; but he was quivering with happiness. Lucy, for the first and last time, did what she had always wanted to do, taking him in her arms and caressing him. Then hastily he got into his cora-cle and took his paddle, and the current caught it and away he went, very black against the lilies. But no lilies grew on the wave; it was a smooth green slope. The coracle went more and more quickly, and beautifully it rushed up the wave's side. For one split second they saw its shape and Reepicheep's on the very top. Then it vanished, and since that moment no one can truly claim to have seen Reepicheep the Mouse. But my belief is that he came safe to Aslan's country and is alive there to this day.

As the sun rose the sight of those mountains outside the world faded away. The wave remained but there was only blue sky behind it.

The children got out of the boat and waded—not toward the wave but southward with the wall of water on their left. They could not have told you why they did this; it was their fate. And though they had felt—and been—very grown-up on the *Dawn Treader*, they now felt just the opposite and held hands as they waded through the lilies. They never felt tired. The water was warm and all the time it got shallower. At last they were on dry sand, and then on grass—a huge plain of very fine short grass, almost level with the Silver Sea and spreading in every direction without so much as a molehill.

And of course, as it always does in a perfectly flat place without trees, it looked as if the sky came down to meet the grass in front of them. But as they went on they got the strangest impression that here at last the sky did really come down and join the earth—a blue wall, very bright, but real and solid: more like glass than anything else. And soon they were quite sure of it. It was very near now.

But between them and the foot of the sky there was something so white on the green grass that even with their eagles' eyes they could

hardly look at it. They came on and saw that it was a Lamb.

"Come and have breakfast," said the Lamb in its sweet milky voice.

Then they noticed for the first time that there was a fire lit on the grass and fish roasting on it. They sat down and ate the fish, hungry now for the first time for many days. And it was the most delicious food they had ever tasted.

"Please, Lamb," said Lucy, "is this the way to Aslan's country?"

"Not for you," said the Lamb. "For you the door into Aslan's country is from your own world."

"What!" said Edmund. "Is there a way into

Aslan's country from our world too?"

"There is a way into my country from all the worlds," said the Lamb; but as he spoke his snowy white flushed into tawny gold and his size changed and he was Aslan himself, towering above them and scattering light from his mane.

"Oh, Aslan," said Lucy. "Will you tell us how to get into your country from our world?"

"I shall be telling you all the time," said Aslan. "But I will not tell you how long or short the way will be; only that it lies across a river. But do not fear that, for I am the great Bridge Builder. And now come; I will open the door in the sky and send you to your own land."

"Please, Aslan," said Lucy. "Before we go, will you tell us when we can come back to Narnia again? Please. And oh, do, do, do make it soon."

"Dearest," said Aslan very gently, "you and your brother will never come back to Narnia."

"Oh, *Aslan*!!" said Edmund and Lucy both together in despairing voices.

"You are too old, children," said Aslan, "and you must begin to come close to your own world now."

"It isn't Narnia, you know," sobbed Lucy. "It's *you*. We shan't meet *you* there. And how can we live, never meeting you?"

"But you shall meet me, dear one," said Aslan.

"Are—are you there too, Sir?" said Edmund.

"I am," said Aslan. "But there I have another name. You must learn to know me by that name. This was the very reason why you were brought to Narnia, that by knowing me here for a little, you may know me better there."

"And is Eustace never to come back here either?" said Lucy.

"Child," said Aslan, "do you really need to know that? Come, I am opening the door in the sky." Then all in one moment there was a rending of the blue wall (like a curtain being torn) and a terrible white light from beyond the sky, and the feel of Aslan's mane and a Lion's kiss on their foreheads and then—the back bedroom in Aunt Alberta's home at Cambridge.

Only two more things need to be told. One is that Caspian and his men all came safely back to Ramandu's Island. And the three lords woke from their sleep. Caspian married Ramandu's daughter and they all reached Narnia in the end, and she became a great queen and the mother and grandmother of great kings. The other is that back in our own world everyone soon started saying how Eustace had improved, and how "You'd never know him for the same boy": everyone except Aunt Alberta, who said he had become very commonplace and tiresome and it must have been the influence of those Pevensie children.

A VIVID ADVENTURE IN PARALLEL TIME

Corporal Calvin Morrison, of the Pennsylvania State Police, was scared. Unsnapping the retaining strap of his holster, he started towards the old farmhouse where a murderer with a rifle was waiting.

He was within a few feet of the little brook when it happened.

There was a blinding flash, and a hemisphere of flickering light glowed all around him, and an oval desk with an instrument-panel appeared, and a young man was rising from a swivel-chair with a weapon in his hand . . . .

Morrison fired, flung himself to one side and rolled, rolled until he was out of the nacreous dome of light, and came bumping up against a tree. The light disappeared, and he lay still for a moment in relief, until he realized that there weren't any trees here! Not in twentieth-century Pennsylvania, anyway.

And Corporal Calvin Morrison had to absorb the fact that he knew *where* he was, but he hadn't the slightest inkling of *when* he was!

LORD KALVAN
OF OTHERWHEN

LORD
KALVAN OF
OTHERWHEN

H. BEAM PIPER

SF
ace books
A Division of Charter Communications Inc.
A GROSSET & DUNLAP COMPANY
51 Madison Avenue
New York, New York 10010

LORD KALVAN OF OTHERWHEN

An ACE Book

This Ace Printing: June 1981
Printed in U.S.A.

Printed Simultaneously in Canada

ONE

I

TORTHA KARF, Chief of Paratime Police, told himself to stop fretting. He was only three hundred years years old, so by the barest life-expectancy of his race he was good for another two centuries. Two hundred more days wouldn't matter. Then it would be Year-End Day, and, precisely at midnight, he would rise from this chair, and Verkan Vall would sit down in it, and after that he would be free to raise grapes and lemons and wage guerrilla war against the rabbits on the island of Sicily, which he owned outright on one uninhabited Fifth Level time-line. He wondered how long it would take Vall to become as tired of the Chief's seat as he was now.

Actually, Karf knew, Verkan Vall had never wanted to be Chief. Prestige and authority meant little to him, and freedom much. Vall liked to work outtime. But it was a job somebody had to do, and it was the job for which Vall had been trained, so he'd take it, and do it, Karf suspected, better than he'd done it himself. The job of policing a near-infinity

1

of worlds, each of which was this same planet Earth, would be safe with Verkan Vall.

Twelve thousand years ago, facing extinction on an exhausted planet, the First Level race had discovered the existence of a second, lateral, time-dimension and a means of physical transposition to and from a near-infinity of worlds of alternate probability parallel to their own. So the conveyers had gone out by stealth, bringing back wealth to Home Time Line—a little from this one, a little from that, never enough to be missed anywhen.

It all had to be policed. Some Paratimers were less than scrupulous in dealing with outtime races—he'd have retired ten years ago except for the discovery of a huge paratemporal slave-trade, only recently smashed. More often, somebody's bad luck or indiscretion would endanger the Paratime Secret, or some incident—nobody's fault, something that just happened—would have to be explained away. But, at all costs, the Paratime Secret must be preserved. Not merely the actual technique of transposition—that went without saying—but the very existence of a race possessing it. If for no other reason (and there *were* many others), it would be utterly immoral to make any outtime race live with the knowledge that there were among them aliens indistinguishable from themselves, watching and exploiting. It was a big police-beat.

Second Level: that had been civilized almost as long as the First, but there had been dark-age interludes. Except for paratemporal transposition, most of its sectors equaled First Level, and from many Home Time Line had learned much. The Third Level civilizations were more recent, but still of respectable antiquity and advancement. Fourth Level had started late and progressed slowly; some Fourth Level genius was first domesticating animals long after the steam engine was obsolescent all over the Third. And Fifth Level: on a few sectors, subhuman brutes, speechless and fireless, were cracking nuts and each other's heads with stones, and on most of it nothing even vaguely humanoid had appeared.

Fourth Level was the big one. The others had devolved

from low-probability genetic accidents; it was the maximum probability. It was divided into many sectors and subsectors, on most of which human civilization had first appeared in the valleys of the Nile and Tigris-Euphrates, and on the Indus and Yangtze. Europo-American Sector: they might have to pull out of that entirely, but that would be for Chief Verkan to decide. Too many thermonuclear weapons and too many competing national sovereignties. That had happened all over Third Level at one time or another within Home Time Line experience. Alexandrian-Roman: off to a fine start with the pooling of Greek theory and Roman engineering talent, and then, a thousand years ago, two half-forgotten religions had been rummaged out of the dustbin and fanatics had begun massacring one another. They were still at it, with pikes and matchlocks, having lost the ability to make anything better. Europo-American could come to that if its rival political and economic sectarians kept on. Sino-Hindic: that wasn't a civilization; it was a bad case of cultural paralysis. And so was Indo-Turanian—about where Europo-American had been ten centuries ago.

And Aryan-Oriental: the Aryan migration of three thousand years ago, instead of moving west and south, as on most sectors, had rolled east into China. And Aryan-Transpacific, an offshoot: on one sector, some of them had built ships and sailed north and east along the Kuriles and the Aleutians and settled in North America, bringing with them horses and cattle and iron-working skills, exterminating the Amerinds, warring with one another, splitting into diverse peoples and cultures. There was a civilization, now decadent, on the Pacific coast, and nomads on the central plains herding bison and crossbreeding them with Asian cattle, and a civilization around the Great Lakes and one in the Mississippi Valley, and a new one, five or six centuries old, along the Atlantic and in the Appalachians. Technological level pre-mechanical, water-and-animal power; a few subsectors had gotten as far as gunpowder.

But Aryan-Transpacific was a sector to watch. They were going forward; things were ripe to start happening soon.

Let Chief Verkan watch it, for the next couple of centuries. After Year-End Day, ex-Chief Tortha would have his vine-yards and lemon-groves to watch.

II

Rylla tried to close her mind to the voices around her in the tapestried room, and stared at the map spread in front of her and her father. There was Tarr-Hostigos overlooking the gap, only a tiny fleck of gold on the parchment, but she could see it in her mind's eye—the walled outer bailey with the sheds and stables and workshops inside, the inner bailey and the citadel and keep, the watchtower pointing a blunt finger skyward. Below, the little Darro flowed north to join the Listra and, with it, the broad Athan to the east. Hostigos Town, white walls and slate roofs and busy streets; the checkerboard of fields to the west and south; the forest, broken by farms, to the west.

A voice, louder and harsher than the others, brought her back to reality. Her cousin, Sthentros.

"He'll do nothing at all? Well, what in Dralm's holy name is a Great King for, but to keep the peace?"

She looked along the table, from one to another. Phosg, the speaker for the peasants, at the foot, uncomfortable in his feast-day clothes and ill at ease seated among his betters. The speakers for the artisans' guilds, and for the merchants and the townsfolk; the lesser family members and marriagekin; the barons and landholders. Old Chartiphon, the chief-captain, his golden beard streaked with gray like the lead-splotches on his gilded breastplate, his long sword on the table in front of him. Xentos, the cowl of his priestly robe thrown back from his snowy head, his blue eyes troubled. And beside her, at the table's head, her father, Prince Ptosphes, his mouth tight between pointed gray mustache and pointed gray beard. How long it had been since she had seen her father smile!

Xentos passed a hand negatively across his face.

"King Kaiphranos said that it was every Prince's duty to guard his own realm; that it was for Prince Ptosphes, not for him, to keep bandits out of Hostigos."

"Bandits? They're Nostori soldiers!" Sthentros shouted. "Gormoth of Nostor means to take all Hostigos, as his grandfather took Sevenhills Valley after the traitor we don't name sold him Tarr-Dombra."

That was a part of the map her eyes had shunned: the bowl valley to the east, where Dombra Gap split the Mountains of Hostigos. It was from thence that Gormoth's mercenary cavalry raided into Hostigos.

"And what hope have we from Styphon's House?" her father asked. He knew the answer; he wanted the others to hear it at first hand.

"The Archpriest wouldn't talk to me; the priests of Styphon hold no speech with priests of other gods," Xentos said.

"The Archpriest wouldn't talk to me, either," Chartiphon said. "Only one of the upperpriests of the temple. He took our offerings and said he would pray to Styphon for us. When I asked for fireseed, he would give me none."

"None at all?" somebody down the table cried. "Then we are indeed under the ban."

Her father rapped with the pommel of his poignard. "You've heard the worst, now. What's in your minds that we should do? You first, Phosg."

The peasant representative rose and cleared his throat.

"Lord Prince, this castle is no more dear to you than my cottage is to me. I'll fight for mine as you would for yours."

There was a quick mutter of approval along the table. "Well said, Phosg!" "An example for all of us!" The others spoke in turn; a few tried to make speeches. Chartiphon said only: "Fight. What else."

"I am a priest of Dralm," Xentos said, "and Dralm is a god of peace, but I say, fight with Dralm's blessing. Submission to evil men is the worst of all sins."

"Rylla," her father said.

"Better die in armor than live in chains," she replied.

"When the time comes, I will be in armor with the rest of you."

Her father nodded. "I expected no less from any of you." He rose, and all with him. "I thank you. At sunset we will dine together; until then servants will attend you. Now, if you please, leave me with my daughter. Chartiphon, you and Xentos stay."

Chairs scraped and feet scuffed as they went out. The closing door cut off the murmur of voices. Chartiphon had begun to fill his stubby pipe.

"I know there's no use looking to Balthar of Beshta," she said, "but wouldn't Sarrask of Sask aid us? We're better neighbors to him than Gormoth would be."

"Sarrask of Sask's a fool," Chartiphon said shortly. "He doesn't know that once Gormoth has Hostigos, his turn will come next."

"He knows that," Xentos differed. "He'll try to strike before Gormoth does, or catch Gormoth battered from having fought us. But even if he wanted to help us, he dares not. Even King Kaiphranos dares not aid those whom Styphon's House would destroy."

"They want that land in Wolf Valley, for a temple-farm," she considered. "I know that would be bad, but . . ."

"Too late," Xentos told her. "They have made a compact with Gormoth, to furnish him fireseed and money to hire mercenaries, and when he has conquered Hostigos he will give them the land." He paused and added: "And it was on my advice, Prince, that you refused them."

"I'd have refused against your advice, Xentos," her father said. "Long ago I vowed that Styphon's House should never come into Hostigos while I lived, and by Dralm and by Galzar neither shall they! They come into a princedom, they build a temple, they make temple-farms, and slaves of everybody on them. They tax the Prince, and make him tax the people, till nobody has anything left. Look at that temple-farm in Sevenhills Valley!"

"Yes, you'd hardly believe it," Chartiphon said. "Why, they even make the peasants for miles around cart their manure in, till they have none left for their own fields. Dralm only knows what they do with it.'' He puffed at his pipe. ''I wonder why they want Sevenhills Valley.''

''There's something in the ground there that makes the water of those springs taste and smell badly,'' her father said.

''Sulfur,'' said Xentos. ''But why do they want sulfur?''

III

Corporal Calvin Morrison, Pennsylvannia State Police, squatted in the brush at the edge of the old field and looked across the small brook at the farmhouse two hundred yards away. It was scabrous with peeling yellow paint, and festooned with a sagging porch-roof. A few white chickens pecked uninterestedly in the littered barnyard; there was no other sign of life, but he knew that there was a man inside. A man with a rifle, who would use it; a man who had murdered once, broken jail, would murder again.

He looked at his watch; the minute-hand was squarely on the nine. Jack French and Steve Kovac would be starting down from the road above, where they had left the car. He rose, unsnapping the retaining-strap of his holster.

''Watch that middle upstairs window,'' he said. ''I'm starting now.''

''I'm watching it.'' Behind him, a rifle-action clattered softly as a cartridge went into the chamber. ''Luck.''

He started forward across the seedling-dotted field. He was scared, as scared as he had been the first time, back in '51, in Korea, but there was nothing he could do about that. He just told his legs to keep moving, knowing that in a few moments he wouldn't have time to be scared.

He was within a few feet of the little brook, his hand close to the butt of the Colt, when it happened.

There was a blinding flash, followed by a moment's darkness. He thought he'd been shot; by pure reflex, the .38-special was in his hand. Then, all around him, a flickering iridescence of many colors glowed, a perfect hemisphere fifteen feet high and thirty across, and in front of him was an oval desk with an instrument-panel over it, and a swivel-chair from which a man was rising. Young, well-built; a white man but, he was sure, not an American. He wore loose green trousers and black ankle-boots and a pale green shirt. There was a shoulder holster under his left arm, and a weapon in his right hand.

He was sure it was a weapon, though it looked more like an electric soldering-iron, with two slender rods instead of a barrel, joined, at what should be the muzzle, by a blue ceramic or plastic knob. It was probably something that made his own Colt Official Police look like a kid's cap-pistol, and it was coming up fast to line on him.

He fired, held the trigger back to keep the hammer down on the fired chamber, and flung himself to one side, coming down, on his left hand and left hip, on a smooth, polished floor. Something, probably the chair, fell with a crash. He rolled, and kept on rolling until he was out of the nacreous dome of light and bumped hard against something. For a moment he lay still, then rose to his feet, letting out the trigger of the Colt.

What he'd bumped into was a tree. For a moment he accepted that, then realized that there should be no trees here, nothing but low brush. And this tree, and the ones all around, were huge; great rough columns rising to support a green roof through which only a few stray gleams of sunlight leaked. Hemlocks; must have been growing here while Columbus was still conning Isabella into hocking her jewelry. He looked at the little stream he had been about to cross when this had happened. It was the one thing about this that wasn't completely crazy. Or maybe it was the craziest thing of all.

He began wondering how he was going to explain this.

"While approaching the house," he began, aloud and in a formal tone, "I was intercepted by a flying saucer landing in front of me, the operator of which threatened me with a ray-pistol. I defended myself with my revolver, firing one round . . ."

No. That wouldn't do at all.

He looked at the brook again, and began to suspect that there might be nobody to explain to. Swinging out the cylinder of his Colt, he replaced the fired round. Then he decided to junk the regulation about carrying the hammer on an empty chamber, and put in another one.

IV

Verkan Vall watched the landscape outside the almost invisible shimmer of the transposition-field; now he was in the forests of the Fifth Level. The mountains, of course, were always the same, but the woods around flickered and shifted. There was a great deal of randomness about which tree grew where, from time-line to time-line. Now and then he would catch fleeting glimpses of open country, and the buildings and airports installations of his own people. The red light overhead went off and on, a buzzer sounding each time. The conveyer dome became a solid iridescence, and then a mesh of cold inert metal. The red light turned green. He picked up a sigma-ray needler from the desk in front of him and holstered it. As he did, the door slid open and two men in Paratime Police green, a lieutenant and a patrolman, entered. When they saw him, they relaxed, holstering their own weapons.

"Hello, Chief's Assistant," the lieutenant said. "Didn't pick anything up, did you?"

In theory, the Ghaldron-Hesthor transposition-field was impenetrable; in practice, especially when two paratemporal vehicles going in opposite "directions" interpenetrated, the field would weaken briefly, and external objects, sometimes alive and hostile, would intrude. That was why Paratimers kept weapons ready to hand, and why conveyers were checked immediately upon materializing. It was also why some Paratimers didn't make it home.

"Not this trip. Is my rocket ready?"

"Yes, sir. Be a little delay about an aircar for the rocket-port." The patrolman had begun to take the transposition record-tapes out of the cabinet. "They'll call you when it's ready."

He and the lieutenant strolled out into the noise and color-ful confusion of the conveyor-head rotunda. He got out his cigarette case and offered it; the lieutenant flicked his lighter.

They had only taken a few puffs when another conveyer quietly materialized in a vacant circle a little to their left.

A couple of Paracops strolled over as the door opened, drawing their needlers, and peeped inside. Immediately, one backed away, snatching the handphone of his belt radio and speaking quickly into it. The other went inside. Throwing away their cigarettes, he and the lieutenant hastened to the conveyer.

Inside, the chair at the desk was overturned. A Paracop lay on the floor, his needler a few inches from his outflung hand. His tunic was off and his shirt, pale green, was darkened by blood. The lieutenant, without touching him, bent over him.

"Still alive," he said. "Bullet, or sword-thrust."

"Bullet. I smell nitro powder." Then he saw the hat lying on the floor, and stepped around the fallen man. Two men were entering with an antigrav stretcher; they got the wounded man onto it and floated him out. "Look at this, Lieutenant."

The lieutenant looked at the hat—gray felt, wide-brimmed, the crown peaked by four indentations.

"Fourth Level," he said. "Europo-American, Hispano-Columbian Subsector."

He picked up the hat and glanced inside. The lieutenant was right. The sweat-band was stamped in golden Roman-alphabet letters, JOHN B. STETSON COMPANY, PHILADELPHIA, PA., and, hand-inked, *Cpl. Calvin Morrison, Penn'a State Police,* and a number.

"I know that crowd," the lieutenant said. "Good men, every bit as good as ours."

"One was a split second better than one of ours." He got out his cigarette case. "Lieutenant, this is going to be a real baddie. This pickup's going to be missed, and the people who'll miss him will be one of the ten best constabulary organizations in the world, on their time-line. We won't satisfy them with the kind of lame-brained explanations that usually get by in that sector. And we'll have to find out where he emerged, and what he's doing. A man who can beat a Paracop to the draw after being sucked into a conveyer won't just sink into obscurity on any time-line. By the time we get to him, he'll be kicking up a small fuss.''

"I hope he got dragged out of his own subsector. Suppose he comes out on a next-door time-line, and reports to his police post, where a duplicate of himself, with duplicate fingerprints, is on duty.''

"Yes. Wouldn't that be dandy, now?'' He lit a cigarette. "When the aircar comes, send it back. I'm going over the photo-records myself. Have the rocket held; I'll need it in a few hours. I'm making this case my own personal baby.''

TWO

CALVIN MORRISON dangled his black-booted legs over the edge of the low cliff and wished, again, that he hadn't lost his hat. He knew exactly where he was: he was right at the same place he had been, sitting on the little cliff above the road where he and Larry Stacey and Jack French and Steve Kovac had left the car, only there was no road there now, and never had been one. There was a hemlock, four feet thick at the butt, growing where the farmhouse should have been, and no trace of the stonework of the foundations of house or barn. But the really permanent features, like the Bald Eagles to the north and Nittany Mountain to the south, were exactly as they should be.

That flash and momentary darkness could have been subjective; put that in the unproven column. He was sure the strangely beautiful dome of shimmering light had been real, and so had the desk and the instrument-panel, and the man with the odd weapon. And there was nothing at all subjective about all this virgin timber where farmlands should have been. So he puffed slowly on his pipe and tried to remember and to analyze what had happened to him.

He hadn't been shot and taken to a hospital where he was now lying delirious, he was sure of that. This wasn't delirium. Nor did he consider for an instant questioning either his sanity or his senses, nor did he indulge in dirty language like "incredible" or "impossible." Extraordinary—now there was a good word. He was quite sure that something extraordinary had happened to him. It seemed to break into two parts: one, blundering into that dome of pearly light, what had happened inside of it, and rolling out of it; and two, this same-but-different place in which he now found himself.

What was wrong with both was anachronism, and the anachronisms were mutually contradictory. None of the first part belonged in 1964 or, he suspected, for many centuries to come; portable energy-weapons, for instance. None of the second part belonged in 1964, either, or for at least a century in the past.

His pipe had gone out. For awhile he forgot to relight it, while he tossed those two facts back and forth in his mind. He still didn't use those dirty words. He used one small boys like to scribble on privy walls.

In spite—no, because—of his clergyman father's insistence that he study for and enter the Presbyterian ministry, he was an agnostic. Agnosticism, for him, was refusal to accept or to deny without proof. A good philosophy for a cop, by the way. Well, he wasn't going to reject the possibility of time-machines; not after having been shanghaied aboard one and having to shoot his way out of it. That thing had been a time-machine, and whenever he was now, it wasn't the Twentieth Century, and he was never going to get back to it. He settled that point in his mind and accepted it once and for all.

His pipe was out; he started to knock out the heel, then stirred it with a twig and relit it. He couldn't afford to waste anything now. Sixteen rounds of ammunition; he couldn't do a hell of a lot of Indian-fighting on that. The blackjack might be some good at close quarters. The value of the handcuffs and the whistle was problematical. When he had smoked the contents of his pipe down to ash, he emptied and pocketed it and climbed down from the little cliff, going to the brook and following it down to where it joined a larger stream.

A bluejay made a fuss at his approach. Two deer ran in front of him. A small black bear regarded him suspiciously and hastened away. Now, if he could only find some Indians who wouldn't throw tomahawks first and ask questions afterward . . . .

A road dipped in front of him to cross the stream. For an instant he accepted that calmly, then caught his breath. A real, wheel-rutted road. And brown horse-droppings in it—they were the most beautiful things he had ever seen. They meant he hadn't beaten Columbus here, after all. Maybe he might have trouble giving a plausible account of himself, but at least he could do it in English. He waded through the little ford and started down the road, toward where he thought Bellefonte ought to be. Maybe he was in time to get into the Civil War. That would be more fun than Korea had been.

The sun went down in front of him. By now he was out of the big hemlocks; they'd been lumbered off on both sides of the road, and there was a respectable second growth, mostly hardwoods. Finally, in the dusk, he smelled freshly turned earth. It was full dark when he saw a light ahead.

The house was only a dim shape; the light came from one window on the end and two in front, horizontal slits under the roof overhang. Behind, he thought, were stables. And a pigpen—his nose told him that. Two dogs, outside, began whauff-whauffing in the road in front of him.

"Hello, in there!" he called.

Through the open windows, too high to see into, he heard voices: a man's, a woman's, another man's. He called again, and came closer. A bar scraped, and the door swung open. For a moment a heavy-bodied woman in a sleeveless dark dress stood in it. Then she spoke to him and stepped aside. He entered.

It was a big room, lighted by two candles, one on a table spread with a meal and the other on the mantel, and by the fire on the hearth. Double-deck bunks along one wall, fireplace with things stacked against it. There were three men and

another, younger, woman, beside the one who had admitted
him. Out of the corner of his eye he could see children
peering around a door that seemed to open into a shed-annex.
One of the men, big and blonde-bearded, stood with his back
to the fireplace, holding what looked like a short gun.

No, it wasn't, either. It was a crossbow, bent, with a
quarrel in the groove.

The other two men were younger—probably his sons.
Both were bearded, though one's beard was only a blonde
fuzz. He held an axe; his older brother had a halberd. All
three wore sleeveless leather jerkins, short-sleeved shirts,
and cross-gartered hose. The older woman spoke in a
whisper to the younger woman, who went through the door at
the side, hustling the children ahead of her.

He had raised his hands pacifically as he entered. "I'm a
friend," he said. "I'm going to Bellefonte; how far is it?"

The man with the crossbow said something. The woman
replied. The youth with the axe said something, and they all
laughed.

"My name's Morrison. Corporal, Pennsylvania State
Police." Hell, they wouldn't know the State Police from the
Swiss Marines. "Am I on the road to Bellefonte?" They
ought to know where that was, it'd been settled in 1770, and
this couldn't be any earlier than that.

More back-and-forth. They weren't talking Pennsylvania
Dutch—he knew a little of it. Maybe Polish . . . no, he'd
heard enough of that in the hard-coal country to recognize it,
at least. He looked around while they argued, and noticed, on
a shelf in the far corner, three images. He meant to get a
closer look at them. Roman Catholics used images, so did
Greek Catholics, and he knew the difference.

The man with the crossbow laid the weapon down, but
kept it bent with the quarrel in place, and spoke slowly and
distinctly. It was no language he had ever heard before. He
replied, just as distinctly, in English. They looked at one
another, and passed their hands back and forth across their
faces. On a thousand-to-one chance, he tried Japanese. It

didn't pay off. By signs, they invited him to sit and eat with them, and the children, six of them, trooped in.

The meal was ham, potatoes and succotash. The eating tools were knives and a few horn spoons; the plates were slabs of corn-bread. The men used their belt-knives. He took out his jackknife, a big switchblade he'd taken off a j.d. arrest, and caused a sensation with it. He had to demonstrate several times. There was also elderberry wine, strong but not particularly good. When they left the table for the women to clear, the men filled pipes from a tobacco-jar on the mantel, offering it to him. He filled his own, lighting it, as they had, with a twig from the hearth. Stepping back, he got a look at the images.

The central figure was an elderly man in a white robe with a blue eight-pointed star on his breast. Flanking him, on the left, was a seated female figure, nude and exaggeratedly pregnant, crowned with wheat and holding a cornstalk; and on the right a masculine figure in a mail shirt, holding a spiked mace. The only really odd thing about him was that he had the head of a wolf. Father-god, fertility-goddess, war-god. No, this crowd weren't Catholics—Greek, Roman or any other kind.

He bowed to the central figure, touching his forehead, and repeated the gesture to the other two. There was a gratified murmur behind him; anybody could see he wasn't any heathen. Then he sat down on a chest with his back to the wall.

They hadn't re-barred the door. The children had been herded back into the annex by the younger woman. Now that he recalled, there'd been a vacant place, which he had taken, at the table. Somebody had gone off somewhere with a message. As soon as he finished his pipe, he pocketed it, managing, unobtrusively, to unsnap the strap of his holster.

Some half an hour later, he caught the galloping thud of hooves down the road—at least six horses. He pretended not to hear it; so did the others. The father moved to where he had put down the crossbow; the older son got hold of the halberd, and the fuzz-chinned youth moved to the door. The horses stopped outside; the dogs began barking frantically. There was a clatter of accoutrements as men dismounted. He slipped the .38 out and cocked it.

The youth went to the door, but before he could open it, it flew back in his face, knocking him backward, and a man—bearded face under a high-combed helmet, steel long sword in front of him. There was another helmeted head behind, and the muzzle of a musket. Everybody in the room shouted in alarm; this wasn't what they'd been expecting, at all. Outside, a pistol banged, and a dog howled briefly.

Rising from the chest, he shot the man with the sword. Half-cocking with the double-action and thumbing the hammer back the rest of the way, he shot the man with the musket, which went off into the ceiling. A man behind him caught a crossbow quarrel in the forehead and pitched forward, dropping a long pistol unfired.

Shifting the Colt to his left hand, he caught up the sword the first man had dropped. Double-edged, with a swept guard, it was lighter than it looked, and beautifully balanced. He stepped over the body of the first man he had shot, to be confronted by a swordsman from outside, trying to get over the other two. For a few moments they cut and parried, and then he drove the point into his opponent's unarmored face, then tugged his blade free as the man went down. The boy, who had gotten hold of the dropped pistol, fired past him and hit a man holding a clump of horses in the road. Then he was outside, and the man with the halberd along with him, chopping down another of the party. The father followed; he'd gotten the musket and a powder-flask, and was reloading it.

Driving the point of the sword into the ground, he holstered his Colt and as one of the loose horses passed, caught the reins, throwing himself into the saddle. Then, when his feet had found the stirrups, he stooped and retrieved the sword, thankful that even in a motorized age the State Police taught their men to ride.

The fight was over, at least here. Six attackers were down, presumably dead; two more were galloping away. Five loose horses milled about, and the two young men were trying to catch them. Their father had charged the short musket, and was priming the pan.

This had only been a sideshow fight, though. The main event was a half mile down the road; he could hear shots, yells and screams, and a sudden orange glare mounted into the night. While he was quieting the horse and trying to accustom him to the change of owership, a couple more fires blazed up. He was wondering just what he had cut himself in on when the fugitives began streaming up the road. He had no trouble identifying them as such; he'd seen enough of that in Korea.

There were more than fifty of them—men, women and children. Some of the men had weapons: spears, axes, a few bows, one musket almost six feet long. His bearded host shouted at them, and they paused.

"What's going on down there?" he demanded.

Babble answered him. One or two tried to push past; he cursed them luridly and slapped at them with his flat. The words meant nothing, but the tone did. That had worked for him in Korea, too. They all stopped in a clump, while the beared man spoke to them. A few cheered. He looked them over; call it twenty effectives. The bodies in the road were stripped of weapons; out of the corner of his eye he saw the two women passing things out the cottage door. Four of the riderless horses had been caught and mounted. More fugitives came up, saw what was going on, and joined.

"All right, you guys! You want to live forever?" He swung his sword to include all of them, then pointed down the road, to where a whole village must now be burning. "Come on, let's go get them!"

A general cheer went up as he started his horse forward, and the whole mob poured after him, shouting. They met more and more fugitives, who saw that a counter-attack had been organized, if that was the word for it. The shooting ahead had stopped. Nothing left in the village to shoot at, he supposed.

Then, when they were within four or five hundred yards of

the burning houses, there was a blast of forty or fifty shots in
less than ten seconds, and loud yells, some in alarm. More
shots, and then mounted men came pelting toward them.
This wasn't an attack; it was a rout. Whoever had raided that
village had been hit from behind. Everybody with guns or
bows let fly at once. A horse went down, and a saddle was
emptied. Remembering how many shots it had taken for one
casualty in Korea, that wasn't bad. He stood up in his
stirrups, which were an inch or so too short for him to begin
with, waved his sword, and shouted, *"Chaaarge!"* Then he
and the others who were mounted kicked their horses into a
gallop, and the infantry—axes, scythes, pitchforks and
all—ran after them.

A horseman coming in the opposite direction aimed a
sword-cut at his bare head. He parried and thrust, the point
glancing from a breastplate. Before either could recover, the
other man's horse had carried him on past and among the
spears and pitchforks behind. Then he was trading thrusts for
cuts with another rider, wondering if none of these imbeciles
had ever heard that a sword had a point. By this time the road
for a hundred yards in front, and the fields on either side,
were full of horsemen, chopping and shooting at one another
in the firelight.

He got his point in under his opponent's arm, the
memory-voice of a history professor of long ago reminded
him of the gap in a cuirass there, and almost had the sword
wrenched from his hand before he cleared it. Then another
rider was coming at him, unarmored, wearing a cloak and a
broad hat, aiming a pistol almost as long as the arm that held
it. He swung back for a cut, urging his horse forward, and
knew he'd never make it. *All right, Cal; your luck's run out!*

There was an upflash from the pan, a belch of flame from
the muzzle, and something hammered him in the chest. He
hung onto consciousness long enough to kick his feet free of
the stirrups. In that last moment, he realized that the rider
who had shot him had been a girl.

THREE

I

RYLLA SAT with her father at the table in the small study. Chartiphon was at one end and Xentos at the other, and Harmakros, the cavalry captain, in a chair by the hearth, his helmet on the floor beside him. Vurth, the peasant, stood facing them, a short horseman's musketoon slung from his shoulder and a horn flask and bullet-bag on his belt.

"You did well, Vurth," her father commended. "By sending the message, and in the fighting, and by telling Princess Rylla that the stranger was a friend. I'll see you're rewarded."

Vurth smiled. "But, Prince, I have this gun, and fireseed for it," he replied. "And my son caught a horse, with all its gear, even pistols in the holsters, and the Princess says we may keep it all."

"Fair battle-spoil, yours by right. But I'll see that something's sent to your farm tomorrow. Just don't waste that fireseed on deer. You'll need it to kill more Nostori before long."

He nodded in dismissal, and Vurth grinned and bowed, and backed out, stammering thanks. Chartiphon looked after him, remarking that there went a man Gormoth of Nostor would find costly to kill.

"He didn't pay cheaply for anything tonight," Harmakros said. "Eight houses burned, a dozen peasants butchered, four of our troopers killed and six wounded, and we counted better than thirty of his dead in the village on the road, and six more at Vurth's farm. And the horses we caught, and the weapons." He thought briefly. "I'd question if a dozen of them got away alive and hale."

Her father gave a mirthless chuckle. "I'm glad some did. They'll have a fine tale to carry back. I'd like to see Gormoth's face at the telling."

"We owe the stranger for most of it," she said. "If he hadn't rallied those people at Vurth's farm and led them back, most of the Nostori would have gotten away. And then I had to shoot him myself!"

"You couldn't know, kitten," Chartiphon told her. "I've been near killed by friends myself, in fights like that." He turned to Xentos. "How is he?"

"He'll live to hear our thanks," the old priest said. "The ornament on his breast broke the force of the bullet. He has a broken rib, and a nasty hole in him—our Rylla doesn't load her pistols lightly. He's lost more blood than I'd want to, but he's young and strong, and Brother Mytron has much skill. We'll have him on his feet again in a half-moon."

She smiled happily. It would be terrible for him to die, and at her hand, a stranger who had fought so well for them. And such a handsome and valiant stranger, too. She wondered who he was. Some noble, or some great captain, of course.

"We owe much to Princess Rylla," Harmakros insisted. "When this man from the village overtook us, I was for riding back with three or four to see about this stranger of Vurth's, but the Princess said, 'We've only Vurth's word there's but one; there may be a hundred Vurth hasn't seen.' So back we all went, and you know the rest."

"We owe most of all to Dralm." Old Xentos' face lit with

a calm joy. "And Galzar Wolfhead, of course," he added. "It is a sign that the gods will not turn their backs upon Hostigos. This stranger, whoever he may be, was sent by the gods to be our aid."

II

Verkan Vall put the lighter back on the desk and took the cigarette from his mouth, blowing a streamer of smoke.

"Chief, it's what I've been saying all along. We'll have to do something." After Year-End Day, he added mentally, I'll do something. "We know what causes this: conveyers interpenetrating in transposition. It'll have to be stopped."

Tortha Karf laughed. "The reason I'm laughing," he explained, "is that I said just that, about a hundred and fifty years ago, to old Zarvan Tharg, when I was taking over from him, and he laughed at me just as I'm laughing at you, because he'd said the same thing to the retiring Chief when he was taking over. Have you ever seen an all-time-line conveyer-head map?"

No. He couldn't recall. He blanked his mind to everything else and concentrated with all his mental power.

"No, I haven't."

"I should guess not. With the finest dots, on the biggest map, all the inhabited areas would be indistinguishable blotches. There must be a couple of conveyers interpenetrating every second of every minute of every day. You know," he added gently, "we're rather extensively spread out."

"We can cut it down." There had to be *something* that could be done. "Better scheduling, maybe."

"Maybe. How about this case you're taking an interest in?"

"Well, we had one piece of luck. The pickup time-line is one we're on already. One of our people, in a newspaper office in Philadelphia, messaged us that same evening. He says the press associations have the story, and there's nothing we can do about that."

"Well, just what did happen?"

"This man Morrison, and three other State Police officers, were closing in on a house in which a wanted criminal was hiding. He must have been a dangerous man—they don't go out in force like that for chicken-thieves. Morrison and another man were in front; the other two were coming in from behind. Morrison started forward, with his companion covering for him with a rifle. This other man is the nearest thing to a witness there is, but he was watching the front of the house and only marginally aware of Morrison. He says he heard the other two officers pounding on the back door and demanding admittance, and then the man they were after burst out the front door with a rifle in his hands. This officer—Stacey's his name—shouted to him to drop the rifle and put up his hands. Instead, the criminal tried to raise it to his shoulder; Stacey fired, killing him instantly. Then, he says, he realized that Morrison was nowhere in sight.

"He called, needless to say without response, and then he and the other two hunted about for some time. They found nothing, of course. They took this body in to the county seat and had to go through a lot of formalities; it was evening before they were back at the substation, and it happened that a reporter was there, got the story, and phoned it to his paper. The press associations then got hold of it. Now the State Police refuse to discuss the disappearance, and they're even trying to deny it.

"They think their man's nerve snapped, he ran away in a panic, and is ashamed to come back. They wouldn't want a story like that getting around; they'll try to cover up."

"Yes. This hat he lost in the conveyer, with his name in it—we'll plant it about a mile from the scene, and then get hold of some local, preferably a boy of twelve or so, give him narco-hyp instructions to find the hat and take it to the State Police substation, and then inform the reporter responsible for the original news-break by an anonymous phone call. After that, there will be the usual spate of rumors of Morrison being seen in widely separated localities."

"How about his family?"

"We're in luck there, too. Unmarried, parents both dead, no near relatives."

The Chief nodded. "That's good. Usually there are a lot of relatives yelling their heads off. Particularly on sectors where they have inheritance laws. Have you located the exit timeline?"

"Approximated it; somewhere on Aryan-Transpacific. We can't determine the exact moment at which he broke free of the field. We have one positive indication to look for at the scene."

The Chief grinned. "Let me guess. The empty revolver cartridge."

"That's right. The things the State Police use don't eject automatically; he'd have to open it and take the empty out by hand. And as soon as he was outside the conveyer and no longer immediately threatened, that's precisely what he'd do: open his revolver, eject the empty, and replace it with a live round. I'm as sure of that as though I watched him do it. We may not be able to find it, but if we do it'll be positive proof."

FOUR

MORRISON WOKE, stiff and aching, under soft covers, and for a moment lay with his eyes closed. Near him, something clicked with soft and monotonous regularity; from somewhere an anvil rang, and there was shouting. Then he opened his eyes. It was daylight, and he was on a bed in a fairly large room with paneled walls and a white plaster ceiling. There were two windows at one side, both open, and under one of them a woman, stout and gray-haired, in a green dress, sat knitting. It had been her needles that he had heard. Nothing but blue sky was visible through the windows. There was a table, with things on it, and chairs, and, across the room, a chest on the top of which his clothes were neatly piled, his belt and revolver on top. His boots, neatly cleaned, stood by the chest, and a long unsheathed sword with a swept guard and a copper pommel leaned against the wall.

The woman looked up quickly as he stirred, then put her knitting on the floor and rose. She looked at him, and went to the table, pouring a cup of water and bringing it to him. He thanked her, drank, and gave it back. The cup and pitcher were of heavy silver, elaborately chased. This wasn't any peasant cottage. Replacing the cup on the table, she went out.

27

He ran a hand over his chin. About three days' stubble. The growth of his fingernails checked with that. The whole upper part of his torso was tightly bandaged. Broken rib, or ribs, and probably a nasty hole in him. He was still alive after three days. Estimating the here-and-now medical art from the general technological level as he'd seen it so far, that probably meant that he had a fair chance of continuing so. At least he was among friends and not a prisoner. The presence of the sword and the revolver proved that.

The woman returned, accompanied by a man in a blue robe with an eight-pointed white star on the breast, the colors of the central image on the peasants' god-shelf reversed. A priest, doubling as doctor. He was short and chubby, with a pleasant round face; advancing, he laid a hand on Morrison's brow, took his pulse, and spoke in a cheerfully optimistic tone. The bedside manner seemed to be a universal constant. With the woman's help, he got the bandages, yards of them, off. He did have a nasty wound, uncomfortably close his heart, and his whole left side was black and blue. The woman brought a pot from the table; the doctor-priest smeared the wound with some dirty-looking unguent, they put on fresh bandages, and the woman took out the old ones. The doctor-priest tried to talk to him: he tried to talk to the doctor-priest. The woman came back with a bowl of turkey-broth, full of finely minced meat, and a spoon. While he was finishing it, two more visitors arrived.

One was a man, robed like the doctor, his cowl thrown back from his head, revealing snow-white hair. He had a gentle, kindly face, and was smiling. For a moment Morrison wondered if this place might be a monastery of some sort, and then saw the old priest's definitely un-monastic companion.

She was a girl, twenty, give or take a year or so, with blonde hair cut in what he knew as a page-boy bob. She had blue eyes and red lips and an impudent tilty little nose dusted with golden freckles. She wore a jerkin of something like brown suede, sewn with gold thread, and a yellow undertunic with a high neck and long sleeves, and brown knit hose and thigh-length jackboots. There was a gold chain around her neck, and a gold-hilted dagger on a belt of gold links. No, this wasn't any monastery, and it wasn't any peasant hovel, either.

As soon as he saw her, he began to laugh. He'd met that young lady before.

"You shot me!" he accused, aiming an imaginary pistol and saying "Bang!" and then touching his chest.

She said something to the older priest, he replied, and she said something to Morrison, pantomiming sorrow and shame, covering her face with one hand, and winking at him over it. Then they both laughed. Perfectly natural mistake—how could she have known which side he'd been on?

The two priests held a colloquy, and then the younger brought him about four ounces of something dark brown in a glass tumbler. It tasted alcoholic and medicinally bitter. They told him, by signs, to go back to sleep, and left him, the girl looking back over her shoulder as she went out.

He squirmed a little, decided that he was going to like it, here-and-now, and dozed off.

Late in the afternoon he woke again. A different woman, thin, with mouse-brown hair, sat in the chair under the window, stitching on something that looked like a shirt. Outside, a dog was barking, and farther off somebody was drilling troops—a couple of hundred, from the amount of noise they were making. A voice was counting cadence: *Heep, heep, heep, heep!* Another universal constant.

He smiled contentedly. Once he got on his feet again, he didn't think he was going to be on unemployment very long. A soldier was all he'd ever been, since he'd stopped being a theological student at Princeton between sophomore and junior years. He'd owed a lot of thanks to the North Korean Communists for starting that war; without it, he might never have found the moral courage to free himself from the career into which his father had been forcing him. His enlisting in the Army had probably killed his father; the Rev. Alexander

Morrison simply couldn't endure not having his own way. At least, he died while his son was in Korea.

Then there had been the year and a half, after he came home, when he'd worked as a bankguard, until his mother died. That had been soldiering of a sort; he'd worked armed and in uniform, at least. And then, when he no longer had his mother to support, he'd gone into the State Police. That had really been soldiering, the nearest anybody could come to it in peacetime.

And then he'd blundered into that dome of pearly light, that time-machine, and come out of it into—into here-and-now, that was all he could call it.

Where *here* was was fairly easy. It had to be somewhere within, say, ten or fifteen miles of where he had been time-shifted, which was just over the Clinton County line, in Nittany Valley. They didn't use helicopters to evacuate the wounded, here-and-now, that was sure.

When *now* was was something else. He lay on his back, looking up at the white ceiling, not wanting to attract the attention of the woman sewing by the window. It wasn't the past. Even if he hadn't studied history—it was about the only thing at college he had studied—he'd have known that Penn's Colony had never been anything like this. It was more like Sixteenth Century Europe, though any Sixteenth Century French or German cavalryman who was as incompetent a swordsman as that gang he'd been fighting wouldn't have lived to wear out his first pair of issue boots. And enough Comparative Religion had rubbed off on him to know that those three images on that peasant's shelf didn't belong in any mythology back to Egypt and Sumeria.

So it had to be the future. A far future, long after the world had been devastated by atomic war, and man, self-blasted back to the Stone Age, had bootstrap-lifted himself back this far. A thousand years, ten thousand years; ten dollars if you guess how many beans in the jar. The important thing was that here-and-now was when-where he would stay, and he'd have to make a place for himself. He thought he was going to like it.

That lovely, lovely blonde! He fell asleep thinking about her.

Breakfast the next morning was cornmeal mush cooked with meat-broth and tasting rather like scrapple, and a mug of sassafras tea. Coffee, it seemed, didn't exist here-and-now, and *that* he was going to miss. He sign-talked for his tunic to be brought, and got his pipe, tobacco and lighter out of it. The woman brought a stool and set it beside the bed to put things on. The lighter opened her eyes a trifle, and she said something, and he said something in a polite voice, and she went back to her knitting. He looked at the tunic; it was torn and blood-soaked on the left side, and the badge was lead-splashed and twisted. That was why he was still alive.

The old priest and the girl were in about an hour later. This time she was wearing a red and gray knit frock that could have gone into Bergdorf-Goodman's window with a $200 price-tag any day, though the dagger on her belt wasn't exactly Fifth Avenue. They had slates and soapstone sticks with them; paper evidently hadn't been rediscovered yet. They greeted him, then pulled up chairs and got down to business.

First, they taught him the words for *you* and *me* and *he* and *she,* and, when he had that, names. The girl was Rylla. The old priest was Xentos. The younger priest, who dropped in for a look at the patient, was Mytron. The names, he thought, sounded Greek; it was the only point of resemblance in the language.

Calvin Morrison puzzled them. Evidently they didn't have surnames, here-and-now. They settled on calling him Kalvan. There was a lot of picture-drawing on the slates, and play-acting for verbs, which was fun. Both Rylla and Xentos smoked; Rylla's pipe, which she carried on her belt with her dagger, had a silver-inlaid redstone bowl and a cane stem. She was intrigued by his Zippo, and showed him her own lighter. It was a tinderbox, with a flint held down by a spring against a quarter-circular striker pushed by hand and returned by another spring for another push. With a spring to drive instead of return the striker it would have done for a gunlock. By noon, they were able to tell him that he was their friend, because he had killed their enemies, which seemed to be the definitive test of friendship, here-and-now, and he was able to assure Rylla that he didn't blame her for shooting him in the skirmish on the road.

They were back in the afternoon, accompanied by a gentleman with a gray imperial, wearing a garment like a fur-collared bathrobe and a sword-belt over it. He had a most impressive gold chain around his neck. His name was Ptosphes, and after much sign-talk and picture-making, it emerged that he was Rylla's father, and also Prince of this place. This place, it seemed, was Hostigos. The raiders with whom he had fought had come from a place called Nostor, to the north and east. Their Prince was named Gormoth, and Gormoth was not well thought of in Hostigos.

The next day, he was up in a chair, and they began giving him solid food, and wine to drink. The wine was excellent; so was the local tobacco. Maybe he'd get used to sassafras tea instead of coffee. The food was good, though sometimes odd. Bacon and eggs, for instance; the eggs were turkey eggs. Evidently they didn't have chickens, here-and-now. They had plenty of game, though. The game must have come back nicely after the atomic wars.

Rylla was in to see him twice a day, sometimes alone and sometimes with Xentos, or with a big man with a graying beard, Chartiphon, who seemed to be Ptosphes' top soldier. He always wore a sword, long and heavy, with a two-hand grip; not a real two-hander, but what he'd known as a hand-and-a-half, or bastard, sword. Often he wore a gilded back-and-breast, ornately wrought but nicked and battered. Sometimes, too, he visited alone, or with a young cavalry officer, Harmakros.

Harmakros wore a beard, too, obviously copied after Prince Ptosphes'. He decided to stop worrying about getting a shave; you could wear a beard, here-and-now, and nobody'd think you were either an Amishman or a beatnik. Harmakros had been on the patrol that had hit the Nostori raiders from behind at the village, but, it appeared, Rylla had been in command.

"The gods," Chartiphon explained, "did not give our Prince a son. A Prince should have a son, to rule after him, so our little Rylla must be as a son to her father."

The gods, he thought, ought to provide Prince Ptosphes with a son-in-law, name of Calvin Morrison . . . or just Kalvan. He made up his mind to give the gods some help on that.

There was another priest in to see him occasionally: a red-nosed, gray-bearded character named Tharses, who had a slight limp and a scarred face. One look was enough to tell which god he served; he wore a light shirt of finely linked mail and a dagger and a spiked mace on his belt, and a wolfskin hood topped with a jewel-eyed wolf head. As soon as he came in, he would toss that aside, and as soon as he sat down somebody would provide him with a drink. He almost always had a cat or a dog trailing him. Everybody called him Uncle Wolf.

Chartiphon showed him a map, elaborately illuminated on parchment. Hostigos was all Centre County, the southern corner of Clinton, and all Lycoming south of the Bald Eagles. Hostigos Town was exactly on the site of otherwhen Bellefonte; they were at Tarr-Hostigos, or Hostigos Castle, overlooking it from the end of the mountain east of the gap. To the south, the valley of the Juniata, the Besh, was the Princedom of Beshta, ruled by a Prince Valthar. Nostor was Lycoming County north of the Bald Eagles, Tioga County to the north, and parts of Northumberland and Montour Counties, to the forks of the Susquehanna. Nostor Town would be about Hughesville. Potter and McKean Counties were Nyklos, ruled by a Prince Armanes. Blair and parts of Clearfield, Huntington and Bedford Counties made up Sask, whose prince was called Sarrask.

Prince Gormoth of Nostor was a deadly enemy. Armanes was a friendly neutral. Sarrask of Sask was no friend of Hostigos; Balthar of Beshta was no friend of anybody's.

On a bigger map, he saw that all this was part of the Great

Kingdom of Hos-Harphax—all of Pennsylvania, Maryland, Delaware and southern New Jersey—ruled by a King Kaiphranos at Harphax City, at the mouth of the Susquehanna, the Harph. No, he substituted—just reigned over lightly. To judge from what he'd seen on the night of his arrival, King Kaiphranos' authority would be enforced for about a day's infantry march around his capital and ignored elsewhere.

He had a suspicion that Hostigos was in a bad squeeze between Nostor and Sask. He could hear the sounds of drilling soldiers every day, and something was worrying these people. Too often, while Rylla was laughing with him—she was teaching him to read, now, and that was fun—she would remember something she wanted to forget, and then her laughter would be strained. Chartiphon seemed always preoccupied; at times he'd forget, for a moment, what he'd been talking about. And he never saw Ptosphes smile.

Xentos showed him a map of the world. The world, it seemed, was round, but flat like a pancake. Hudson's Bay was in the exact center, North America was shaped rather like India, Florida ran almost due east, and Cuba north and south. Asia was attached to North America, but it was all blankly unknown. An illimitable ocean surrounded everything. Europe, Africa and South America simply weren't.

Xentos wanted him to show the country from whence he had come. He'd been expecting that to come up, sooner or later, and it had worried him. He couldn't risk lying, since he didn't know on what point he might be tripped up, so he had decided to tell the truth, tailored to local beliefs and preconceptions. Fortunately, he and the old priest were alone at the time.

He put his finger down on central Pennsylvania. Xentos thought he misunderstood.

"No, Kalvan. This is your home now, and we want you to stay with us always. But from what place did you come?"

"Here," he insisted. "But from another time, a thousand years in the future. I had an enemy, an evil sorcerer, of great power. Another sorcerer, who was not my friend but was my enemy's enemy, put a protection about me, so that I might not be sorcerously slain. So my enemy twisted time for me, and hurled me far back into the past, before my first known ancestor had been born, and now here I am and here I must stay."

Xentos' hand described a quick circle around the white star on his breast, and he muttered rapidly. Another universal constant.

"How terrible! Why, you have been banished as no man ever was!"

"Yes. I do not like to speak, or even think, of it, but it is right that you should know. Tell Prince Ptosphes, and Princess Rylla, and Chartiphon, pledging them to secrecy, and beg them not to speak of it to me. I must forget my old life, and make a new one here and now. For all others, it may be said that I am from a far country. From here." He indicated what ought to be the location of Korea on the blankness of Asia. "I was there, once, fighting in a great war."

"Ah! I knew you had been a warrior." Xentos hesitated, then asked: "Do you also know sorcery?"

"No. My father was a priest, as you are, and our priests hated sorcery." Xentos nodded in agreement with that. "He wished me also to become a priest, but I knew that I would not be a good one, so when this war came, I left my studies and joined the army of my Great King, Truman, and went away to fight. After the war, I was a warrior to keep the peace in my own country."

Xentos nodded again. "If one cannot be a good priest, one should not be a priest at all, and to be a good warrior is the next best thing. What gods did your people worship?"

"Oh, my people had many gods. There was Conformity, and Authority, and Expense Account, and Opinion. And there was Status, whose symbols were many, and who rode in the great chariot Cadillac, which was almost a god itself. And there was Atom-bomb, the dread destroyer, who would some day come to end the world. None were very good gods, and I worshipped none of them. Tell me about your gods, Xentos."

Then he filled his pipe and lit it with the tinderbox that

replaced his now fuelless Zippo. He didn't need to talk any
more; Xentos was telling him about his gods. There was
Dralm, to whom all men and all other gods bowed; he was a
priest of Dralm himself. Yirtta Allmother, the source of all
life. Galzar the Wargod, all of whose priests were called
Uncle Wolf; lame Tranth, the craftman-god; fickle Lytris,
the Weather-Goddess; all the others.

"And Styphon," he added grudgingly. "Styphon is an
evil god, and evil men serve him, but to them he gives wealth
and great power."

FIVE

AFTER THAT, he began noticing a subtle change in manner toward him. Occasionally he caught Rylla regarding him in awe tinged with compassion. Chartiphon merely clasped his hand and said, "You'll like it here, Lord Kalvan." It amused him that he had accepted the title as though born to it. Prince Ptosphes said casually, "Xentos tells me there are things you don't want to talk about. Nobody will speak of them to you. We're all happy that you're with us; we'd like you to make this your home always."

The others treated him with profound respect; the story for public consumption was that he was a Prince from a distant country, beyond the Western Ocean and around the Cold Lands, driven from his throne by treason. That was the ancient and forgotten land of wonder; that was the Home of the Gods. And Xentos had told Mytron, and Mytron told everybody else, that the Lord Kalvan had been sent to Hostigos by Dralm.

As soon as he was on his feet again, they moved him to a suite of larger rooms, and gave him personal servants. There were clothes for him, more than he had ever owned at one

time in his life, and fine weapons. Rylla contributed a pair of
her own pistols, all of two feet long but no heavier than his
Colt .38-special, the barrels tapering to almost paper thinness
at the muzzles. The locks worked like the tinderboxes, flint
held tightly against moving striker, like wheellocks but with
simpler and more efficient mechanism.

"I shot you with one of them," she said.

"If you hadn't," he said, "I'd have ridden on, after the
fight, and never come to Tarr-Hostigos."

"Maybe it would have been better for you if you had."

"No, Rylla. This is the most wonderful thing that ever
happened to me."

As soon as he could walk unaided, he went down and
outside to watch the soldiers drilling. They had nothing like
uniforms, except blue and red scarves or sashes, Prince
Ptosphes' colors. The flag of Hostigos was a blue halberd-
head on a red field. The infantry wore canvas jacks sewn
with metal plates, or brigandines, and a few had mail shirts;
their helmets weren't unlike the one he had worn in Korea. A
few looked like regulars; most of them were peasant levies.
Some had long pikes; more had halberds or hunting-spears
or scythe-blades with the tangs straightened and fitted to
eight-foot staves, or woodcutters' axes with four-foot
helves.

There was about one firearm to three polearms. Some were
huge muskets, five to six feet long, 8- to 6-bore, aimed and
fired from rests. There were arquebuses, about the size and
weight of an M-1 Garrand, 16- to 20-bore, and calivers about
the size of the Brown Bess musket of the Revolution and the
Napoleonic Wars. All were fitted with the odd back-acting
flintlocks; he wondered which had been adapted from which,
the gunlock or the tinderbox. There were also quite a few
crossbowmen.

The cavalry wore high-combed helmets and cuirasses;
they were armed with swords and pistols, a pair in saddle-
holsters and, frequently, a second pair down the boot-tops.
Most of them also carried short musketoons or lances. They
all seemed to be regulars. One thing puzzled him: while the

crossbowmen practiced constantly, he never saw a firearm discharged at a target. Maybe a powder-shortage was one of the things that was worrying the people here.

The artillery was laughable; it would have been long out of date in the Sixteenth Century of his own time. The guns were all wrought-iron, built up by welding bars together and strengthened with shrunk-on iron rings. They didn't have trunnions; evidently nobody here-and-now had ever thought of that. What passed for field-pieces were mounted on great timbers, like oversized gunstocks, and hauled on four-wheel carts. They ran from four to twelve pound bore. The fixed guns on the castle walls were bigger, some huge bombards firing fifty, one hundred, and even two-hundred pound stone balls.

Fifteenth Century stuff; Henry V had taken Harfleur with just as good, and John of Bedford had probably bombarded Orleans with better. He decided to speak to Chartiphon about this.

He took the broadsword he had captured on the night of his advent here-and-now to the castle bladesmith, to have it ground down into a rapier. The bladesmith thought he was crazy. He found a pair of wooden practice swords and went outside with a cavalry lieutenant to demonstrate. Immediately, the lieutenant wanted a rapier, too. The blade-smith promised to make real ones, to his specifications, for both of them. His was finished the next evening, and by that time the bladesmith was swamped with orders for rapiers.

Almost everything these people used could be made in the workshops inside the walls of Tarr-Hostigos, or in Hostigos Town, and he seemed to have an unlimited expense-account with them. He began to wonder what, besides being the guest from the Land of the Gods, he was supposed to do to earn it. Nobody mentioned that; maybe they were waiting for him to mention it.

He brought the subject up, one evening, in Prince Ptosphes' study, where he and the Prince and Rylla and Xentos and Chartiphon were smoking over a flagon of after-dinner wine.

"You have enemies on both sides—Gormoth of Nostor and Sarrask of Sask—and that's not good. You have taken me in and made me one of you. What can I do to help against them?"

"Well, Kalvan," Ptosphes said, "perhaps you could better tell us that. We don't want to talk of what distresses you, but you must come of a very wise people. You've already taught us new things, like the thrusting-sword"—he looked admiringly at the new rapier he had laid aside—"and what you've told Chartiphon about mounting cannon. What else can you teach us?"

Quite a lot, he thought. There had been one professor at Princeton whose favorite pupil he had been, and who had been his favorite teacher. A history prof, and an unusual one. Most academic people at the middle of the Twentieth Century took the same attitude toward war that their Victorian opposite numbers had toward sex: one of those deplorable facts nice people don't talk about, and maybe if you don't look at the horrid thing it'll go away. This man had been different. What happened in the cloisters and the guildhalls and the parliaments and council-chambers was important, but none of them went into effect until ratified on the battlefield. So he had emphasized the military aspect of history in a freshman from Pennsylvania named Morrison, a divinity student, of all unlikely things. So, while he should have been studying homiletics and scriptural exegesis and youth-organization methods, that freshman, and a year later that sophomore, had been reading Sir Charles Oman's *Art of War*.

"Well, I can't tell you how to make weapons like that sixshooter of mine, or ammunition for it," he began, and then tried, as simply as possible, to explain about mass production and machine industry. They only stared in incomprehension and wonder. "I can show you a few things you can do with the things you have. For instance, we cut spiral grooves inside the bores of our guns, to make the bullet spin. Such guns shoot harder, straighter and farther than smoothbores. I can show you how to build cannon that can be moved rapidly and loaded and fired much more rapidly than what you have. And another thing.'' He mentioned never having seen any practice firing. ''You have very little powder—fireseed, you call it. Is that it?''

''There isn't enough fireseed in all Hostigos to load all the cannon of this castle for one shot,'' Chartiphon told him. ''And we can get no more. The priests of Styphon have put us under the ban and will let us have none, and they send cartload after cartload to Nostor.''

''You mean you get your fireseed from the priests of Styphon? Can't you make your own?''

They all looked at him though he were a cretin.

''Nobody can make fireseed but the priests of Styphon,'' Xentos told him. ''That was what I meant when I told you that Styphon's House has great power. With Styphon's aid, they alone can make it, and so they have great power, even over the Great Kings.''

''Well I'll be Dralm-damned!''

He gave Styphon's House that grudging respect any good cop gives a really smart crook. Brother, what a racket! No wonder this country, here-and-now, was divided into five Great Kingdoms, and each split into a snakepit of warring Princes and petty barons. Styphon's House wanted it that way; it was good for business. A lot of things became clear. For instance, if Styphon's House did the weaponeering as well as the powder-making, it would explain why small-arms were so good; they'd see to it that nobody without fireseed stood an outside chance against anybody with it. But they'd keep the brakes on artillery development. Styphon House wouldn't want bloody or destructive wars—they'd be bad for business. Just wars that burned lots of fireseed; that would be why there were all these great powder-hogs of bombards around.

And no wonder everybody in Hostigos had monkeys on their backs. They knew they were facing the short end of a war of extermination. He set down his goblet and laughed.

"You think nobody but those priests of Styphon can make fireseed?" There was nobody here that wasn't security-cleared for the inside version of his cover-story. "Why, in my time, everybody, even the children, could do that." (Well, children who'd gotten as far as high school chemistry; he'd almost been expelled, once . . . .) "I can make fireseed right here on this table." He refilled his goblet.

"But it is a miracle; only by the power of Styphon . . ." Xentos began.

"Styphon's a big fake!" he declared. "A false god; his priests are lying swindlers." That shocked Xentos; good or bad, a god was a god and shouldn't be talked about like that. "You want to see me do it? Mytron has everything in his dispensary I'll need. I'll want sulfur, and saltpeter." Mytron prescribed sulfur and honey (they had no molasses here-and-now), and saltpeter was supposed to cool the blood. "And charcoal, and a brass mortar and pestle, and a flour-sieve and something to sift into, and a pair of balance-scales." He picked up an unused goblet. "This'll do to mix it in."

Now they were all staring at him as though he had three heads, and a golden crown on each one.

"Go on, man! Hurry!" Ptosphes told Xentos. "Have everything brought here at once."

Then the Prince threw back his head and laughed—maybe a trifle hysterically, but it was the first time Morrison had heard Ptosphes laugh at all. Chartiphon banged his fist on the table.

"Ha, Gormoth!" he cried. "Now see whose head goes up over whose gate!"

Xentos went out. Morrison asked for a pistol, and Ptosphes brought him one from a cabinet behind him. It was loaded; opening the pan, he spilled out the priming on a sheet of parchment and touched a lighted splinter to it. It scorched the parchment, which it shouldn't have done, and left too much black residue. Styphon wasn't a very honest powder maker; he cheapened his product with too much charcoal and not enough saltpeter. Morrison sipped from his goblet. Saltpeter was seventy-five percent, charcoal fifteen, sulfur ten.

After awhile Xentos returned, accompanied by Mytron, bringing a bucket of charcoal, a couple of earthen jars, and the other things. Xentos seemed slightly dazed; Mytron was frightened and making a good game try at not showing it. He put Mytron to work grinding saltpeter in the mortar. The sulfur was already pulverized. Finally, he had about a half pint of it mixed.

"But it's just dust," Chartiphon objected.

"Yes. It has to be moistened, worked into dough, pressed into cakes, dried, and ground. We can't do all that here. But this will flash."

Up to about 1500, all gunpowder had been like that—meal powder, they had called it. It had been used in cannon for a long time after grain powder was being used in smallarms. Why, in 1588, the Duke of Medina-Sidonia had been very happy that all the powder for the Armada was corned arquebus powder, and not meal powder. He primed the pistol with a pinch from the mixing goblet, aimed at a half-burned log in the fireplace, and squeezed. Outside somebody shouted, feet pounded up the hall, and a guard with a halberd burst into the room.

"The Lord Kalvan is showing us something about a pistol," Ptosphes told him. "There may be more shots; nobody is to be alarmed."

"All right," he said, when the guard had gone out and closed the door. "Now let's see how it'll fire." He loaded with a blank charge, wadding it with a bit of rag, and handed it to Rylla. "You fire the first shot. This is a great moment in the history of Hostigos. I hope."

She pushed down the striker, set the flint down, aimed at the fireplace, and squeezed. The report wasn't quite as loud, but it did fire. Then they tried it with a ball, which went a half inch into the log. Everybody thought that was very good. The room was full of smoke, and they were all coughing, but nobody cared. Chartiphon went to the door and shouted into the hall for more wine.

Rylla had her arms around him. "Kalvan! You really did it!" she was saying.

"But you said no prayers," Mytron faltered. "You just made fireseed."

"That's right. And before long, everybody'll be just making fireseed. Easy as cooking soup." And when that day comes, he thought, the priests of Styphon will be out on the sidewalk, beating a drum for pennies.

Chartiphon wanted to know how soon they could march against Nostor. "It will take more fireseed than Kalvan can make on this table," Ptosphes told him. "We will need saltpeter, and sulfur, and charcoal. We will have to teach people how to get the sulfur and the saltpeter for us, and how to grind and mix them. We will need many things we don't have now, and tools to make them. And nobody knows all about this but Kalvan, and there is only one of him."

Well, glory be! Somebody had gotten something from his lecture on production, anyhow.

"Mytron knows a few things, I think." He pointed to the jars of sulfur and saltpeter. "Where did you get these?" he asked.

Mytron had gulped his first goblet of wine without taking it from his lips. He had taken three gulps to the second. Now he was working on his third, and coming out of shock nicely. It was about as he thought. The saltpeter was found in crude lumps under manure-piles, then refined; the sulfur was evaporated out of water from the sulfur springs in Wolf Valley. When that was mentioned, Ptosphes began cursing Styphon's House bitterly. Mytron knew both processes, on a quart-jar scale. He explained how much of both they would need.

"But that'll take time," Chartiphon objected. "And as soon as Gormoth hears that we're making our own fireseed, he'll attack at once."

"Don't let him hear about it. Clamp down the security." He had to explain about that. Counter-intelligence seemed to be unheard of, here-and-now. "Have cavalry patrols on all the roads out of Hostigos. Let anybody in, but let nobody out. Not just to Nostor; to Sask and Beshta, too." He thought for a moment. "And another thing. I'll have to give orders people aren't going to like. Will I be obeyed?"

"By anybody who wants to keep his head on his shoulders," Ptosphes said. "You speak with my voice."

"And mine, too!" Chartiphon cried, reaching his sword across the table for him to touch the hilt. "Command me and I will obey, Lord Kalvan."

He established himself, the next morning, in a room inside the main gateway to the citadel, across from the guardroom, a big flagstone-floored place with the indefinable but unmistakable flavor of a police-court. The walls were white plaster; he could write and draw diagrams on them with charcoal. Nobody, here-and-now, knew anything about paper. He made a mental note to do something about that, but no time for it now. Rylla appointed herself his adjutant and general Girl Friday. He collected Mytron, the priest of Tranth, all the master-craftsmen in Tarr-Hostigos, some of the craftsmen's guild people from Hostigos Town, a couple of Chartiphon's officers, and half a dozen cavalrymen to carry messages.

Charcoal would be no problem—there was plenty of that, burned exclusively in the iron-works in the Listra Valley and extensively elsewhere. There was coal, from surface outcroppings to the north and west, and it was used for a number of purposes, but the sulfur content made it unsuitable for iron-furnaces. He'd have to do something about coke some time. Charcoal for gunpowder, he knew, ought to be willow or alder or something like that. He'd do something about that, too, but at present he'd have to use what he had available.

For quantity evaporation of sulfur he'd need big iron pans, and sheet-metal larger than skillets and breastplates didn't seem to exist. The iron-works were forges, not rolling mills. So they'd have to beat the sheet-iron in two-foot squares and weld them together like patch quilts. He and Mytron got to work on planning the evaporation works. Unfortunately,

Mytron was not pictorial-minded, and made little or no sense
of the diagrams he drew.

Saltpeter could be accumulated all over. Manure-piles
would be the best source, and cellars and stables and under-
ground drains. He set up a saltpeter commission, headed by
one of Chartiphon's officers, with authority to go anywhere
and enter any place, and orders to behead any subordinate
who misused his powers and to deal just as summarily with
anybody who tried to obstruct or resist. Mobile units, wagons
and oxcarts loaded with caldrons, tubs, tools and the like, to
go from farm to farm. Peasant women to be collected and
taught to leech nitrated soil and purify nitrates. Equipment,
manufacture of.

Grinding mills: there was plenty of water-power, and by
good fortune he didn't have to invent the waterwheel. That
was already in use, and the master-millwright understood
what was needed in the way of converting a gristmill to a
fireseed mill almost at once. Special grinding equipment,
invention of. Sifting screens, cloth. Mixing machines; these
would be big wine-casks, with counter-revolving paddle-
wheels inside. Presses to squeeze dough into cakes. Mills to
grind caked powder; he spent considerable thought on regulations to prevent anything from striking a spark around them,
with bloodthirsty enforcement threats.

During the morning he managed to grind up the cake he'd
made the evening before from what was left of the first
experimental batch, running it through a sieve to about FFFg
fineness. A hundred grains of that drove a ball from an 8-bore
musket an inch deeper into a hemlock log than an equal
charge of Styphon's Best.

By noon he was almost sure that almost all of his War
Production Board understood most of what he'd told them. In
the afternoon there was a meeting, in the outer bailey, of as
many people who would be working on fireseed production
as could be gathered. There was an invocation of Dralm by
Xentos, and an invocation of Galzar by Uncle Wolf, and an
invocation of Tranth by his priest. Ptosphes spoke, emphasizing that the Lord Kalvan had full authority to do

anything, and would be backed to the limit, by the headsman if necessary. Chartiphon made a speech, picturing the howling wilderness they would shortly make of Nostor. (Prolonged cheering.) He made a speech, himself, emphasizing that there was nothing of a supernatural nature whatever about fireseed, detailing the steps of manufacture, and trying to give some explanation of what made it explode. The meeting then broke up into small groups, everybody having his own job explained to him. He was kept running back and forth, explaining to the explainers.

In the evening they had a feast. By that time he and Rylla had gotten a rough table of organization charcoaled onto the wall of his headquarters.

Of the next four days, he spent eighteen hours each in that room, talking to six or eight hundred people. Some of them he suffered patiently if not gladly; they were trying to do their best at something they'd never been expected to do before. Some he had trouble with. The artisans' guilds bickered with one another about jurisdiction, and they all complained about peasants invading their crafts. The masters complained that the journeymen and apprentices were becoming intractable, meaning that they'd started thinking for themselves. The peasants objected to having their byres invaded and their dunghills forked down, and to being put to unfamiliar work. The landlords objected to having their peasants taken out of the fields, predicting that the year's crop would be lost.

"Don't worry about that," he told them. "If we win, we'll eat Gormoth's crops. If we lose, we'll all be too dead to eat."

And the Iron Curtain went down. Within a few days, indignant pack-traders and wagoners were being collected in Hostigos Town, trapped for the duration, protesting vehemently but unavailingly. Sooner or later, Gormoth and Sarrask would begin to wonder why nobody was coming out of Hostigos, and would send spies slipping through the woods to find out. *Counter-espionage; organize soonest.* And a few of his own spies in Sask and Nostor. And an anti-Styphon fifth column in both princedoms. *Discuss with Xentos.*

By the fifth day, the Wolf Valley sulfur-evaporation plant

was ready to go into operation, and saltpeter production was up to some ten pounds a day. He put Mytron in charge at Tarr-Hostigos, hoping for something better than the worst, and got into his new armor. He and Rylla and a half dozen of Harmakros' cavalrymen trotted out the gate and down the road from the castle into Hostigos Gap. It was the first time he'd been outside the castle since he had been brought there unconscious, tied onto a horse-litter.

It was not until they were out of the gap and riding toward the town, spread around the low hill above the big spring, that he turned in his saddle to look back at the castle. For a moment he couldn't be certain what was wrong, but he knew something was. Then it struck him.

There was no trace whatever of the great stone-quarries.

There should have been. No matter how many thousands of years had passed since he had been in and out of that dome of shifting light that had carried him out of his normal time, there would have been some evidence of quarrying there. Normal erosion would have taken, not thousands, but hundreds of thousands, of years to obliterate those stark man-made cliffs, and enough erosion to have done that would have reduced the whole mountain by half. He remembered how unchanged the little cliff, under which he and Larry and Jack and Steve had parked the car, had been when he had . . . emerged. No. That mountain had never been quarried, at any time in the past.

So he wasn't in the future; that was sure. And he wasn't in the past, unless every scrap of history everybody had ever written or taught was an organized lie, and that he couldn't swallow.

Then when the hell was he?

Rylla had reined in her horse and stopped beside him. The six troopers came to an unquestioning halt.

"What is it, Kalvan?"

"I was just . . . just thinking of the last time I saw this place."

"You mustn't think about that, any more." Then, after a

moment: "Was there somebody . . . somebody you didn't want to leave?"

He laughed. "No, Rylla. The only somebody like that is right beside me, now."

They shook their reins and started off again, the six troopers clattering behind them.

SIX

VERKAN VALL watched Tortha Karf spin the empty revolver cartridge on his desk. It was a very valuable empty cartridge; it had taken over forty days and cost ten thousand man-hours of crawling on hands and knees and pawing among dead hemlock needles to find it.

"That was a small miracle, Vall," the Chief said. "Aryan-Transpacific?"

"Oh, yes; we were sure of that from the beginning. Styphon's House Subsector." He gave the exact numerical designation of the time-line. "They're all basically alike; the language, culture, taboo and situation-response tapes we have will do."

The Chief was fiddling with the selector for the map screen; when he had gotten geographical area and run through Level and Sector, he lit it with a map of eastern North America, divided into five Great Kingdoms. First, Hos-Zygros—he chose to identify it in the terms the man he was hunting would use—its use—its capital equivalent with Quebec, taking in New England and southeastern Canada to Lake Ontario. Second, Hos-Agrys: New York, western

Quebec Province and northern New Jersey. Third, Hos-Harphax, where the pickup incident had occurred. Fourth, Hos-Ktemnos: Virginia and North Carolina. Finally, Hos-Bletha, south from there to the tip of Florida and west along the Gulf to Mobile Bay. And also Trygath, which was not Hos-, or *great*, in the Ohio Valley. Glancing at a note in front of him, Tortha Karf made a dot of light in the middle of Hos-Harphax.

"That's it. Of course, that was over forty days ago. A man can go a long way, even on foot, in that time."

The Chief knew that. "Styphon's House," he said. "That's that gunpowder theocracy, isn't it?"

It was. He'd seen theocracies all over Paratime, and liked none of them; priests in political power usually made themselves insufferable, worse than any secular despotism. Styphon's House was a particularly nasty case in point. About five centuries ago, Styphon had been a minor healer-god; still was on most of Aryan-Transpacific. Some deified ancient physician, he supposed. Then, on one time-line, some priest experimenting with remedies had mixed a batch of saltpeter, sulfur and charcoal—a small batch, or he wouldn't have survived it.

For a century or so, it had merely been a temple miracle, and then the propellant properties had been discovered, and Styphon had gone out of medical practice and into the munitions business. Priestly researchers had improved the powder and designed and perfected weapons to use it. Nobody had discovered fulminating powder and invented the percussion-cap, but they had everything short of that. Now, through their monopoly on this essential tool for maintaining or altering the political status quo, Styphon's House ruled the whole Atlantic seaboard, while the secular sovereigns merely reined.

He wondered if Calvin Morrison knew how to make gunpowder, and while he was wondering silently, the Chief did so aloud, adding:

"If he does, we won't have any trouble locating him. We may, afterward, though."

That was how pickup jobs usually were, on the exit end; the pickup either made things easy or impossibly difficult. Many of these paratemporal DP's, suddenly hurled into an unfamiliar world, went hopelessly insane, their minds refusing to cope with what common sense told them was impossible. Others were quickly killed through ignorance. Others would be caught by the locals, and committed to mental hospitals, imprisoned, sold as slaves, executed as spies, burned as sorcerers, or merely lynched, depending on local mores. Many accepted and blended into their new environment and sank into traceless obscurity. A few created commotions and had to be dealt with.

"Well, we'll find out. I'm going outtime myself to look into it."

"You don't need to, Vall. You have plenty of detectives who can do that."

He shook his head obstinately. "On Year-End Day, that'll be a hundred and seventy-four days, I'm going to be handcuffed to that chair you're sitting in. Until then, I'm going to do as much outtime work as I possibly can." He leaned over and turned a dial on the map-selector, got a large-scale map of Hos-Harphax and increased the magnification and limited the field. He pointed. "I'm going in about there. In the mountains in Sask, next door. I'll be a pack-trader—they go everywhere and don't have to account for themselves to anybody. I'll have a saddle-horse and three pack-horses loaded with wares. It'll take about five or six days to collect and verify what I'll take with me. I'll travel slowly, to let word seep ahead of me. It may be that I'll hear something about this Morrison before I enter Hostigos."

"What'll you do about him when you find him?"

That would depend. Sometimes a pickup could be taken alive, moved to Police Terminal on the Fifth Level, given a complete memory obliteration, and then returned to his own time-line. An amnesia case; that was always a credible explanation. Or he would be killed, with a sigma-ray needler which left no traceable effects. Heart failure, or, "He just died." Amnesia and heart-failure were wonderful things, from the Paratime Police viewpoint. Anybody with any common sense would accept either. Common sense was a wonderful thing, too.

"Well, I don't want to kill the fellow; after all, he's a police officer, too. But with the explanation we're cobbling up for his disappearance, returning him to his own time-line wouldn't be any favor to him." He paused, thinking. "We'll have to kill him, I'm afraid. He knows too much."

"What does he know, Vall?"

"One, he's seen the inside of a conveyer, something completely alien to his own culture's science. Two, he knows he's been shifted in time, and time-travel is a common science-fiction concept in his own world. If he can disregard verbalisms about fantasies and impossibilities, he will deduce a race of time-travelers.

"Only a moron, which no Pennsylvania State Police officer is, would be so ignorant of his own world's history as to think for a moment that he'd been shifted into the past. And he'll know he hasn't been shifted into the future, because that area, on all of Europo-American, is covered with truly permanent engineering works of which he'll find no trace. So what does that leave?"

"A lateral shift in time, and a race of lateral time travelers," the Chief said. "Why, that's the Paratime Secret itself!"

II

They were feasting at Tarr-Hostigos that evening. All morning, pigs and cattle had been driven in, lowing and squealing, to be slaughtered in the outer bailey. Axes thudded for firewood; the roasting-pits were being cleaned out from the last feast; casks of wine were coming up from the cellars. Morrison wished the fireseed mills were as busy as the castle bakery and kitchen.

A whole day's production shot to hell. He said as much to Rylla.

"But, Kalvan, they're all so happy." She was pretty happy, herself. "And they've worked so hard."

He had to grant that, and maybe the morale gain would offset the production loss. And they did have something to celebrate: a full hundredweight of fireseed, fifty percent better than Styphon's Best, and half of it made in the last two days.

"It's been so long since any of us had anything to be really happy about," she was saying. "When we'd have a feast, everybody'd try to get drunk as soon as they could, to keep from thinking about what was coming. And now maybe it won't come at all."

And now, they were all drunk on a hundred pounds of black powder. Five thousand caliver or arquebus rounds at most. They'd have to do better than twenty-five pounds a day—get it up above a hundred at least. Saltpeter production was satisfactory, and Mytron had figured a couple of angles at the evaporation plant that practically gave them sulfur running out their ears. The bottleneck was mixing and caking, and grinding the cakes. That meant more machinery, and there weren't enough men competent to build it. It would mean stopping work on the other things.

The carriages for the new light four-pounders. The iron-works had turned out four of them, so far—welded wrought-iron, of course, since nobody knew how to cast iron, here-and-now, and neither did he—but made with trunnions. They only weighed four hundred pounds, the same as Gustavus Adolphus', and with four horses the one prototype already completed could keep up with cavalry on any kind of decent ground. He was happier about that little gun than anything else—except Rylla, of course.

And they were putting trunnions on some old stuff, big things, close to a ton metal-weight but only six and eight pounders, and he hoped to get field-carriages under them, too. They'd take eight horses apiece, and they would never keep up with cavalry.

And rifling-benches—long wooden frames in which the

barrel would be clamped, with grooved wooden cylinders to slide in guides to rotate the cutting-heads. One turn in four feet—that, he remembered, had been the usual pitch for the Kentucky rifles. So far, he had one, in the Tarr-Hostigos gunshop.

And drilling troops—he had to do most of that himself, too, till he could train some officers. Nobody knew anything about foot-drill by squads; here-and-now troops maneuvered in columns of droves.

It would take a year to build the sort of an army he wanted. And Gormoth of Nostor would give him a month, at most.

He brought that up at the General Staff meeting that afternoon. Like rifled firearms and trunnions on cannon, General Staffs hadn't been invented here-and-now, either. You just hauled a lot of peasants together and armed them; that was Mobilization. You picked a reasonably passable march-route; that was Strategy. You lined up your men and shot or hit anything in front of you; that was Tactics. And Intelligence was what mounted scouts, if any, brought in at the last minute from a mile ahead. It cheered him to recall that that would probably be Prince Gormoth's notion of the Art of War. Why, with twenty thousand men, Gustavus Adolphus, or the Duke of Parma, or Gonzalo de Córdoba, could have gone through all five of these Great Kingdoms like a dose of croton oil. And what Turenne could have done!

Ptosphes and Rylla were present as Prince and Heiress-Apparent. The Lord Kalvan was Commander-in-Chief of the Armed Forces of Hostigos. Chartiphon, gratifyingly unresentful at seeing an outlander promoted over his head, was Field Marshal and Chief of Operations. An elderly ''captain''—actual functioning rank about brigadier-general—was quartermaster, paymaster, drillmaster, inspector-general and head of the draft board. A civilian merchant, who wasn't losing any money at it, had charge of procurement and supply. Mytron was surgeon-general, and the priest of Tranth had charge of production. Uncle Wolf Tharses was Chief of Chaplains. Harmakros was G2, mainly because his cavalry were patrolling the borders and keeping the Iron

Curtain tight, but he'd have to be moved out of that. He was too good a combat man to be stuck with a Pentagon Job, and Xentos was now doing most of the Intelligence work. Besides his ecclesiastical role as highpriest of Dralm, and his political function as Ptosphes' Chancellor, he was in contact with his co-religionists in Nostor, all of whom hated Styphon's House inexpressibly and were organizing an active Fifth Column. Like Iron Curtain, Fifth Column was now part of the local lexicon.

The first blaze of optimism, he was pleased to observe, had died down on the upper echelon.

"Dralm-damn fools!" Chartiphon was growling. "One keg of fireseed—they'll want to shoot that all away tonight celebrating—and they think we're saved. Making our own fireseed's given us a chance, and that's all." He swore again, this time an oath that made Xentos frown. "We have three thousand under arms; if we take all the boys with bows and arrows and all the old peasants with pitchforks, we might get that up to five thousand, but not another child or dotard more. And Gormoth'll have ten thousand: four thousand of his own people and those six thousand mercenaries he has."

"I'd call it eight thousand," Harmakros said. "He won't take the peasants out of the fields; he needs them there."

"Then he won't wait till the harvest's in; he'll invade sooner," Ptosphes said.

He looked at the relief-map on the long table. The idea that maps were important weapons of war was something else he'd had to introduce. This one was only partly finished; he and Rylla had done most of the work on it, in time snatched from everything else that ought to have been done last week at the latest. It was based on what he remembered from the U.S. Geological Survey quadrangle sheets he'd used on the State Police, on interviews with hundreds of soldiers, woodsmen, peasants and landlords, and on a good bit of personal horseback reconnaissance.

Gormoth could invade up the Listra Valley, crossing the river at the equivalent of Lock Haven, but that wouldn't give him a third of Hostigos. The whole line of the Bald Eagles

was strongly defended everywhere but at Dombra Gap.
Tarr-Dombra, guarding it, had been betrayed, seventy-five
years ago, to Prince Gormoth's grandfather, and Sevenhills
Valley with it.

"Then we'll have to do something to delay him. This
Tarr-Dombra . . . say we take that, and occupy Sevenhills
Valley. That'll cut off his best invasion route."

They all stared at him, just as he'd been stared at when
he'd first spoken of making fireseed. It was Chartiphon who
first found his voice:

"Man! You never saw Tarr-Dombra, or you wouldn't talk
like that! Nobody can take Tarr-Dombra, unless they buy it,
like Prince Galtrath did, and we haven't enough money for
that."

"That's right," said the retread "captain" who was G1
and part of G4. "It's smaller than Tarr-Hostigos, of course,
but it's twice as strong."

"Do the Nostori think it can't be taken, too? Then it can
be. Prince, are there any plans of that castle here?"

"Well, yes. On a big scroll, in one of my coffers. It was
my grandfather's, and we've always hoped that some time
. . ."

"I'll want to see that. Later will do. Do you know if any
changes have been made since the Nostori got it?"

None on the outside, at least. He asked about the garrison;
five hundred, Harmakros thought. A hundred of Gormoth's
regulars, and four hundred mercenary cavalry, to patrol
Sevenhills Valley and raid into Hostigos.

"Then we stop killing raiders who can be taken alive.
Prisoners can be made to talk." He turned to Xentos. "Is
there a priest of Dralm in Sevenhills Valley? Can you get in
touch with him, and will he help us? Explain to him that this
is not a war against Prince Gormoth, but against Styphon's
House."

"He knows that, and he will help as much as he can, but he
can't get into Tarr-Dombra. There is a priest of Galzar there,
for the mercenaries, and a priest of Styphon for the lord of the

castle and his gentlemen, but among the Nostori, Dralm is but a god for the peasants.''

Yes, and that rankled, too. The priests of Dralm would help, all right.

''Good enough. He can talk to people who can get inside, can't he? And he can send messages, and organize an espionage apparatus. I want to know everything that can be found out about Tarr-Dombra, no matter how trivial. Particularly, I want to know the guard-routine, and I want to know how the castle is supplied. And I want it observed at all times. Harmakros, you find men to do that. I take it we can't storm the place. Then we'll have to get in by trickery.''

III

Verkan the pack-trader went up the road, his horse plodding unhurriedly and the three pack-horses on the lead-line trailing behind. He was hot and sticky under his steel back-and-breast, and sweat ran down his cheeks from under his helmet into his new beard, but nobody ever saw an unarmed pack-trader, so he had to endure it. A Paratimer had to be adaptable, if nothing else. The armor was from an adjoining, nearly identical time-line, and so were his clothes, the short carbine in the saddle-sheath, his sword and dagger, the horse-gear, and the loads of merchandise—all except the bronze coffer on one pack-load.

Reaching the brow of the hill, he started slowly down the other side, and saw a stir in front of a whitewashed and thatch-roofed roadside cottage. Men mounting horses, sun-glints on armor, and the red and blue colors of Hostigos. Another cavalry post, the third since he'd crossed the border from Sask. The other two had ignored him, but this crowd meant to stop him. Two had lances, and a third a musketoon, and a fourth, who seemed to be in command, had his holsters open and his right hand on his horse's neck. Two more, at the cottage, were getting into the road on foot with musketoons.

He pulled up; the pack-horses, behind, came to a well-trained stop.

"Good cheer, soldiers," he greeted.

"Good cheer, trader," the man with his hand close to his pistol-butt replied. "From Sask?"

"Sask latest. From Ulthor, this trip; Grefftscharr by birth." Ulthor was the lake port in the north; Grefftscharr was the kingdom around the Great Lakes. "I'm for Agrys City."

One of the troopers chuckled. The sergeant asked: "Have you fireseed?"

He touched the flask on his belt. "About twenty charges. I was going to buy some in Sask Town, but when the priests heard I was passing through Hostigos they'd sell me none. Doesn't Styphon's House like you Hostigi?"

"We're under the ban." The sergeant didn't seem greatly distressed about it. "But I'm afraid you'll not get out of here soon. We're on the edge of war with Nostor, and Lord Kalvan wants no tales carried to him, so he's ordered that none may leave Hostigos."

He cursed; that was expected of him. The Lord Kalvan, now?

"I'd feel ill-used, too, in your place, but you know how it is," the sergeant sympathized. "When lords command, commonfolk obey, if they want to keep their heads on. You'll make out all right, though. You'll find ready sale for all your wares at good price, and then if you're skilled at any craft, work for good pay. Or you might take the colors. You're well horsed and armed, and Lord Kalvan welcomes all such."

"Lord Kalvan? I thought Ptosphes was Prince of Hostigos. Or have there been changes?"

"No; Dralm bless him, Ptosphes is still our Prince. But the Lord Kalvan, Dralm bless him too, is our new warleader. It's said he's a Prince himself, from a far land, which he well could be. It's also said he's a sorcerer, but that I doubt."

"Yes. Sorcerers are more heard of than seen," Vall commented. "Are there many more traders caught here as I am?"

"Oh, the Styphon's own lot of them; the town's full of them. You'd best go to the Sign of the Red Halberd; the better sort of them all stay there. Give the landlord my name''—he repeated it several times to make sure it would be remembered—"and you'll fare well.''

He chatted pleasantly with the sergeant and his troopers, about the quality of local wine and the availability of girls and the prices things fetched at sale, and then bade them good luck and rode on.

The Lord Kalvan, indeed! Deliberately, he willed himself no longer to think of the man in any other way. And a Prince from a far country, no less. He passed other farmhouses; around them some work was going on. Men were forking down dunghills and digging under them, and caldrons steamed over fires. He added that to the cheerfulness with which the cavalrymen had accepted the ban of Styphon's House.

Styphon, it appeared, had acquired a competitor.

Hostigos Town, he saw, was busier and more crowded than Sask Town had been. There were no mercenaries around, but many local troops. The streets were full of carts and wagons, and the artisans' quarter was noisy with the work of smiths and joiners. He found the inn to which the sergeant had directed him, mentioning his name to make sure he got his rake-off, put up his horses, safe-stowed his packs and had his saddlebags, valise and carbine carried to his room. He followed the inn-servant with the bronze coffer on his shoulder. He didn't want anybody else handling that and finding out how light it was.

When he was alone, he went to the coffer, an almost featureless rectangular block without visible lock or hinges, and pressed his thumbs on two bright steel ovals on the top. The photoelectric lock inside responded to his thumb-print patterns with a click, and the lid rose slowly. Inside were four globes of gleaming coppery mesh, a few instruments with dials and knobs, and a little sigma-ray needler, a ladies' model, small enough to be covered by his hand but as deadly as the big one he usually carried.

There was also an antigrav unit attached to the bottom of
the coffer; it was on, with a tiny red light glowing. When he
switched it off, the floorboards under the coffer creaked.
Lined with collapsed metal, it now weighed over half a ton.
He pushed down the lid which only his thumbprints could
open, and heard the lock click.

The common-room downstairs was crowded and noisy.
He found a vacant place at one of the long tables, across from
a man with a bald head and a straggling red beard, who
grinned at him.

"New fish in the net?" he asked. "Welcome, brother.
Where from?"

"Ulthor, with three horse-loads of Grefftscharr wares. My
name's Verkan."

"Mine's Skranga." The bald man was from Agrys City,
on the island at the mouth of the Hudson. He had been trading
for horses in the Trygath country.

"These people here took the lot, fifty of them. Paid me
less than I asked, but more than I expected, so I guess I got a
fair price. I had four Trygathi herders—they all took the
colors in the cavalry. I'm working in the fireseed mill, till
they let me leave here."

"The what?" He made his voice sound incredulous.
"You mean they're making their own fireseed? But only the
priests of Styphon can do that."

Skranga laughed. "That's what I used to think, too, but
anybody can do it. It's easy as boiling maple-sugar. See, they
get saltpeter from under dunghills . . ."

He detailed the process step by step. The man next to him
joined the conversation; he even understood, roughly, the
theory: the charcoal was what burned, the sulfur was the
kindling, and the saltpeter made the air to blow up the fire and
blow the bullet out of the gun. And there was no secrecy
about it, Vall mused as he listened. If a man who had been a
constabulary corporal, and a combat soldier before that,
wasn't keeping any better security it was because he didn't
care. Lord Kalvan just didn't want word getting into Nostor
till he had enough fireseed to fight a war with.

"I bless Dralm for bringing me here," Skranga was saying. "When I can leave here, I'm going somewhere and set up making fireseed myself. Hos-Ktemnos—no, I don't want too close to Styphon's House Upon Earth. Maybe Hos-Bletha, or Hos-Zygros. But I'll make myself rich at it. So can you, if you keep your eyes and ears open."

The Agrysi finished his meal, said he had to go back to work, and left. A cavalry officer, a few places down, promptly picked up his goblet and flagon and moved into the vacated seat.

"You just got in?" he asked. "From Nostor?"

"No, from Sask." The answer seemed to disappoint the cavalryman; he went into the Ulthor-Grefftscharr routine again. "How long will I have to stay here?"

The officer shrugged. "Dralm and Galzar only know. Till we fight the Nostori and beat them. What do the Saski think we're doing here?"

"Waiting for Gormoth to cut your throats. They don't know you're making your own fireseed."

The officer laughed. "Ha! Some of those buggers'll get theirs cut, if Prince Sarrask doesn't mind his step. You say you have three pack-loads of Grefftscharr wares. Any sword-blades?"

"About a dozen; I sold a few in Sask Town. Some daggers, a dozen gunlocks, four good shirts of rivet-link mail, a lot of bullet-moulds. And jewelry, and tools, and brassware."

"Well, take your stuff up to Tarr-Hostigos. They have a little fair in the outer valley each evening; you can get better prices from the castle-folk than here in town. Go early. Use my name." He gave it, and his cavalry unit. "See Captain Harmakros; he'll be glad of any news you can give him."

Late in the afternoon, he re-packed his horses and went up the road to the castle on the mountain above the gap. The workshops along the wall of the outer bailey were all busy. Among other things, he saw a new carriage for a field-piece being put together—not a four-wheel cart, but two big wheels and a trail, to be hauled with a limber, which was also being built. The gun was a welded iron four-pounder, which was normal for Styphon's House Subsector, but it had trunnions, which was not. Lord Kalvan, again.

Like all the local gentry, Harmakros had a small neat beard. His armor was rich but commendably well battered; his sword, instead of the customary cut-and-thrust (mostly cut) broadsword, was a long rapier, quite new. Kalvan had evidently introduced the revolutionary concept that swords had points, which should be used. He asked a few exploratory questions, then listened to a detailed account of what the Grefftscharr trader had seen in Sask, including mercenary companies Prince Sarrask had lately hired, with the names of the captains.

"You've kept your eyes and ears open," he commended, "and you know what's worth telling about. I wish you'd come through Nostor instead. Were you ever a soldier?"

"All free-traders are soldiers, in their own service."

"Yes; that's so. Well, when you've sold your loads, you'll be welcome in ours. Not as a common trooper—I know you traders too well for that. As a scout. You want to sell your pack-horses, too? We'll give you a good price for them."

"If I can sell my loads, yes."

"You'll have no trouble doing that. We'll buy the mail, the gunlocks, the sword-blades and that sort of thing ourselves. Stay about; have your meals with the officers here. We'll find something for you."

He had some tools, both for wood and metal work. He peddled them among the artisans in the shops along the outer wall, for a good price in silver and a better one in information. Besides rapiers and cannon with trunnions, Lord Kalvan had introduced rifling in firearms. Nobody knew whence he had come, except that it was far beyond the Western Ocean. The more pious were positive that he had been guided to Hostigos by the very hand of Dralm.

The officers with whom he ate listened avidly to what he had picked up in Sask Town. Nostor first and then Sask seemed to be the schedule. When they talked about Lord Kalvan, the coldest expressions were of deep respect, shading from there up to hero-worship. But they knew nothing about him before the night he had appeared to rally some fleeing peasants for a counter-attack on Nostori raiders and had been shot, by mistake, by Princess Rylla herself.

Vall sold the mail and sword-blades and gunlocks as a lot, and spread his other wares for sale in the bailey. There was a crowd, and the stuff sold well. He saw Lord Kalvan, strolling about from display to display, in full armor—probably wearing it all the time to accustom himself to the weight, Vall decided. Kalvan was carrying a .38 Colt on his belt along with his rapier and dagger, and clinging to his arm was a beautiful blonde girl in male riding-dress. That would be Prince Ptosphes' daughter, Rylla. The happy possessiveness with which she clung to him, and the tenderness with which he looked at her, made him smile. Then the thought of his mission froze the smile on his lips. He didn't want to kill that man, and break that girl's heart, but . . .

They came over to his display, and Lord Kalvan picked up a brass mortar and pestle.

"Where did you get this?" he asked. "Where did it come from?"

"It was made in Grefftscharr, Lord; shipped down the lakes by boat to Ulthor."

"It's cast. Are there no brass foundries nearer than Grefftscharr?"

"Oh, yes, Lord. In Zygros City there are many." Lord Kalvan put down the mortar. "I see. Thank you. Captain Harmakros tells me he's been talking to you. I'd like to talk to you, myself. I think I'll be around the castle all morning, tomorrow; ask for me, if you're here."

Returning to the Red Halberd, Vall spent some time and a little money in the common-room. Everybody, as far as he could learn, seemed satisfied that the mysterious Lord Kalvan had come to Hostigos in a perfectly normal manner, with or without divine guidance. Finally, he went up to his room.

Opening the coffer, he got out one of the copper-mesh globes, and from it drew a mouthpiece on a small wire, into which he spoke for a long time.

''So far,'' he concluded, ''there seems to be no suspicion of anything paranormal about the man in anybody's mind. I have been offered an opportunity to take service with his army as a scout. I intend doing this; assistance can be given me in performing this work. I will find a location for an antigrav conveyer to land, somewhere in the woods near Hostigos Town; when I do, I will send a message-ball through from there.''

Then he replaced the mouthpiece, set the timer for the transposition-field generator, and switched on the antigrav. Carrying the ball to an open window, he tossed it outside, and then looked up as it vanished in the night. After a few seconds, high above, there was an instant's flash among the many visible stars. It looked like a meteor; a Hostigi, seeing it, would have made a wish.

SEVEN

KALVAN SAT on a rock under a tree, wishing he could smoke, and knowing that he was getting scared again. He cursed mentally. It didn't mean anything—as soon as things started happening he'd forget about it but it always happened, and he hated it. That sort of thing was all right for a buck private, or a platoon-sergeant, or a cop going to arrest some hillbilly killer, but, for Dralm's sake, a five-star general, now!

And that made him think of what Churchill had called Hitler: the lance-corporal who had promoted himself to commander-in-chief at one jump. Corporal Morrison had done that, cut Hitler's time by quite a few years, and gotten into the peerage, which Hitler hadn't.

It was quiet on the mountain top, even though there were two hundred men squatting or lying around him, and another five hundred, under Chartiphon and Prince Ptosphes, five hundred yards behind. And, in front, at the edge of the woods, a skirmish line of thirty riflemen, commanded by Verkan, the Grefftscharr trader.

There had been some objections to giving so important a

command to an outlander; he had informed the objectors
rather stiffly that until recently he had been an outlander and a
stranger himself. Verkan was the best man for it. Since
joining Harmakros' scouts, he had managed to get closer to
Tarr-Dombra than anybody else, and knew the ground ahead
better than any. He wished he could talk the Grefftscharrer
into staying in Hostigos. He'd fought bandits all over, as any
trader must, and Trygathi, and nomads on the western plains,
and he was a natural rifle-shot and a born guerrilla. Officer
type, too. But free-traders didn't stay anywhere, they all had
advanced cases of foot-itch and horizon-fever.

And out in front of Verkan and his twenty rifled calivers at
the edge of the woods, the first on any battlefield in here-
and-now history, were a dozen men with rifled 8-bore muskets, fitted with peep-sights and carefully zeroed in, in what
was supposed to be the cleared ground in front of the castle
gate. The condition of that approach ground was the most
promising thing about the whole operation.

It had been cleared, all right—at least, the trees had been
felled and the stumps rooted out. But the Nostori thought
Tarr-Dombra couldn't be taken and they'd gone slack: the
ground hadn't been brushed for a couple of years. There were
bushes all over it as high as a man's waist, and not a few that a
man could hide behind standing up. And his men would have
been hard enough to see even if it had been kept like a
golf-course.

The helmets and body-armor had all been carefully rusted;
there'd been anguished howls about that. So had every gun-
barrel and spearhead. Nobody wore anything but green or
brown, and most of them had bits of greenery fastened to
helmets and clothing. The whole operation had been re-
hearsed four times back of Tarr-Hostigos, starting with
twelve hundred men and eliminating down to the eight
hundred best.

There was a noise, about what a wild-turkey would make
feeding, and a soft voice called, "Lord Kalvan!" It was
Verkan; he carried a rifle and wore a dirty gray-green smock

with a hood; his sword and belt were covered with green and brown rags.

"I never saw you till you spoke," Morrison commended him.

"The wagons are coming up. They're at the top switch-back now."

He nodded. "We start, then." His mouth was dry. What was that thing in *For Whom the Bell Tolls* about spitting to show you weren't afraid? He couldn't have done that now. He nodded to the boy squatting beside him; the boy picked up his arquebus and started back to where Ptosphes and Chartiphon were waiting.

And Rylla. He cursed vilely—in English, since he still couldn't get much satisfaction out of taking the names of these local gods in vain. She'd announced that she was coming along. He'd told her she'd do nothing of the sort; so had her father and Chartiphon. She'd thrown a tantrum, and thrown other things as well. She had come along. He was going to have his hands full with that girl, after they were married.

"All right," he said softly to the men around him. "Let's start earning our pay."

The men around and behind him rose quietly, two spears or halberds or long-handled scythe-blades to every caliver or arquebus, though some of the spearmen had pistols in their belts. He and Verkan advanced to the edge of the woods, where riflemen crouched in pairs behind trees. Across four hundred yards of clearing rose the limestone walls of Tarr-Dombra, the castle that couldn't be taken, above the chasm that had been quarried straight across the mountain top. The drawbridge was down and the portcullis up, and a few soldiers with black and orange scarves and sashes—his old college colors; he ought to be ashamed to shoot them—loitered in the gateway or kept perfunctory watch from the battlements.

Ptosphes and Chartiphon—and Rylla, damn it!— came up with the rest of the force, with a frightful clatter and brush-

crashing which nobody at the castle seemed to hear. There
was one pike or spear or halberd or something—too often
something—to every two arquebuses or calivers. Chartiphon
wore a long brown sack with arm and neck holes over his
armor. Ptosphes wore brown, and browned armor; so did
Rylla. They nodded greetings, and peered through the bushes
to where the road from Sevenhills Valley came up to the
summit of the mountain.

Finally, four cavalrymen, with black and orange pennons
and scarves, came into view. They were only fake Princeton
men; he hoped they'd get rid of that stuff before some other
Hostigi shot them by mistake. A long ox-wagon, piled high
with hay which covered eight Hostigi infantrymen, followed. Then a few false-color cavalry, another big hay-
wagon, more cavalry, and two more wagons, and a dozen
cavalry behind.

The first four clattered over the drawbridge, spoke to the
guards, and rode through the gate. Two wagons followed
vanishing through the gate. Great Galzar, if anybody noticed
anything, now! The third rumbled onto the drawbridge and
stopped directly below the portcullis; that was the one with
the log framework under the hay, and the log slung underneath; the driver must have cut the strap to let it drop,
jamming the wagon. The fourth, the one loaded with rocks to
the top of the bed, stopped on the end of the drawbridge,
weighting it down.

Then a pistol banged inside, and another; there were
shouts of "Hostigos!" and "Ptosphes!" He blew his State
Police whistle, and six of the big elephant-size muskets went
off in front, from places where he'd have sworn there'd been
nobody at all. The rest of Verkan's rifle-platoon began firing,
sharp whipcrack reports entirely different from the
smoothbores. He hoped they'd remember to patch their bullets when they reloaded; that was something new for them.
He blew his whistle twice and started running forward.

The men who had been showing themselves on the walls
were gone, now, but a musket-shot or so showed that the
snipers in front hadn't gotten all of them. He ran past a man

with fishnet over his helmet stuck full of twigs, ramming a ball into his musket; another, near him, who had been waiting till he was half through, fired. Gray powdersmoke hung in the gateway; all the Hostigi were inside now, and there was an uproar of shouting—*"Hostigos!"* *"Nostor!"* —and shots and blade-clashing. He broke step to look behind him; his two hundred were pouring after him and Ptosphes' spearmen; the arquebusiers and calivermen had advanced to two hundred yards and were plastering the battlements as fast as they could load and fire, without bothering to aim. Aimed smoothbore fire at that range was useless; they were just trying to throw as much lead as they could.

A cannon went off above him when he was almost to the end of the drawbridge, and then, belatedly, the portcullis slammed down and stopped eight feet from the ground on the log framework hidden under the hay of the third wagon. They'd tested that a couple of times with the portcullis at Tarr-Hostigos, first. All six of the oxen on the last wagon were dead; the drivers and the infantrymen inside had been furnished short broadaxes to make sure of that. The oxen of the portcullis wagon had been cut loose and driven inside. There were a lot of ripped-off black and orange scarves on the ground, and more on corpses. The gate, and the two gate-towers, had been secured.

But shots were coming from the citadel, across the bailey, and a mob of Nostori was pouring out the gate from it. This, he thought, was the time to expend some .38-specials. Standing with his feet apart and his left hand on his hip, he drew the Colt and began shooting, timed-fire rate. He killed six men with six shots (he'd done that well on silhouette targets often enough), and they were the front six men. The rest stopped, just long enough for the men behind him to come up and sweep forward, arquebuses banging. Then he holstered the empty Colt—he had only eight rounds left for it—and drew his rapier and poignard. Another cannon thundered from the outside wall; he hoped Rylla and Chartiphon hadn't been in front of it. Then he was fighting his way through the citadel gate, shoulder to shoulder with Prince Ptosphes.

Behind, in the bailey, something else besides *"Ptosphes!"* and *"Gormoth!"* and *"Hostigos!"* was being shouted. It was:

"Mercy, comrade! Mercy; I yield! Oath to Galzar!"

There was much more of that as the morning passed; before noon, all the garrison had either cried for mercy or hadn't needed it. There had only been those two cannon-shots, though between them they had killed or wounded fifty men. Nobody would be crazy enough to attack Tarr-Dombra, so the cannon had been left empty, and they'd only had time to load and fire two.

The hardest fighting was inside the citadel. He ran into Rylla there, with Chartiphon hurrying to keep up with her. There was a bright sword-nick on her brown helmet, and blood on her light rapier; she was laughing happily. Then the melee swept them apart. He had expected that taking the keep would be even grimmer work, but as soon as they had the citadel, it surrendered. By that time, he had used the last of his irreplaceable cartridges. Muzzle-loaders for him, from now on.

They hauled down Gormoth's black flag with the orange lily and ran up the halberd-head of Hostigos. They found four huge bombards, throwing hundred-pound stone balls, loaded them, hand-spiked them around, and sent the huge gunstones crashing into the roofs of the town of Dyssa, at the mouth of Gorge River, to announce that Tarr-Dombra was under new management. They set the castle cooks to work skinning and cutting up the dead wagon-oxen for a barbecue. Then they turned their attention to the prisoners, herded into the inner bailey.

First, there were the mercenaries. They all agreed to enter Prince Ptosphes' service. They couldn't be used against Gormoth until the term of their contract with him expired; they would be sent to patrol the Sask border. Then there were Gormoth's own subject troops. They couldn't be made to bear arms at all, but they could be put to work, as long as they were given soldiers' pay and soldierly treatment. Then there was the governor of the castle, a Count Pheblon, cousin to

Gormoth, and his officers. They would be released, on oath to send their ransoms to Hostigos. The castle priest of Galzar, after administering the oaths, elected to go to Hostigos with his parishioners.

As for the priest of Styphon, Chartiphon wanted to question him under torture, and Ptosphes thought he should be beheaded out of hand.

"Send him to Nostor with Pheblon," Morrison said. "No, send him to Balph, in Hos-Ktemnos, with a letter to the Supreme Priest, Styphon's Voice, telling him that we make our own fireseed, that we will teach everybody else to make it, and that we are the enemies of Styphon's House until Styphon's House is destroyed."

Everybody, including those who had been suggesting novel and interesting ways of putting the priest to death, shouted approval.

"And a letter to Gormoth," he continued, "offering him peace and friendship. Tell him we'll put his soldiers to work in the fireseed mill and teach them the whole art, and when we release them, they can teach it in Nostor."

Ptosphes was horrified. "Kalvan! What god has addled your wits, man? Gormoth's our enemy by birth, and he'll be our enemy as long as he lives."

"Well, if he tries to make his own fireseed without joining us, that won't be long. Styphon's House will see to that."

EIGHT

I

VERKAN THE Grefftscharrer led the party that galloped back to Hostigos Town in the late afternoon with the good news—Tarr-Dombra taken, with over two hundred prisoners, a hundred and fifty horses, four tons of fireseed, twenty cannon, and rich booty of smallarms, armor and treasure. And Sevenhills Valley was part of Hostigos again. Harmakros had defeated a large company of mercenary cavalry, killing over twenty of them and capturing the rest. And he had taken the Styphon temple-farm, a nitriary, freeing the slaves and putting the priests to death. And the long-despised priest of Dralm had gathered his peasant flock and was preaching to them that the Hostigi had come not as conquerors but as liberators.

That sounded familiar to Verkan Vall; he'd heard the like on quite a few time-lines, including Morrison/Kalvan's own. Come to think of it, in the war in which Morrison had fought, both sides had made that claim.

He also brought copies of the letters Prince Ptosphes had written—more likely, that Kalvan had written and Ptosphes had signed—to Gormoth and to Sesklos, Styphon's Voice.

The man was clever; those letters would do a lot of harm, where harm would do the most good.

Dropping a couple of troopers to spread the news in the town, he rode up to the castle; as he approached the gate, the great bell of the town hall began pealing. It took some time to tell the whole story to Xentos, counting interruptions while the old priest-chancellor told Dralm about it. When he got away from Xentos, he was dragged bodily into the officers' mess, where a barrel of wine had already been broached. Fortunately, he had some First Level alcodote-vitamin pills with him. By the time he got down to Hostigos Town it was dark, everybody was roaring drunk, the bell was still ringing, and somebody was wasting fireseed in the square with a little two-pounder.

He was mobbed there, too; the troopers who had come in with him betrayed him as one of the heroes of Tarr-Dombra. Finally he managed to get into the inn and up to his room. Getting another message-ball and a small radio-active beacon from his coffer, he hid them under his cloak, got his horse, and managed to get out of town, riding to a little clearing two miles away.

Pulling out the mouthpiece, he recorded a message, concluding:

"I wish especially to thank Skordran Kirv and the people with him for the reconnaissance work at Tarr-Dombra, on this and adjoining time-lines. The information so secured, and the success this morning resulting from it, places me in an excellent position to carry out my mission.

"I will need the assistants, and the equipment, at once. The people should come in immediately; there is a big victory celebration in the town, everybody's drunk, and they could easily slip in unnoticed. There will be a formal thanksgiving ceremony in the temple of Dralm, followed by a great feast, three days from now. At this time the betrothal of Lord Kalvan to the Princess Rylla will be announced."

Then he set the transposition timer, put the ball on anti-grav, and tossed it up with a gesture like a falconer releasing his hawk. There was a slight overcast, and it flashed just below the ceiling, but that didn't matter. On this night, nobody would be surprised at portents in the sky over Hostigos. Then, after tripping the shielding from the beacon and planting it to guide the conveyer in, he sat down with his back to a tree and lit his pipe. Half an hour transposition time to Police Terminal, maybe an hour to get the men and equipment together, and another half hour to transpose in.

He wouldn't be bored waiting. First Level people never were. He had too many interesting things in his memory, all of which were available to total recall.

II

Invited to sit, the Agrysi horse-trader took the chair facing the desk in the room that had been fitted up as Lord Kalvan's private office. He was partly bald, with a sparse red beard; about fifty, five-eight, a hundred and forty-five. The sort of character Corporal Calvin Morrison would have taken a professional interest in: he'd have a record, was probably wanted somewhere, for horse-theft at a guess. Shave off that beard and he'd double for a stolen-car fence he had arrested a year ago. A year before he'd gone elsewhen, anyhow. The horse-trader, Skranga, sat silently, wondering why he'd been brought in, and trying to think of something they might have on him. Another universal constant, he thought.

"Those were excellent horses we got from you," he began. "The officers snapped most of them up before they could get to the remount corrals."

"I'm glad to hear you say so, Lord Kalvan," Skranga said cautiously. "I try to deal only in the best."

"You've been working in the fireseed mill, since. I'm told you've learned all about making fireseed."

"Well, Lord, I try to learn what I'm doing, when I'm supposed to do something."

"Most commendable. Now, we're going to open the frontiers. There's no point in keeping them closed since we took Tarr-Dombra. Where had you thought of going?"

Skranga shrugged. "Back to the Trygath country for more horses, I suppose."

"If I were you, I'd go to Nostor, before Gormoth closes his frontiers. Speak to Prince Gormoth privately, and be sure the priests of Styphon don't find out about it. Tell him you can make fireseed, and offer to make it for him. You'll be making your fortune if you do."

That was the last thing Skranga had expected. He was almost successful in concealing his surprise.

"But, Lord Kalvan! Prince Gormoth is your enemy." Then he stopped, scenting some kind of top-level double-crossing. "At least, he's Prince Ptosphes' enemy."

"And Prince Ptosphes' enemies are mine. But I like my enemies to have all the other enemies possible, and if Styphon's House find out that Gormoth is making his own fireseed, they'll be his. You worship Dralm? Then, before you speak to Prince Gormoth, go to the Nostor temple of Dralm, speak secretly to the highpriest there, tell him I sent you, and ask his advice. You mustn't let Gormoth know about that. Dralm, or somebody, will reward you well."

Skranga's eyes widened for a moment, then narrowed craftily.

"Ah. I understand, Lord Kalvan. And if I get into Gormoth's palace, I'll find means of sending word to the priests of Dralm, now and then. Is that it, Lord Kalvan?"

"You understand perfectly, Skranga. I suppose you'd like to stay for the great feast, but if I were you, I'd not. Go the first thing in the morning, tomorrow. And before you go, speak to Highpriest Xentos; ask the blessing of Dralm before you depart."

He'd have to get somebody into Sask and start Prince Sarrask up in fireseed production, too, he thought. That might be a little harder. And after the feast, all these traders and wagoners who'd been caught in the Iron Curtain would be leaving, fanning out all over the five Great Kingdoms. He watched Skranga go out, and then filled and lit a pipe—not the otherwhen Dunhill, but a local corncob, regular Douglas MacArthur model—and lit it at the candle on his desk.

Styphon's House was the real enemy. Beat Gormoth properly, on his own territory, and he'd stay beaten. Sarrask of Sask was only a Mussolini to Gormoth's Hitler; a decisive defeat of Nostor would overawe him. But Styphon's House wouldn't stop till Hostigos was destroyed; their prestige, which was their biggest asset, demanded it. And Styphon's House was big; it spread over all the Great Kingdoms, from the St. Lawrence to the Gulf.

Big but vulnerable, and he knew, by now, the vulnerable point. Styphon wasn't a popular god, like Dralm or Galzar or Yirtta Allmother. The priests of Styphon never tried for a following among the people, or even the minor nobility and landed gentry who were the backbone of here-and-now society. They ruled by pressure on the Great Kings and the Princes, and as soon as the pressure was relieved, as soon as the fireseed monopoly was broken, those rulers and their people with them would turn on Styphon's House. The war against Styphon's House was going to be won in little independent powder mills all over the Five Kingdoms.

But beating Gormoth was the immediate job. He didn't know how much good Skranga would be able to do, or Xentos' Dralm-temple Fifth Column. You couldn't trust that kind of thing. Gormoth would have to be beaten on the battlefield. Taking Tarr-Dombra had been a good start. The next morning, two thousand Nostori troops, mostly mercenaries, had tried to force a crossing at Dyssa Ford, at the mouth of Pine Creek; they'd been stopped by artillery fire. That night, Harmakros had taken five hundred cavalry across the West Branch at Vryllos Gap, and raided western Nostor, firing thatches, running off cattle, and committing all the usual atrocities.

He frowned slightly. Harmakros was a fine cavalry leader, and a nice guy to sit down and drink with, but Harmakros was just a trifle atrocity-prone. That massacre at the Sevenhills temple-farm, for instance. Well, if that was the way they made war, here-and-now, that would be the way to make it.

Then he sat for a while longer, thinking about the Art of War, here-and-now. He hoped taking Tarr-Dombra would hold Gormoth off for the rest of this year, and give him a chance to organize a real army, trained in the tactics he could remember from the history of the Sixteenth and Seventeenth Centuries of his own time.

Light cannon, the sort Gustavus Adolphus had smashed Tilly's unwieldy tercios at Breitenfeld with. And plenty of rifles, and men trained to use them. There was a lot of forest country, here-and-now, and oddly, no game laws to speak of; everybody was a hunter. And bore-standardization, so that bullets could be issued, instead of every soldier having to carry his own bullet-mould and make his own bullets. He wondered how soon he could get socket bayonets, unknown here-and-now, produced. Not by the end of this year, not along with everything else. But if he could get rid of all these bear spears, and these scythe-blade things, whatever they were called, and get the spearmen armed with eighteen-foot Swiss pikes, then they'd keep the cavalry off his arquebusiers and calivermen.

He dug the heel out of his pipe and put it down, rising and looking at his watch (the only one in the world, and what would he do if he broke it?). It was 1700; dinner in an hour and a half. He went out, returning the salute of the halberdier at the door, and up the stairway.

His servant had the things piled on a table in his parlor, on a white sheet. The tunic with the battered badge that had saved his life; the gray shirt, torn and blood-stained. The breeches; he left the billfold in the hip pocket. He couldn't spend the paper currency of a nonexistent United States, and the identification cards belonged to a man similarly nonexistent here-and-now. He didn't want the boots, either; the castle cordwainer did better work, now that he had learned to make right and left feet. The Sam Browne belt, with the empty cartridge-loops and the holster and the handcuff-pouch. Anybody you needed handcuffs for, here-and-now, you knocked on the head or shot. He tossed the blackjack down contemptuously; blackjacks didn't belong, here-and-now. Rapiers and poignards did.

He picked up the .38 Colt Official Police, swung out the

cylinder and checked it by habit-reflex, and dry-practiced a few rounds at a knot-hole in the paneling. He didn't want to part with that, even if there were no more cartridges for it, but the rest of this stuff would be rather meaningless without it. He slipped it into the holster and buttoned down the retaining-strap.

"That's the lot," he told the servant. "Take them to Highpriest Xentos."

The servant put them compactly together, one boot on either side, and wrapped them in the sheet. Tomorrow, at the thanksgiving ceremony, they would be deposited as votive offerings in the temple of Dralm. He didn't believe in Dralm, or any other god, but now, besides being a general and an ordnance engineer and an industrialist, he had to be a politician and no politician can afford to slight his constituents' religion. If nothing else, a parsonage childhood had given him a talent for hypocritical lip-service.

He watched the servant carry the bundle out. There goes Corporal Calvin Morrison, he thought. Long live Lord Kalvan of Hostigos.

III

Verkan Vall, his story finished, relaxed in his chair and sipped his tall drink. There was no direct light on the terrace, only a sky-reflection of the city lights below, dim enough that the tip of Tortha Karf's cigarette glowed visibly. There were four of them around the low table: the Chief of Paratime Police; the Director of the Paratime Commission, who acted only on the Chief's suggestion; the Chairman of the Paratemporal Trade Board, who did as the Commission Director told him; and himself, who, in a hundred and twenty-odd days, would have all Tortha Karf's power and authority—and all his headaches.

"You took no action?" the Paratime Commission Director was asking.

"None whatever. None was needed. The man knows he was in some kind of a time-machine, which shifted him, not into the past or future of his own world, but laterally, in another time-dimension, and from that he can deduce the existence, somewhen, of a race of lateral time-travelers. That, in essence, is the Paratime Secret, but this Calvin Morrison—Lord Kalvan, now—is no threat to it. He's doing a better job of protecting it in his own case than we could. He has good reason to.

"Look what he has, on his new time-line, that his old one could never have given him. He's a great nobleman; they've gone out of fashion on Europo-American, where the Common Man is the ideal. He's going to marry a beautiful princess, and they've even gone out of fashion for children's fairy-tales. He's a sword-swinging soldier of fortune, and they've vanished from a nuclear-weapons world. He's commanding a good little army, and making a better one of it, the work he loves. And he has a cause worth fighting for, and an enemy worth beating. He's not going to jeopardize his position with those people.

"You know what he did? He told Xentos, under pledge of secrecy, that he had been banished by sorcery from his own time, a thousand years in the future. Sorcery, on that time-line, is a perfectly valid explanation for anything. With his permission, Xentos gave that story to Rylla, Ptosphes and Chartiphon; they handed it out that he is an exiled Prince from a country completely outside local geographical knowledge. See what he has? Regular defense in depth; we couldn't have done nearly as well outselves."

"Well, how'd it leak to you?" the Board Chairman wanted to know.

"From Xentos, at the big victory feast. I got him off to one side, got him into a theological discussion, and spiked his drink with some hypno truth-drug. He doesn't even remember, now, that he told me."

"Nobody on that time-line'll get it that way," the Board Chairman agreed. "But didn't you take a chance on getting that stuff of his out of the temple?"

He shook his head. "We ran a conveyer in, the night of the feast, when it was empty. The next morning, when the priests discovered that the uniform and the revolver and the other things had vanished, they cried, 'Lo! Dralm has accepted the offering! A miracle!' I was there, and saw it. Kalvan doesn't believe in any miracles; he thinks some of these transients that left Hostigos that day when the borders were opened stole the stuff. I know Harmakros' cavalry were stopping people at all the exit roads and searching wagons and packs. Publicly, of course, Kalvan had to give thanks to Dralm for accepting the offering.''

"Well, was it necessary?''

"Not on that time-line. On the pickup line, yes. The stuff will be found . . . first the clothing and the badge with his number on it. Not too far from where he vanished; I think at Altoona. We have a man planted on the city police force there. Later, maybe in a year, the revolver will turn up, in connection with a homicide we will arrange. The Sector Regional Subchief can take care of that. There are always plenty of prominent people on any time-line who wouldn't be any great loss.''

"But that won't explain anything,'' the Commission Director objected.

"No; it'll be an unsolved mystery. Unsolved mysteries are just as good as explanations, as long as they're mysterious within a normal framework.''

"Well, gentlemen, all this is very interesting, but how does it concern me officially?'' the Paratime Trade Board Chairman asked.

The Commission Director laughed. "You disappoint me! This Styphon's House racket is perfect for penetration of that subsector, and in a couple of centuries, long before either of us retire, it'll be a good area to have penetrated. We'll just move in on Styphon's House and take over the same way we did the Yat-Zar temples on the Hulgun Sector, and build that up to general political and economic control.''

"You'll have to stay off Morrison's—Kalvan's—time-line,'' Tortha Karf said.

"I should say they will! You know what's going to be done with that? We're going to turn that over to the University of

Dhergabar, as a study-area, and five adjoining time-lines for controls. You know what we have here?" He was becoming excited about it. "We have the start of an entirely new subsector, identified from the exact point of divarication, something we've never been able to do before, except from history. I'm already established on that time-line as Verkan the Grefftscharr trader; Kalvan thinks that I'm traveling on horseback to Zygros City to recruit brass-founders for him, to teach his people how to cast brass cannon. In about forty or so days, I can return with them. They will, of course, be the University study-team. And I will be back, every so often, as often as horse travel rates would plausibly permit. I'll put in a trade depot, which can mask the conveyer-head . . ."

Tortha Karf began laughing. "I knew you'd figure yourself some way! And, of course, it's such a scientifically important project that the Chief of Paratime Police would have to give it his personal attention, so you'll be getting outtime even after I retire and you take over."

"Well, all right. We all have our hobbies; you've been going to that farm of yours on Fifth Level Sicily for as long as I've been on the Paracops. Well, my hobby farm's going to be Kalvan Subsector, Fourth Level Aryan Transpacific. I'm only a hundred and thirty; by the time I'm ready to retire . . ."

NINE

I

IN THE quiet of the Innermost Circle, in Styphon's House Upon Earth, at Balph, the great image looked down, and Sesklos, Supreme Priest and Styphon's Voice, returned the carven stare almost as stonily. Sesklos did not believe in Styphon or in any other god; if he had, he would not be sitting here. The policies of Styphon's House were too important to entrust to believers, and such could never hope to rise above the white robed outer circle, or at most don the black robes of underpriests. None might wear the yellow robe, let along the flame-colored robe of primacy. The image, he knew, was of a man—the old highpriest who had, by discovering the application of a minor temple secret, taken the cult of a minor healer-god out of its mean back-street shrines and made it the power that ruled the rulers of all the Five Kingdoms. If it had been in Sesklos to worship anything, he would have worshipped the memory of that man.

And now, the first Supreme Priest looked down upon the last one. Sesklos lowered his eyes to the sheets of parchment in front of him, flattening one with his hands to read again:

85

PTOSPHES, Prince of Hostigos, to SESKLOS, calling himself Styphon's Voice, these:

False priest of a false god, impudent swindler, liar and cheat!

Know that we in Hostigos, by simple mechanic arts, now make for ourselves that fireseed which you pretend to be the miracle of your fraudulent god, and that we propose teaching these arts to all, that hereafter Kings and Princes minded to make war may do so for their own defense and advancement, and not to the enrichment of Styphon's House of Iniquities.

In proof thereof, we send fireseed of our own make, enough for twenty musket charges, and set forth how it is made, thus:

To three parts of refined saltpeter and three fifths of one part of charcoal and two fifths of one part of sulfur, all ground to the fineness of bolted wheat flour. Mix thoroughly, moisten the mixture, and work it to a heavy dough, then press into cakes and dry them, and when they are fully dry, grind and sieve them.

And know that we hold you and all in Styphon's House of Iniquities our deadly enemies, and the enemies general of all men, to be dealt with as wolves are, and that we will not rest content until Styphon's House of Iniquities is utterly cast down and destroyed.

PTOSPHES,
Prince of and for the nobles and people of Hostigos.

That had been the secret of the power of Styphon's House. No ruler, Great King or petty lord, could withstand his enemies if they had fireseed and he had none; no ruler sat secure upon his throne except by the favor of Styphon's House. Given here, armies marched to victory; withheld there, terms of peace were accepted. In every council of state, Styphon's House spoke the deciding word. Wealth poured in to be loaned out again at usury and return more wealth.

And now, the contemptible Prince of a realm a man could

ride across without tiring his horse was bringing it down, and
Styphon's House had provoked him to it. There had been
sulfur springs in Hostigos, and of Styphon's Trinity, sulfur
was hardest to get. Well, they'd demanded the land of him,
and he'd refused, and none could be allowed to defy
Styphon's House, so his enemy, Prince Gormoth, had been
given gifts of money and fireseed. Things like that were done
all the time.

Three moons ago, Ptosphes and his people had been desperate; now he was writing thus, to Styphon's Voice Himself. The impiety of it shocked Sesklos. Then he pushed aside
Ptosphes' letter and looked again at the one from Vyblos, the
highpriest at Nostor Town. Three moons ago, a stranger,
calling himself Kalvan and claiming to be an exiled Prince
from a far country, had appeared in Hostigos. A moon later,
Ptosphes had made this Kalvan commander of all his soldiers, and had set guards on his borders, that none might
leave. He had been informed of that, but had thought nothing
of it.

Then, six days ago, the Hostigi had taken Tarr-Dombra,
the castle securing Gormoth's best route of invasion into
Hostigos, and a black-robe priest who had been there had
been released to bear this letter to him. Vyblos had sent the
letter on by swift couriers; the priest was following more
slowly to tell his tale in person.

It had, of course, been this Kalvan who had given Ptosphes
the fireseed secret. He wondered briefly if this Kalvan might
be some renegade from Styphon's House, then shook his
head. No; the full secret, as Ptosphes had set it down, was
known only to yellow-robe priests of the Inner Circle, upperpriests, highpriests and Archpriests. If one of these had
absconded, the news would have reached him as fast as
relays of galloping horses could bring it. Some Inner Circle
priest might have written it down, a thing utterly forbidden,
and the writing might have fallen into unconsecrated hands,
but he doubted that. The proportions were different: more
saltpeter and less charcoal. He would have Ptosphes' sample
tried; he suspected that it might be better than their own.

A man, then, who had rediscovered the secret for himself? That could be, though it had taken many years and the work of many priests to perfect the process, especially the caking and grinding. He shrugged. That was not important. The important thing was that the secret was out. Soon everybody would be making fireseed, and then Styphon's House would be only a name, and a name of mockery at that.

He might, however, postpone that day for as long as mattered to him. He was near his ninetieth year; he would not live to see many more, and for each man the world ends when he dies.

Letters of urgency to the Archpriests of the five Great Temples, plainly telling them all, each to tell those under him as much as he saw fit. A story to be circulated among the secular rulers, that fireseed stolen by bandits was being smuggled and sold. Prompt investigation of reports of anyone gathering sulfur or saltpeter, or building or altering grinding-mills. Death by assassination of anyone suspected of knowing the secret.

That would only do for the moment; he knew that. Something better must be devised, and quickly. And care must be taken not to spread, while trying to suppress, the news that someone outside Styphon's House was making fireseed. A Great Council of all the Archpriests, but that later.

And, of course, immediate destruction of Hostigos, and all in it, not one to be spared even for slavery. Gormoth had been waiting until his own people could harvest their crops; he must be made to move at once. An Archpriest of Styphon's House Upon Earth to be sent to Nostor, since this was entirely beyond poor Vyblos' capacities. Krastokles, he thought. Lavish gifts of fireseed and silver and arms for Gormoth.

He glanced again at Vyblos' letter. A copy of Ptosphes' letter to himself had gone to Gormoth, by the hand of the castellan of Tarr-Dombra, released on ransom-oath. Why, Ptosphes had given his enemy the fireseed secret! He rebuked himself for not having noticed that before. That had been a daring, and a fiendishly clever, thing to do.

So, with Krastokles would go fifty mounted Guardsmen of the Temple, their captain to be an upperpriest without robe. And more silver, to corrupt Gormoth's courtiers and mercenary captains.

And a special letter to the highpriest of the Sask Town temple. It had been planned to use Prince Sarrask as a counterpoise to Gormoth, when the latter had grown too great by the conquest of Hostigos. Well, the time for that was now. Gormoth was needed to destroy Hostigos; as soon as that was accomplished, he, too, must be destroyed.

Sesklos struck the gong thrice, and as he did, he thought again of this mysterious Kalvan. That was nothing to shrug off. It was important to learn who he was, and whence he had come, and with whom he had been in contact before he had appeared—he was intrigued by Vyblos' choice of the word—in Hostigos. He could have come from some far country where the making of fireseed was commonly known. He knew of none such, but the world might well be larger than he thought.

Or could there be other worlds? The idea had occurred to him, now and then, as an idle speculation.

II

The man called Lord Kalvan—except in retrospect, he never thought of himself as anything else now—sipped from the goblet and set it on the stand beside his chair. It was what they called winter-wine: set out in tubs to freeze, and the ice thrown off until it was sixty to seventy proof, the nearest they had to spirits, here-and-now. *Distillation,* he added to the long list of mental memos; *invent and introduce.* Bourbon, he thought; they grew plenty of corn.

It was past midnight; a cool breeze fluttered the curtains at the open windows, and flickered the candles. He was tired, and he knew that he would have to rise at dawn tomorrow, but he knew that he would lie awake a long while if he went to bed now. There was too much to think about.

Troop strengths: better than two to one against Hostigos. If

Gormoth waited till his harvests were in and used all his peasant levies, more than that. Of course, if he waited, they'd be a little better prepared in training and matériel, but not much. Three thousand regular infantry, meaning they had been organized into companies and given a modicum of drill. Two thousand were pikemen and halberdiers, and too many of the pikes were short hunting-spears, and too many of the halberds were those scythe-blade things (he still didn't know what else to call them), and a thousand calivermen, arquebusiers and musketeers. And fifty riflemen, though in another thirty days there would be a hundred more. And eight hundred cavalry, all of whom could be called regulars— nobles and gentlemen-farmers, and their attendants.

Artillery—there was the real bright spot. Four of the light four-pounders were finished and in service, gun-crews training with them, and two more would be finished in another eight or ten days. And the old guns had been remounted; they were at least three hundred percent better than anything Gormoth would have.

All right, they couldn't do anything about numbers; then cut the odds by concentrating on mobility and firepower. It didn't really matter who had the mostest; just git th'ar fustest and fire the most shots and score the most hits with them. But he didn't want to think about that right now.

He emptied the goblet and debated pouring himself more, lighting his pipe. Instead, he turned to something he hadn't had time to think about lately: the question of just when now was.

He wasn't at any time in the past, or the future, of May 19, 1964, when he'd walked into that dome of light. He'd settled that in his mind definitely. So what did that leave? Another time-dimension.

Say time was a plane, like a sheet of paper. *Paper; experiment with manufacture of;* that mental memo popped up automatically, and was promptly shoved down again. He wished he'd read more science fiction; time-dimensions were a regular science fiction theme, and a lot of it carefully thought out. Well, say he was an insect, capable of moving only in one direction, crawling along a line on the paper, and say somebody picked him up and set him down on another line.

That figured. And say, long ago, one of these lines of time had forked, maybe before the beginning of recorded history. Or say these lines had always existed, an infinite number of them, and on each one, things happened differently. That could be it. He was beginning to be excited; Dralm-dammit, now he'd be awake half the night, thinking about this. He got up and filled the goblet with almost-brandy.

He'd found out a little about these people's history. Their ancestors had been living on the Atlantic Coast for over five hundred years; they all spoke the same language, and were of the same stock: Zarthani. They hadn't come from across the Atlantic, but from the west, across the continent. Some of that was recorded history he had read, and some was legend; all of it was supported by the maps, which showed all the important seacoast cities at the mouths of rivers. There were no cities on the sites of such excellent harbors as Boston, Baltimore or Charleston. There was the Grefftscharr Kingdom, at the west end of the Great Lakes, and Dorg at the confluence of the Mississippi and Missouri, and Xiphlon at the site of New Orleans. But there was nothing but a trading town at the mouth of the Ohio, and the Ohio valley was full of semi-savages. Rivers flowing east and south had been the pathway.

So these people had come from across the Pacific. But they weren't Asiatics, as he used the word; they were blond Caucasians. Aryans! Of course; the Aryans had come out of Central Asia, thousands of years ago, sweeping west and south into India and the Mediterranean basin, and west and north to Scandinavia. On this line of events, they'd gone the other way.

The names sounded Greek—all those -os and -es and-on endings—but the language wasn't even the most corrupt Greek. It wasn't even grammatically the same. He'd had a little Greek in college, dodging it as fast as it was thrown at him, but he knew that.

Wait a minute. The words for "father" and "mother".
German, *vater*; Spanish, *padre*; Latin, *pater*; Greek, as near
that as didn't matter; Sanskrit, *pitr*. German, *mutter*;
Spanish, *madre*; Latin, *mater*; Greek, *meter*; Sanskrit, *matr*.
In Zarthani, they were *phadros* and *mavra*.

III

It was one of those small late-afternoon gatherings, nobody seeming to have a care in the world, lounging indo-
lently, sipping tall drinks, nibbling canapes, talking and
laughing. Verkan Vall held his lighter for his wife, Hadron
Dalla, then applied it to his own cigarette. Across the low
table, Tortha Karf was mixing himself a drink, with the
concentrated care of an alchemist compounding the Elixir of
Life. The Dhergabar University people—the elderly professor of Paratemporal Theory, the lady professor of Outtime
History(IV), and the young man who was director of outtime
study operations—were all smiling like three pussy-cats at a
puddle of spilled cream.

"You'll have it all to yourselves," Vall told them. "The
Paratime Commission has declared that time-line a study-
area, and it's absolutely quarantined to everybody but University personnel and accredited students. I'm making it my
personal business to see that the quarantine is enforced."

Tortha Karf looked up. "After I retire, I'm taking a seat on
the Paratime Commission," he said. "I'll see to it that the
quarantine isn't revoked or modified."

"I wish we could account for those four hours from the
time he got out of that transposition field until he stopped at
that peasant's cottage," the paratemporal theorist said. "We
have no idea what he was doing."

"Wandering in the woods, trying to orient himself,"
Dalla said. "Sitting and thinking, most of the time, I'd say.
Getting caught in a conveyer field must be a pretty shattering
experience, if you don't know what it is, and he seems to
have adjusted very nicely by the time he had those Nostori to

fight. I don't believe he was changing history all by himself."

"You can't say that," the old professor chided. "He could have shot a rattlesnake which would otherwise have bitten and killed a child who would otherwise have grown up to be an important personage. That sounds far-fetched and trivial, but paratemporal alternate probability is built on different trivialities. Who knows what started the Aryan migration eastward on that sector, instead of westward as on all the others? Some tribal chief's hangover; some wizard's nightmare."

"Well, that's why you're getting those five adjoining time-lines for controls," the outtime study operations director said. "And I'd keep out of Hostigos on all of them. We don't want our people massacred along with the resident population by Gormoth's gang, or forced to defend themselves with Home Time Line weapons."

"What bothers me," the lady professor of history said, "is Vall's beard."

"It bothers me, too," Dalla said, "but I'm getting used to it."

"He hasn't shaved it off since he came back from Kalvan's time-line, and it begins to look like a permanent fixture. And I notice that Dalla's a blonde, now. Blondes are less conspicuous on Aryan-Transpacific. They're both going to be on and off that time-line all the time."

"Well, nobody's exclusive rights to anything outtime excludes the Paratime Police. I told you I was going to give that time-line my personal attention. And Dalla is officially Special Chief's Assistant's Special Assistant, now; she'll be promoted automatically along with me."

"Well, you won't introduce a lot of probability contamination, will you?" the elderly theorist asked anxiously. "We want to observe the effect of this man's appearance on that time-line . . ."

"You know any kind of observation that doesn't contaminate the thing observed, professor?" Tortha Karf, who had gotten the drink mixed, asked.

"If anything, I'll be able to minimize the amount of contamination his study-teams introduce. I'm already well established with these people, as Verkan the Grefftscharr trader. Why, Lord Kalvan offered me a commission in his army, commanding a rifle regiment he's raising, and right now I'm supposed to be recruiting brass-founders for him in Zygros." Vall turned to the operations director. "I can't plausibly get back to Hostigos for another thirty days. Can you have your first team ready by then? They'll have to know their trade; if they cast cannon that blow up on the first shot, I know where their heads will go, and I won't try to intervene for them."

"Oh, yes. They have everything now but local foundry techniques and correct Zygrosi accent. Thirty days will be plenty."

"But that's contamination!" the professor of Paratemporal Theory objected. "You're teaching his people to make cannon, and . . ."

"Just to make better cannon, and if I didn't bring in fake Zygrosi founders, Kalvan would send somebody else to bring in real ones. I will help him in any other way a wandering pack-trader could; information and things like that. I may even go into battle with him, again—with one of those back-acting flintlocks. But I want *him* to win. I admire the man too much to want to hand him an unearned victory on a platter."

"He sounds like a lot of man to me," the lady historian said. "I'd like to meet him, myself."

"Better not, Eldra," Dalla warned. "That princess of his is handy with a pistol, and I don't think she cares much who she shoots."

TEN

I

THE GENERAL STAFF had a big room of their own to meet in, just inside the door of the keep, and the relief map was finished and set up. The General Staff were all new at it. So was he, but he had some vague idea of what a General Staff was supposed to do, which put him several up on any of the rest of them. Xentos was reporting what he had gotten from the Nostori Fifth Column.

"The bakeries work night and day," he said. "And milk cannot be bought at any price—it is all being made into cheese. And most of the meat is being made into smoked sausages."

Stuff a soldier could carry in a haversack and eat uncooked: field-rations. That stuff, even the bread, could be stored, Kalvan thought, but Xentos was also reporting that wagons and oxen were being commandeered, and peasants impressed as drivers. They wouldn't do that too long in advance.

"Then Gormoth isn't waiting to get his harvests in,"

Ptosphes said. "He'll strike soon, and taking Tarr-Dombra didn't stop him at all."

"It delayed him, Prince," Chartiphon said. "He'd be pouring mercenaries into Nostor now through Sevenhills Valley if we hadn't."

"I grant that." There was a smile on Ptosphes' lips. He'd been learning to smile again, since the powder mills had gone into operation, and especially since Tarr-Dombra had fallen. "We'll have to be ready for him a little sooner than I'd expected, that's all."

"We'll have to be ready for him yesterday at the latest," Rylla said. She'd picked that expression up from him. "What do you think he'll hit us with?"

"Well, he's been shifting troops around," Harmakros said. "He seems to be moving all his mercenaries east, and all his own soldiers west."

"Marax Ford," Ptosphes guessed. "He'll throw the mercenaries at us first."

"Oh, no, Prince!" Chartiphon dissented. "Go all the way around the mountains and all the way up through East Hostigos? He wouldn't do that. Here's how he'll come in."

He drew his big hand-and-a-half sword—none of these newfangled pokers for him—and gave it a little toss in his hand to get the right grip on it, then pointed on the map to where the Listra flowed into the Athan.

"There—Listra-Mouth. He can move his whole army up the river in his own country, force a crossing here—if we let him—and take all Listra Valley to the Saski border. That's where all our iron-works are."

Now that was something. Not so long ago, to Chartiphon, weapons had been just something you fought with; he'd taken them for granted. Now he was realizing that they had to be produced.

That started an argument. Somebody thought Gormoth would try to force one of the gaps. Not Dombra; that was too strong. Maybe Vryllos Gap.

"He'll attack where we don't expect him, that's where," Rylla declared.

"Well, that means we have to expect him everywhere."

"Great Galzar!" Ptosphes exploded, drawing his rapier. "That means we have to expect him everywhere from here"—he touched the point to the map to the mouth of the Listra—"to here," which was about where Lewisburg had been in Calvin Morrison's world. "That means that with half Gormoth's strength, we'll have to be stronger than he is at every point."

"Then we'll have to move what men we have around faster," his daughter told him.

Well, good girl! She'd seen what none of the others had, what he'd been thinking about last night, that mobility could make up for lack of numbers.

"Yes," he said. "Harmakros, how many infantrymen could you put horses under? They don't have to be good horses, just good enough to take them where they'll fight on foot."

Harmakros was scandalized. Mounted soldiers were *cavalry*; everybody knew it took years to train a cavalryman; he had to be practically born at it. Chartiphon was scandalized, too. Infantrymen were *foot* soldiers; they had no business on horses.

"It'll mean," he continued, "that in action about one out of four will have to hold horses for the others, but they'll get into action before the battle's over, and they can wear heavier armor. Now, how many infantry can you find mounts for?"

Harmakros looked at him, decided that he was serious, thought for a moment, then grinned. It always took Harmakros a moment or so to recover from the shock of a new idea, but he always came up punching before the count was over.

"Just a minute; I'll see."

He pulled the remount officer aside; Rylla joined them with a slate and soapstone. Among other things, Rylla was the mathematician. She'd learned Arabic numerals, even the reason for having a symbol for nothing at all. Very high on the *I love Rylla, reasons why* list was the fact that the girl had a brain and wasn't afraid to use it.

He turned to Chartiphon and began talking about the

defense of Listra-Mouth. They were still discussing it when Rylla and Harmakros came over and joined them.

"Two thousand," Rylla said. "They all have four legs, and we think they were all alive last evening."

"Eighteen hundred," Harmakros cut it. "We'll need some for pack-train and replacements."

"Sixteen hundred," Kalvan decided. "Eight hundred pikemen, with pikes and not hunting-spears or those scythe-blade things, and eight hundred arquebusiers, with arquebuses and not rabbit-guns. Can you do that, Chartiphon?"

Chartiphon could. All men who wouldn't fall off their horses, too.

"It'll make a Styphon's own hole in the army, though," he added.

Aside from the Mobile Force, that would leave twelve hundred pikemen and two hundred with firearms. Of course, there was the militia: two thousand peasant levies, anybody who could do an hour's foot-drill without dropping dead, armed with anything at all. They would fight bravely if unskillfully. A lot of them were going to get killed.

And, according to best intelligence estimates, Gormoth had six thousand mercenaries, of whom four thousand were cavalry, and four thousand of his own subjects, including neither the senile nor the adolescent and none of them armed with agricultural implements or crossbows. He looked at the map again. Gormoth would attack where he could use his cavalry superiority to best advantage. Either Listra-Mouth or Marax Ford.

"Good. And all the riflemen." All fifty of them. "Put them on the best horses, they'll have to be everywhere at once. And five hundred regular cavalry."

Everybody howled at that. There weren't that many, not uncommitted. Swords flashed over the map, indicating places where they only had half enough now. Contradictions were shouted. One of these days somebody was going to use a sword for something besides map-pointing in one of these arguments. Finally, by robbing Peter and Paul both, they scraped up five hundred for the Mobile Force.

"And I want all those musketoons and lances turned in," he said. "The lances are better pikes than half our pikemen have, and the musketoons are almost as good as arquebuses. We won't have cavalrymen burdened with infantry weapons when the infantry need them as desperately as they do."

Harmakros wanted to know what the cavalry would fight with.

"Swords and pistols. The purpose of cavalry is to scout and collect information, neutralize enemy cavalry, harass enemy movement and communications, and pursue fugitives. It is not to fight on foot—that's why we're organizing mounted infantry—and it is not to commit suicide by making attacks on massed pikemen—that's why we're building these light four-pounders. The lances and musketoons will go to the infantry, and the fowling-pieces and scythe-blade things they replace can go to the militia.

"Now, you'll command this Mobile Force, Harmakros. Turn all your intelligence work over to Xentos; Prince Ptosphes and I will help him. You'll have all four of the four-pounders, and the two being built as soon as they're finished, and pick out the lightest four of the old eight-pounders. You'll be based in Sevenhills Valley; be prepared to move either east or west as soon as you have orders.

"And another thing: battle-cries." They had to be shouted constantly, to keep friend from killing friend. "Besides 'Ptosphes!' and 'Hostigos!' we will shout 'Down Styphon!' "

That met with general approval. They all knew who the real enemy was.

II

Gormoth, Prince of Nostor, set down the goblet, wiping his bearded lips on the back of his hand. The candles in front of him and down the long tables at the sides flickered. Tableware clattered, and voices were loud.

"Lost everything!" The speaker was a baron driven from Sevenhills Valley when Tarr-Dombra had fallen almost a moon ago. "My house, a score of farms, a village . . ."

"You think we've lost nothing?" another noble demanded. "They crossed the river the night after they chased you out, and burned everything on my land. It was Styphon's own miracle I got out with my own blood unspilled."

"For shame!" cried Vyblos, the highpriest of the temple of Styphon, sitting with him at the high table. "You speak of cow-byres and peasant-huts; what of the temple-farm of Sevenhills, a holy place pillaged and desecrated? What of fifteen consecrated priests and novices, and a score of lay guards, all cruelly murdered? 'Dealt with as wolves are,' " he quoted.

"That's Styphon's business; let him look to his own," the lord from western Nostor said. "I want to know why our Prince isn't looking to the protection of Nostor."

"It can be stopped, Prince." That was the mayor, and wealthiest merchant, of Nostor Town. "Prince Ptosphes had offered peace, now that Hostigos has Tarr-Dombra again. He's a man of his word."

"Peace tossed like a bone to a cur?" yelled Netzigon, the chief captain of Nostor. "Friendship shot at us out of cannon?"

"Peace with a desecrator of holy places, and a butcher of Styphon's priests?" Vyblos fairly screamed. "Peace with a blasphemer who pretends, with his mortal hands, to work Styphon's own miracle, and make fireseed without Styphon's aid?"

"More than pretends!" That was Gormoth's cousin, Count Pheblon. He still hadn't taken Pheblon back into his favor after losing Tarr-Dombra, but for those words he was close to it. "By Dralm, the Hostigi burned more fireseed taking Tarr-Dombra than we thought they had in all Hostigos. I was there, which you weren't. And when they opened the magazines, they only sneered and said, 'That filthy trash; don't get it mixed with ours.' "

"That's all aside," the baron from Listra-Mouth said. "I want to know what's being done to keep their raiders out of Nostor. Why, they've harried all the strip between the mountains and the river; there isn't a house standing there now."

Weapons clattered at the door. Somebody else sneered: "That's Ptosphes, now! Under the tables, everybody!" A man in mail and black leather strode in, advancing and saluting; the captain of the dungeons.

"Lord Prince, the special prisoner has been made to talk. He will tell all."

"Ha!" Gormoth knew what that meant. Then he laughed at the looks of concern on faces down the side tables. Not a few at his court had cause to dread somebody telling all about something. He drew his poignard and cut a line across the candle in front of him, a thumb's breadth from the top.

"You bring good news. I'll go to hear him in that time."

As he nodded dismissal, the captain bowed and backed away. He rapped loudly on the table with the pommel of the dagger.

"Be silent, all of you; I've little time, so give heed. Klestreus," he addressed the elected captain-general of the mercenary free-companies, "You have four thousand horse, two thousand foot, and ten cannon. Add to them a thousand of my infantry and such guns of mine as you think fit. You'll cross the Athan at Marax Ford. Be on the road before the dew's off the grass tomorrow; before dawn of the next day, take and hold the ford, put the best of your cavalry across at once, and let the others follow as speedily as they can.

"Netzigon," he told his own chief-captain, "you'll gather every man you can, down to the very peasant rabble, and such cannon as Klestreus leaves you. Post companies to confront every pass in the mountains from across the river; use the peasants for that. With the rest of your force, march to Listra-Mouth, and Vryllos Gap. As Klestreus moves west through East Hostigos, he will attack each gap from behind;

when he does, your people will cross over and give aid.
Tarr-Dombra we'll have to starve out; the rest must be taken
by storm. When Klestreus is as far as Vryllos Gap, you will
cross the Athan and move up Listra Valley. After that, we'll
have Tarr-Hostigos to take. Galzar only knows how long
we'll be at that, but by the end of the moon-half all else in
Hostigos should be ours.''

There were gratified murmurs all along the table; this
made good hearing, and they had waited long to hear it. Only
the highpriest, Vyblos, was ill-pleased.

''But why so soon, Prince?''

''Soon? By the Mace of Galzar, you've been bawling for it
like a branded calf since greenleaf-time. Well, now you have
your invasion—yet you object. Why?''

''A few more days would cost nothing, Prince,'' Vyblos
said. ''Today I had word from Styphon's House Upon Earth,
from the pen of His Divinity, Styphon's Voice Himself. An
Archpriest, His Sanctity Krastokles, is traveling hither with
rich gifts and the blessing of Styphon. It were poor reverence
not to await His Sanctity's coming.''

Another cursed temple-rat, bigger and fatter and more
insolent than this one. Well, let him come after the victory,
and content himself with what bones were tossed to him.

''You heard me,'' he told the two captains. ''I rule here,
not this priest. Be about it; send out your orders now, and
move in the morning.''

Then he rose, pushing back the chair before the servant
behind him could touch it. The line was still visible at the top
of the candle.

Guards with torches attended him down the winding stairs
into the dungeons. The air stank. His breath congealed; the
heat of summer never penetrated here. From the torture
chamber shrieks told of some wretch being questioned; idly
he wondered who. Stopping at an iron-bound door, he un-
locked it with a key from his belt and entered alone, closing it
behind him.

The room within was large, warmed by a fire on a hearth in

the corner and lighted by a great lantern from above. Under it, a man bent over a littered table, working with a mortar and pestle. As the door closed, he straightened and turned. He had a bald head and a red beard, and wore a most unprisoner-like dagger on his belt. A key for the door lay on the table, and by them a pair of heavy horseman's pistols. He smiled.

"Greetings, Prince; it's done. I tried some, and it's as good as they make in Hostigos, and better than the dirt the priests sell."

"And no prayers to Styphon, Skranga?"

Skranga was chewing tobacco. He spat brownly on the floor.

"That in the face of Styphon! You want to try it, Prince? The pistols are empty."

There was a bowl half full of fireseed on the table. He measured a charge and poured it into one, loaded and wadded a ball on top of it, primed the pan, readied the flint and striker. Aiming at a billet of wood by the hearth, he fired, then laid the pistol down and went to probe the hole with a straw. The bullet had gone in almost a little finger's length; Styphon's powder wouldn't do that much.

"Well, Skranga!" he laughed. "We'll have to keep you hidden for awhile yet, but from this hour you're first noble-man of Nostor after myself. Style yourself Duke. There'll be rich lands for you in Hostigos, when Hostigos is mine."

"And in Nostor the Styphon temple-farms?" Skranga asked. "If I'm to make fireseed for you, there's all there that I'll need."

"Yes, by Galzar, that too! After I've dealt with Ptosphes, I'll have a reckoning with Vyblos, and before I let him die, he'll be envying Ptosphes."

Snatching up a pewter cup without looking to see if it were clean, he went to the wine-barrel and drew it full. He tasted the wine, then spat it out.

"Is this the swill they've given you to drink?" he demanded. "Whoever's at fault won't see tomorrow's sun set!" He flung open the door and bellowed into the hall:

"Wine! Wine for Prince Gormoth and Duke Skranga! And silver cups!" He hurled the pewter, still half full of wine, at a guard. "Move your feet, you bastard! And see it's fit for nobles to drink!"

ELEVEN

I

MOBILE FORCE HQ had been the mansion of a Nostori noble driven from Sevenhills Valley on D-for-Dombra Day. Kalvan's name had been shouted ahead as he rode to it through the torchlit, troop-crowded village, and Harmakros and some of his officers met him at the door.

"Great Dralm, Kalvan!" Harmakros laughed. "Don't tell me you're growing wings on horses, now. Our messengers only got off an hour ago."

"Yes, I met them at Vryllos Gap." They crossed the outer hall and entered the big room beyond. "We got the news at Tarr-Hostigos just after dark. What have you heard since?"

At least fifty candles burned in the central chandelier. Evidently the cavalry had gotten here before the peasants, on D-Day, and hadn't looted too destructively themselves. Harmakros led him to an inlaid table on which a map, scorched with hot needles on white deerskin, was spread.

"We have reports from all the watchtowers along the mountains. They're too far back from the river for anything but dust to be seen, but the column's over three miles long.

First cavalry, then infantry, then guns and wagons, and then the more infantry and some cavalry. They halted at Nirfë at dusk and built hundreds of campfires. Whether they left them burning and moved on after dark, and how far ahead the cavalry are now, we don't know. We expect them at Marax Ford by dawn.''

''We got a little more than that. The Nostor priest of Dralm got a messenger off a little after noon, but he didn't get across the river till twilight. Your column's commanded by Klestreus, the mercenary captain-general. All Gormoth's mercenaries, four thousand cavalry and two thousand infantry, a thousand of his own infantry, and fifteen guns, he didn't say what kind, and a train of wagons that must be simply creaking with loot. At the same time, Netzigon's moving west on Listra-Mouth with an all-Nostori army; dodging them was what delayed this messenger. Chartiphon's at Listra-Mouth with what he can scrape up; Ptosphes is at Vryllos Gap with a small force.''

''That's it,'' Harmakros said. ''Double attack, but the one from the east will be the heavy one. We can't do anything to help Chartiphon, can we?''

''Beat Klestreus as badly as we can; that's all I can think of.'' He had gotten out his pipe; as soon as he had it filled, one of the staff officers was offering a light. That was another universal constant. ''Thank you. What's been done here, so far?''

''I started my wagons and the eight-pounders east on the main road; they'll halt just west of Fitra, here.'' He pointed on the map to a little farming village. ''As soon as I'm all collected, here, I'll start down the back road, which joins the main road at Fitra. After I'm past, the heavy stuff will follow on. I have two hundred militia—the usual odd-and-sods, about half with crossbows—marching with the wagons.''

''That was all smart.''

He looked again at the map. The back road, adequate for cavalry and four-pounders but not for wagons or the heavy guns, followed the mountain and then bent south to join the main valley road. Harmakros had gotten the slow stuff off first, and wouldn't be impeded by it on his own march, and he was waiting to have all his force together, instead of feeding it in to be chopped up by detail.

"Where had you thought of fighting?"

"Why, on the Athan, of course." Harmakros was surprised that he should ask. "Klestreus will have some of his cavalry across before we get there, but that can't be helped. We'll kill them or run them back, and then defend the line of the river."

"No." Kalvan touched the stem of his corncob on the Fitra road-junction. "We fight here."

"But, Lord Kalvan! That's miles inside Hostigos!" one of the officers expostulated. Maybe he owned an estate down there. "We can't let them get that far!"

"Lord Kalvan," Harmakros began stiffly. He was going to be insubordinate; he never bothered with titles otherwise. "We cannot give up a foot of Hostigi ground. The honor of Hostigos forbids it."

Here we are, back in the Middle Ages! He seemed to hear the voice of the history professor, inside his head, calling a roll of battles lost on points of honor. Mostly by the French, though they weren't the only ones. He decided to fly into a rage.

"To Styphon with that!" he yelled, banging his fists on the table. "We're not fighting this war for honor, and we're not fighting this war for real-estate. We're fighting this Dralm-damned war for survival, and the only way we can win it is to kill all the damned Nostori we can, and get as few of our men killed doing it as we can.

"Now, here," he continued quietly, the rage having served its purpose. "Here's the best place to do it. You know what the ground's like there. Klestreus will cross here at Marax. He'll rush his best cavalry ahead, and after he's secured the ford, he'll push on up the valley. His cavalry'll want to get in on the best looting before the infantry come up. By the time the infantry are over, they'll be strung out all up East Hostigos.

"And they'll be tired, and, more important, their horses

will be tired. We'll all have gotten to Fitra by daylight, and
by the time they begin coming up, we'll have our position
prepared, our horses will be fresh again, all the men will have
at least an hour or so sleep, and a hot meal. You think that
won't make a difference? Now, what troops have we east of
here?''

A hundred-odd cavalry along the river; a hundred and fifty
regular infantry, and about twice as many militia. Some five
hundred, militia and some regulars, at posts in the gaps.

''All right . . . get riders off at once, somebody who
won't be argued with. Have that force along the river move
back, the infantry as rapidly as possible, and the cavalry a
little ahead of the Nostori, skirmishing. They will not attempt
to delay them; if the ones in front are slowed down, the ones
behind will catch up with them, and we don't want that.''

Harmakros had been looking at the map, and also looking
over the idea. He nodded.

''East Hostigos,'' he declared, ''will be the graveyard of
the Nostori.''

That took care of the honor of Hostigos.

''Well, mercenaries from Hos-Agrys and Hos-Ktemnos.
Who hired those mercenaries, anyhow—Gormoth, or
Styphon's House?''

''Why, Gormoth. Styphon's House furnished the money,
but the mercenary captains contracted with Gormoth.''

''Stupid of Styphon. The reason I asked, the Rev.
What's-his-name, in Nostor, included an interesting bit of
gossip in his report. It seems that this morning Gormoth had
one of his understewards put to death. Forced a funnel into
his mouth, and had close to half a keg of wine poured into
him. The wine was of inferior quality, and had been furnished to a prisoner, or supposed prisoner, for whom Gormoth had commanded good treatment.''

One of the officers made a face. ''Sounds like Gormoth.''
Another laughed and named a couple of innkeepers in Hostigos town who deserved the same. Harmakros wanted to
know who this pampered prisoner was.

''You know him. That Agrysi horse-trader, Skranga.''

"Yes, we got some good horses from him. I'm riding one, myself," Harmakros said. "Hey! He was working in the fireseed mill. Do you think he's making fireseed for Gormoth, now?"

"If he's doing what I told him to he is." There was an outcry; even Harmakros stared at him in surprise. "If Gormoth starts making his own fireseed, Styphon's House will find it out, and you know what'll happen then. That's why I was wondering who'd be able to use those mercenaries against whom. That's another thing. We can't be bothered with Nostori prisoners, but take all the mercenaries who'll surrender. We'll need them when Sarrask's turn comes up."

II

Dawn was only a pallor in the east, and the whitewashed walls were dim blurs under dark thatches, but the village of Fitra was awake, and the shouting began as he approached: "Lord Kalvan! Dralm bless Lord Kalvan!" He was used to it, now; it didn't give him the thrill it had at first. Light streamed from open doors and windows, and a fire blazed on the little common, and there was a crowd of villagers and cavalrymen who had ridden on ahead. Behind him, hooves thudded on the road, and far back he could hear the four-pounders clattering over the pole bridge at the mill. He had to make a speech from the saddle, while orders were shouted and reshouted to the rear and men and horses crowded off the road to make way for the guns.

Then he and Harmakros and four or five other officers rode forward, reining in where the main road began to dip into the little hollow. The eastern pallor had become a bar of yellow light. The Mountains of Hostigos were blackly plain on the left, and the jumble of low ridges on the right were beginning to take shape. He pointed to a ravine between two of them.

"Send two hundred cavalry around that ridge and into that little valley, where those three farms are clumped together," he said. "They're not to make fires or let themselves be seen. They're to wait till we're engaged, here, and the second batch of Nostori come up. Then they'll come out and hit them from behind.''

·An officer galloped away to attend to it. The yellow light spread; only a few of the larger and brighter stars were still visible. In front, the ground fell away to the small brook that ran through the hollow, to join a larger stream that flowed east along the foot of the mountain. The mountain rose steeply to a bench, then sloped up to the summit. On the right was broken ground, mostly wooded. In front, across the hollow, was mostly open farmland. There were a few trees around them, in the hollow, and on the other side. This couldn't have been better if he'd had Dralm create it to special order.

The yellow light had reached the zenith, and the eastern horizon was a dazzle. Harmakros squinted at it and said something about fighting with the sun in their eyes.

''No such thing; it'll be overhead before they get here. Now, you go take a nap. I'll wake you in time to give me some sack-time. As soon as the wagons get here, we'll give everybody a hot meal.''

An ox-cart appeared on the brow of the hill across the hollow, piled high, a woman and a boy trudging beside the team and another woman and some children riding. Before they were down to the brook, a wagon had come into sight. This was only the start; there'd be a perfect stream of them soon. They couldn't be allowed on the main road west of Fitra until the wagons and the eight-pounders were through.

''Have them turned aside,'' he ordered. ''And use the wagons and carts for barricades, and the oxen to drag trees.''

The village peasants were coming out now, with four-and six-ox teams dragging chains. Axes began thudding. More refugees were coming in; there were loud protests at being diverted and at having wagons and oxen commandeered. The axemen were across the hollow now, and men shouted at straining oxen as felled trees were dragged in to build an abatis.

He strained his eyes against the sunrise; he couldn't see any smoke. Too far away, but he was sure it was there. The enemy cavalry had certainly crossed the Athan by now, and pyromania was as fixed in the mercenary character as kleptomania. The abatis began to take shape, trees dragged into line with the tops to the front and the butts to the rear, with spaces for three of the six four-pounders on either side of the road and a barricade of wagons and farmcarts a little in advance at either end. He rode forward now and then to get an enemy's-eye view of it. He didn't want it to look too formidable from in front, or too professional—for one thing, he wanted to make sure that the guns were completely camouflaged. Finally he began to notice smears of smoke against the horizon, maybe six or eight miles away. Klestreus' mercenaries weren't going to disappoint him after all.

A company of infantry came up. They were regulars, a hundred and fifty of them, with two pikes (and one of them a real pike) to every caliver, marching in good order. They'd come all the way from the Athan, reported fighting behind them, and were disgusted at marching away from it. He told them they'd get all they wanted before noon, and to fall out and rest. A couple of hundred militia, some with crossbows, dribbled in. There were more smokes on the eastern horizon, but he still couldn't hear firing. At seven-thirty, the supply wagons, the four eight-pounders, and the two hundred militia arrived. That was good. The refugees, now a steady stream, could be sent on up the road. He saw to it that fires were lit and a hot meal started, and then went into the village.

He found Harmakros asleep in one of the cottages, wakened him, and gave him the situation to date.

"Send somebody to wake me," he finished, "as soon as you see smoke within three miles, as soon as our cavalry skirmishers start coming in, and in any case in two and a half hours."

Then he pulled off his helmet and boots, unbuckled his sword-belt, and lay down in the rest of his armor on the cornshuck tick Harmakros had vacated, hoping that it had no small inhabitants or, if so, that none of them would find lodgement under his arming-doublet. It was cool in here behind the stone walls and under the thick thatch. The wet

heat of his body became a clammy chill. He shifted positions
a few times, decided that fewer things gouged into him when
lying on his back, and closed his eyes.

So far, everything had gone nicely; all he was worried
about was who was going to let him down, and how badly.
He hoped some valiant fool wouldn't get a rush of honor to
the head and charge when he ought to stand fast, like the
Saxons at Hastings.

If he could bring this off just half as well as he'd planned it,
which would be about par for any battle, he could go to
Valhalla when he died and drink at the same table with
Richard Coeur-de-Lion, the Black Prince and Henry of
Navarre. A complete success would entitle him to take a
salute from Stonewall Jackson. He fell asleep receiving the
commendation of George S. Patton.

III

An infantry captain wakened him at a little before ten.

"They're burning Systros, now," he said. That was a
town of some two thousand, two and a half miles away. "A
couple of the cavalry who've been keeping contact with them
just came in. The first batch, about fifteen hundred, are
coming up fast, and there's another lot, about a thousand, a
mile and a half behind them. And we've been hearing those
big bombards at Narza Gap."

Between Montoursville and Muncy; that would be Klestreus' infantry on this side, and probably some of Netzigon's
ragtag and bobtail on the other. He pulled on his boots and
buckled on his belt, and somebody brought him a bowl of
beef stew with plenty of onion in it, and a mug of sour red
wine. When his horse was brought, he rode forward to the
line, noticing in passing that the Mobile Force Uncle Wolf
and the village priest of Dralm and priestess of Yirtta had set
up a field hospital in the common, and that pole-and-blanket
stretchers were being made. He hoped he wouldn't be

wounded. No anesthetics, here-and-now, though the priests of Galzar used sandbags.

A big cloud of smoke dirtied the sky over Systros. Silly buggers—first crowd in had fired it. Here-and-now mercenaries were just the same as Tilly's or Wallenstein's. Now the ones behind would have to bypass it, which would bring them to Fitra in even worse order.

The abatis was finished, and he cantered forward for a final look at it. He couldn't see a trace of any of the guns, and it looked, as he had wanted it to, like the sort of thing a lot of peasant home-guards would throw up. At each end, between the abatis itself and the short barricades of carts, was an opening big enough for cavalry to sortie out. The mounted infantry horse-lines were back of the side road, with the more poorly armed militia holding horses.

Away off, one of the Narza Gap bombards boomed; they were still holding out. Then he began to hear the distant, and then not-so-distant, pop of smallarms. Cavalry drifted up the road, some reloading pistols as they came. The shots grew louder; more cavalry, in more of a hurry, arrived. Finally, four of them topped the rise and came down the slope; the last one over the top turned in his saddle and fired a pistol behind him. A dozen Nostori cavalry appeared as they were splashing through the brook.

Immediately, a big 8-bore rifled musket bellowed from behind the abatis, and then another and another. His horse dance-stepped daintily. Across the hollow, a horse was down, kicking, another reared, riderless, and a third, also empty saddled, trotted down to the brook and stopped to drink. The mercenaries turned and galloped away out of sight into the dead ground beyond the rise. He was wondering where Harmakros had put the rest of the riflemen when a row of smoke-puffs blossomed along the edge of the bench above the stream on the left, and shots cracked like a string of firecrackers. There were yells from out of sight across the hollow, and musketoons thumped in reply. Wasting Styphon's good fireseed—at four hundred yards, they couldn't have hit Grant's Tomb with smoothbores.

He wished he had five hundred rifles up there. Hell, why not wish for twenty medium tanks and half a dozen Sabre-Jets, while he was at it?!

Then Klestreus' mercenary cavalry came up in a solid front on the brow of the hill—black and orange pennons and helmet-plumes and scarves, polished breastplates. Lancers all in front, musketoon-men behind. A shiver ran along the front as the lances came down.

As though that had been the signal, and it probably had been, six four-pounders and four eight-pounders went off together. It wasn't a noise, but a palpable blow on the ears. His horse started to buck; by the time he had him under control the smoke was billowing out over the hollow, and several perfect rings were floating up against the blue, and everybody behind the abatis was yelling, *"Down Styphon!"*

Roundshot; he could see where it had torn furrows back into the group of black and orange cavalry. Men were yelling, horses rearing, or down and screaming horribly, as only wounded horses can. The charge had stopped before it had started. On either side of him, gun-captains were shouting, "Grapeshot! Grapeshot!" and cannoneers were jumping to their pieces before they had stopped recoiling with double-headed swabs, one end wet to quench lingering powder-bag sparks and one end dry.

The cavalry charge slid forward in broken chunks, down the slope and into the hollow. When they were twenty yards short of the brook, four hundred arquebuses crashed. The whole front went down, horses behind falling over dropped horses in front. The arquebusiers who had fired stepped back, drawing the stoppers of their powder-flasks with their teeth. *Spring powder-flasks, self-measuring; get made and issued soonest.* He also added cartridge-paper to the paper memo.

When they were half reloaded, the other four hundred arquebuses crashed. The way those cavalry were jammed down there, it would take an individual miracle for any bullet to miss something. The smoke was clogging the hollow like spilled cotton now, but through it he could see another wave of cavalry coming up on the brow of the opposite hill. A four-pounder spewed grapeshot into them, then another and another, till the whole six had fired.

Gustavus Adolphus' four-pounder crews could load and fire faster than musketeers, the dry lecture-room voice was telling him. Of course, the muskets they'd been timed against had been matchlocks; that had made a big difference. Lord Kalvan's were doing almost as well: the first four-pounder had fired on the heels of the third arquebus volley. Then one of the eight-pounders fired, and that was a small miracle.

A surprising number of Klestreus' cavalry had survived the fall of their horses. Well, not so surprising; horses were bigger targets, and they didn't wear breastplates. Having nowhere else to go, the men were charging on foot, using their lances as pikes. A few among them had musketoons; they'd been in the rear. Quite a few were shot coming up, and more were piked trying to get through the abatis. A few did get through. As he galloped to help deal with one of these parties, he heard a trumpet sound on the left, and another on the right, and there was a clamor of *Down Styphon!* at both ends. That would be the cavalry going out; he hoped the artillery wouldn't get excited.

Then he was in front of a dozen unhorsed Nostori cavalrymen, pulling up his horse and aiming a pistol at them.

"Yield, comrades! We spare mercenaries!"

An undecided second and a half, then one of them lifted a reversed musketoon.

"We yield; oath to Galzar."

That, he thought, they would keep. Galzar didn't like oath-breaking soldiers; he let them get killed at the next opportunity. *Cult of Galzar; encourage.*

Some peasants ran up, brandishing axes and pitchforks. He waved them back with his pistol, letting them have a look at the muzzle.

"Keep your weapons," he told the mercenaries. "I'll find somebody to guard you."

He detailed a couple of Mobile Force arquebusiers; they

impressed some militia. Then he had to save a wounded
mercenary from having his throat cut. Dralm-damned civil-
ians! He'd have to detail prisoner-guards. Disarm these
mercenaries and the peasants'd cut their throats; leave them
armed, and the temptation might overcome the fear of Galzar.

Along the abatis, the firing had stopped, but the hollow
below was a perfect hell's bedlam—pistol shots, clashing
steel, *Down Styphon!* and, occasionally, *Gormoth!* Over his
shoulder he could see villagers, even women and children,
replacing militiamen on the horse-lines. Captains were
shouting, "Pikes forward!" and pikemen were dodging
among the branches to get through the abatis. Dimly, through
the smoke, he could see red and blue on horsemen at the brow
of the opposite hill. *Uniforms; do something about. Brown,
or dark green.*

The road had been left unobstructed, and he trotted
through and down toward the brook. What he saw in the
hollow made his stomach heave, and it didn't heave easily. It
was the horses that bothered him more than anything else,
and he wasn't the only one. The infantry, going forward,
were stopping to cut wounded horses' throats, or brain them,
or shoot them with pistols from saddle-holsters. They
shouldn't do that, they ought to keep on, but they couldn't
stand seeing horses suffer.

Stretcher-bearers were coming forward to, and villagers
to loot. Corpse-robbing was the only way the here-and-now
civil population had of getting a little of their own back after a
battle. Most of them had clubs or hatchets, to make sure that
what they were robbing really were corpses.

There were a lot of good weapons lying around. They
ought to be collected, before they rusted into uselessness, but
there was no time for that now. Stopping to do that, once, had
been one of Stonewall Jackson's few mistakes. Something
was being done toward that, though: he saw crossbows lying
around, and each one meant a militiaman who had armed
himself with an enemy cavalry musketoon.

The battle had passed on eastward; unopposed infantry

were forming up, blocks of pikemen with blocks of arquebusiers between, and men were running back to bring up horses. Away ahead, there was an uproar of battle; that would be the two hundred cavalry he had posted on the far right hitting another batch of Gormoth's mercenaries, who, by now, would be disordered by fugitives streaming back from the light at the hollow. The riflemen on the bench were drifting eastward, too, firing as they went.

And enemy cavalry were coming in in groups, holding their helmets up on their sword-points, calling out, "We yield, oath to Galzar." One of the officers of the flanking party, with four troopers, was coming in with close to a hundred of them, regretting that so many had gotten away. And all the infantry who had marched in from the Athan, and many of the local militia, had mounted themselves on captured horses.

There was a clatter behind him, and he got his horse off the road to let the four-pounders pass in column. Their captain waved to him and told him, laughing, that the eights would be along in a day or so.

"Where do we get some more shooting?" he asked.

"Down the road a piece; just follow along and we'll show you plenty to shoot at."

He slipped back the knit cuff under his mail sleeve and looked at his watch. It was still ten minutes to noon, Hostigos Standard Sundial Time.

TWELVE

I

BY 1730, they were down the road a really far piece, and there had been considerable shooting on the way. Now they were two miles west of the Athan, on the road to Marax Ford, and the Nostori wagons and cannon were strung out for half a mile each way. He was sitting, with his helmet off, on an upended wine keg at a table made by laying a shed-door across some boxes, with Harmakros' pyrographed deerskin map spread in front of him, and a mug where he could reach it. Beside the road, some burned out farm buildings were still smoking, and the big oaks which shaded him were yellowed on one side from heat. Several hundred prisoners squatted in the field beyond, eating rations from their own wagons.

Harmakros, and the commander of mounted infantry, Phrames—he'd be about two-star rank—and the brigadier-general commanding cavalry, and the Mobile Force Uncle Wolf—somewhat younger than the Tarr-Hostigos priest of Galzar and about chaplain major equivalent—sat or squatted around him. The messenger from Sevenhills Valley, who had just caught up with him, paced back and forth, trying to walk the stiffness out of his legs. He drank from a mug as he talked. He was about U.S. first lieutenant equivalent.

Titles of rank; regularize. This business of calling everybody from company commander up to Commander-in-chief a captain just wouldn't do. He'd made a start with that, on the upper echelons; he'd have to carry it down to field and company level. *Rank, insignia of; establish.* He thought he'd adopt the Confederate Army system—it was simpler, with no oak and maple leaves and no gold and silver distinctions. Then he pulled his attention back to what the messenger was saying.

"That's all we know. All morning, starting before mess call, there was firing up the river. Cannon-fire, and then smallarms, and, when the wind was right, we could hear shouting. About first morning drillbreak, some of our cavalry, who'd been working up the river along the mountains, came back and reported that Netzigon had crossed the river in front of Vryllos Gap, and they couldn't get through to Ptosphes and Princess Rylla."

He cursed, first in Zarthani and then in English. "Is she at Vryllos Gap too?"

Harmakros laughed. "You ought to know that girl by now, Kalvan; you're going to marry her. Just try and keep her out of battles."

That he would, by Dralm! With how much success, though, was something else.

The messenger, having taken time out for a deep drink, continued:

"Finally, a rider came in from this side of the mountain. He said that the Nostori were across and pushing Prince Ptosphes back into the gap. He wanted to know if the captain of Tarr-Dombra could send him help."

"Well?"

The messenger shrugged. "We only had two hundred regulars and two hundred and fifty militia, and it's ten miles to Vryllos along the river, and an even longer way around the mountains on the south side. So the captain left a few cripples and kitchen-women to hold the castle, and crossed the river at Dyssa. They were just starting when I left; I could hear cannon-fire as I was leaving Sevenhills Valley.''

"That was about the best thing he could do.''

Gormoth would have a couple of hundred men at Dyssa. Just a holding-force; they'd given up the idea of any offensive operations against Dombra Gap. If they could be run out and the town burned, it would start a scare that might take a lot of pressure off Ptosphes and Chartiphon both.

"Well, I hope nobody expects any help from us," Harmakros said. "Our horses are ridden into the ground; half our men are mounted on captured horses, and they're in worse shape than what we have left of our own.''

"Some of my infantrymen are riding two to a horse," Phrames said. "You can figure what kind of a march they'd make. They'd do almost as well on foot.''

"And it would be midnight before any of us could get to Vryllos Gap, and that would be less than a thousand.''

"Five hundred, I'd make it," the cavalry brigadier said. "We've been losing by attrition all the way east.''

"But I'd heard that your losses had been very light.''

"You heard? From whom?''

"Why, the men guarding prisoners. Great Galzar, Lord Kalvan, I never saw so many prisoners . . .''

"That's been our losses: prisoner-guard details. Every one of them is as much out of it as though he'd been shot through the head.''

But the army Klestreus had brought across the Athan had ceased to exist. Not improbably as many as five hundred had re=crossed at Marax Ford. Six hundred had broken out of Hostigos at Narza Gap. There would be several hundred more, singly and in small bands, dodging through the woods to the south; they'd have to be mopped up. The rest had all either been killed or captured.

First, there had been the helter-skelter chase east from Fitra. For instance, twenty riflemen, firing from behind rocks and trees, had turned back two hundred trying to get through at the next gap down. Mostly, anybody who was overtaken had simply pulled off his helmet or held up a reversed weapon and cried for quarter.

He'd only had to fight once, himself; he and two Mobile Force cavalrymen had caught up to ten fleeing mercenaries and shouted to them to yield. Maybe this crowd were tired of running, maybe they were insulted at the demand from so few, or maybe they'd just been bullheaded. Instead, they had turned and charged. He had half-dodged and half parried a lance and spitted the lancer in the throat, and then had been fighting two swordsmen, and good ones, when a dozen mounted had come up.

Then, they'd had a small battle a half-mile west of Systros. Fifteen hundred infantry and five hundred cavalry, all mercenaries, had just gotten onto the main road again after passing on both sides of the burning town when the Fitra fugitives came dashing into them. Their own cavalry were swept away, and the infantry were trying to pike off the fugitives, when mounted Hostigi infantry arrived, dismounted, gave them an arquebus volley, and then made a pike charge, and then a couple of four-pounders came up and began throwing case-shot, leather tubes full of pistol balls. The Fitra fugitives had never been exposed to case-shot before, and after about two hundred were casualties they began hoisting their helmets and invoking Galzar.

Galzar was being a big help today. Have to do something nice for him.

That had been where the mercenary general, Klestreus, had been captured. Phrames had taken his surrender; Kalvan and Harmakros had been too busy chasing fugitives. A lot of these had turned toward Narza Gap.

Hestophes, the Hostigi CO there, had been a real cool cat. He'd had two hundred and fifty men, two old bombards, and a few lighter pieces. Klestreus' infantry had attacked Nirfë Gap, the last one down, and, with the help of Netzigon's people from the other side, swamped it. A few survivors had managed to get away along the mountain top and brought him warning. An hour later, he was under attack from both sides, too.

He had beaten off three attacks, by a probable total of two thousand, and was bracing for a fourth when his lookouts on the mountain reported seeing the fugitives from Fitra and Systros streaming east. Immediately he had spiked his guns and pulled his men up the mountain. The besieging infantry on the south were swept through by fleeing cavalry, and they threw the Nostori on the other side into confusion. Hestophes spattered them generously with smallarms fire to discourage loitering and let them go to spread panic on the other side. By now, they would be spreading it in Nostor Town.

Then, just west of the river, they had run into the wagon train and artillery, inching along under ox-power, accompanied by a thousand of Gormoth's subject troops and another five hundred mercenary cavalry. This had been Systros over again, except it had been a massacre. The fugitive cavalry had tried to force a way past, the infantry had resisted them, the four-pounders—only five of them, now; one was off the road just below Systros with a broken axle—arrived and began firing case-shot, and then two eight-pounders showed up. Some of the mercenaries attempted to fight— when they later found the paychests in one of the wagons, they understood why—but the Nostori simply emptied their arquebuses and calivers and ran. Along with *Down Styphon!* the pursuers were shouting *Dralm and no Quarter!* He wondered what Xentos would think of that; Dralm wasn't supposed to be that kind of a god, at all.

"You know," he said, getting out his pipe and tobacco, "we didn't have a very big army to start with. What do we have now?"

"Five hundred, and four hundred along the river," Phrames said. "We lost about five hundred, killed and wounded. The rest are guarding prisoners all the way back to Fitra." He looked up at the sun. "Back almost to Hostigos Town, by now."

"Well, we can help Ptosphes and Chartiphon from here," he said. "That gang Hestophes let through Narza Gap will be in Nostor Town by now, panting their story out, and the way they'll tell it, it will be five times worse than it really was."

He looked at his watch. "By this time, Gormoth should be getting ready to fight the Battle of Nostor." He turned to Phrames. "You're in charge of this stuff here. How many men do you really need to guard it? Two hundred?"

Phrames looked up and down the road, and then at the prisoners, and then, out of the corner of his eye, at the boxes under the improvised table. They hadn't gotten around to weighing that silver yet, but there was too much of it to be careless with.

"I ought to have twice that many."

"The prisoners are mercenaries, and have agreed to take Prince Ptosphes' colors," the priest of Galzar said. "Of course, they may not bear arms against Prince Gormoth or any in his service until released from their oaths to him. In the sight of the Wargod, helping guard these wagons would be the same, for it would release men of yours to fight. But I will speak to them, and I will answer that they will not break their surrender. You will need some to keep the peasants from stealing, though."

"Two hundred," Phrames agreed. "We have some walking wounded who can help."

"All right. Take two hundred; men with the worst beat up horses and those men who are riding double, and mind the store. Harmakros, you take three hundred and two of the four-pounders, and cross at the next ford down. I'll take the other four hundred and three guns and work north and east. You might split into two columns, a hundred men and one gun, but no smaller. There'll be companies and parts of companies over there, trying to re-form. Break them up. And burn the whole country out—everything that'll catch fire and make a smoke by daylight or a blaze at night. Any refugees, head them up the river, give them a good scare and let them go. We want Gormoth to think we're across the river with three or four thousand men. By Dralm, that'll take some pressure off Ptosphes and Chartiphon!"

He rose, and Phrames took his seat. Horses were brought, and he and Harmakros mounted. The messenger from Sevenhills Valley sat down, stretching his legs in front of him. He rode slowly along the line of wagons, full of food the Nostori wouldn't eat this winter, and would curse Gormoth for it, and fireseed the Styphon temple-farm slaves would have to toil to replace. Then he came to the guns, and saw one that caught his eye. It was a long brass eighteen-pounder, on a two-wheel cart, with the long tail of the heavy timber stock supported by a four-wheel cart. There were two more behind it, and an officer with a ginger-brown beard sat morosely smoking a pipe on the limber-cart of the middle one. He pulled up.

"Your guns, Captain?"

"They were. They're Prince Ptosphes' guns now, I suppose."

"They're still yours, if you take our colors, and good pay for the use of them. We have other enemies besides Gormoth, you know."

The captain grinned. "So I've heard. Well, I'll take Ptosphes' colors. You're the Lord Kalvan? Is it true that you people make your own fireseed?"

"What do you think we were shooting at you, sawdust? You know what the Styphon stuff's like. Try ours and see the difference."

"Well, Down Styphon, then!"

They chatted for a little. The mercenary artilleryman's name was Alkides; his home, to the extent that any free-captain had one, was in Agrys City, on Manhattan Island. His guns, of which he was inordinately proud, and almost tearfully happy at being able to keep, had been cast in Zygros City. They were very good; if Verkan could collect a few men capable of casting guns like that, with trunnions . . .

"Well, go back there by that burned house, by those big trees. You'll find one of my officers, Count Phrames, and our Uncle Wolf, there. You'll find a keg of something, too. Where are your men?"

"Well, some were killed, before we cried quits. The rest are back with the other prisoners."

"Gather them up. Tell Count Phrames you're to have oxen—we have no horses to spare—and get your company and guns on the road for Hostigos Town as soon as you can. I'll talk to you later. Good luck, Captain Alkides.''

Or *Colonel* Alkides; if he was as good as he seemed to be, maybe Brigadier-General Alkides.   -

There were dead infantry all along the road, mostly killed from behind. Another case of cowardice carrying its own penalty; infantry who stood against cavalry had a chance, often a good one, but infantry who turned tail and ran had none. He didn't pity them a bit.

It grew progressively worse as he neared the river, where the crews of the four-pounders and the two eight-pounders were swabbing and polishing their pieces, and dark birds rose cawing and croaking and squawking when disturbed. Must be every crow and raven and buzzard in Hos-Harphax; he even saw eagles.

The river, horse-knee deep at the ford, was tricky; his mount continually stumbled on armor-weighted corpses. That had been case-shot, mostly, he thought.

THIRTEEN

I

"SO YOUR BOY did it, all by himself," the lady history professor was saying.

Verkan Vall grinned. They were in a seminar room at the University, their chairs facing a big map of Fourth Level Aryan-Transpacific Hostigos, Nostor, northeastern Sask and northern Beshta. The pin-points of light he had been shifting back and forth on it were out, now.

"Didn't I tell you he was a genius?"

"Just how much genius did it take to lick a bunch of klunks like that?" said Talgan Dreth, the outtime studies director. The way I heard it, they licked themselves."

"Well, considerable, to predict their errors accurately and plan to exploit them," argued old Professor Shalgro, the paratemporal probability theorist. To him, it was a brilliant theoretical achievement, and the battle was merely the experiment which had vindicated it. "I agree with Chief's Assistant Verkan; the man is a genius, and the fact that he was only able to become a minor police officer on his own time-line shows how these low-order cultures allow genius to go to waste.''

"He knew the military history of his own time-line, and he knew how to apply it on Aryan-Transpacific.'' The historian wasn't letting her own subject be slighted. "Actually, I think Gormoth planned an excellent campaign—against people like Ptosphes and Chartiphon. If it hadn't been for Kalvan, he'd have won.''

"Well, Chartiphon and Ptosphes fought a battle of their own and won it, didn't they?''

"More or less.'' He began punching buttons on the arm of his chair and throwing on red and blue lights. "Netzigon was supposed to wait here, at Listra-Mouth, till Klestreus got up to here. Chartiphon began cannonading him—ordnance engineering by Lord Kalvan—and Netzigon couldn't take it. He attacked prematurely.''

"Why didn't he just pull back? He had that river in front of him. Chartiphon couldn't have gotten his guns across that, could he?'' Talgan Dreth asked.

"Oh, that wouldn't have been honorable. Besides, he didn't want the mercenaries to win the war; he wanted the glory of winning it himself.''

The historian laughed. "How often I've heard *that*!'' she said. "But don't these Hostigi go in for all this honor and glory jazz too?''

"Sure—till Kalvan talked them out of it. As soon as he started making fireseed, he established a moral ascendancy. And then, the new tactics, the new swordplay, the artillery improvements; now it's 'Trust Lord Kalvan. Lord Kalvan is always right.' ''

"He'll have to work at that, now,'' Dreth said. "He won't dare make any mistakes. What happened to Netzigon?''

"He made three attempts to cross the river, which is a hundred yards wide, in the face of artillery superiority. That was how he lost most of his cavalry. Then he threw his infantry across here at Vryllos, pushed Ptosphes back into the gap, and started a flank attack up the south bank on Chartiphon. Ptosphes wouldn't stay pushed; he waited till Netzigon was between the river and the mountain, and then counter-attacked. Then Rylla took what cavalry they had across the river, burned Netzigon's camp, butchered some camp-followers, and started a panic in his rear. That was when everything came apart and the pieces began breaking up, and then the commander at Tarr-Dombra, there, took some of his men across, burned Dyssa, and started another panic.''

"It was too bad about Rylla," the lady historian said.

"Yes." He shrugged. "Things like that happen, in battles." That was why Dalla was always worried when she heard he'd been in one. "We had a couple of antigrav conveyers in, after dark. They had to stay up to twenty thousand feet, since we didn't want any heavenly portents on top of everything else, but they got some good infrared telephoto views. Big fires all over western Nostor, and around Dyssa, and more of them, the whole countryside, in the southwest—that was Kalvan and Harmakros. And a lot of hasty fortifying and entrenching around Nostor Town; Gormoth seems to think he's going to have to fight the next battle there.''

"Oh, that's ridiculous," Talgan Dreth said. "It'll be a couple of weeks before Kalvan has his army in shape for an offensive, after those battles. And how much powder do you think he has left?''

"Six or seven tons. That came in just before I came here, from our people in Hostigos Town. After he crossed the river last evening, Harmakros captured a big wagon train. A Styphon's House Archpriest, on his way to Nostor Town, with four tons of fireseed and seven thousand ounces of gold. Subsidies for Gormoth.''

"Now that's what's called making war support war," the history professor commented.

"And another ton or so in Klestreus' supply train, and the pay-chests for his army," he added. "Hostigos came out of this all right.''

"Wait till I get this all worked up," old Professor Shalgro was gloating. "Absolute proof of the decisive effect of one

superior individual on the course of history. Kalthar Morth
and his Historical Inevitability, and his vast, impersonal
social forces, indeed!''

"Well, what are we going to do, now?" Talgan Dreth
asked. "We have the study-team organized, the five men
who'll be the brass-founders, and the three girls who'll be the
patternmakers.''

"Well, we have horseback travel-time between Zygros
City and Hostigos Town to allow for. They've been
familiarizing on adjoining near-identical time-lines? Send
them all to Zygros City on the Kalvan time-line. I have a
couple of Paracops planted there already. Let them make
local contacts and call attention to themselves. Dalla and I
will do the same. Then we won't have to worry about some
traveler from Zygros showing up in Hostigos Town and
punching holes in our stories.''

"How about conveyer-heads?"

He shook his head. "You'll have to have your team
established in Hostigos Town before they can put one in
there. You have a time-line for operations on Fifth Level, of
course; work from there. You'll have to get onto Kalvan
Time-Line by an antigrav conveyer drop.''

"Horses and all?"

"Horses and all. That will be mounts for myself and Dalla,
for two Paracops who will pose as hired guards, and for your
team. Seventeen saddle-horses. And twelve pack horses,
with loads of Zygrosi and Grefftscharr wares. Lord Kalvan's
friend Verkan is a trader; traders have to have merchandise.''

Talgan Dreth whistled softly. "That'll mean at least two
hundred-foot conveyers. Where had you thought of landing
them?''

"Up here." He twisted the dial; the map slid down, until
he had the southern corner of the Princedom of Nyklos,
north and west of Hostigos. "About here," he said, making a
spot of light.

II

Gormoth of Nostor stood inside the doorway of his presence-chamber, his arm over the shoulder of the newly ennobled Duke Skranga, and together they surveyed the crowd within. Netzigon, who had come stumbling in after midnight with all his guns and half his army lost and the rest a frightened rabble. His cousin, Count Pheblon, his ransom still unpaid; he'd hoped Ptosphes wouldn't be alive to be paid by the moon's end. The nobles of the Elite Guard, who had attended him here at Tarr-Hostigos, waiting for news of victory until news of defeat had come in. Three of Klestreus' officers, who had broken through at Narza Gap to bring it, and a few more who had gotten over Marax Ford and back to Nostor alive. And Vyblos, the Highpriest, and with him the Archpriest Krastokles from Styphon's House Upon Earth, and his black-armored guard-captain, who had arrived at dawn with half a dozen troopers on broken-down horses.

He hated the sight of all of them, and the two priests most of all. He cut short their greetings.

"This is Duke Skranga," he told them. "Next to me, he is first nobleman of Nostor. He takes precedence over all here." The faces in front of his went slack with amazement, then stiffened angrily. A mutter of protest was hushed almost as soon as it began. "Do any object? Then it had better be one who's served me at least half as well as this man, and I see none such here." He turned to Vyblos. "What do you want, and who's this with you?"

"His Sanctity, the Archpriest Krastokles, sent by His Divinity, Styphon's Voice," Krastokles began furiously. "And how has he fared since entering your realm? Set upon by Hostigi heathens, hounded like a deer through the hills, his people murdered, his wagons pillaged . . ."

"His wagons, you say? Well, great Galzar, what of my gold and my fireseed, sent me by Styphon's Voice in his care, and look how he's cared for them, he and Styphon between them."

"You blaspheme!" Archpriest Krastokles cried. "And it was not your gold and fireseed, but the god's, to be given you in the god's service at my discretion."

"And lost at your indiscretion. You witless fool in a yellow bedgown, didn't you know a battle when you were riding into one?"

"Sacrilege!"

A dozen voices said it at once: Vyblos' and Krastokles', and, among others, Netzigon's. By the Mace of Galzar, now didn't he have a fine right to open his mouth here? Anger almost sickened him; in a moment he was afraid that he would vomit pure bile. He strode to Netzigon, snatching the golden chief-captain's chain from over his shoulder.

"All the gods curse you, and all the devils take you! I told you to wait at Listra-Mouth for Klestreus, not to throw your army away along with his. By Galzar, I ought to have you flayed alive!" He struck Netzigon across the face with the chain. "Out of my sight, while you're still alive!" Then he turned to Vyblos. "You, too—out of here, and take the Archpimp Krastokles with you. Go to your temple and stay there; return here either at my bidding or at your peril."

He watched them leave: Netzigon shaken, the black-armored captain stolidly, Vyblos and Krastokles stiff with rage. A few of Netzigon's officers and gentlemen attended him; the rest drew back from them as though from contamination. He went to Pheblon and threw the golden chain over his head.

"I still don't thank you for losing me Tarr-Dombra, but that's a handful of dried peas to what that son of a horse-leech's daughter cost me. Now, Galzar help you, you'll have to make an army out of what he left you."

"My ransom still needs paying," Pheblon reminded him. "Till that's done, I'm oath-bound to Prince Ptosphes and Lord Kalvan."

"So you are; twenty thousand ounces of silver for you and those taken with you. You know where to find it? I don't."

"I do, Prince," Duke Skranga said. "There's ten times that in the treasure-vault of the temple of Styphon."

III

Count Netzigon waited until he was outside to touch a handkerchief to his cheek. It was bleeding freely, and had dripped onto his doublet. Now by Styphon, the cleaning of that would cost Gormoth dear!

It wasn't his fault, anyhow. Great Styphon, was he to sit still while Chartiphon cannonaded him from across the river? And how had he known what sort of cannon Chartiphon had? The Hostigi really must be making fireseed; he hadn't believed that until yesterday. Three times he had sent his cavalry splashing into the river, and three times the guns had murdered them. He'd never seen guns throw small-shot so far. So then he'd sent his infantry over at Vryllos, and driven those with Prince Ptosphes back into the gap, and then, while he was driving against Chartiphon's right and the day had seemed won, Ptosphes had brought his beaten soldiers back, fighting like panthers, and that she-devil daughter of his— he'd heard, later, that she'd been killed. Styphon bless whoever did it!

Then everything had gone down in bloody ruin. Driven back across the river again, the Hostigi pouring after them, and then riders from Nostor Town with word that Klestreus' army was beaten in East Hostigos and orders to fall back, and they had retreated, with the whole country burning around them, fire and smoke at Dyssa and fugitives screaming that a thousand Hostigi were pouring out of Dombra Gap, and his worthless peasant levies throwing away their weapons and taking to their heels . . . .

Sorcery, that's what it was! That cursed foreign wizard, Kalvan!

Someone touched his arm. His hand flew to his poignard, and then he saw that it was the Archpriest's guard-captain. He relaxed.

"You were ill-used, Count Netzigon," the man in black armor said. "By Styphon, it ired me to see a brave soldier used like a thievish serf!"

"His Sanctity wasn't reverently treated, nor His Holiness Vyblos. It shocked me to hear such words to the consecrated of Styphon," he replied. "What good can come to a realm whose Prince so insults the anointed of the god?"

"Ah!" The captain smiled. "It's a pleasure, in such a court, to hear such piety. Now, Count Netzigon, if you could have a few words with His Sanctity—this evening, say, at the temple. Come after dark, cloaked and in commoner's dress."

FOURTEEN

I

KALVAN'S HORSE stumbled, jerking him awake. Behind him, fifty-odd riders clattered, many of them more or less wounded, none seriously. There had been a score on horse-litters, or barely able to cling to their mounts, but they had been left at the base hospital in Sevenhills Valley. He couldn't remember how long it had been since he had had his clothes, or even all his armor, off; except for quarter-hour pauses, now and then, he had been in the saddle since daylight, when he had recrossed the Athan with the smoke of southern Nostor behind him.

That had been as bad as Phil Sheridan in the Shenandoah, but every time some peasant's thatching blazed up, he knew it was burning another hole in Prince Gormoth's morale. He'd felt better about it, today, after following the mile-wide swath of devastation west from Marax Ford and seeing it stop, with dramatic suddenness, at Fitra.

And the story Harmakros' stragglers had told him: fifteen eight-horse wagons, four tons of fireseed, seven thousand ounces of gold—that would come to about $150,000—two

wagon-loads of armor, three hundred new calivers, six
hundred pistols, and all of a Styphon's House Archpriest's
personal baggage and vestments. He was sorry the Archpriest had gotten away; his execution would have been an
interesting feature of the victory celebration.

He had passed prisoners marching east, all mercenaries,
under arms and in good spirits, at least one pike or lance in
each detachment sporting a red and blue pennon. Most of
them shouted, "Down Styphon!" as he rode by. The back
road from Fitra to Sevenhills Valley hadn't been so bad, but
now, in what he had formerly known as Nittany Valley,
traffic had become heavy again. Militia from Listra-Mouth
and Vryllos, marching like regulars, which was what they
were, now. Trains of carts and farm-wagons, piled with
sacks and barrels or loaded with cabbages and potatoes, or
with furniture that must have come from manor-houses.
Droves of cattle, and droves of prisoners, not armed, not in
good spirits, and under heavy guard: Nostori subjects headed
for labor-camps and intensive Styphon-is-a-fake indoctrina-
tion. And guns, on four-wheel carts, that he couldn't remember from any Hostigi ordnance inventory.

Hostigos Town was in an all-time record traffic-jam. He
ran into Alkides, the mercenary artilleryman, with a strip of
blue cloth that seemed to have come from a bedspread and a
strip of red from the bottom of a petticoat. He was magnifi-
cently drunk.

"Lord Kalvan!" he shouted. "I saw your guns; they're
wonderful! What god taught you that? Can you mount mine
that way?"

"I think so. I'll have a talk with you about it tomorrow, if
I'm awake then."

Harmakros was on his horse in the middle of the square,
his rapier drawn, trying to untangle the chaos of wagons and
carts and riders. Kalvan shouted to him, above the din:

"What the Styphon—when did we start using three-star
generals for traffic-cops?"

*Military Police; organize soonest. Mercenaries, tough
ones.*

"Just till I get a detail here. I sent all my own crowd up with the wagons." He started to say something else, then stopped short and asked, "Did you hear about Rylla?"

"No, for Dralm's sake." He went cold under his scalding armor. "What about her?"

"Well, she was hurt—late yesterday, across the river. Her horse threw her; I only know what I got from one of Chartiphon's aides. She's at the castle."

"Thanks; I'll see you there later."

He swung his horse about and plowed into the crowd, drawing his sword and yelling for way. People crowded aside, and yelled his name to others beyond. Outside town, the road was choked with troops, and with things too big and slow to get out of the way; he rode mostly in the ditch. The wagons Harmakros had captured, great canvas-covered things like Conestogas, were going up to Tarr-Hostigos. He thought he'd never get past them: there always seemed to be more ahead. Finally he got through the outer gate and galloped across the bailey.

Throwing his reins to somebody at the foot of the keep steps, he stumbled up them and through the door. From the Staff Room, he heard laughing voices, Ptosphes' among them. For an instant he was horrified, then reassured; if Ptosphes could laugh, it couldn't be too bad.

He was mobbed as soon as he entered, everybody shouting his name and thumping him on the back; he was glad for his armor. Chartiphon, Ptosphes, Xentos, Uncle Wolf, most of the General Staff crowd. And a dozen officers he had never seen before, all wearing new red and blue scarves. Ptosphes was presenting a big man with a florid face and gray hair and beard.

"Kalvan, this is General Klestreus, late of Prince Gormoth's service, now of ours."

"And most happy at the change, Lord Kalvan," the mercenary said. "An honor to have been conquered by such a soldier."

"Our honor, General. You fought most brilliantly and valiantly." He'd fought like a damned imbecile, and gotten his army chopped to hamburger, but let's be polite. "I'm sorry I hadn't time to meet you earlier, but things were a trifle pressing." He turned to Ptosphes. "Rylla? What happened to her?"

"Why, she broke a leg," Ptosphes began.

That frightened him. People had died from broken legs in his own world when the medical art was at least equal to its here-and-now level. They used to amputate . . . .

"She's in no danger, Kalvan," Xentos assured him. "None of us would be here if she were. Brother Mytron is with her. If she's awake, she'll want to see you."

"I'll go to her at once." He clinked goblets with the mercenary and drank. It was winter-wine, aged quite a few winters, and evidently frozen down in a very cold one. It warmed and relaxed him. "To your good fortune in Hostigos, General. Your capture," he lied, "was Gormoth's heaviest loss, yesterday, and our greatest gain." He set down the goblet, took off his helmet and helmet-coif and detached his sword from his belt, then picked up the wine again and finished it. "If you'll excuse me, now, gentlemen. I'll see you all later."

Rylla, whom he had expected to find gasping her last, sat propped against a pile of pillows in bed, smoking one of her silver-inlaid redstone pipes. She was wrapped in a loose gown, and her left leg, extended, was buckled into a bulky encasement of leather—no plaster casts, here-and-now. Mytron, the chubby and cherubic physician-priest, was with her, and so were several of the women who functioned as midwives, hexes, herb-boilers and general nurses. Rylla saw him first, and her face lighted like a sunrise.

"Hi, Kalvan! Are you all right? When did you get in? How was the battle?"

"Rylla, darling!" The women sprayed away from in front of him like grasshoppers. She flung her arms around his neck as he bent over her; he thought Mytron stepped in to relieve her of her pipe. "What happened to you?"

"You stopped in the Staff Room," she told him, between kisses. "I smell it on you."

"How is she, Mytron?" he asked over his shoulder.

"Oh, a beautiful fracture, Lord Kalvan!" the doctor enthused. "One of the priests of Galzar set it; he did an excellent job . . ."

"Gave me a fine lump on the head, too," Rylla added. "Why, my horse fell on me. We were burning a Nostori village, and he stepped on a hot ember. He almost threw me, and then fell over something, and down we both went, the horse on top of me. I was carrying an extra pair of pistols in my boots and I fell on one of them. The horse broke a leg, too. They shot him. I guess they thought I was worth making an effort about . . . . Kalvan! Never hug a girl so tight when you're wearing mail sleeves!"

"It's nothing to worry about, Lord Kalvan," Mytron was saying. "Not the first time for this young lady, either. She broke an ankle when she was eight, trying to climb a cliff to rob a hawk's nest, and a shoulder when she was twelve, firing a musket-charge out of a carbine."

"And now," Rylla was saying, "it'll be a moon, at least, till we can have the wedding."

"We could have it right now, sweetheart . . ."

"I will not be married in my bedroom," she declared. "People make jokes about girls who have to do that. And I will not limp to the temple of Dralm on crutches."

"All right, Princess; it's your wedding." He hoped the war with Sask that everybody expected would be out of the way before she was able to ride again. He'd have a word with Mytron about that. "Somebody," he said, "go and have a hot bath brought to my rooms, and tell me when it's ready. I must stink to the very throne of Dralm."

"I was wondering when you were going to mention that, darling," Rylla said.

II

He did speak to Mytron, the next day, catching him between a visit to Rylla and his work at the main army hospital in Hostigos Town. Mytron thought, at first, that he was impatient for Rylla's full recovery and the wedding.

"Oh, Lord Kalvan, quite soon. You know, of course, that broken bones take time to knit, but our Rylla is young and young bones knit fast. Inside a moon, I'd say."

"Well, Mytron; you know we're going to have to fight Sarrask of Sask, now. When war with Sask comes, I'd be most happy if she were still in bed, with that thing on her leg. So would Prince Ptosphes."

"Yes. Our Rylla, shall we say, is a trifle heedless of her own safety." That was a generous five hundred percent understatement. Mytron put on his professional portentous frown. "You must understand, of course, that it is not good for any patient to be kept too long in bed. She should be able to get up and walk about as soon as possible. And wearing the splints is not pleasant."

He knew that. It wasn't any light plaster cast; it was a frame of heavily padded steel splints, forged from old sword-blades, buckled on with a case of saddle leather. It weighed about ten pounds, and it would be even more confining and hotter than his armor. But the next thing she broke might be her neck, or she might stop a two-ounce musket ball, and then his luck would run out along with hers. His mind shied like a frightened horse from the thought of no more happy, lovely Rylla.

"I'll do my best, Lord Kalvan, but I can't keep her in bed forever."

War with Sask wouldn't wait that long, either. Xentos was in contact with the priests of Dralm in Sask Town; they reported that the news of Fitra and Listra-Mouth had stunned Sarrask's court briefly, then thrown Sarrask into a furor of activity. More mercenaries were being hired, and some sort of negotiations, the exact nature undetermined, were going on between Sarrask and Balthar of Beshta. A Styphon Archpriest, one Zothnes, had arrived in Sask Town, with a train of wagons as big as the one taken by Harmakros in southern Nostor.

A priest of Galzar arrived at Tarr-Hostigos from Nostor

Town with an escort and a thousand ounces of gold—gold and silver seemed to be on a twenty-to-one ratio, here-and-now—to pay the ransoms of Count Pheblon and the other gentlemen taken at Tarr-Dombra. The news was that Pheblon was now Gormoth's chief-captain and was trying to reorganize what was left of the Nostori army. Gormoth would be back in the ring for another bout in the spring; that meant that Sarrask must be dealt with this fall.

He was having his own reorganization problems. They'd taken heavier losses than he'd liked, mostly the poorly armed and partly trained militia who'd fought at Listra-Mouth. On the other hand, they'd acquired over a thousand mercenary infantry and better than two thousand cavalry. They were a headache; they'd have to be integrated into the army of Hostigos. He didn't want any mercenary troops at all. Mercenary soldiers, as individual soldiers, were as good as any; in fact, any regular army man was simply a mercenary in the service of his own country. But mercenary troops, as troops, weren't good at all. They didn't fight for the Prince who hired them; they fought for their own captains, who paid them from what the Prince had paid him. *Mercenary captains,* he could hear his history professor quoting Machiavelli, *are either very capable men or not. If they are, you cannot rely upon them, for they will always aspire to their own greatness, either by oppressing you, their master, or by oppressing others against your intentions; but if the captain is not an able man, he will generally ruin you.* Most of the captains captured in East Hostigos seemed to be quite able.

Klestreus was one exception. As a battle commander, he was an incompetent—Fitra had proven that. He wasn't a soldier at all; he was a military businessman. He could handle sales, promotion and public relations, but not management and operations. That was how he'd gotten elected captain-general in Nostor. But he did have a wide knowledge of political situations, knew most of the Princes of Hos-Harphax, and knew the composition and command of all the mercenary outfits in the Five Kingdoms. So Kalvan appointed him Chief of Intelligence, where he could really be of

use, and wouldn't be able to lead troops in combat. He was
quite honored and flattered.

Nothing could be done about breaking up the mercenary
cavalry companies, numbering over two thousand men. The
mercenary infantry, however, were broken up, and put into
militia companies, one mercenary to three militiamen. This
almost started a mutiny, until he convinced them that they
were being given posts of responsibility and the rank of
private first class, with badges. The sergeants were all collected into a quickie OCS company, to emerge second
lieutenants.

Alkides, the artilleryman, was made captain of Tarr-
Esdreth-of-Hostigos, and sent there with his three long brass
eighteens, now fitted with trunnions on welded-on iron bands
and mounted on proper field-carriages. Tarr-Esdreth-of-
Hostigos was a sensitive spot. The Sask-Hostigos border
followed the east branch of the Juniata, the Besh, and ran
through Esdreth gap. Two castles dominated the gap, one on
either side; until one or the other could be taken, the gap
would be closed both to Hostigos and Sask.

Ten days after Fitra and Listra-Mouth, an unattached
mercenary, wearing the white and black colors of unemployment, put in an appearance at Tarr-Hostigos. There
were many such; they were equivalent to the bravos of
Renaissance Italy. This one produced letters of credence,
which Xentos found authentic, from Prince Armanes of
Nyklos. His client, he said, wanted to buy fireseed, but
wished to do so secretly; he was not ready for an open break
with Styphon's House. When asked if he would trade cavalry
and artillery horses, the unofficial emissary instantly agreed.

Well, that was a beginning.

FIFTEEN

I

SESKLOS RESTED his elbows on the table and palmed his smarting eyes. Around him, pens scratched on parchment and tablets clattered. He longed for the cool quiet and privacy of the Innermost Circle, but there was so much to do, and he must order the doing of all of it himself.

There were frantic letters from everywhere; the one before him was from the Archpriest of the Great Temple of Hos-Agrys. News of Gormoth's defeat was spreading rapidly, and with it rumors that Prince Ptosphes, who had defeated him, was making his own fireseed. Agents-inquisitory were reporting that the ingredients, and even the proportions, were being bandied about in taverns; it would take an army of assassins to deal with everybody who seemed to know them. Even a pestilence couldn't wipe out everybody who knew at least some of the secret. Oddly, it was even better known in far northern Zygros City than elsewhere. And they all wanted him to tell them how to check the spread of such knowledge.

Curse and blast them! Did they have to ask him about anything? Couldn't any of them think for themselves?

143

He opened his eyes. Why, admit it; better that than try to deny what would soon be proven everywhere. Let everyone in Styphon's House, even the lay Guardsmen, know the full secret, but for those outside, and for the few believers within, insist that special rites and prayers, known only to the yellow-robes of the Inner Circle, were essential.

But why? Soon it would be known that fireseed made by unconsecrated hands would fire just as well, and, to judge from Prince Ptosphes' sample, with more force and less fouling.

Well, there were devils, malignant spirits of the nether-world; everybody knew that. He smiled, imagining them thronging about—scrawny bodies, bat-wings, bristling beards, clawed and fanged. In fireseed, there were many— they made it explode—and only the prayers of anointed priests of Styphon could slay them. If fireseed were made without the aid of Styphon, the devils would be set free as soon as the fireseed burned, to work manifold evils and frights in the world of men. And, of course, the curse of Styphon was upon any who presumed profanely to make fireseed.

But Ptosphes had made fireseed, and he had pillaged a temple-farm, and put consecrated priests cruelly to death, and then he had defeated the army of Gormoth, which had marched under Styphon's blessing. How about that?

But wait! Gormoth himself was no better than Ptosphes. He too had made fireseed—both Krastokles and Vyblos were positive of that. And Gormoth had blasphemed Styphon and despitefully used a holy Archpriest, and forced a hundred thousand ounces of silver out of the Nostor temple, at as close to pistol-point as made no difference. To be sure, most of that had happened after the day of battle, but outside Nostor who knew that? Gormoth, he decided, had suffered defeat for his sins.

He was smiling happily now, wondering why he hadn't thought of that before. And what was known in Nostor would matter little more than what was known in Hostigos before long. Both would have to be destroyed utterly.

He wondered how many more Princedoms he would have to doom to fire and sword. Not too many—a few sharp examples at the start ought to be enough. Maybe just Hostigos and Nostor, and Sarrask of Sask and Balthar of Beshta could attend to both. An idea began to seep up in his mind, and he smiled.

Balthar's brother, Balthames, wanted to be a Prince, himself; it would take only a poisoned cup or a hired dagger to make him Prince of Beshta, and Balthar knew it. He should have had Balthames killed long ago. Well, suppose Sarrask gave up a little corner of Sask, and Balthar gave up a similar piece of Beshta, adjoining and both bordering on western Hostigos, to form a new Princedom; call it Sashta. Then, to that could be added all western Hostigos south of the mountains; why, that would be a nice little Princedom for any young couple. He smiled benevolently. And the father of the bride and the brother of the groom could compensate themselves for their generosity, respectively, with the Listra Valley, rich in iron, and East Hostigos, manured with the blood of Gormoth's mercenaries.

This must be done immediately, before winter put an end to campaigning. Then, in the spring, Sarrask, Balthar and Balthames could hurl their combined strength against Nostor.

And something would have to be done about fireseed making in the meantime. The revelation about the devils would have to be made public everywhere. And call a Great Council of Archpriests, here at Balph—no, at Harphax City: let Great King Kaiphranos bear the costs—to consider how they might best meet the threat of profane fireseed making, and to plan for the future. It could be, he thought hopefully, that Styphon's House might yet survive.

II

Verkan Vall watched Dalla pack tobacco into a little cane-stemmed pipe. Dalla preferred cigarettes, but on Aryan-Transpacific they didn't exist. No paper; it was a

wonder Kalvan wasn't trying to do something about that.
Behind them, something thumped heavily; voices echoed
in the barnlike pre-fab shed. Everything here was
temporary—until a conveyor-head could be established at
Hostigos Town, nobody knew where anything should go at
Fifth Level Hostigos Equivalent.

Talgan Dreth, sitting on the edge of a packing case with a
clipboard on his knee, looked up, then saw what Dalla was
doing and watched as she got out her tinderbox, struck
sparks, blew the tinder aflame, lit a pine splinter, and was
puffing smoke, all in fifteen seconds.

"Been doing that all your life," he grinned.

"Why, of course," Dalla deadpanned. "Only savages
have to rub sticks together, and only sorcerers can make fire
without flint and steel."

"You checked the pack-loads, Vall?" he asked.

"Yes. Everything perfectly in order, all Kalvan time-line
stuff. I liked that touch of the deer and bear skins. We'd have
to shoot for the pot, on the way south, and no trader would
throw away saleable skins."

Talgan Dreth almost managed not to show how pleased he
was. No matter how many outtime operations he'd run, a
back-pat from the Paratime Police still felt good.

"Well, then we make the drop tonight," he said. "I had
a reconnaissance-crew checking it on some adjoining time-
lines, and we gave it a looking over on the target time-line
last night. You'll go in about fifteen miles east of the
Hostigos-Nyklos road."

"That's all right. They're hauling powder to Nyklos and
bringing back horses. That road's being patrolled by Harmakros' cavalry. We make camp fifteen miles off the road
and start around sunrise tomorrow; we ought to run into a
Hostigi patrol before noon."

"Well, you're not going to get into any more battles, are
you?" Dalla asked.

"There won't be any more battles," Talgan Dreth told
her. "Kalvan won the war while Vall was away."

"He won a war. How long it'll stay won I don't know, and

neither does he. But *the* war won't be over till he's destroyed Styphon's House. That is going to take a little doing.''

"He's destroyed it already," Talgan Dreth said. "He destroyed it by proving that anybody can make fireseed. Why, it was doomed from the start. It was founded on a secret, and no secret can be kept forever.''

"Not even the Paratime Secret?" Dalla asked innocently.

"Oh, Dalla!" the University man cried. "You know that's different. You can't compare that with a trick like mixing saltpeter and charcoal and sulfur.''

III

The late morning sun baked the open horsemarket; heat and dust and dazzle, and flies at which the horses switched constantly. It was hot for so late in the year; as nearly as Kalvan could estimate it from the way the leaves were coloring, it would be mid-October. They had two calendars here-and-now—lunar, for daily reckoning, and solar, to keep track of the seasons—and they never matched. *Calendar reform; do something about.* He seemed to recall having made that mental memo before.

And he was sweat-sticky under his armor, forty pounds of it—quilted arming-doublet with mail sleeves and skirt, quilted helmet-coif with mail throat-guard, plate cuirass, plate tassets down his thighs into his jackboots, high combed helmet, rapier and poignard. It wasn't the weight—he'd carried more, and less well distributed, as a combat infantryman in Korea—but he questioned if anyone ever became inured to the heat and lack of body ventilation. *Like a rich armor worn in heat of day, That scalds with safety*—if Shakespeare had never worn it himself except on the stage, he'd known plenty of men who had, like that little Welsh pepperpot Williams, who was the original of Fluellen.

"Not a bad one in the lot!" Harmakros, riding beside him, was enthusing. "And a dozen big ones that'll do for gun-horses.''

And fifty-odd cavalry horses; that meant, at second or

third hand, that many more infantrymen who could get into line when and where needed, in heavier armor. And another lot coming in tonight; he wondered where Prince Armanes was getting all the horses he was trading for bootleg fireseed. He turned in his saddle to say something about it to Harmakros.

As he did, something hit him a clanging blow on the breastplate, knocking him almost breathless and nearly unhorsing him. He thought he heard the shot; he did hear the second, while he was clinging to his seat and clawing a pistol from his saddlebow. Across the alley, he could see two puffs of smoke drifting from back upstairs windows of one of a row of lodginghouse-wineshop-brothels. Harmakros was yelling; so was everybody else. There was a kicking, neighing confusion among the horses. His chest aching, he lifted the pistol and fired into one of the windows. Harmakros was firing, too, and behind him an arquebus roared. Hoping he didn't have another broken rib, he holstered the pistol and drew its mate.

"Come on!" he yelled. "And Dralm-dammit, take them alive! We want them for questioning."

Torture. He hated that, had hated even the relatively mild third-degree methods of his own world, but when you need the truth about something, you get it, no matter how. Men were throwing poles out of the corral gate; he sailed past them, put his horse over the fence across the alley, and landed in the littered back yard beyond. Harmakros took the fence behind him, with a Mobile Force arquebusier and a couple of horse-wranglers with clubs following on foot.

He decided to stay in the saddle; till he saw how much damage the bullet had done, he wasn't sure how much good he'd be on foot. Harmakros flung himself from his horse, shoved a half-clad slattern out of the way, drew his sword, and went through the back door into the house, the others behind him. Men were yelling, women screaming; there was commotion everywhere except behind the two windows from which the shots had come. A girl was bleating that Lord Kalvan had been murdered. Looking right at him, too.

He squeezed his horse between houses to the street, where a mob was forming. Most of them were pushing through the front door and into the house; from within came yells, screams, and sounds of breakage. Hostigos Town would be the better for one dive less if they kept at that.

Up the street, another mob was coagulating; he heard savage shouts of "Kill! Kill!" Cursing, he holstered the pistol and drew his rapier, knocking a man down as he spurred forward, shouting his own name and demanding way. The horse was brave and willing, but untrained for riot work; he wished he had a State Police horse under him, and a yard of locust riot-stick instead of this sword. Then the combination provost-marshal and police chief of Hostigos Town arrived, with a dozen of his men laying about them with arquebus-butts. Together they rescued two men, bloodied, half-conscious and almost ripped naked. The mob fell back, still yelling for blood.

He had time, now, to check on himself. There was a glancing dent on the right side of his breastplate, and a lead-splash, but the plate was unbroken. *That scalds with safety*—Shakespeare could say that again. Good thing it hadn't been one of those great armor-smashing brutes of 8-bore muskets. He drew the empty pistol and started to reload it, and then he saw Harmakros approaching on foot, his rapier drawn and accompanied by a couple of soldiers, herding a pot-bellied, stubble-chinned man in a dirty shirt, a blowsy woman with "madam" stamped all over her, and two girls in sleazy finery.

"That's them! That's them!" the man began, as they came up, and the woman was saying, "Dralm smite me dead, I don't know nothing about it!"

"Take these two to Tarr-Hostigos," Kalvan directed the provost-marshal. "They are to be questioned rigorously." Euphemistic police-ese; another universal constant. "This lot, too. Get their statements, but don't harm them unless you catch them trying to lie to you."

"You'd better go to Tarr-Hostigos, yourself, and let My-tron look at that," Harmakros told him.

"I think it's only a bruise; plate isn't broken. If it's another broken rib, my back-and-breast'll hold it for awhile. First we go to the temple of Dralm and give thanks for my escape. Temple of Galzar, too." He'd been building a reputation for piety since the night of his appearance, when he'd bowed down to those three graven images in the peasant's cottage; not doing that would be out of character, now. "And we go slowly, and roundabout. Let as many people see me as possible. We don't want it all over Hostigos that I've been killed."

SIXTEEN

I

AS A CHILD, he had heard his righteous Ulster Scots father speak scornfully of smoke-filled-room politics and boudoir diplomacy. The Rev. Alexander Morrison should have seen this—it was both, and for good measure, two real idolatrous heathen priests were sitting in on it. They were in Rylla's bedroom because it was easier for the rest of Prince Ptosphes' Privy Council to gather there than to carry her elsewhere, they were all smoking, and because the October nights were as chilly as the days were hot, the windows were all closed.

Rylla's usually laughing eyes were clouded with anxiety. "They could have killed you, Kalvan." She'd said that before. She was quite right, too. He shrugged.

"A splash on my breastplate, and a big black-and-blue place on me. The other shot killed a horse; I'm really provoked about that."

"Well, what's being done with them?" she demanded.

"They were questioned," her father said distastefully. He didn't like using torture, either. "They confessed. Guardsmen of the Temple—that's to say, kept cutthroats of

151

Styphon's House—sent from Sask Town by Archpriest Zothnes, with Prince Sarrask's knowledge. They told us there's a price of five hundred ounces gold on Kalvan's head, and as much on mine. Tomorrow,'' he added, ''they will be beheaded in the town square.''

''Then it's war with Sask.'' She looked down at the saddler's masterpiece on her leg. ''I hope I'm out of this before it starts.''

Not between him and Mytron she wouldn't; Kalvan set his mind at rest on that.

''War with Sask means war with Beshta,'' Chartiphon said sourly. ''And together they outnumber us five to two.''

''Then don't fight them together,'' Harmakros said. ''We can smash either of them alone. Let's do that, Sask first.''

''Must we always fight?'' Xentos implored. ''Can we never have peace?''

Xentos was a priest of Dralm, and Dralm was a god of peace, and in his secular capacity as Chancellor Xentos regarded war as an evidence of bad statesmanship. Maybe so, but statesmanship was operating on credit, and sooner or later your credit ran out and you had to pay off in hard money or get sold out.

Ptosphes saw it that way, too. ''Not with neighbors like Sarrask of Sask and Balthar of Beshta we can't,'' he told Xentos. ''And we'll have Gormoth of Nostor to fight again in the Spring, you know that. If we haven't knocked Sask and Beshta out by then, it'll be the end of us.''

The other heathen priest, alias Uncle Wolf, concurred. As usual, he had put his wolfskin vestments aside; and as usual, he was nursing a goblet, and playing with one of the kittens who made Rylla's room their headquarters.

''You have three enemies,'' he said. *You,* not *we;* priests of Galzar advised, but they never took sides. ''Alone, you can destroy each of them; together, they will destroy you.''

And after they had beaten all three, what then? Hostigos was too small to stand alone. Hostigos, dominating Sask and Beshta, with Nostor beaten and Nyklos allied, could, but then there would be Great King Kaiphranos, and back of him, back of everything, Styphon's House.

So it would have to be an empire. He'd reached that conclusion long ago.

Klestreus cleared his throat. "If we fight Balthar first, Sarrask of Sask will hold to his alliance and deem it an attack on him," he pronounced. "He wants war with Hostigos anyhow. But if we attack Sask, Balthar will vacillate, and take counsel of his doubts and fears, and consult his sooth-sayers, whom we are bribing, and do nothing until it is too late. I know them both." He drained his goblet, refilled it, and continued:

"Balthar of Beshta is the most cowardly, and the most miserly, and the most suspicious, and the most treacherous Prince in the world. I served him, once, and Galzar keep me from another like service. He goes about in an old black gown that wouldn't make a good dustclout, all hung over with wizards' amulets. His palace looks like a pawnshop, and you can't go three lance-lengths anywhere in it without having to shove some impudent charlatan of a soothsayer out of your way. He sees murderers in every shadow, and a plot against him whenever three gentlemen stop to give each other good day."

He drank some more, as though to wash the taste out of his mouth.

"And Sarrask of Sask's a vanity-swollen fool who thinks with his fists and his belly. By Galzar, I've known Great Kings who hadn't half his arrogance. He's in debt to Styphon's House beyond belief, and the money all gone for pageants and feasts and silvered armor for his guards and jewels for his light-o'-loves, and the only way he can get quittance is by conquering Hostigos for them."

"And his daughter's marrying Balthar's brother," Rylla added. "They're both getting what they deserve. The Prin-cess Amnita likes cavalry troopers, and Duke Balthames likes boys."

And he, and all of them, knew what was back of that

marriage—this new Princedom of Sashta that there was talk of, to be the springboard for conquest and partition of Hostigos, and when that was out of the way, a concerted attack on Nostor. Since Gormoth had started making his own fireseed, Styphon's House wanted him destroyed, too.

It all came back to Styphon's House.

"If we smash Sask now, and take over some of these mercenaries Sarrask's been hiring on Styphon's expense-account, we might frighten Balthar into good behavior without having to fight him." He didn't really believe that, but Xentos brightened a little.

Ptosphes puffed thoughtfully at his pipe. "If we could get our hands on young Balthames," he said, "we could depose Balthar and put Balthames on the throne. I think we could control him."

Xentos was delighted. He realized that they'd have to fight Sask, but this looked like a bloodless—well, almost—way of conquering Beshta.

"Balthames would be willing," he said eagerly. "We could make a secret compact with him, and loan him, say, two thousand mercenaries, and all the Beshtan army and all the better nobles would join him."

"No, Xentos. We do not want to help Balthames take his brother's throne," Kalvan said. "We want to depose Balthar ourselves, and then make Balthames do homage to Ptosphes for it. And if we beat Sarrask badly enough, we might depose him and make him do homage for Sask."

That was something Xentos seemed not to have thought of. Before he could speak, Ptosphes was saying, decisively:

"Whatever we do, we fight Sarrask now; beat him before that old throttlepurse of a Balthar can send him aid."

Ptosphes, too, wanted war now, before Rylla could mount a horse again. Kalvan wondered how many decisions of state, back through the history he had studied, had been made for reasons like that.

"I'll make sure of that," Chartiphon promised. "He won't send any troops up the Besh."

That was why Hostigos now had two armies: the Army of

the Listra, which would make the main attack on Sask, and the Army of the Besh, commanded by Chartiphon in person, to drive through southern Sask and hold the Beshtan border.

"How about Tarr-Esdreth?" Harmakros asked.

"You mean Tarr-Esdreth-of-Sask? Alkides can probably shoot rings around anybody they have there. Chartiphon can send a small force to hold the lower end of the gap, and you can do the same from the Listra side."

"Well, how soon can we get started?" Chartiphon wanted to know. "How much sending back and forth will there have to be, first?"

Uncle Wolf put down his goblet, and then lifted the kitten from his lap and set her on the floor. She mewed softly, looked around, and then ran over to the bed and jumped up with her mother and brothers and sisters who were keeping Rylla company.

"Well, strictly speaking," he said, "you're at peace with Prince Sarrask, now. You can't attack him until you've sent him letters of defiance, setting forth your causes of enmity."

Galzar didn't approve of undeclared wars, it seemed. Harmakros laughed.

"Now, what would they be, I wonder?" he asked. "Send them Kalvan's breastplate."

"That's a just reason," Uncle Wolf nodded. "You have many others. I will carry the letter myself." Among other things, priests of Galzar acted as heralds. "Put it in the form of a set of demands, to be met on pain of instant war—that would be the quickest way."

"Insulting demands," Klestreus specified.

"Well, give me a slate and a soapstone, somebody," Rylla said. "Let's see how we're going to insult him."

"A letter to Balthar, too," Xentos said thoughtfully. "Not of defiance, but of friendly warning against the plots and treacheries of Sarrask and Balthames. They're scheming to involve him in war with Hostigos, let him bear the brunt of it, and then fall on him and divide his Princedom between them. He'll believe that—it's what he'd do in their place."

"Your job, Klestreus," Kalvan said. A diplomatic as-

signment would be just right for him, and would keep him
from combat command without hurting his feelings. "Leave
with it for Beshta Town tomorrow. You know what Balthar
will believe and what he won't; use your own judgment."

"We'll get the letters written tonight," Ptosphes said. "In
the morning, we'll hold a meeting of the Full Council of
Hostigos. The nobles and people should have a voice in the
decision for war."

As though the decision hadn't been made already, here in
Princess Rylla's smoke-filled boudoir. Real democracy, this
was. Just like Pennsylvania.

II

The Full Council of Hostigos met in a long room, with
tapestries on one wall and windows opening onto the inner
citadel garden on the other. The speaker for the peasants, a
work-gnarled graybeard named Phosg, sat at the foot of the
table, flanked by the speaker for the shepherds and herdsmen
on one side, and for the woodcutters and charcoal burners on
the other. They graded up from there, through the artisans,
the master-craftsmen, the merchants, the yeomen farmers,
the professions, the priests, the landholding gentry and nobility, to Prince Ptosphes, at the head of the table, in a magnificent fur robe, with a heavy gold chain on his shoulders. He
was flanked, on the left, by the Lord Kalvan, in a no less
magnificent robe and an only slightly less impressive gold
chain. The place on his right was vacant, and everybody was
looking at it.

It had been talked about—Kalvan and Xentos and Chartiphon and Harmakros had seen to that—that the Princess
Rylla would, because of her injury, be unable to attend. So,
when the double doors were swung open at the last moment
and six soldiers entered carrying Rylla propped up on a
couch, there were exclamations of happiness and a general
ovation. Rylla was really loved in Hostigos.

She waved her hand in greeting and replied to them, and
the couch was set down at Ptosphes' right. Ptosphes waited

until the clamor had subsided, then drew his poignard and rapped on the table with the pommel.

"You all know why we're here," he began without preamble. "The last time we met, it was to decide whether to have our throats cut like sheep or die fighting like men. Well, we didn't have to do either. Now, the question is, shall we fight Sarrask of Sask now, at our advantage, or wait and fight Sarrask and Balthar together at theirs? Let me hear what is in your minds about it."

It was like a council of war; junior rank first. Phosg was low man on the totem-pole. He got to his feet.

"Well, Lord Prince, it's like I said the last time. If we have to fight, let's fight."

"Different pack of wolves, that's all," the shepherds' and herdsmen's speaker added. "We'll have another wolf-hunt like Fitra and Listra-Mouth."

It went up the table like that. The speaker for the lawyers, naturally, wanted to know if they were really sure Prince Sarrask was going to attack. Somebody asked him why not wait and have his throat cut, his house burned and his daughters raped, so that he could really be sure. The priestess of Yirtta abstained; a servant of the Allmother could not vote for the shedding of the blood of mothers' sons. Uncle Wolf just laughed. Then it got up among the nobility.

"Well, who wants this war with Sask?" one of them demanded. "That is, besides this outlander who has grown so great in so short a time among us, this Lord Kalvan."

He leaned right a little to look. Yes, Sthentros. He was some kind of an in-law of Ptosphes . . . had a barony over about where Boalsburg ought to be. He'd made trouble when the fireseed mills were being started—refused to let his peasants be put to work collecting saltpeter. Kalvan had threatened to have his head off, and Sthentros had run sputtering to Ptosphes. The interview had been private, nobody knew exactly what Ptosphes had told him, but he had emerged from it visibly shaken. The peasants had gone to work collecting saltpeter.

"Just who is this Kalvan?" Sthentros persisted. "Why,

until five moons ago, nobody in Hostigos had even heard of him!''

A couple of other nobles, including one who had just sworn to wade to his boottops in Saski blood, muttered agreement. Another, who had fought at Fitra, said:

"Well, nobody'd ever heard of *you* in Hostigos, either, till your uncle's wife's sister married our Prince.''

Uncle Wolf laughed again. "They've heard of Kalvan since, and in Nostor, too, by the Wargod's Mace!''

"Yes,'' another noble said, "I grant that. But you'll have to grant that the man's an outlander, and it's a fine thing indeed to see him rise so swiftly over the heads of nobles of old Hostigi family. Why, when he came among us, he couldn't speak a word that anybody could understand.''

"By Dralm, we understand him well enough now!'' That was another newcomer to the Full Council—the speaker for the fireseed makers. There were murmurs of agreement; quite a few got the point.

Sthentros refused to be silenced. "How do we know that he isn't some runaway priest of Styphon himself?''

Mytron, present as speaker for the physicians, surgeons and apothecaries, rose.

"When Kalvan came among us, I tended his wounds. He is not circumcised, as all priests of Styphon are.''

Then he sat down. That knocked that on the head. It was a good thing the Rev. Morrison had refused to let the doctor load the bill with what he'd considered non-essentials, when his son had been born. He'd never say another word against Scotch-Irish frugality. Sthentros, however, was staying with it.

"Well, maybe that's worse,'' he argued. "It's flatly against nature for anything to act like fireseed. I think there are devils in it, that make it explode, and maybe the priests of Styphon do something to keep the devils from getting out when it explodes . . . something that we don't know anything about.''

The speaker for the fireseed makers was on his feet.

"I make the stuff; I know what goes in it. Saltpeter and
sulfur and charcoal, and there aren't any devils in any of
them." He didn't know anything about oxidization, but he
knew that the saltpeter made the rest of it burn fast. "Next
thing, he'll be telling us there are devils in wine, or in dough
to make the bread rise, or in . . ."

"Has anybody heard of any devils around Fitra?" somebody else asked. "We burned plenty of fireseed there."

"What in Galzar's name does Sthentros know about
Fitra?—he wasn't there!"

"I'm going to have a little talk with that fellow, after this
is over," Ptosphes said quietly to Kalvan. "All he is in
Hostigos, he is by my favor, and my favor to him is getting
frayed now."

"Well, devils or not, the question is Lord Kalvan's place
among us," the noble who had sided with Sthentros
said. "He is no Hostigi—what right has he to sit at the
Council table?"

"Fitra!" somebody cried, from a place or two above
Sthentros; "Tarr-Dombra!" added another voice, from
across the table.

"He sits here," Rylla said icily, "as my betrothed hus-
band, by my choice. Do you question that, Euklestes?"

"He sits here as heir-matrimonial to the throne of Hostigos, and as my son-adoptive," Ptosphes added. "I hope
none of you presume to question that."

"He sits here as commander of our army," Chartiphon
roared, "and as a soldier I am proud to obey. If you want to
question that, do it with your sword against mine!"

"He sits here as one sent by Dralm. Do you question the
Great God?" Xentos asked.

Euklestes gave Sthentros a look-what-you-got-me-into
look.

"Great Dralm, no!"

"Well, then. We still have the question of war with Sask to
be voted," Ptosphes said. "How vote you, Lord Sthentros?"

"Oh, war, of course; I'm as loyal a Hostigi as any here."

There was no more argument. The vote was unanimous. As soon as Ptosphes had thanked them, Harmakros was on his feet.

"Then, to show that we are all in loyal support of our Prince, let us all vote that whatever decision he may make in the matter of our dealings with Sask, with Beshta, or with Nostor, either in making war or in making peace afterward, shall stand approved in advance by the Full Council of Hostigos."

"*What?*" Ptosphes asked in a whisper. "Is this some idea of yours, Kalvan?"

"Yes. We don't know what we're going to have to do, but whatever it is, we may have to do it in a hurry, and afterward we won't want anybody like Sthentros or Euklestes whining that they weren't consulted."

"That's probably wise. We'd do it anyhow, but this way there'll be no argument."

Harmakros' motion was also carried unanimously. The organization steamroller ran up the table without a bump.

III

Verkan, the free-trader from Grefftscharr, waited till the others—Prince Ptosphes, old Xentos, and the man of whom he must never under any circumstances think as Calvin Morrison—were seated, and then dropped into a chair at the table in Ptosphes' study.

"Have a good trip?" Lord Kalvan was asking him.

He nodded, and ran quickly over the fictitious details of the journey to Zygros City, his stay there, and his return to Hostigos, checking them with the actual facts. Then he visualized the panel, and his hand reaching out and pressing the black button. Other Paratimers used different imagery, but the result was the same. The pseudo-memories fed to him under hypnosis took over, the real memories of visits on this time-line to Zygros City were suppressed, and a complete blockage imposed on anything he knew about Fourth Level Europo-American, Hispano-Columbian Subsector.

"Not bad," he said. "I had a little trouble at Glarth Town, in Hos-Agrys. I'd sold those two kegs of Tarr-Dombra fireseed to a merchant, and right away they were after me, the Prince of Glarth's soldiers and Styphon's House agents. It seems Styphon's House had put out a story about one of their wagon-trains being robbed by bandits, and everybody's on the lookout for unaccountable fireseed. They'd arrested and tortured the merchant; he put them onto me. I killed one and wounded another, and got away."

"When was that?" Xentos asked sharply.

"Three days after I left here."

"Eight days after we took Tarr-Dombra and sent that letter to Sesklos," Ptosphes said. "That story'll be all over the Five Kingdoms by now."

"Oh, they've dropped that. They have a new story, now. They admit that some Prince in Hos-Harphax is making his own fireseed, but it isn't good fireseed."

Kalvan laughed. "It only shoots half again as hard as theirs, with half as much fouling."

"Ah, but there are devils in your fireseed. Of course, there are devils in all fireseed—that's what makes it explode—but the priests of Styphon have secret rites that cause the devils to die as soon as they've done their work. When yours explodes, the devils escape alive. I'll bet East Hostigos is full of devils, now."

He laughed, then stopped when he saw that none of the others were. Kalvan cursed; Ptosphes mentioned a name.

"That story has appeared here," Xentos said. "I hope none of our people believe it. It comes from Sask Town."

"This Sthentros, a kinsman by marriage of mine," Ptosphes said. "He's jealous of Kalvan's greatness among us. I spoke to him, gave him a good fright. He claimed he thought of it himself, but I know he's lying. Somebody from Sask's been at him. Trouble is, if we tortured him, all the other nobles would be around my ears like a swarm of hornets. We're having him watched."

"They move swiftly," Xentos said, "and they act as one. Their temples are everywhere, and each temple has its post station, with relays of fast horses. Styphon's Voice can speak today at Balph, in Hos-Ktemnos, and in a moon-quarter his words are heard in every temple in the Five Kingdoms. Their lies can travel so fast and far that the truth can never overtake them.''

''Yes, and see what'll happen,'' Kalvan said. ''From now on, everything—plague, famine, drought, floods, hail-storms, forest-fires, hurricanes—will be the work of devils out of our fireseed. Well, you got out of Glarth; what then?''

''After that, I thought it better to travel by night. It took me eight days to reach Zygros City. My wife, Dalla, met me there, as we'd arranged when I started south from Ulthor. In Zygros City, we recruited five brass-founders—two are cannon-founders, one's a bell founder, one's an image-maker and knows the wax-runoff method, and one's a gen-eral foundry foreman. And three girls, woodcarvers and patternmakers, and two mercenary sergeants I hired as guards.

''I gave the fireseed secret to the gunmakers' guild in Zygros City, in exchange for making up twelve long rifled fowling-pieces and rifling some pistols. They'll ship you rifled caliver barrels at the cost of smoothbore barrels. They'd heard the devil story; none of them believe it. And I gave the secret to merchants from my own country; they will spread it there.''

''And by this time next year, Grefftscharr fireseed will be traded down the Great River to Xiphlon,'' Kalvan said. ''Good. Now, how soon can this gang of yours start pouring cannon?''

''Two moons; a special miracle for each day less.''

He started to explain about the furnaces, and moulding sand; Kalvan understood.

''Then we'll have to fight this war with what we have. We'll be fighting in a moon-quarter, I think. We sent our Uncle Wolf off to Sask Town today with demands on Prince Sarrask. As soon as he hears them, they'll have to chain Sarrask up to keep him from biting people.''

''Among other things, we're demanding that Archpriest

Zothnes and the Sask Town highpriest be sent here in chains, to be tried for plotting Kalvan's death and mine," Ptosphes said. "If Zothnes has the influence over Sarrask I think he has, that alone will do it."

"You'll command the Mounted Rifles again, won't you?" Kalvan asked. "It's carried on the Army List as a regiment, so you'll be a colonel. We have a hundred and twenty rifles, now."

Dalla wouldn't approve. Well, that was too bad, but people who didn't help their friends fight weren't well thought of around here. Dalla would just have to adjust to it, the way she had to his beard.

Ptosphes finished his wine. "Shall we go up to Rylla's room?" he asked. "I'm glad you brought your wife with you, Verkan. Charming girl, and Rylla likes her. They made friends at once. She'll be company for Rylla while we're away."

"Rylla's sore at us," Kalvan said. "She thinks we're keeping that bundle of splints on her leg to keep her from going to war with us." He grinned. "She's right; we are. Maybe Dalla'll help keep her amused."

Vall didn't doubt that. Rylla and Dalla would get along together, all right; what he was worried about was what they'd get *into* together. Those two girls were just two cute little sticks of the same brand of dynamite; what one wouldn't think of, the other would.

SEVENTEEN

I

THE COMMON-ROOM of the village inn was hot and stuffy in spite of the open door; it smelled of woolens drying, of oil and sheep-tallow smeared on armor against the rain, of wood smoke and tobacco and wine, unwashed humanity and ancient cooking-odors. The village outside was jammed with the Army of the Listra; the inn with officers, steaming and stinking and smoking, drinking mugs of mulled wine or strong sassafras tea, crowding around the fire at the long table where the map was unrolled, spooning stew from bowls or gnawing meat impaled on dagger-points. Harmakros was saying, again and again, "Dralm damn you, hold that dagger back; don't drip grease on this!" And the priest of Galzar, who had carried the ultimatum to Sask Town and gotten this far on his return, and who had lately been out among the troops, sat in his shirt with his back to the fire, his wolfskin hood and cape spread to dry and a couple of village children wiping and oiling his mail. He had a mug in one hand, and with the other stroked the head of a dog that squatted beside him. He was laughing jovially.

165

"So I read them your demands, and you should have heard them! When I came to the part about dismissing the newly hired mercenaries, the captain-general of free companies bawled like a branded calf. I took it on myself to tell him you'd hire all of them with no loss of pay. Did I do right, Prince?"

"You did just right, Uncle Wolf," Ptosphes told him. "When we come to battle, along with 'Down Styphon,' we'll shout, 'Quarter for mercenaries.' How about the demands touching on Styphon's House?"

"Ha! The Archpriest Zothnes was there, sitting next to Sarrask, with the Chancellor of Sask shoved down one place to make room for him, which shows you who rules in Sask now. He didn't bawl like a calf; he screamed like a panther. Wanted Sarrask to have me seized and my head off right in the throne-room. Sarrask told him his own soldiers would shoot him dead on the throne if he ordered it, which they would have. The mercenary captain-general wanted Zothnes' head off, and half drew his sword for it. There's one with small stomach to fight for Styphon's House. And this Zothnes was screaming that there was no god at all but Styphon; now what do you think of that?"

Gasps of horror, and exclamations of shocked piety. One officer was charitable enough to say that the fellow must be mad.

"No. He's just a—" A monotheist, Kalvan wanted to say, but there was no word in the language for it. "One who respects no gods but his own. We had that in my own country." He caught himself just before saying, "in my own time"; of those present, only Ptosphes was security-cleared for that version of his story. "They are people who believe in only one god, and then they believe that the god they worship is the only true one, and all others are false, and finally they believe that the only true god must be worshipped in only one way, and that those who worship otherwise are vile monsters who should be killed." The Inquisition; the wicked and bloody Albigensian Crusade; Saint Bartholomew's; Haarlem; Magdeburg. "We want none of that here."

"Lord Prince," the priest of Galzar said, "you know how we who serve the Wargod stand. The Wargod is the Judge of Princes, his courtroom the battlefield. We take no sides. We minister to the wounded without looking at their colors; our temples are havens for the war-maimed. We preach only Galzar's Way: be brave, be loyal, be comradely; obey your officers; respect yourselves and your weapons and all other good soldiers; be true to your company and to him who pays you.

"But Lord Prince, this is no common war, of Hostigos against Sask and Ptosphes against Sarrask. This is a war for all the true gods against false Styphon and Styphon's foul brood. Maybe there is some devil called Styphon, I don't know, but if there is, may the true gods trample him under their holy feet as we must those who serve him."

A shout of "Down Styphon!" rose. So this was what he had said they must have none of, and an old man in a dirty shirt, a mug of wine in his hand and a black and brown mongrel thumping his tail on the floor beside him, had spelled it out. A religious war, the vilest form an essentially vile business can take. Priests of Dralm and Galzar preaching fire and sword against Styphon's House. Priests of Styphon rousing mobs against the infidel devil-makers. *Styphon wills it!* Atrocities. Massacres. *Holy Dralm and no quarter!*

And that was what he'd brought to here-and-now. Well, maybe for the best; give Styphon's House another century or so in power and there'd be no gods, here-and-now, but Styphon.

"And then?"

"Well, Sarrask was in a fine rage, of course. By Styphon, he'd meet Prince Ptosphes' demands where they should be met, on the battlefield, and the war'd start as soon as I took my back out of sight across the border. That was just before noon. I almost killed a horse, and myself, getting here. I haven't done much hard riding, lately," he parenthesized. "As soon as I got here, Harmakros sent riders out."

They'd reached Tarr-Hostigos at cocktail time, another alien rite introduced by Lord Kalvan, and found him and

Ptosphes and Xentos and Rylla and Dalla in Rylla's room. Hasty arming and saddling, hastier goodbyes, and then a hard mud-splashing ride up Listra Valley, reaching this village after dark. The war had already started; from Esdreth Gap they could hear the distant dull thump of cannon.

Outside, the Army of the Listra was still moving forward; an infantry company marched past with a song:

> *Roll another barrel out, the party's just begun.*
> *We beat Prince Gormoth's soldiers; you oughta seen them*
> *run!*
> *And then we crossed the Athan, and didn't we have fun,*
> *While we were marching through Nostor!*

Galloping hoofs; cries of "Way! Way! Courier!" The song ended in shouted imprecations from mud-splashed infantrymen. The galloping horse stopped outside. The march, and the song, was resumed:

> *Hurrah! Hurrah! We burned the bastards out!*
> *Hurrah! Hurrah! We put them all to rout!*
> *We stole their pigs and cattle and we dumped their sauer-*
> *kraut,*
> *While we were marching through Noostor!*

A muddy cavalryman stumbled through the door, looked around blinking, and then made for the long table, saluting as he came.

"From Colonel Verkan, Mounted Rifles. He and his men have Fyk; they beat off a counter-attack, and now the whole Saski army's coming at him. I found some Mobiles and a four-pounder on the way back; they've gone to help him."

"By Dralm, the whole Army of the Listra's going to help him. Where is this Fyk place?"

Harmakros pointed on the map—beyond Esdreth Gap, on the main road to Sask Town. There was a larger town, Gour, a little beyond. Kalvan pulled on his quilted coif and fastened the throat-guard; while he was settling his helmet on his head, somebody had gone to the door and was bawling into the dripping night for horses.

II

The rain had stopped, an hour later, when they reached Fyk. It was a small place, full of soldiers and lighted by bonfires. The civil population had completely vanished; all fled when the shooting had started. A four-pounder pointed up the road to the south, with the dim shape of an improvised barricade stretching away in the darkness on either side. Off ahead, an occasional shot banged, and he could distinguish the sharper reports of Hostigos-made powder from the slower-burning stuff put out by Styphon's House. Maybe Uncle Wolf was right that this was a war between the true gods and false Styphon; it was also a war between two makes of gunpowder.

He found Verkan and a Mobile Force major in one of the village cottages; Verkan wore a hooded smock of brown canvas, and a short chopping-sword on his belt and a powder-horn and bullet-pouch slung from his shoulder. The major's cavalry armor was browned and smeared with tallow. They had one of the pyrographed deerskin field-maps spread on the table in front of them. *Paper, invention of;* he'd made that mental memo a thousand times already.

"There were about fifty cavalry here when we arrived," Verkan was saying. "We killed them or ran them out. In half an hour there were a couple of hundred back. We beat them off, and that was when I sent the riders back. Then Major Leukestros came up with his men and a gun, just in time to help beat off another attack. We have some cavalry and mounted arquebusiers out in front and on the flanks; that's the shooting you're hearing. There are some thousand cavalry at Gour, and probably all Sarrask's army following."

"I'm afraid we're going to have to make a wet night of it," Kalvan said. "We'll have to get our battle-line formed now; we can't take chances on what they may do."

He shoved the map aside and began scribbling and dia-
graming an order of battle on the white-scrubbed table top.
Guns to the rear, in column along a side road north of the
village, four-pounders in front; horses to be unhitched, but
fed and rested in harness, ready to move out at once. Infantry
in a line to both sides of the road a thousand yards ahead of
the village, Mobile Force infantry in the middle. Cavalry on
the flank; mounted infantry horses to the rear. A battle-order
that could be converted instantly into a march-order if they
had to move on in the morning.

The army came stumbling in for the next hour or so, in bits
and scraps, got themselves sorted out, and took their positions astride of the road on the slope south of the village. The
air had grown noticeably warmer. He didn't like that; it
presaged fog, and he wanted good visibility for the battle
tomorrow. Cavalry skirmishers began drifting back, reporting pressure of large enemy forces in front.

An hour after he had his line formed, the men lying in the
wet grass on blankets, or whatever bedding they could snatch
from the village, the Saski began coming up. There was a
brief explosion of smallarms fire as they ran into his skirmishers, then they pulled back and began forming their own
battle-line.

Hell of a situation, he thought disgustedly, lying on a
cornshuck tick he and Ptosphes and Harmakros had stolen
from some peasant's abandoned bed. Two blind armies, not a
thousand yards apart, waiting for daylight, and when daylight came . . .

A cannon went off in front and on his left, with a loud, dull
whump! A couple of heartbeats later, something whacked
behind the line. He rose on his hands and knees, counting
seconds as he peered into the darkness. Two minutes later, he
glimpsed an orange glow on his left, and two seconds after
that heard the report. Call it eight hundred yards, give or take
a hundred. He hissed to a quartet of officers on a blanket next
to him.

''They're overshooting us a little. Pass the word along the

line, both ways, to move forward three hundred paces. And not a sound; dagger anybody who speaks above a whisper. Harmakros, get the cavalry and the mounted infantry horses back on the other side of the village. Make a lot of noise about five hundred yards behind us.''

The officers moved off, two to a side. He and Ptosphes picked up the mattress and carried it forward, counting three hundred paces before dropping it. Men were moving up on both sides, with a gratifying minimum of noise.

The Saski guns kept on firing. At first there were yells of simulated fright; Harmakros and his crowd. Finally, a gun fired almost in front of him; the cannonball passed overhead and landed behind with a swish and whack like a headsman's sword coming down. The next shot was far on his left. Eight guns, at two minute intervals—call it fifteen minutes to load. That wasn't bad, in the dark and with what the Saski had. He relaxed, lying prone with his chin rested on his elbows. After awhile Harmakros returned and joined him and Ptosphes on the shuck tick. The cannonade went on in slow procession from left to right and left to right again. Once there was a bright flash instead of a dim glow, and a much sharper crack. Fine! One of the guns had burst! After that, there were only seven rounds to the salvo. Once there was a rending crash behind, as though a roundshot had hit a tree. Every shot was a safe over.

Finally, the firing stopped. The distant intermittent dueling between the two Castles Esdreth had ceased, too. He let go of wakefulness and dropped into sleep.

Ptosphes, stirring besides him, wakened him. His body ached and his mouth tasted foul, as every body and mouth on both battle-lines must. It was still dark, but the sky above was something less than black, and he made out his companions as dim shapes. Fog.

By Dralm that was all they needed! Fog, and the whole Saski army not five hundred yards away, and all their advantages of mobility and artillery superiority lost. Nowhere to move, no room to maneuver, visibility down to less than pistol-shot, even the advantage of their hundred-odd rifled calivers nullified.

This looked like the start of a bad day for Hostigos.

They munched the hard bread and cold pork and cheese they had brought with them and drank some surprisingly good wine from a canteen and talked in whispers, other officers creeping in until a dozen and a half were huddled around the headquarters mattress.

"Couldn't we draw back a little?" That was Mnestros, the mercenary "captain"—approximately major-general—in command of the militia. "This is a horrible position. We're halfway down their throats."

"They'd hear us," Ptosphes said, "and start with their guns again, and this time they'd know where to shoot."

"Bring up our own guns and start shooting first," somebody suggested.

"Same objection; they'd hear us and open fire before we could. And for Dralm's sake keep your voices down," Kalvan snapped. "No, Mnestros said it. We're halfway down their throats. Let's jump the rest of the way and kick their guts out from the inside."

The mercenary was a book-soldier. He was briefly dubious then admitted:

"We are in line to attack, and we know where they are and they don't know where we are. They must think we're back at the village, from the way they were firing last night. Cavalry on the flanks?" He deprecated that. According to the here-and-now book, cavalry should be posted all along the line, between blocks of infantry.

"Yes, half the mercenaries in each end, and a solid line of infantry, two ranks of pikes, and arquebuses and calivers to fire over the pikemen's shoulders," Kalvan said. "Verkan, have your men pass the word along the line. Everybody stay put and keep quiet till we can all go forward together. I want every pan reprimed and every flint tight; we'll all move off together, and no shouting till the enemy sees us. I'll take the extreme right. Prince Ptosphes, you'd better take center;

Mnestros, command the left. Harmakros, you take the regular and Mobile Force cavalry and five hundred Mobile Force infantry, and move back about five hundred yards. If they flank us or break through, attend to it."

By now, the men around him were individually recognizable, but everything beyond twenty yards was fog-swollowed. Their saddle-horses were brought up. He reprimed the pistols in the holsters, got a second pair from a saddlebag, renewed the priming, and slipped one down the top of each jackboot. The line was stirring with a noise that stood his hair on end under his helmet-coif, until he realized that the Saski were making too much noise to hear it. He slipped back the cuff under his mail sleeve and looked at his watch. Five forty-five; sunrise in half an hour. They all shook hands with one another, and he started right along the line.

Soldiers were rising, rolling and slinging cloaks and blankets. There were quilts and ticks and things from the village lying on the ground; mustn't be a piece of bedding left in Fyk. A few were praying, to Dralm or Galzar. Most of them seemed to take the attitude that the gods would do what they wanted to without impertinent human suggestions.

He stopped at the extreme end of the line, on the right of five hundred regular infantry, like all the rest lined four deep, two ranks of pikes and two of calivers. Behind and on the right, the mercenary cavalry were coming up in a block of twenty ranks, fifty to the rank. The first few ranks were heavy-armed, plate rerebraces and vambraces on their arms instead of mail sleeves, heavy pauldrons protecting their shoulders, visored helmets, mounted on huge chargers, real old style brewery-wagon horses. They came to a halt just behind him. He passed the word of readiness left, then sat stroking his horse's neck and talking softly to him.

After awhile the word came back with a moving stir along the line through the fog. He lifted a long pistol from his right-hand holster, readied it to fire, and shook his reins. The line slid forward beside him, front rank pikes waist high, second rank pike-points a yard behind and breast high, calivers behind at high port. The cavalry followed him with a slow fluviatile *clop-clatter-clop*. Things emerged from the fog in front—seedling pines, clumps of tall weeds, a rotting cartwheel, a whitened cow's skull—but the gray nothingness marched just twenty yards in front.

This, he recalled, was how Gustavus Adolphus had gotten killed, riding forward into a fog like this at Lützen.

An arquebus banged on his left; that was a charge of Styphon's Best. Half a dozen shots rattled in reply, most of them Kalvan's Unconsecrated, and he heard yells of *"Down Styphon!"* and *"Sarrask of Sask!"* The pikemen stiffened; some of them lost step and had to hop to make it up. They all seemed to crouch over their weapons, and the caliver muzzles poked forward. By this time, the firing was like a slate roof endlessly sliding off a house, and then, much farther to the left, there was a sudden ringing crash like sheet-steel falling into a scrap-car.

The Fyk corpse-factory was in full production.

But in front, there was only silence and the slowly receding curtain of fog, and pine-dotted pastureland broken by small gullies in which last night's rainwater ran yellowly. Ran straight ahead of them—that wasn't right. The Saski position was up a slope from where they had lain under the midrange trajectory of the guns, and now the noise of battle was not only to the left but behind them. He flung up the hand holding the gold-mounted pistol.

"Halt!" he called out. "Pass the word left to stand fast!"

He knew what had happened. Both battle-lines, formed in the dark, had overlapped the other's left. So he had flanked them, and Mnestros, on the Hostigi left, was also flanked.

"You two," he told a pair of cavalry lieutenants. "Ride left till you come to the fighting. Find a good pivot-point, and one of you stay with it. The other will come back along the line, passing the word to swing left. We'll start swinging from this end. And find somebody to tell Harmakros what's happened, if he doesn't know it already. He probably does. No orders; just use his own judgment."

Everybody would have to use his own judgment, from here out. He wondered what was happening to Mnestros. He hadn't the liveliest confidence in Mnestros' judgment when he ran into something the book didn't cover. Then he sat, waiting for centuries, until one of the lieutenants came thudding back behind the infantry line, and he gave the order to start the leftward swing.

The level pikes and slanting calivers kept line on his left; the cavalry clop-clattered behind him. The downward slope swung in front of them, until they were going steeply uphill, and then the ground was level under their feet, and he could feel a freshening breeze on his cheek.

He was shouting a warning when the fog tore apart for a hundred yards in front and two or three on either side, and out of it came a mob of infantry, badged with Sarrask's green and gold. He pulled his horse back, fired his pistol into them, holstered it, and drew the other from his left holster. The major commanding the regular infantry blew his whistle and screamed above the din:

"Action front! Fire by ranks, odd numbers only!"

The front rank pikemen squatted as though simultaneously stricken with diarrhea. The second rank dropped to one knee, their pikes advanced. Over their shoulders, half the third rank blasted with calivers, then dodged for the fourth rank to fire over them. As soon as the second volley crashed, the pikemen were on their feet and running at the disintegrating front of the Saski infantry, all shouting, *"Down Styphon!"*

He saw that much, then raked his horse with his spurs and drove him forward, shouting, *"Charge!"* The heavily-armed mercenaries thundered after him, swinging long swords, firing pistols almost as big as small carbines, smashing into the Saski infantry from the flank before they could form a new front. He pistoled a pikeman who was thrusting at his horse, then drew his sword.

Then the fog closed down again, and dim shapes were dodging among the horses. A Saski cavalryman bulked in front of him, firing almost in his face. The bullet missed him, but hot grains of powder stung his cheek. Get a coal-miner's tattoo out of that, he thought, and then his wrist hurt as he drove the point into the fellow's throat-guard, spreading the links. *Plate gorgets; issue to mounted troops as soon as can be produced*. He wrenched the point free, and the Saski slid gently out of his saddle.

"Keep moving!" he screamed at the cavalry with him. "Don't let them slow you down!"

In a mess like this, stalled cavalry were all but helpless. Their best weapon was the momentum of a galloping horse, and once lost, that took at least thirty yards to regain. Cavalry horses ought to be crossed with jackrabbits; but that was something he couldn't do anything about at all. One mass of cavalry, the lancers and musketoon-men who had ridden behind the heavily armed men, had gotten hopelessly jammed in front of a bristle of pikes. He backed his horse quickly out of that, then found himself at the end of a line of Mobile Force infantry, with short arquebuses and cavalry lances for pikes. He directed them to the aid of the stalled cavalry, and then realized that he was riding across the road at right angles. That meant that he—and the whole battle, since all the noise was either to his right or left along the road—was now facing east instead of south. Of the heavily armed mercenary cavalry who had been with him at the beginning he could see nothing.

A horseman came crashing at him out of the fog, shouting "Down Styphon!" and thrusting at him with a sword. He had barely time to beat it aside with his own and cry, "Ptosphes!" and a moment later:

"Ptosphes, by Dralm! How did you get here?"

"Kalvan! I'm glad you parried that one. Where are we?"

He told the Prince, briefly. "The whole Dralm-damned battle's turned at right angles; you know that?"

"Well, no wonder. Our whole left wing's gone. Mnestros is dead—I heard that from an officer who saw his body. The regular infantry on our extreme left are all but wiped out; what few are left, and what's left of the militia next to them, reformed on Harmakros, in what used to be our rear. That's our left wing, now."

"Well, their left wing's in no better shape; I swung in on that and smashed it up. What's happened to the cavalry we had on the left?''

''Dralm knows; I don't. Took to their heels out of this, I suppose.'' Ptosphes drew one of his pistols and took a powder-flask from his belt. ''Watch over my shoulder, will you, Kalvan.''

He drew one of his own holster-pair and poured a charge into it. The battle seemed to have moved out of their immediate vicinity, though off in the fog in both directions there was a bedlam of shooting, yelling and steel-clashing. Then suddenly a cannon, the first of the morning, went off in what Kalvan took to be the direction of the village. An eight-pounder, he thought, and certainly loaded with Made-in-Hostigos. On its heels came another, and another.

''That,'' Ptosphes said, ''will be Harmakros.''

''I hope he knows what he's shooting at.'' He primed the pistol, holstered it, and started on its mate. ''Where do you think we could do the most good?''

Ptosphes had his saddle pair loaded, and was starting on one from a boot-top.

''Let's see if we can find some of our own cavalry, and go looking for Sarrask,'' he said. ''I'd like to kill or capture him, myself. If I did, it might give me some kind of a claim on the throne of Sask. If this cursed fog would only clear.''

From off to the right, south up the road, came noises like a boiler-shop starting up. There wasn't much shooting—everybody's gun was empty and no one had time to reload—just steel, and an indistinguishable *waw-waw-waw*-ing of voices. The fog was blowing in wet rags, now, but as fast as it blew away, more closed down. There was a limit to that, though; overhead the sky was showing a faint sunlit yellow.

''Come on, Lytris, come on!'' he invoked the Weather Goddess. ''Get this stuff out of here! Whose side are you fighting on, anyhow?''

Ptosphes finished the second of his spare pair; he had the last one of his own four to prime. Ptosphes said, ''Watch behind you!'' and he almost spilled the priming, then closed the pan and readied the pistol to fire. It was some twenty of the heavy-armed cavalry who had gone in with him. Their sergeant wanted to know where they were.

He hadn't any better idea than they had. Shoving the flint away from the striker, he pushed the pistol into his boot and drew his sword; they all started off toward the noise of fighting. He thought he was still going east until he saw that he was riding, at right angles, onto a line of mud-trampled quilts and bedspreads and mattresses, the things that had been appropriated in the village the night before. He glanced left and right. Ptosphes knew what they were, too, and swore.

Now the battle had made a full 180-degree turn. Both armies were facing in the direction from whence they had come; the route of either would be in the direction of the enemy's country.

Galzar, he thought irreverently, must have overslept this morning.

But at least the fog was definitely clearing, gilded above by sunlight, and the gray tatters around them were fewer and more threadbare, visibility now better than a hundred yards. They found a line of battle extending, apparently, due east of Fyk, and came up behind a hodgepodge of militia, regulars and Mobiles, any semblance of unit organization completely lost. Mobile Force cavalry were trotting back and forth behind them, looking for soft spots where breakthroughs, in either direction, might happen. He yelled to a Mobile Force captain who was fighting on foot:

"Who's in front of you?"

"How should I know? Same mess of odds-and-sods we are. This Dralm-damned battle . . ."

Officially, he supposed, it would be the Battle of Fyk, but nobody who'd been in it would ever call it anything but the Dralm-damned Battle.

Before he could say anything, there was a crash on his left like all the boiler-shops in creation together. He and Ptosphes looked at one another.

"Something new has been added," he commented. "Well, let's go see."

They started to the left with their picked up heavy cavalry, not too rapidly, and with pistols drawn. There was a lot of shouting—*"Down Styphon!"* of course, and *"Ptosphes!"* and *"Sarrask of Sask!"* There were also shouts of *"Balthames!"* That would be the retinue Balthar's brother, the prospective Prince of Sashta, had brought to Sask Town—some two hundred and fifty, he'd heard. Then, there were cries of *"Treason! Treason!"*

Now there was a hell of a thing to yell on any battlefield, let alone in a fog. He was wondering who was supposed to be betraying whom when he found the way blocked by the backs of Hostigi infantry at right angles to the battle-line; not retreating, just being pushed out of the way of something. Beyond them, through the thinning fog, he could see a rush of cavalry, some wearing black and pale yellow surcoats over their armor. They'd be Balthames' Beshtans; they were firing and chopping indiscriminately at anything in front of them, and, mixed with them, were green-and-gold Saski, fighting with them and the Hostigi both. All he and Ptosphes and the mercenary men-at-arms could do was sit their horses and fire pistols at them over the heads of their own infantry.

Finally, the breakthrough, if that was what it had been, was over. The Hostigi infantry closed in behind them, piking and shooting, and there were cries of "Comrade, we yield!" and "Oath to Galzar!" and "Comrade, spare mercenaries!"

"Should we give them a chase?" Ptosphes asked, looking after the Saski-Beshtan whatever-it-had-been.

"I shouldn't think so. They're charging in the right direction. What the Styphon do you think happened?"

Ptosphes laughed. "How should I know? I wonder if it really was treason."

"Well, let's get through here." He raised his voice. "Come on—forward! Somebody's punched a hole for us; let's get through it!"

Suddenly, the fog was gone. The sun shone from a cloudless sky; the mountainside, nearer than he thought, was gaudy with Autumn colors; all the drifting puffs and hanging bands of white on the ground were powdersmoke. The village of Fyk, on his left, was ringed with army wagons like a Boer laager, guns pointing out between them. That was the strongpoint on which Harmakros had rallied the wreckage of the left wing.

In front of him, the Hostigi were moving forward, infantry running beside the cavalry, and in front of them the Saski line was raveling away, men singly and in little groups and by whole companies turning and taking to their heels, trying to join two or three thousand of their comrades who had made a porcupine. He knew it from otherwhen history as a Swiss hedgehog: a hollow circle bristling pikes in all directions. Hostigi cavalry were already riding around it, firing into it, and Verkan's riflemen were sniping at it. There seemed to be no Saski cavalry whatever; they must all have joined the rush to the south at the time of the breakthrough.

Then three four-pounders came out from the village at a gallop, unlimbered at three hundred yards, and began firing case-shot. When two eight-pounders followed more sedately, helmets began going up on pike-points and caliver muzzles.

Behind him, the fighting had ceased entirely. Hostigi soldiers had scattered through the brush and trampled cornstalks, tending to their wounded, securing prisoners, robbing corpses, collecting weapons, all the routine after-battle chores, and the battle wasn't over yet. He was worrying about where all the Saski cavalry had gotten, and the possibility that they might rally and counterattack, when he saw a large mounted column approaching from the south. This is it, he thought, and we're all scattered to Styphon's House and gone—He was shouting at the men nearest him to drop what they were doing and start earning their pay when he saw blue and red colors on lances, saddle-pads, scarves. He trotted forward to meet them.

Some were mercenaries, some were Hostigi regulars; with them were a number of green-and-gold prisoners, their helmets hung on saddlebows. A captain in front shouted a greeting as he came up.

"Well, thank Galzar you're still alive, Lord Kalvan! Where's the Prince?"

"Back at the village, trying to get things sorted out. How far did you go?"

"Almost to Gour. Better than a thousand of them got away; they won't stop short of Sask Town. The ones we have are the ones with the slow horses. Sarrask may have gotten away; we know Balthames did."

"Dralm and Galzar and all the true gods curse that Beshtan bastard!" one of the prisoners cried. "Devils eat his soul forever! The Dralm-damned lackwit cost us the battle, and only Galzar's counted how many dead and maimed."

"What happened? I heard cries of treason."

"Yes, that dumped the whole bagful of devils on us," the Saski said. "You want to know what happened? Well, in the darkness we formed with our right wing far beyond your left; yours beyond ours, I suppose, from the looks of things. On our right, we carried all before us, drove your cavalry from the field and smashed your infantry. Then this boy-lover from Beshta—we can fight our enemies, but Galzar guard us from our allies—took his own men and near a thousand of our mercenary horse off on a rabbit-hunt after your fleeing cavalry, almost to Esdreth.

"Well, you know what happened in the meantime. Our right drove in your left, and yours ours, and the whole battle turned like a wheel, and we were all facing in the way we'd come, and then back comes this Balthames of Beshta, smashing into our rear, thinking that he was saving the day.

"And to make it worse, the silly fool doesn't shout 'Sarrask of Sask,' as he should have; no, he shouts 'Balthames!'—he and all his, and the mercenaries with him took it up to curry favor with him. Well, great Dralm, you know how much anybody can trust anybody from Beshta; we thought the bugger'd turned his coat, and somebody cried treason. I'll not deny crying it myself, after I was near spitted on a Beshtan lance, and me crying 'Sarrask!' at the top of my lungs. So we were carried away in the rout, and I fell in with mercenaries from Hos-Ktemnos. We got almost to Gour and tried to make a stand, and were ridden over and taken.''

"Did Sarrask get away? Galzar knows I want to spill his blood badly enough, but I want to do it honestly.''

The Saski didn't know; none of Sarrask's silver-armored personal guard had been near him in the fighting.

"Well, don't blame Duke Balthames too much.'' Looking around, he saw over a score of Saski and mercenary prisoners within hearing. If we're going to have a religious war, let's start it now. "It was,'' he declared, "the work of the true gods! Who do you think raised the fog, but Lytris the Weather Goddess? Who confounded your captains in arraying your line, and caused your gunners to overshoot, harming not one of us, but Galzar Wolfhead, the Judge of Princes? And who but Great Dralm himself addled poor Balthames' wits, leading him on a fool's chase and bringing him back to strike you from behind? At long last,'' he cried, "the true gods have raised their mighty hands against false Styphon and the blasphemers of Styphon's House!''

There were muttered amens, some from the Saski prisoners. Styphon's stock had dropped quite a few points. He decided to let it go at that, and put them in with the other prisoners and let them talk.

EIGHTEEN

PTOSPHES WAS shocked by the casualties. Well, they *were* rather shocking—only forty-two hundred effectives left out of fifty-eight hundred infantry, and eighteen hundred of a trifle over three thousand cavalry. The body count didn't meet the latter figure, however, and he remembered what the Saski officer had said about Balthames' chase almost to Esdreth Gap. Most of the mercenaries on the left wing had simply bugged out; by now, they'd be fleeing into Listra Valley, spreading tales of a crushing Hostigi defeat. He cursed; there wasn't anything else he could do about it.

Some cavalry arrived from Esdreth Gap: Chartiphon's Army of the Besh men. During the night, they reported, infantry from both the army of the Besh and the Army of the Listra had gotten onto the mountain back of Tarr-Esdreth-of-Sask, and taken it by storm just before daylight. Alkides had moved his three treasured brass eighteen-pounders and some lighter pieces down into the gap, and was holding it at both ends with a mixed force. As the fog had started to blow away, a large body of Saski cavalry had tried to force a way through; they had been driven off by gunfire. Perturbed by the presence of enemy troops so far north, he had sent to find out what was going on. Riders were sent to reassure him, and order him to come up in person and bring his eighteens with him.

There was no telling what they might have to break into before the day was over the long eighteen-pounders were excellent burglar-tools.

Harmakros got off at ten, with the Mobile Force and all the four-pounders, up the main road for Sask Town. All the captured mercenaries agreed to take Prince Ptosphes' colors and were released under oath and under arms. The Saski subjects were disarmed and put to work digging trenches for mass graves and collecting salvageable equipment. Mytron and his staff preempted the better cottages and several of the larger and more sanitary barns for hospitals. Taking five hundred of the remaining cavalry, Kalvan started out a little before noon, leaving Ptosphes to await the arrival of Alkides and the eighteen-pounders.

Gour was a market town of some five thousand. He found bodies, already stripped of armor, in the square, and a mob of townsfolk and disarmed Saski prisoners working to put out several fires, guarded by some lightly wounded mounted arquebusiers. He dropped two squads to help them and rode on.

He thought he knew this section; he'd been stationed in Blair County five otherwhen years ago. He hadn't realized how much the Pennsylvania Railroad Company had altered the face of Logan Valley. At about what ought to be Allegheny Furnace, he was stopped by a picket-post of Mobile Force cavalry and warned to swing right and come in on Sask Town from behind. Tarr-Sask was being held, either by or for Prince Sarrask, and was cannonading the town. While he talked with them, he could hear the occasional distant boom of a heavy bombard.

Tarr-Sask stood on the south end of Brush Mountain, Sarrask's golden-rayed sun on green flying from the watch-tower. The arrival of his cavalry at the other side of the town must have been observed; four bombards let go with strain-everything charges of Styphon's Best, hurling hundred and fifty pound stone cannonballs among the houses. This, he thought, wouldn't do much to improve relations between Sarrask and his subjects. Harmakros, who had nothing but four-pounders, which was to say nothing, was not replying. Wait, he thought, till Alkides gets here.

Battering-pieces, thirty-two-pounders, about six; get cast as soon as Verkan's gang gets a foundry going. And cast shells; do something about.

There had been no fighting inside the town; Harmakros' blitzkrieg had hit it too fast, before resistance could be organized. There had been some looting—that was to be expected—but no fires. Arson for arson's sake, without a valid strategic reason as in Nostor, was discountenanced in the Hostigos army. Most of the civil population had either refugeed out or were down in the cellar.

The temple of Styphon had been taken first of all. It stood on almost the exact site of the Hollidaysburg courthouse, a circular building under a golden dome, with rectangular wings on either side. If, as he suspected, that dome was really gold, it might go a long way toward paying the cost of the war. A Mobile Force infantryman was up a ladder with a tarpot and a brush, painting DOWN STYPHON over the door. Entering, the first thing he saw was a twenty-foot image, its face newly spalled and pitted and lead-splashed. The Puritans had been addicted to that sort of smallarms practice, he recalled, and so had the Huguenots. There was a lot of gold ornamentation around; guards had been posted.

He found Harmakros in the Innermost Circle, his spurred heels resting on the highpriest's desk. He sprang to his feet.

"Kalvan! Did you bring any guns?"

"No, only cavalry. Ptosphes is bringing Alkides' three eighteens. He'l be here in about three hours. What happened here?"

"Well, as you see, Balthames got here a little ahead of us and shut himself up in Tarr-Sask. We sent the local Uncle Wolf up to parley with him. He says he's holding the castle in Sarrask's name, and won't surrender without Sarrask's orders as long as he has fireseed."

"Then he doesn't know where Sarrask is, either."

Sarrask could be dead and his body stripped on the field by common soldiers—it'd be worth stripping—and tumbled anonymously into one of those mass graves. If so, they might never be sure, and then, every year for the next thirty years, some fake Sarrask would be turning up somewhere in the Five Kingdoms, conning suckers into financing a war to recover his throne. That had happened occasionally in otherwhen history.

"Did you get the priests along with this temple?"

"Oh, yes, Zothnes and all. They were packing to leave when we got here, and argued about what to take along. We have them in chains in the town jail, now. Do you want to see them?"

"Not particularly. We'll have their heads off tomorrow or the next day, when we find time for it. How about the fireseed mill?"

Harmakros laughed. "Verkan's surrounding it with his riflemen. As soon as we get a dozen or so men dressed in priestly robes, about a hundred more will chase them in, with a lot of yelling and shooting. If that gets the gate open, we may be able to take the place before some fanatic blows it up. You know, some of these underpriests and novices really believe in Styphon."

"Well, what did you get here?"

Harmakros waved a hand about him. "All this gold and fancywork. Then there's gold and silver, specie and bullion, in the vaults, to about fifty thousand gold ounces, I'd say."

That was a lot of money. Around a million U.S. dollars. He could believe it, though; besides making fireseed, Styphon's House was in the loan-shark business, at something like ten percent per lunar month, compound interest. *Anti-usury laws; do something about.* Except for a few small-time pawnbrokers, they were the only money-lenders in Sask.

"Then," Harmakros continued, "there's a magazine and armory. We haven't taken inventory yet, but I'd say ten tons of fireseed, three or four hundred stand of arquebuses and calivers, and a lot of armor. And one wing's packed full of general merchandise, probably taken in as offerings. We haven't even looked at that, yet; just put it under guard. A lot of barrels that could be wine; we don't want the troops getting at that yet.''

The guns of Tarr-Sask kept on firing slowly, smashing a house now and then. None of the roundshot came near the temple; Balthames was evidently still in awe of Styphon's House. The main army arrived about 1630; Alkides got his brass eighteen-pounders and three twelves in position and began shooting back. They didn't throw the huge granite globes Balthames' bombards did, but they fired every five minutes instead of every half hour, and with something approaching accuracy. A little later, Verkan rode in to report the fireseed mill taken intact. He didn't think much of the equipment—the mills were all slave-powered—but there had been twenty tons of finished fireseed, and over a hundred of sulfur and saltpeter. He had had some trouble preventing a massacre of the priests when the slaves had been unshackled.

At 1815, in the gathering dusk, riders came in from Es-dreth, reporting that Sarrask had ben captured, in Listra Valley, while trying to reach the Nostori border to place himself under the questionable protection of Prince Gor-moth.

''He was captured,'' the sergeant in command finished, ''by the Princess Rylla and Colonel Verkan's wife Dalla.''

He and Ptosphes and Harmakros and Verkan all shouted at once. A moment later, the roar of one of Alkides' eighteens was almost an anticlimax. Verkan was saying, *''That's* the girl who wanted *me* to stay out of battles!''

''But Rylla can't get out of bed,'' Ptosphes argued.

''I wouldn't know about that, Prince,'' the sergeant said. ''Maybe the Princess calls a saddle a bed, because that's what she was in when I saw her.''

''Well, did she have that cast—that leather thing—on her leg?'' Kalvan asked.

''No, sir—just regular riding boots, with pistols in them.''

He and Ptosphes cursed antiphonally. Well, at least they'd

kept her out of that blindfold slaughterhouse at Fyk.

"Sound Cease Fire, and then Parley," he ordered. "Send Uncle Wolf up the hill again; tell Balthames we have his pa-in-law."

They got a truce arranged; Balthames sent out a group of neutrals, merchants and envoys from other princedoms, to observe and report. Bonfires were lit along the road up to the castle. It was full dark when Rylla and Dalla arrived, with a mixed company of mounted Tarr-Hostigos garrison troops, fugitive mercenaries rallied along the road south, and over-age peasants on overage horses. With them were nearly a hundred of Sarrask's elite guard, in silvered harness that looked more like table-service than armor, and Sarrask himself in gilded armor.

"Where's that lying quack of a Mytron?" Rylla demanded, as soon as she was within hearing. "I'll doctor him when I catch him—a double orchidectomy! You know what? Yes, of course you do; you put him up to it! Well, Dalla had a look at my leg this morning, she's forgotten more about doctoring than Mytron ever learned, and she said that thing ought to have been off half a moon ago."

"Well, what's the story?" Kalvan asked. "How did you pick all this up?" He indicated Sarrask, glowering at them from his saddle, with his silver-plated guardsmen behind him.

"Oh, this band of heroes you took to a battle you tried to keep me out of," Rylla said bitterly. "About noon, they came clattering into Tarr-Hostigos—that's the ones with the fastest horses and the sharpest spurs—screaming that all was lost, the army destroyed, you killed, father killed, Harmak-ros killed, Verkan killed, Mnestros killed; why, they even had Chartiphon, down on the Beshtan border, killed!"

"Well, I'm sorry to say that Mnestros *was* killed," her father told her.

"Well, I didn't believe a tenth of it, but even at that something bad could have happened, so I gathered up what men I could mount at the castle, appointed Dalla my lieutenant—she was the best man around—and we started south, gathering up what we could along the way. Just this side of Darax, we ran into this crowd. We thought they were the cavalry screen for a Saski invasion, and we gave them an argument. That was when Dalla captured Prince Sarrask.''

"I did not," Verkan's wife denied. "I just shot his horse. Some farmers captured him, and you owe them a lot of money, or somebody does. We rode into this gang on the road, and there was a lot of shooting, and this big man in gilded armor came at me swinging a sword as long as I am. I fired at him, and as I did his horse reared and caught it in the chest and fell over backward, and while he was trying to get clear some peasants with knives and hatchets and things jumped on him, and began screaming, 'I am Prince Sarrask of Sask; my ransom is a hundred thousand ounces of silver!' Well, right away, they lost interest in killing him.''

"Who are they, do you know?" Ptosphes asked. "I'll have to make that good to them.''

"Styphon will pay," Kalvan said.

"Styphon ought to; he got Sarrask into this mess in the first place," Ptosphes commented. He turned back to Rylla. "What then?''

"Well, when Sarrask surrendered, the rest of them began pulling off helmets and holding swords up by the blades and crying, 'Oath to Galzar!' They all admitted they'd taken an awful beating at Fyk, and were trying to get into Nostor. Now wouldn't that have been nice?''

"Our gold-plated friend here didn't want to come along with us," Dalla said. "Rylla told him he didn't need to; we could take his head along easier than all of him. You know, Prince, your daughter doesn't fool. At least, Sarrask didn't think so.''

She hadn't been fooling, and Sarrask had known it.

"So," Rylla picked it up, "we put him on a horse one of his guards didn't need any more, and brought him along. We thought you might find a use for him. We stopped at Esdreth Gap—I saw our flag on the Sask castle; that looked pretty, but Sarrask didn't think so . . .''

"Prince Ptosphes!" Sarrask burst out. "I am a Prince, as

you are. You have no right to let these—these girls—make sport of me!''

''They're as good soldiers as you are,'' Ptosphes snapped. ''They captured you, didn't they?''

''It was the true gods who made sport of you, Prince Sarrask!'' Kalvan went into the same harangue he had given the captured officers at Fyk, in his late father's best denunciatory pulpit style. ''I pray all the true gods,'' he finished, ''that now that they have humbled you, they will forgive you.''

Sarrask was no longer defiant; he was a badly scared Prince, as badly scared as any sinner at whom the Rev. Alexander Morrison had thundered hellfire and damnation. Now and then he looked uneasily upward, as though wondering what the gods were going to hit him with next.

It was almost midnight before Kalvan and Ptosphes could sit down privately in a small room behind Sarrask's gaudy presence chamber. There had been the takeover of Tarr-Sask, and the quartering of troops, and the surrendered mercenaries to swear into Ptosphes' service, and the Saski troops to disarm and confine to barracks. Riders had been coming and going with messages. Chartiphon, on the Beshtan border, was patching up a field truce with Balthar's officers on the spot, and had sent cavalry to seize the lead mines in Sinking Valley. As soon as things stabilized, he was turning the Army of the Besh over to his second in command and coming to Sask Town.

Ptosphes had let his pipe go out. Biting back a yawn, he leaned forward to relight it from a candle.

''We have a panther by the tail here, Kalvan; you know that?'' he asked. ''What are we going to do now?''

''Well, we clean Styphon's House out of Sask, first of all. We'll have the heads off all those priests, from Zothnes down.'' Counting the lot that had been brought in from the different temple-farms, that would be about fifty. They'd have to gather up some headsmen. ''That will have to be policy, from now on. We don't leave any of that gang alive.''

''Oh, of course,'' Ptosphes agreed. '' 'To be dealt with as

wolves are.' But how about Sarrask and Balthames? If we behead them, the other Princes would criticize us.''

"No, we want both of them alive, as your vassals. Balthames is going to marry that wench of Sarrask's if I have to stand behind him with a shotgun, and then we'll make him Prince of Sashta, and occupy all that territory Balthar agreed to cede him. In return, he'll guarantee us the entire output of those lead mines. Lead, I'm afraid, is going to be our chief foreign-exchange monetary metal for a long time to come.

"To make it a little tighter,'' he continued, ''we'll add a little of Hostigos, east of the mountains, say to the edge of the Barrens—"

"Are you crazy, Kalvan? Give up Hostigi land? Not as long as I'm Prince of Hostigos!"

"Oh, I'm sorry. I must have forgotten to tell you. You're not Prince of Hostigos any more. I am.'' Ptosphes' face went blank, for an instant, with shocked incredulity. Then he was on his feet with an oath, his poignard half drawn. "No,'' Kalvan continued, before his father-in-law-to-be could say anything else. "You are now His Majesty, Ptosphes the First, Great King of Hos-Hostigos. As Prince by betrothal of your Majesty's domain of Old Hostigos, let me be the first to do homage to your Majesty.''

Ptosphes resumed his chair, solely by force of gravity. He stared for a moment, then picked up his goblet and drained it.

This was a Hos-of another color.

"If the people in that section don't want to live under the rule of Balthames, for which I shouldn't blame them, we'll buy them out and settle them elsewhere. We'll fill that country with mercenaries we've had to take over and don't want to carry on the payroll. The officers can be barons, and the privates will all get forty acres and a mule, and we'll make sure they all have something to shoot with. That'll keep them out of worse mischief, and keep Prince Balthames' hands full. If we need them, we can always call them up again. Styphon, as usual, will pay.

"I don't know how long it'll take us to get Beshta—a moon or so. We'll let Balthar find out how much gold and silver we're getting out of this temple here. Balthar is fond of money. Then, after he's broken with Styphon's House, he'll find that he'll have to join us.''

"Armanes, too," Ptosphes considered, toying with his golden chain. "He owes Styphon's House a lot of money. What do you think Kaiphranos will do about this?"

"Well, he won't be happy about it, but who cares? He only has some five thousand troops of his own; if he wants to fight us, he'll either have to raise a mercenary army—and there's a limit to how many mercenaries anybody, even financed by Styphon's House, can hire—or he'll have to levy on his subject Princes. Half of them won't send troops to help coerce a fellow Prince—it might be their turn next—and the rest will all be too jealous of their own dignities to take orders from him. And in any case, he won't move till spring.''

Ptosphes had started to lift the chain from around his neck. He replaced it.

"No, Kalvan," he said firmly. "I will remain Prince of Old Hostigos. You must be Great King.''

"Now, look here, Ptosphes; Dralm-dammit, you *have* to be Great King!'' For a moment, he was ten years old again, arguing who'd be cops and who'd be robbers. "You have some standing; you're a Prince. Nobody in Hos-Harphax knows me from a hole in the ground.''

Ptosphes slapped the table till the goblets jiggled.

"That's just it, Kalvan! They know me all too well. I'm just a Prince, no better than they are; every one of these other Princes would say he had as much right to be Great King as I do. But they don't know who you are; all they know is what you've done. That and the story we told at the beginning, that you come from far across the Western Ocean, around the Cold Lands. Why, that's the Home of the Gods! We can't claim that you're a god, yourself; the real gods wouldn't like that. But anybody can plainly see that you've been taught by the gods, and sent by them. It would be nothing but plain blasphemy to deny it!''

Ptosphes was right; none of these haughty Princes would

kneel to one of their own ilk. But Kalvan, Galzar-taught and Dralm-sent; that was a Hos- of another color, too. Rylla's father had risen to kneel to him.

"Oh, sit down; sit down! Save that nonsense for Sarrask and Balthames to do. We'll have to talk to some of our people tonight; best do that in the presence chamber."

Harmakros was still up and more or less awake. He took the announcement quite calmly; by this time he was beyond surprise at anything. They had to waken Rylla; she'd had a little too much, for her first day up. She merely nodded drowsily. Then her eyes widened. "Hey, doesn't this make me Great Queen, or something?" Then she went back to sleep.

Chartiphon, arriving from the Beshtan border, was informed. He asked, "Why not Ptosphes?" then nodded agreement when the reasons were explained. About the necessity for establishing a Great Kingdom he had no doubt. "What else are we, now? We'll have Beshta next."

A score of others, Hostigi nobles and top army brass, were gathered in the presence chamber. Among them was Sthentros; maybe he hadn't been at Fitra, but nobody could say he hadn't been at Fyk. He might have envied Lord Kalvan, but Great King Kalvan was completely beyond envy. They were all half out on their feet—they'd only marched all day yesterday, tried to sleep in a wet cowpasture with cannon firing over them, fought a "great murthering battle" in the morning, marched fifteen more miles, and taken Sask Town and Tarr-Sask—but they wanted to throw a party to celebrate. They were persuaded to have one drink to their new sovereign and then go to bed.

The rank-and-file weren't in any better shape; half a den of Cub Scouts could have taken Tarr-Sask and run the lot of them out.

NINETEEN

I

THE next morning Kalvan's orderly, who didn't seem to have gotten much sleep, wakened him at nine-thirty. Should have done it earlier, but he'd probably just gotten awake himself. He bathed, put on clothes he'd never seen before—*have things brought from Tarr-Hostigos, soonest*—and breakfasted with Ptosphes, who had also been outfitted from some Saski nobleman's wardrobe. There were more messages: from Klestreus, in Beshta Town, who had bullied Balthar into agreeing to a truce and pulling his troops back to the line agreed on the treaty with Sarrask; and from Xentos, at Tarr-Hostigos. Xentos was disturbed about reports of troop mobilization in Nostor; Gormoth, he knew, had recently hired five hundred mercenary cavalry. Immediately, Ptosphes became equally disturbed. He wanted to march at once down the Listra Valley.

"No, for Dralm's sake!" Kalvan protested. "We have a panther by the tail, here. In a day or so, when we're in control, we can march a lot of these new mercenaries to

Listra-Mouth, but right now we mustn't let anybody know
we're frightened or they'll all jump us."

"But if Gormoth's invading Hostigos—"

"I don't think he is. Just to make sure, we'll send Phrames
off with half the Mobile Force and four four-pounders; they
can hold anything Gormoth's moving against us for a few
days."

He gave the necessary orders, saw to it that the troops left
Sask Town quietly, and tried to ignore the subject. He was
glad, though, that Rylla had gotten out of her splints and
come to Sask Town; she might be safer here.

So they had Sarrask and Balthames brought in.

Both seemed to be expecting to be handed over to the
headsman, and were trying to be nonchalant about it.
Ptosphes informed them abruptly that they were now subjects
of the Great King of Hos-Hostigos.

"Who's he?" Sarrask demanded, with a truculence the
circumstances didn't quite justify. "You?"

"Oh, no. I am Prince of Old Hostigos. His Majesty,
Kalvan the First, is Great King."

They were both relieved. Ptosphes had been right; the
sovereignty of the mysterious and possibly supernatural Kalvan would be acceptable; that of a self-elevated equal would
not. When the conditions under which they would reign as
Princes, respectively, of Sashta and Sask were explained,
Balthames was delighted. He'd come out of this as well as
though Sask had won the war. Sarrask was somewhat less so,
until informed that he was now free of all his debts to
Styphon's House and would share in the loot of the temple
and be given the fireseed mill.

"Well, Dralm save your Majesty!" he cried, and then
loosed a torrent of invective against Styphon's House and all
in it. "You'll let me put these thieving priests to death, won't
you, your Majesty?"

"They are offenders against the Great King; his justice
will deal with them," Ptosphes informed him.

Then they had in the foreign envoys, representatives of
Prince Kestophes of Ulthor, on Lake Erie, and Armanes of

Nyklos, and Tythanes of Kyblos, and Balthar of Beshta, and other neighboring Princes. There had been no such diplomatic corps at Tarr-Hostigos, because of the ban of Styphon's House. The Ulthori minister immediately wanted to know what the new Great Kingdom included.

"Well, at the moment, the Princedom of Old Hostigos, the Princedom of Sask, and the new Princedom of Sashta. Any other Princes who may elect to join us will be made welcome under our rule and protection; those which do not will be respected in their sovereignty as long as they respect us in ours. Or what they may conceive to be their sovereignty as subjects of this Great King of Hos-Harphax, Kaiphranos."

He shrugged Kaiphranos off as too trivial for consideration. Several of them laughed. The Beshtan minister began to bristle:

"This Princedom of Sashta, now; does that include territory ruled by my master, Prince Balthar of Beshta?"

"It includes territory your master ceded to our subject, Prince Balthames, in a treaty with our subject Prince Sarrask, which we recognized and confirm, and which we are prepared to enforce. As to how we are prepared to enforce it, I trust I don't have to remind you of what happened at Fyk yesterday morning."

He turned to the others. "Now, if your respective Princes don't wish to acknowledge our sovereignty, we hope they will accept our friendship and extend their own," he said. "We also hope that mutually satisfactory arrangements for trade can be made. For example, before long we expect to be producing fireseed in sufficient quantities for export, of better quality and at lower price than Styphon's House."

"We know that," the Nyklosi envoy said. "I can't, of course, commit my Prince to accepting the sovereignty of Hos-Hostigos, though I will strongly advise it. We've been paying tribute to King Kaiphranos and getting absolutely nothing in return for it. But in any case, we'll be glad to get all the fireseed you can send us."

"Well, look here," the Beshtan began. "What's all this about devils? The priests of Styphon make the devils in fireseed die when it burns, and yours lets them loose.''

The Ulthori nodded. ''We've heard about that, too,'' he said. ''We have no use for King Kaiphranos; for all he does, we might as well not have a Great King. But we don't want Ulthor being filled with evil spirits.''

''We've been using Hostigos fireseed in Nyklos, and we haven't had any trouble with devils,'' the Nyklosi said.

''There are no devils in fireseed,'' Kalvan declared. ''It's nothing but saltpeter and charcoal and sulfur, mixed without any prayers or rites or magic whatever. You know how much of it we burned at Fitra and Listra-Mouth. Nobody's seen any devils there, since.''

''Well, but you can't see the devils,'' the envoy from Kyblos said. ''They fill the air, and make bad weather, and make the seed rot in the ground. You wait till Spring, and see what kind of crops you have around Fitra. And around Fyk.''

The Beshtan was frankly hostile, the Ulthori unconvinced. That devil story was going to have to be answered, and how could you prove the nonexistence of something, especially an invisible something, that didn't exist? That was why he was an agnostic instead of an atheist.

They got rid of the diplomatic corps, and had in the priests and priestesses of all the regular, non-Styphon, pantheon. The one good thing about monotheism, he thought, was that it reduced the priesthood problem. Hadn't the Romans handled that through a government-appointed pontifex maximus? *Think over, seriously*. The good thing about polytheism was that the gods operated in non-competitive fields, and their priests had a common basis of belief, and mutual respect for each other's deities. The highpriest of Dralm seemed to be the acknowledged dean of the sacred college. Assisted by all his colleagues, he would make the invocation and proclaim Kalvan Great King in the name of all the gods. Then they had in a lot of Sarrask's court functionaries, who bickered endlessly about protocol and precedence. And they made sure that each of the mercenary captains swore a new oath of service to the Great King.

After noon-meal, they assembled everybody in Prince Sarrask's throne-room.

In Korea, another sergeant in Calvin Morrison's company had seen the throne room of Napoleon at Fontainebleau.

"You know," his comrade had said, "I never really understood Napoleon till I saw that place. If Al Capone had ever seen it, he'd have gone straight back to Chicago and ordered one for himself, twice as big, because he couldn't possibly have gotten one twice as flashy or in twice as bad taste."

That described Sarrask's throne room exactly.

The highpriest of Dralm proclaimed him Great King, chosen by all the true gods; the other priests and priestesses ratified that on behalf of their deities. Divine right of kings was another innovation, here-and-now. He then seated Rylla on the throne beside him, and then invested her father with the throne of Old Hostigos, emphasizing that he was First Prince of the Great Kingdom. Then he accepted the homage of Sarrask and Balthames, and invested them with their Princedoms. The rest of the afternoon was consumed in oaths of fealty from the more prominent nobles.

When he left the throne, he was handed messages from Klestreus, in Beshta Town, and Xentos. Klestreus reported that Prince Balthar had surrounded the temple of Styphon with troops, to protect it from mobs incited by priests of Dralm and Galzar. Xentos reported confused stories of internal fighting in Nostor, and no incidents on the border, where Phrames was on watch.

That evening, they had a feast.

The next morning, after assembling the court, the priests and priestesses of all the regular deities, and all the merchants, itinerant traders and other travelers in Sask Town, the priests of Styphon, from Zothnes down, were hustled in. They were a sorry-looking lot, dungeon-soiled, captivity-scuffed, and loaded with chains. Prodded with pike-butts, they were formed into a line facing the throne, and booed enthusiastically by all.

"Look at them!" Balthames jeered. "See how Styphon cares for his priests!"

"Throw their heads in Styphon's face!" Sarrask shouted.

Other suggestions were forthcoming, most of which would have horrified the Mau-Mau. A few, black-robe priests and white-robe underpriests, were defiant. He remembered what Harmakros had said about some on the lower echelons really believing in Styphon. Most of them didn't, and were in no mood for martyrdom. Zothnes, who should have been setting an example, was in a pitiable funk.

Finally, he commanded silence. "These people," he said, "are criminals against all men and against all the true gods. They must be put to death in a special manner, reserved for them and those like them. Let them be blown from the muzzles of cannon!"

Well, the British had done that during the Sepoy Mutiny, in the reign of her enlightened Majesty, Victoria, and could you get any more respectable than that? He was making a bad pun about cannon-ized martyrs. There was a general shout of approval—original, effective, uncomplicated, and highly appropriate. A yellow-robe upperpriest fainted.

Kalvan addressed his mercenary Chief of Artillery: "Alkides, say we use the three eighteens and three twelve; how long would it take your men to finish off this lot?"

"Six at a time." Alkides looked the job-lot over. "Why, if we started right after noon-meal, we could be through in time for dinner." He thought for a moment. "Look, Lord Kal—Pardon, your Majesty. Suppose we use the big bombards, here. We could load the skinny ones all the way in, and the fat ones up to the hips." He pointed at Zothnes. "I think that one would go all the way in a fifty-pounder, almost."

Kalvan frowned. "But I'd wanted to do it in the town square. The people ought to watch it."

"But it would make an awful mess in the square," Rylla objected.

"The people could come out from town to watch," Sarrask suggested helpfully. "More than could see it in the square. And vendors could come out and sell honey-cakes and meat-pies.''

Another priest fainted. Kalvan didn't want too many of them doing that, and nodded unobtrusively to Ptosphes.

''Your Majesty,'' the First Prince of the Great Kingdom said, ''I understand this is a fate reserved only for the priests of the false god Styphon. Now, suppose, before they can be executed, some of these criminals abjure their false god, recant their errors, and profess faith in the true gods. What then?''

''Oh, in that case we'd have no right to put them to death at all. If they make public abjuration of Styphon, renounce their priesthood, profess faith in Dralm and Galzar and Yirtta Allmother and the other true gods, and recant all their false teachings, we would have to set them free. To those willing to enter our service, honorable employment, appropriate to their condition, would be given. If Zothnes, say, were to do so, I'd think something around five hundred ounces of gold a year—''

A white-robe underpriest shouted that he would never deny his god. A yellow-robe upperpriest said, ''Shut your fool's mouth!'' and hit him across the face with the slack of his fetter-chain. Zothnes was giggling in half-hysterical relief.

''Dralm bless your Majesty; of course we will, all of us!'' he babbled. ''Why, I spit in the face of Styphon! You think any true god would suffer his priests to be treated as we've been?''

Xentos reached Sask Town that evening. The news from Nostor was a little more definite: according to his sources there, Gormoth had started mobilizing for a blitz attack on Hostigos on hearing the first, false, news of a Hostigi disaster at Fyk. As soon as he had learned better, he had used his troops to seize the Nostor Town temple of Styphon and the temple-farm up Lycoming Creek. Now there was savage fighting all over Nostor, between Gormoth's new mercenaries and supporters of Styphon's House, and the Nostori regular army was split by mutiny and counter-mutiny. There had been an unsuccessful attack on Tarr-Nostor. Gormoth still seemed to be in control.

The Sask Town priestcraft all deferred to Xentos; it was evident that he was Primate of the Great Kingdom, Archbishop of Canterbury or something of the sort. *Established Church of Hos-Hostigos; think over carefully.* He immediately called an ecclesiastical council and began working out a program for the auto-da-fé.

Held the next day, it was a great success. Procession of the penitents from Tarr-Sask to the Sask Town temple of Dralm, in sackcloth and ashes, guarded by enough pikemen to keep the mob from pelting them with anything more lethal than rotten cabbage and dead cats. Token flagellation. Recantation of all heresies, special emphasis on fireseed, supernatural nature and devil content of. He was pleased to observe the reactions of the diplomatic corps to this. Sermon of the Faith, preached by the Hostigos Uncle Wolf; as a professional performance, at least, the Rev. Alexander Morrison would have approved. And, finally, after profession of faith in the true gods and absolution, a triumphant march through the streets, the new converts robed in white and crowned with garlands. And free wine for everybody. This was even more fun than shooting them out of cannons would have been. The public was delighted.

They had another feast that evening.

The next day, Klestreus reported that Balthar had seized the temple of Styphon and massacred the priests; the mob was parading their heads on pike-points. He refused, however, to renounce his sovereignty and accept the rule of Great King Kalvan. Evidently he never considered his vassalage to Great King Kaiphranos, which wasn't surprising. Late in the afternoon, a troop of cavalry from Nyklos Town arrived, escorting one of Prince Armanes' chief nobles with a petition that Nyklos be annexed to the Great Kingdom of Hos-Hostigos, and also a packhorse loaded with severed heads. Prince Armanes was more interested in liquidating his debts by liquidating the creditors than he was in winning converts for the true gods. Prince Kestophes of Ulthor blew his priests of Styphon off the guns of his lakeside fort; along with his allegiance he gave Hos-Hostigos a port on the Great Lakes. By that time the demolition of the Sask Town temple of Styphon had begun, starting with the gold dome. It was real gold, twelve thousand ounces, of which Sarrask, after his ransom was paid, received three thousand.

When he returned to Tarr-Hostigos, Klestreus was there, seeking instructions. Prince Balthar was now ready to accept the sovereignty of King Kalvan. It seemed that, after seizing the temple, massacring the priests, and incurring the ban of Styphon's House, he discovered that there was no fireseed mill at all in Beshta; all the fireseed the priests had furnished him had been made in Sask. He was, in spite of the Sask Town auto-da-fé, still worried about the possible devil content of Kalvan's Unconsecrated. The ex-Archpriest Zothnes, now with the Ministry of State at six thousand ounces, gold, a year, was sent to reassure him.

It took more reassurance to induce him to come to Tarr-Hostigos to do homage; outside Tarr-Beshta, Balthar was violently agorophobic. He came, however, in a mail-curtained wagon, guarded by two hundred of Harmakros' cavalry.

The news from Nostor was still confused. A civil war was raging, that was definite, but exactly who against whom was less clear. It sounded a little like France at the time of the War of the Three Henries. Netzigon, the former chief-captain, and Krastokles, who had escaped the massacre when Gormoth had taken the temple, were in open revolt, though relations between them were said to be strained. Fighting continued in the streets of Nostor Town after the abortive attack on the castle. Count Pheblon, Gormoth's cousin and Netzigon's successor, commanded about half the army; the other half adhered to their former commander. The nobles, each with a formidable following, were split about evenly. Then there were minor factions: anti-Gormoth-and-anti-Styphon, pro-Styphon-and-pro-Gormoth, anti-Gormoth-

and-pro-Pheblon. In addition, several large mercenary companies had invaded Nostor on their own and were pillaging
indiscriminately, committing all the usual atrocities, while
trying to auction their services.

Not liking all this anarchy next door, Kalvan wanted to
intervene. Chartiphon and Harmakros were in favor of that;
so was Armanes of Nyklos, who hoped to pick up a few bits
of real estate on his southeast border. Xentos, of course,
wanted to wait and see, and, rather surprisingly, he was
supported by Ptosphes, Sarrask and Klestreus. Klestreus
probably knew more about the situation in Nostor than any of
them. That persuaded Kalvan to wait and see.

Tythanes of Kyblos arrived to do homage, attended by a
large retinue, and bringing with him twenty-odd priests of
Styphon, yoked neck-and-neck like a Guinea Coast slave-
kaffle. Baron Zothnes talked to them; there was an auto-da-
fé and public recantation. Some went to work in the fireseed
mill and some became novices in the temple of Dralm, all
under close surveillance. Kestophes of Ulthor came in a few
days later. Balthar of Beshta was still at Tarr-Hostigos,
which, by then, was crowded like a convention hotel. *Royal
palace; get built.* Something that could accommodate a mob
of subject Princes and their attendants, but not one of these
castles. Castles, once he began making cast iron roundshot
and hollow explosive shells and heavy brass guns, would
become scenic features, just as these big hooped iron bombards would become war memorials. Something simple and
homelike, he thought. On the order of Versailles.

When the Princes were all at Tarr-Hostigos, he and Rylla
were married, and there was a two-day feast, with an extra
day for hangovers. He'd never been married before. He liked
it. It couldn't possibly have happened with anybody nicer
than Rylla.

Some time during the festivities, Prince Balthames and
Sarrask's daughter Amnita were married. There was also a
minor and carefully hushed scandal about Balthames and a
page boy.

Then they had the Coronation. Xentos, who was shaping

up nicely as a prelate-statesman of the Richelieu type, crowned him and Rylla. Then he crowned Ptosphes as First Prince of the Great Kingdom, and the other Princes in order of their submission. Then the Proclamation of the Great Kingdom was read. Quite a few hands, lifting goblets between phrases, had labored on that. His own contributions had been cribbed from The Declaration of Independence and, touching Styphon's House, from Martin Luther. Everybody cheered it enthusiastically.

Some of the Princes were less enthusiastic about the Great Charter. It wasn't anything like the one that Tammany Hall in chain mail had extorted from King John at Runnymede; Louis XIV would have liked it much better. For one thing, none of them liked having to renounce their right, fully enjoyed under Great King Kaiphranos, of making war on one another, though they did like the tightening of control over their subject lords and barons, most of whom were an unruly and troublesome lot. The latter didn't like the abolition of serfdom and, in Beshta and Kyblos, outright slavery. But it gave everybody security without having to hire expensive mercenaries or call out peasant levies when they were most needed in the fields. The regular army of the Great Kingdom would take care of that.

And everybody could see what was happening in Nostor at the moment. He understood, now, why Xentos had opposed intervention; Nostor was too good a horrible example to sacrifice.

So they all signed and sealed it. *Secret police, to make sure they live up to it; think of somebody for chief.*

Then they feasted for a couple more days, and there were tournaments and hunts. There was also a minor scandal, carefully hushed, about Princess Amnita and one of Tythanes' cavalry officers. Finally they all began taking their leave and drifting back to their own Princedoms, each carrying the flag of the Great Kingdom, dark green with a red keystone on it.

Darken the green a little more and make the scarlet a dull maroon and they'd be good combat uniform colors.

II

The weather stayed fine until what he estimated to be the first week in November—*calendar reform; get onto this now*—and then turned cold, with squalls of rain which finally turned to snow. Outside, it was blowing against the window panes—*clear glass; why can't we do something about this?*—and candles had been lighted, but he was still at work. Petitions, to be granted or denied. Reports. Verkan's Zygrosi were going faster than anybody had expected with the brass foundry; they'd be pouring the first heat in ten or so days, and he'd have to go and watch that. The rifle shop was up to fifteen finished barrels a day, which was a real miracle. Fireseed production up, too, sufficient for military and civilian hunting demands in all the Princedoms of the Great Kingdom, and soon they would be exporting in quantity. Verkan and his wife were gone, now, returning to Greffscharr to organize lake trade with Ulthor; he and Rylla both missed them.

And King Kaiphranos was trying to raise an army for the reconquest of his lost Princedoms, and getting a very poor response from the Princes still subject to him. There'd be trouble with him in the spring, but not before. And Sesklos, Styphon's Voice, had summoned all his Archpriests to meet in Harphax city. Council of Trent, Kalvan thought, nodding; now the Counter Reformation would be getting into high gear.

And rioting in Kyblos; the emancipated slaves were beginning to see what Samuel Johnson had meant when he defined freedom as the choice of working or starving.

And the Prince of Phaxos wanted to join the Great Kingdom, but he was making a lot of conditions he'd have to be talked out of.

And pardons, and death-warrants. He'd have to be careful not to sign too many of the former and too few of the latter; that was how a lot of kings lost their thrones.

A servant announced a rider from Vryllos Gap, who,

ushered in, informed him that a party from Nostor had just crossed the Athan. A priest of Dralm, a priest of Galzar, twenty mercenary cavalry, and Duke Skranga, the First Noble of Nostor.

He received Duke Skranga in his private chambers, and remembered how he had told the Agrysi horse-trader that Dralm, or somebody, would reward him. Dralm, or somebody, with substantial help from Skranga, evidently had. He was richly clad, his robe lined with mink-fur, a gold chain about his neck and a gold-hilted poignard on a gold link belt. His beard was neatly trimmed.

"Well, you've come up in the world," he commented.

"So, if your Majesty will pardon me, has your Majesty." Then he produced a signet-ring—the one given as pledge token by Count Pheblon when captured and released at Tarr-Dombra, and returned to him when his ransom had been delivered. "So has the owner of this. He is now Prince Pheblon of Nostor, and he sends me to declare for him his desire to submit himself and his realm to your Majesty's sovereignty and place himself, and it, under your Majesty's protection."

"Well, your Grace, I'm most delighted. But what, if it's a fair question, has become of Prince Gormoth?"

The ennobled horse-trader's face was touched with a look of deepest sorrow.

"Prince Gormoth, Dralm receive his soul, is no longer with us, your Majesty. He was most foully murdered."

"Ah. And who appears to have murdered him, if that's a fair question too?"

Skranga shrugged. "The then Count Pheblon, and the Nostor priest of Dralm, and the Nostor Uncle Wolf were with me in my private apartments at Tarr-Nostor when suddenly we heard a volley of shots from the direction of Prince Gormoth's apartments. Snatching weapons, we rushed thither, to find the Princely rooms crowded with guardsmen who had entered just ahead of us, and, in his bedchamber, our beloved Prince lay weltering in his gore, bleeding from a dozen wounds. He was quite dead," Skranga said sadly.

"Uncle Wolf and the highpriest of Dralm, whom your Majesty knows, will both testify that we were all together in my rooms when the shots were fired, and that Prince Gormoth was dead when we entered. Surely your Majesty will not doubt the word of such holy men."

"Surely not. And then?"

"Well, by right of nearest kinship, Count Pheblon at once declared himself Prince of Nostor. We tortured a couple of servants lightly—we don't do so much of that in Nostor, since our beloved and gentle Prince . . . Well, your Majesty, they all agreed that a band of men in black cloaks and masks had suddenly forced their way into Prince Gormoth's chambers, shot him dead, and then fled. In spite of the most diligent search, no trace of them could be found."

"Most mysterious. Fanatical worshipers of false Styphon, without doubt. Now, you say that Prince Pheblon, whom we recognize as the rightful Prince of Nostor, will do homage to us?"

"On certain conditions, of course, the most important of which your Majesty has already met. Then, he wishes to be confirmed in his possession of the temple of Styphon in Nostor Town, and the fireseed mills, nitriaries and sulfur springs which his predecessor confiscated from Styphon's House."

"Well, that's granted. And also the act of his late Highness, Prince Gormoth, in elevating you to the title of Duke and First Noble of Nostor."

"Your Majesty is most gracious!"

"Your Grace has earned it. Now, about these mercenary companies in Nostor?"

"Pure brigands, your Majesty! His highness begs your Majesty to send troops to deal with them."

"That'll be done; I'll send Duke Chartiphon, our Grand Constable, to attend to that. What's happened to Krastokles, by the way?"

"Oh, we have him, and Netzigon too, in the dungeons at Tarr-Nostor. They were both captured a moon-quarter ago. If your Majesty wishes, we'll bring both of them to Tarr-Hostigos.''

''Well, don't bother about Netzigon; take his head off yourselves, if you think he needs it. But we want that Archpriest. I hope that our faithful Baron Zothnes can spare us the mess of blowing him off a cannon by talking some sense into him.''

''I'm sure he can, your Majesty.''

He wondered just who had arranged the killing of Gormoth, Skranga or Pheblon, or both together. He didn't care; Nostor hadn't been his jurisdiction then. It was now, though, and if either of that pair had ideas about having the other killed, he'd do something about it in a hurry. Court intrigues, he supposed, were something he'd have with him always, but no murders, not inside the Great Kingdom.

After he showed Skranga out, he returned to his desk, opened a box, and got out a cigar—a stogie, rather, and a very crudely made stogie at that. It was a beginning, however. He bit the end and lit it at one of the candles, and picked up another report, a wax-covered wooden tablet. He still hadn't gotten anything done on paper-making. Maybe he'd better not invent paper; if he did, some Dralm-damned bureaucrat would invent paper-work, and then he'd have to spend all his time endlessly reading and annotating reports.

He was happy about Nostor, of course; that meant they wouldn't have a little war to fight next door in the spring, when King Kaiphranos would begin being a problem. And it was nice Pheblon had Krastokles and would turn him over. Two Archpriests, about equivalent to cardinals, defecting from Styphon's House was a serious blow. It weakened their religious hold on the Great Kings and their Princes, which was the only hold they had left now that they had lost the fireseed monopoly. Priests, and especially the top level of the hierarchy, were supposed to believe in their gods.

Xentos believed in Dralm, for instance. Maybe he'd have trouble with the old man, some day, if Xentos found his duty to Dralm conflicting with his duty to the Great Kingdom. But he hoped that would never happen.

He'd have to find out more about what was going on in the other Great Kingdoms. Spies—there was a job for Duke Skranga, one that would keep him out of mischief in Nostori local politics. Chief of Secret Service. Skranga was crooked enough to be good at that. And somebody to watch Skranga, of course. That could be one of Klestreus' jobs.

And find out just what the situation was in Nostor. Go there himself; Machiavelli always recommended that for securing a new domain. Make the Nostori his friends—that wouldn't be hard, after they'd lived under the tyranny of Gormoth. And . . .

General Order, to all Troops: Effective immediately, it shall be a court-martial offence for any member of the Armed Forces of the Great Kingdom of Hos-Hostigos publicly to sing, recite, play, whistle, hum, or otherwise utter the words and/or music of the song known as Marching Through Nostor.

TWENTY

VERKAN VALL looked at his watch and wished Dalla would hurry, but Dalla was making herself beautiful for the party. A waste of time, he thought; Dalla had been born beautiful. But try and tell any woman that. Across the low table, Tortha Karf also looked at his watch, and smiled happily. He'd been doing that all through dinner and ever since, and each time had been broader and happier as more minutes till midnight leaked away.

He hoped Dalla's preparations would still permit them to reach Paratime Police Headquarters with an hour to spare before midnight. There'd be a big crowd in the assembly room—everybody who was anybody on the Paracops and the Paratime Commission, politicians, society people, and, by special invitation, the Kalvan Project crowd from the University. He'd have to shake hands with most of them, and have drinks with as many as possible, and then, just before midnight, they'd all crowd into the Chief's office, and Tortha Karf would sit down at his desk, and, precisely at 2400, rise, and they'd shake hands, and Tortha Karf would step aside and he'd sit down, and everybody would start that Fourth Level barbarian chant they used on such occasions.

And from then on, he'd be stuck there—Dralm-dammit!

He must have said that aloud. The soon-to-retire Chief grinned unsympathetically.

"Still swearing in Aryan-Transpacific Zarthani. When do you expect to get back there?"

"Dralm knows, and he doesn't operate on Home Time Line. I'm going to have a lot to do here. One, I'm going to start a flap, and keep it flapping, about this pickup business. Ten new cases in the last eight days. And don't tell me what you told Zarvan Tharg when he was retiring, or what Zarvan Tharg told Hishan Galth when *he* was retiring. I'm going to do something about this, by Dralm I am!"

"Well, fortunately for the working cops, we're a longev-ous race. It's a long time between new Chiefs."

"Well, we know what causes it. We'll have to work on eliminating the cause. I'm a hundred and four; I can look forward to another two centuries in that chair of yours. If we don't have enough men, and enough robots, and enough computers to eliminate some of these interpenetrations, we might as well throw it in and quit."

"It'll cost like crazy."

"Look, I don't make a practice of preaching moral ethics, you know that. I just want you to think, for a moment, of the morality of snatching people out of the only world they know and dumping them into an entirely different world, just enough like their own . . ."

"I've thought about it, now and then," Tortha Karf said, in mild understatement. "This fellow Morrison, Lord Kal-van, Great King Kalvan, is one in a million. That was the best thing that could possibly have happened to him, and he'd be the first to say so, if he dared talk about it. But for the rest, the ones the conveyer operators ray down with their needlers are the lucky ones.

"But what are we going to do, Vall? We have a population of ten billion, on a planet that was completely exhausted twelve thousand years ago. I don't think more than a billion and a half are on Home Time Line at any one time; the rest are scattered all over Fifth Level, and out at conveyer-heads all over Fourth, Third and Second. We can't cut them loose; there's a slight moral issue involved there, too. And we can't haul them all in to starve after we stop paratiming. That little Aryan-Transpacific expression you picked up fits. We have a panther by the tail."

"Well, we can do all we can. I saw to it that they did it on the University Kalvan Operation. We checked all the conveyer-heads equivalent with Hostigos Town on every Paratime penetrated time-line, and ours doesn't coincide with any of them."

"I'll bet you had a time." Tortha Karf sipped some more of the after-dinner coffee they were dragging out, and lit another cigarette. "I'll bet they love you in Conveyer Registration Office, too. How many were there?"

"A shade over three thousand, inside four square miles. I don't know what they'll do about the conveyer-head for Agrys City, when they go to put one in there. There's a city on that river-mouth island on every time line that builds cities, and tribal villages on most of the rest."

"Then they aren't just establishing a conveyer-head at Hostigos Town?"

"Oh, no; they're making a real operation out of it. We have five police posts, here and there, including one at Greffa, the capital of Grefftscharr, where Dalla and I are supposed to come from. The University will have study teams, or at least observers, in the capital cities of all the Five Great Kingdoms. Six Kingdoms, now, with Hos-Hostigos. They'll have to be careful; by spring, there'll be a war that'll make the Conquest of Sask look like a schoolyard brawl."

They were both silent for awhile. Tortha Karf, smiling contentedly, was thinking of his farm on Fifth Level Sicily; he'd be there this time tomorrow, with nothing to worry about but what the rabbits were doing to his truck-gardens. Verkan Vall was thinking about his friend, the Great King Kalvan, and everything Kalvan had to worry about. Now *there* was a man who had a panther by the tail.

Then something else occurred to him; a disquieting thought that had nagged him ever since a remark Dalla had made, the morning before they'd made the drop as Verkan and his party.

"Chief," he said, and remembered that in a couple of hours people would be calling him that. "This pickup problem is only one facet, and a small one, of something big and serious, and fundamental. We're supposed to protect the Paratime Secret. Just how good a secret is it?"

Tortha Karf looked up sharply, his cup halfway to his lips.

"What's wrong with the Paratime Secret, Vall?"

"How did we come to discover Paratime transposition?"

Tortha Karf had to pause briefly. He had learned that long ago, and there was considerable mental overlay.

"Why, Ghaldron was working to develop a spacewarp drive, to get us out to the stars, and Hesthor was working on the possibility of linear time-travel, to get back to the past, before his ancestors had worn the planet out. Things were pretty grim, on this time-line, twelve thousand years ago. And a couple of centuries before, Rhogom had worked up a theory of multidimensional time, to explain the phenomenon of precognition. Dalla could tell you all about that; that's her subject.

"Well, science was pretty tightly compartmented, then, but somehow Hesthor read some of Rhogom's old papers, and he'd heard about what Ghaldron was working on and got in touch with him. Between them, they discovered paratemporal transposition. Why?"

"As far as I know, nobody off Home Time Line has ever developed any sort of time-machine, linear or lateral. There are Second Level civilizations, and one on Third, that have over-light-speed drives for interstellar ships. But the idea of multidimensional time and worlds of alternate probability is all over Second and Third Levels, and you even find it on Fourth—a mystical concept on Sino-Hindic, and a science-fiction idea on Europo-American."

"And you're thinking, suppose some Sino-Hindic mystic, or some Europo-American science-fiction writer, gets picked up and dumped onto, say, Second Level Interworld Empire?"

"That could do it. It mightn't even be needed. You know, there is no such thing as a single-shot discovery; anything that's been discovered once can be discovered again. That's why it always amuses me to see some technological warfare office classifying a law of nature as top-secret. Gunpowder was the secret of Styphon's House, and look what's happening to Styphon's House now. Of course, gunpowder is a simple little discovery; it's been made tens of thousands of times, all over Paratime. Paratemporal transposition is a big, complicated, discovery; it was made just once, twelve thousand years ago, on one time-line. But no secret can be kept forever. One of the University crowd said that, speaking of Styphon's House. He became quite indignant when Dalla mentioned the Paratime Secret in that connection."

"I'll bet you didn't. That's a nice thought to give a retiring Chief of Paratime Police. Now I'll be having nightmares about—"

He broke off, rising to his feet with a smile. A Paratimer could always produce a smile when one was needed.

"Well, now, Dalla! That gown! And how did you achieve that hairdo?"

He rose and turned. Dalla had come out onto the terrace and was pirouetting slowly in the light from the room behind her. It hadn't been a waste of time, after all.

"But I kept you waiting ages! You're both dears, to be so patient. Do we go, now?"

"Yes, the party will have started; we'll get there just at the right time. Not too early, and not too late."

And in two hours, Verkan Vall, Chief of Paratime Police, would begin to assume responsibility for guarding the Paratime Secret.

A panther by the tail. And he was holding it.

H. BEAM PIPER

POUL ANDERSON

78657	**A Stone in Heaven**	$2.50
20724	**Ensign Flandry**	$1.95
48923	**The Long Way Home**	$1.95
51904	**The Man Who Counts**	$1.95
57451	**The Night Face**	$1.95
65954	**The Peregrine**	$1.95
91706	**World Without Stars**	$1.50

Available wherever paperbacks are sold or use this coupon

ACE SCIENCE FICTION
P.O. Box 400, Kirkwood, N.Y. 13795

Please send me the titles checked above. I enclose _____.
Include 75¢ for postage and handling if one book is ordered; 50¢ per
book for two to five. If six or more are ordered, postage is free. Califor-
nia, Illinois, New York and Tennessee residents please add sales tax.

NAME_____

ADDRESS_____

CITY_____STATE_____ZIP_____

120

Ursula K. Le Guin

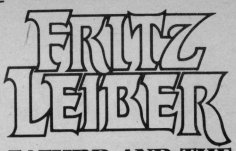

FRITZ LEIBER

FAFHRD AND THE GRAY MOUSER SAGA

☐ 79176	SWORDS AND DEVILTRY	$2.25
☐ 79156	SWORDS AGAINST DEATH	$2.25
☐ 79185	SWORDS IN THE MIST	$2.25
☐ 79165	SWORDS AGAINST WIZARDRY	$2.25
☐ 79223	THE SWORDS OF LANKHMAR	$1.95
☐ 79169	SWORDS AND ICE MAGIC	$2.25

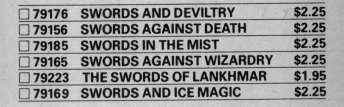

Available wherever paperbacks are sold or use this coupon

ACE SCIENCE FICTION
P.O. Box 400, Kirkwood, N.Y. 13795

Please send me the titles checked above. I enclose $_____.
Include 75¢ for postage and handling if one book is ordered; $1.00 if
two to five are ordered. If six or more are ordered, postage is free.

NAME_____

ADDRESS_____

CITY_____STATE_____ZIP_____